THE FRAGMENT OF
LIGHT

By Ben Hale

To my family and friends,

Who believed

And to my wife,

Who is perfect

The Chronicles of Lumineia

By Ben Hale

—The Shattered Soul—

The Fragment of Water
The Fragment of Shadow
The Fragment of Light
The Fragment of Fire
The Fragment of Mind
The Fragment of Power

—The Master Thief—

Jack of Thieves
Thief in the Myst
The God Thief

—The Second Draeken War—

Elseerian
The Gathering
Seven Days
The List Unseen

—The Warsworn—

The Flesh of War
The Age of War
The Heart of War

—The Age of Oracles—

The Rogue Mage
The Lost Mage
The Battle Mage

—The White Mage Saga—

Table of Contents

Chapter 1: The Fragment of Distraction

The fragment of Light yawned. He hated the Deep, with its labyrinth of caverns, tunnels, and incessant darkness. It made him exhausted just thinking about it, and now here he was, trudging on a dark ledge next to an even darker ravine.

Mushrooms, moss, and clinging vines adorned walls and ceilings, their colors vibrant blue, white, and green. The fluorescent display revealed the plunging canyon at their side and the curve of the ledge ahead. More moss grew on the walls of the shallow ravine, the light flickering off the surface of the underground stream.

"How are you doing?" Willow asked.

He looked to Willow and brightened. The dark elf strode at his side, her eyes filled with concern. A gifted soldier and swordswoman, her bladecraft was lethal enough without her magic, which came from her tattoos. Weapons lined her flesh, covering her body in ink. A crossbow curved across her back, the hilt on her shoulder, while the bow extended onto her bare abdomen. A short sword was visible on her hip, the blade appearing below her skirt where it extended to her knee.

Her arms were covered in knives and daggers and a multitude of tools. A whip coiled around her other leg, the handle near the tattoo of her sword. Her most prominent weapon connected to a second whip, the hilt on her stomach, curving above the sword hilt to the circular blade on her back.

"Tired," Light said, yawning again. "I hate the darkness."

"You get used to it," Willow said, touching his arm to offer comfort.

"I'm a guardian of light," he replied. "I don't think I'll ever get used to the darkness."

From behind them, the last member of their party offered a quiet chuckle. "You may be uncomfortable, but I'm on my way to visit a dark elf city, a place where they hate my kind."

"Don't pretend like you're not enjoying this," Light grumbled.

Jeric grinned and raised his hands as if he'd been caught. Like the rest of the elven race, he was tall and slender. Unlike the rest of his race, he had a compulsion for adventure that bordered on dangerous. If life became too dull, he was likely to incite a battle just to watch the ensuing conflict.

Jeric was dressed in dark elf clothing. His tunic and pants were black, and he'd insisted on carrying his customary weapons, two hilts with aquaglass blades. The hilts were fastened to straps on his chest, making him appear unarmed at first glance.

Light's thoughts shifted to Elenyr, the woman who had trained the five fragments of Draeken. Known as the Hauntress, Elenyr could turn herself ethereal to pass through solid objects, and she had lived for thousands of years. She'd also favored Jeric at one time, an attraction Light had thought dead, until recently.

Light poked Jeric in the shoulder. "Why do you still pursue Elenyr?"

"I've lived for nine hundred years," he replied, "and never met a woman with such gravity."

"She is formidable," Willow said.

Light didn't appreciate his tone about Elenyr. "I don't like how you talk about her—look! A deep hawk!"

Light's scowl turned into a smile when the hawk fluttered across the pool of illumination. The bird had large eyes that allowed it to catch every scrap of light emanating from the rich plant life unique to the depths.

On impulse, Light used the brightness in the room to cast a pair of wings and leapt over the ledge. He soared upward, catching the deep hawk by his claws and bringing him back to the ledge. The bird screeched in his grip as he examined it with interest.

The bird had leathery wings and a streak of feathers down its back. Its claws were sharp, as was its beak, which it used on Light's arm. Ignoring the sting, Light lifted the bird closer and watched the large eyes turn.

"It's beautiful," he said in awe.

"I wouldn't know," Jeric said wryly.

Light suddenly realized he'd used all the nearby light, plunging the section of trail into darkness. He sought to draw on more light, only to make the situation worse. The light of the bird's wings sputtered before dying, leaving them in total darkness.

"Sorry," he said, his tone apologetic.

"And I don't think the bird likes to be touched."

Light squinted to see the screeching bird, and released it. Squawking in fury, it flew upward, returning to its nest. Light sighed, then snapped his fingers, igniting a flameless candle from his thumb.

"I'm not certain I can do this," Light muttered.

His voice was too soft to echo, but it seemed to reverberate off the walls, reminding him of the task assigned to him by Elenyr. *Become Serak*, she'd said. But donning the persona of another was more than shaping their face, a talent Light could perform with ease. Serak was vicious and methodical, tactical and terrifying. Light possessed none of those attributes.

"Do not forget our purpose," Willow said, her soft expression barely visible in the gloom. "The dark elf queen has been taken by Princess Melora. If she is not returned before the people notice her absence, there will be war in the Deep."

Willow's face tightened with concern, both for her queen, and for Light. Despite his fears, he allowed a small smile, grateful for her presence. He leaned down and kissed the woman. Jeric snorted in amusement.

"A fragment of a guardian and a dark elf," he said. "Love truly has no boundaries."

11

Light grinned, his emotions brightening. Seized with a desire to see the dark elf city, he accelerated down the path, forcing his companions to hasten to keep up. As they descended into the earth, Willow told him everything she knew about Serak.

"As you know, I infiltrated the Order of Ancients at my queen's request," she said. "But there are many areas to which I am not permitted access because I am just an initiate, not a senior acolyte . . ."

Vacillating between excitement and fatigued irritability, Light struggled to pay attention. He'd always feared the Deep. On the surface he could cast anything out of sunlight and relished the wealth of power—when it wasn't overcast. He hated the rain.

But he was also excited to see the Deep, where the fragment of Shadow always got to visit. Shadow would always tell of wondrous cities and exotic foods. The other fragments of Mind, Fire, and Water had all gone to the Deep, and Light had struggled to hide his envy—

Did it have to be so exhausting in the Deep? His eyes drooped, and he yearned for a pillow to cradle his head. Like the soft one at the Oracle's Respite in Herosian. They always had the nicest pillows, made of down feathers . . .

"Are you snoring?"

Willow's voice was incredulous, and Light managed a quick reply. "Of course not."

"You were," Jeric supplied from behind them.

"Not helping," Light growled.

"I know you're tired," Willow said softly. "But what I'm telling you about Serak will make the difference between the Order of Ancients believing you, or killing you."

"They'll kill us too," Jeric said. "And I'd like to avoid that eventuality. I have a lot of life to live, you know."

"You're nine hundred years old," Light said. "Elves never live beyond a thousand."

"Do you know what I could do with a hundred years?" Jeric asked, his tone wistful. "A hundred years with Elenyr would be—"

"Stop!" Light said, his voice tinged with panic. "Whatever you were about to say, I don't want to hear it." He shuddered. "Elenyr *raised* us, remember. She's like my mother."

"She trained you," Jeric reasoned. "Which means I can talk about the curves of her—"

The sword came to a stop on Jeric's throat, and he stopped speaking. Light struggled to control the burst of rage, and Willow put a calming hand on his arm. He lowered the glittering sword and it withdrew back into his flesh.

"You are quite volatile," Jeric said, his tone amused as he rubbed his neck.

"Try not to die before we arrive," Willow said to Jeric. "You know he has a hard time controlling his impulses."

"You make it sound like that's a bad thing," Light said, his anger switching to laughter.

"It is when you are about to impersonate the Father of Guardians," Jeric said.

Light caught the tone in his voice, and realized Jeric had pushed him on purpose, wanting to test his boundaries. A touch of rage returned, but he realized the elf was right. Light did not like to control his shifting emotions, and the coming task would test him to his limit. When he spoke his voice was small.

"Why don't you start back at the beginning?" he said. "It's possible I wasn't listening."

Willow smiled, the expression touched with understanding. "Serak is a man to be feared, but if you want to know him, you must know his habits."

"Tell me," he said.

Willow held his gaze, and he tried not to watch the flutter of her hair. Was she always so beautiful? But of course she was. No, he needed to pay attention. He wouldn't let Willow die because he couldn't pay attention.

For the next few hours he listened to Willow speak of Serak, of how he rarely visited the Deep. When he did, he always met with Princess Melora, who tested acolytes she thought were loyal enough to know the secrets of the Order.

Serak ate the same foods, drank the same ale, even spoke to the same people. He kept a close circle of his most loyal. To the rest of the Order he was almost a demigod, a man with enormous power, one who'd lived for five thousand years.

Light managed to hear most of it but was frequently distracted by the wondrous architecture of the Deep. The endless network of underground caves, caverns, and tunnels were broken by canyons, lakes, and streams.

"Serak does not smile often," Willow said.

"But I like to smile," Light lamented, tearing his eyes off a giant glowing mushroom that cast silver light onto a pool of water.

"Restrain it," Jeric said. "Or we'll be the first ones killed because an evil mastermind began to giggle."

Light chuckled, and then offered a stern expression. "I'll try."

"We're nearly there," Willow said.

"We're not going to Elsurund?" Jeric asked.

Willow shook her head. "The capitol lies west of here. We're going to Kordune, the second largest city in the dark elf kingdom."

"But I wanted to see the capitol," Light complained.

"Another time," Willow said. "I promise."

Light brightened at that, and then Willow slowed their gait. "You'll want to be a regular dark elf for now," she said.

14

"Why?" Light asked.

"Because we can't just walk into the Order's tower," Willow said. "Serak always arrives through the Gate."

"So what do you suggest?" Light asked.

"Change your features to a dark elf, and Jeric too," Willow said. "And if you can, make Jeric look better."

"You can't improve on these features," Jeric protested.

Light waved a hand to Jeric, bending the light so he looked like a grizzled dark elf, right down to a broken nose and scars. Then he enlarged the chin, making him look borderline hideous.

"You made me ugly," Jeric sighed. "Didn't you?"

"That's for talking about Elenyr's curves," Light said.

He cast the same charm on himself, arcing the light so his features morphed into that of another. He recalled a dark elf they'd met in the outpost before entering the Deep and modeled his features after the soldier.

"How do I look?" he asked.

"Not as handsome," Willow said. "But it will do."

"How long do I have to look like this?" Jeric asked.

"We'll have to enter the city unseen, and then infiltrate the Order's location. Once we're in the Gate room, we can walk out and pretend we used the Gate to arrive."

"And if Serak is there?" Light asked.

"I suggest we run," Jeric said, examining his new face in a pool of water. "Fighting might get the queen killed."

Light adjusted Jeric's nose again, smiling at the result. Doing so dimmed the light in the chamber, and the elf glared at him, making Light giggle at the overly large nostrils. Willow poked him and he modified it to its previous shape.

15

"And no magic," Willow warned. "Serak does not possess light magic."

"How soon will we get there?" Light asked.

"Now," Willow said.

The tunnel curved sharply, abruptly coming to an end. Light sucked in his breath as they stepped into a massive cavern, and his gaze lifted to the glittering city. He veritably bounced on his feet, prompting Jeric to sigh.

"I think this was a bad idea," he murmured.

Chapter 2: Kordune

A vast lake stretched across the base of the cavern, the water as still as glass, and a great city filled the opposite bank. Towers of stone rose to an impressive height, each containing balconies and arches, some connecting to neighboring towers. Channels of glowing water circled the towers, providing light and beauty to the city.

Bridges of stone connected many of the structures and extended to the back wall of the giant cavern, where great windows and archways allowed Light to catch a glimpse of the inner city. More light spilled from the Inner Kordune, the light coming from black trees, their strange leaves a vibrant purple. Protrusions of crystal clung to the ceiling of the enormous cavern, the bright stones flickering like underground stars.

"Kordune is the oldest of the dark elf cities," Willow said, "and dates back to the Dawn of Magic."

"Which explains why Serak favors it," Jeric said.

"Are you ready?" Willow asked.

"Can't wait!" Light bounded forward.

The group circled the lake until they reached a grand archway at its shore. Two lines of light crossed the lake, the barrier glowing faintly, marking the border of the bridge. The aquaglass span was on the same level as the lake, making it appear as if they walked on water.

Light struggled to contain his excitement, but the dark elves passing them cast Light strange looks. Some were astride deep lizards, the mounts larger than a horse, and pulled carts and wagons.

"We're just a day's journey from Elsurund," Willow murmured. "And many make the journey to sell their wares or visit relatives."

"Is that how the Order smuggled the queen here?" Jeric asked, equally as quiet.

"I suspect the Order has a Gate in the capitol," she said. "But they placed me here, so I am unfamiliar with other locations. Serak likes to keep the different factions of the Order isolated in order to maintain control. Only senior acolytes are permitted to use the Gates to travel."

"How does he choose his loyal?"

"A test," Willow said. "It's where initiates are invited to become senior acolytes."

Light barely heard them, his eyes on the glass as they advanced across the bridge. The bridge was perfectly clear, and he watched large shapes glide in the depths, the sleek fish rising and then plunging into the deeper waters.

"Are those Gorthon fish?" he breathed.

"They are," Willow said, and motioned to the strands of light bordering the bridge. "Those keep the fish from attacking us."

"They're beautiful," he breathed in awe.

"Not when you're in the water with them," Jeric said wryly. "They're as big as a bull, with more teeth than a shark."

"But rather tasty," Willow said.

She noticed Light veritably shaking with the desire to speak, and leaned in. "How many questions do you have?"

"A million," Light breathed.

He wanted to know about the fish, what they tasted like, how many dark elves were in the city, why did some women wear a sash across their tunics while others preferred it around their necks? And could he ride a deep lizard? He saw a green one and a grey one, and then wanted to know why they were different colors—

"Calm yourself," Jeric advised. "Once we're inside, you can speak your mind."

"Promise?" Light asked, seeming about to burst.

"I promise," Jeric said.

Light glanced his way and spotted a child pointing at Jeric's oversized chin. "Look, mother, at his face . . ."

The mother hushed the child. Jeric glared at Light. Light struggled not to giggle. They reached the end of the bridge and ascended into the streets of Outer Kordune, the paths wide enough for lizards and dark elves, carts and caravans.

Light lifted his gaze to the towers on all sides, shocked by their height. Built above and inside what had once been a natural rock formation, the towers rose halfway towards the roof of the cavern.

The bottom level of the towers was dedicated to commerce, with shops selling goods of every kind. Strange plants, glowing stones, and barrels of dark elf ale were on display. Taverns were frequently on the second level, and deep lizards climbed the outside of the tower like it was flat ground, carrying their riders to the higher levels.

Garbed in light armor, the dark elves stood in groups according to their affiliation. A mercenary guild walked together, the warriors laughing and talking. A knot of soldiers eyed them suspiciously, while a collection of mages avoided them both, keeping to themselves as they purchased supplies for their school.

Jeric noticed the current of tension between the various factions. He asked Willow about the difficult climate. Light heard the conversation but did not care, his eyes on the group of men shouting in the nearby street. Guards rushed to the scene and sought to separate them, and the men reluctantly parted.

"The High Council has enacted heavy taxes," Willow was saying, "and only the queen has kept the taxes from escalating further. The people have grown sullen and angry, and sides are being chosen."

"Which explains why we need the queen," Jeric said, his eyes on a group of elves glaring at the city guard.

"The Outer City contains the merchants and most of the populace," Willow murmured, and motioned them into an alley between two towers. From that vantage point, she swept a hand to the Inner City. "Those with means take up residence on the back wall, or the caverns beyond. Inner Kordune houses a large army, and patrols are—"

"*So good*," Light breathed.

He held a plate of fried gorthon, which he'd retrieved as they'd passed a roofless tavern. Both Jeric and Willow looked at him in disapproval. Light glanced down at the plate. Then looked back to them, his expression guilty.

"Sorry." His voice was muffled by the bite he'd just taken. "Would you like some?"

"Would you like to finish eating *before* we discuss the kidnapped queen and the fate of my entire race?"

"Would you be mad if I said yes?" Light asked.

"Yes."

Light grimaced, and reluctantly set the plate onto a decorative section of rock. Willow turned back and pointed upward, where a tower rose from a knobby outcropping of stone that resembled a fist. Windows in the outcropping were evenly placed around the exterior, with decorative and defensive balconies overlooking the streets.

Dark elf guards stood on the balconies, or wound their way inside the foundation. Most were armed with crossbows, while some patrolled with a variety of entities. Dark elves could possess any type of magic, albeit few had more than a single talent.

At the top of the knoll, adjacent to the tower, two beasts prowled. Each was the size of a jungle cat, their bodies layered in dark red scales. Light grew excited when he saw they had fangs. He loved creatures with fangs.

"Don't touch the deragoths," Willow said. "They are small, but they are fearsome predators. Their skin secretes a poison that will paralyze you in seconds."

"Even me?" Light asked.

"Perhaps not you," Willow allowed, and then glanced to Jeric. "Dark elves can withstand the poison longer, but I wouldn't suggest you go patting their heads."

"Don't worry," Jeric said with a wry smile. "I've already seen one up close. It tried to paralyze me and then eat me alive."

"They like to do that," she said.

"Where's the Gate Chamber?" Jeric asked.

"Top of the tower," Willow said.

"How do you suppose we get in . . ."

Jeric frowned as he noticed Light. Willow turned as well, and found Light with his plate in hand, savoring the last morsel. He looked to Willow, to Jeric, and then back to his plate. Guilt washed over him and he swallowed.

"Please don't be mad," he said in a small voice.

Willow released a long breath and then surprised him by leaning up to kiss him on the cheek. "I've helped you many times, my love. This time I need you."

Light stared into the dark eyes of Willow, and saw a yearning he'd never seen before. She needed him to stand with her, and he'd taken a break to eat a meal. Fine friend he was. He shook himself and set the plate down again.

"How do we get in?"

"The nearest tower is too far," Jeric said, eyeing the closest structures to the refuge. "And very few are taller. You want to climb past the deragoths?"

"We'd never make it," Willow said.

"Can't you just walk us inside the front door?" Light asked.

He pointed to the large opening flanked by a quartet of soldiers. The space beyond seemed welcoming, with a small forest of the purple trees in the entrance hall. Interspersed with glowing white mushrooms, it was artistic and pleasant.

Willow shook her head. "All Order members are recognized by name at the door—"

"I can do that," Light said.

"—and must pass through the anti-magic trees."

"I can't do that," Light said.

Willow pointed to the trees in the entrance hall. "Walk past those and you'll lose any active charm. We'll be spotted before we go five steps."

"*You* can walk in, though."

"So I'm supposed to leave you outside?" she asked, smiling faintly.

"If you go in, you can open a window for us," Light said.

"And how are we supposed to get to the window?" Jeric asked.

"From there," Light said, pointing upward.

They followed his gaze to the roof of the cavern, where luminescent vines covered the stone, crisscrossing in glowing patterns. A small protrusion pointed downward, directly above the Order tower.

"What do you expect us to do," Jeric said with a laugh. "Fall five hundred feet and land on the roof?"

"Why not?" Light asked.

"Because I like my bones *inside* my body," Jeric said.

"I won't let you shatter," Light said.

"Unless you get distracted," Jeric said.

Light laughed. "That probably won't happen."

"That's comforting."

"Even if no one sees you fall," Willow said, "you'll have to use your magic to land."

"So we'll use a distraction," Light said, his eyes glowing with excitement as the idea formed.

He wasn't used to being the one to come up with ideas, but he thought this was a good one. He gathered the light from the area and pulled it into his hands, compressing it into a small sphere.

He reached for more light, but recalled their warning about using too much magic, so he kept the draw slow, gradually pulling the sources on the street. Light orbs dimmed, both in the street and in the buildings nearby. Dark elves paused and glanced about, so he stopped pulling and let the orbs regain their magic.

The orb in his hands pulsed, so Light forced the magic to point inward. The exterior darkened, but the sphere trembled in his hand, occasionally spitting sparks of power, illuminating their faces.

"Ignite this just before we land," Light said, turning to Willow. "Everyone will look and no one will see us."

"How bright is this going to be?" she asked, gingerly accepting the sphere like it might explode in her palm.

"Just touch the rune on the top when you are ready," Light said. "And then get away."

"How far?"

"And cover your eyes," he advised. "Or it will take a few days for your vision to come back."

She turned her eyes away from it. "There's an old arena nearby that should suit our purposes nicely."

"Are we actually considering this?" Jeric asked.

"It's a good plan," Willow said, nodding her approval to Light.

"For both of you," Jeric said. "I get to fall five hundred feet and trust my landing to a distracted, impulsive fragment of a guardian."

"It will be a tale for the ages," Willow said.

Her tone was quiet, but a hint of a challenge had crept into her voice. Light looked to Jeric, delighted with Willow's effort to poke Jeric's sense of adventure. Jeric's eyes narrowed and he leveled an accusing finger at the dark elf.

"I know you're trying to manipulate me," Jeric said.

"Good," Willow said. "Because it wouldn't be fun if you didn't realize what I was doing."

"You think you can appeal to my sense of adventure?" Jeric folded his arms. "Or maybe you think I'm old and I've lost my wits."

"So you won't do it?"

"Of course I'm going to do it," Jeric said. "I just want it remembered that if I die with my body broken in a thousand pieces, I went out the way I lived."

"Don't worry," Light said, "I won't let you fall to your—hey, is that cocoa sauce on stone fried bread and dwarven spiced cheese?"

Jeric sighed. "So this is how I die . . ."

Chapter 3: A Risky Venture

"Have I told you that you're my favorite?"

Light threw Jeric a surprised look. "You always said Shadow was your favorite fragment."

"He is," Jeric said. "But I really would like to survive this."

Light laughed, and then smothered it before it could be heard. After separating from Willow, Light and Jeric worked their way through the towers of Outer Kordune and passed into the more modest homes on the slopes of the outer wall. Also built on outcroppings of rock, the smaller structures dotted the sides, interior, and summit.

Dark elf children sought amusement in the streets, those with magic playing with small orbs of power, tossing them about in games that elicited shouts and laughter. Light wanted to join them, but Jeric discouraged the notion.

The homes had given way to small shanties for the poor and destitute of the city. The streets grew dingier and darker, lacking the brighter plants that illuminated the rest of the city. Normally Light enjoyed it when thieves attempted to steal from him, but this time they only lurked in the alleys.

Light and Jeric reached the end of the city and ducked behind a building, ascending to the roof of an abandoned home. Jeric eyed the curving wall, tilting his head back to see the long ascent to the ceiling of the great cavern.

"Tales of your exploits don't really matter if you're dead," Jeric murmured.

"Are you still worried?" Light asked.

"You're not?"

Light merely laughed and drew on the magic emanating from the luminescent vines and mushrooms, shaping the power into spider legs large enough to support his body. Then he added straps like a pack. Handing it to Jeric, he crafted his own set of spider legs.

At Jeric's request, he shielded the light of the legs, making them less visible. Two dark shapes ascending the outer wall would be hard to spot, especially if they stuck to the patches of bare stone, where the illumination would not reveal them, but sixteen shiny legs would be spotted in moments.

The legs darkened as Light redirected the magic to point inward, shielding the illumination. Then he fastened one set of legs to his back and Jeric did the same. A smile spread on his face as he turned toward the city, and the legs reached for the wall.

The legs snagged the wall and began to climb, lifting his feet off the roof of the empty house, carrying him aloft. Jeric's spider legs did the same, and the ground gradually receded as they glided up the wall.

One of Jeric's legs slipped, and he cursed under his breath. Excitement flooded Light's blood and he released a high laugh. Jeric glared at him, a reminder to stay silent, and Light gave an apologetic look.

"I've never done anything as insane as this," he said in an excited whisper.

"You won't get to do anything ever again if you don't focus," Jeric said, his voice tense.

The spider legs continued to climb, carrying them up the curving slope of the cavern wall, navigating the cracks and crevasses and keeping them in the many patches of darkness. Several times they passed crystals, and he tried to break one off for a souvenir. Instead he dropped it, and it fell into the city. He winced when it shattered on a roof, drawing the eyes of several in the street. Jeric looked daggers at him as they waited. They were two hundred feet off the ground and the curve of the roof left them dangling over the streets.

"Look at the view," Light breathed.

"Let's not see it up close," Jeric said.

Annoyed, Light looked to Jeric. "Why are you being so depressing? You're the one that likes adventure, but you're acting like a frightened child. If we fall, I'll just cast wings and we'll fly down."

"Would that it could be so easy," Jeric said tensely. "There's not enough light for you to cast wings."

"Of course there's enough to . . ."

His eyes widened as he looked to the plants clinging to the uneven rock around them. Although the covering of vines helped to illuminate the cavern, there were not enough for him to cast wings capable of slowing their descent.

He looked down at the three hundred-foot fall with new eyes, panic rising in his blood and making his hands shake. What had he been thinking? This plan was madness, and why had they trusted him? He didn't have the tactical mind of his fragment brothers.

"You let me do this?" Light demanded.

"I thought you knew what was at stake," Jeric said.

"I *never* think of what's at stake," Light said, his voice tinged with fear. "And now I'm about to fall to my death—!"

One of his legs slipped, and he squeaked in surprise and terror. The legs continued to climb, clinging to crevasses that now seemed tiny, cracks that could break at any moment. He wished he'd cast more legs, or more spiders—or never opened his mouth.

"We're half way," Jeric said, clenching the band of light wrapping around his chest. "We'll be there soon."

"We should go back!" Light cried. "I like my bones in my body too!"

Jeric grinned but shook his head. "I don't like saying it, but your plan was actually pretty sound."

Light rounded on the elf. "How can you say that? Look at where we are, with nothing to save us if we fall."

"Light," Jeric said, his voice urgent, "most have nothing to save them. That's why they live so cautiously."

Light's panic skidded to a halt, and he regarded his companion with surprise. Jeric's words had the ring of truth, especially coming from one with no magic. Jeric had only his wits and skills to keep him alive, yet he'd adventured across the world. Every risk he'd taken, every battle he'd fought, could have claimed his life.

The fragments of Draeken were each powerful in their own way, and Light had rarely been tested to an extreme—and never by choice. He'd always assumed he would survive, that his magic, or his brothers, would bring victory.

"Yet you chose to follow my idea?" Light asked slowly.

"Like I said," Jeric replied. "It was a good plan. Dangerous and terrifying, but good."

Light gazed down upon the city, on the great towers that continued to shrink in size. The enormous cavern stretched away from them, the towers, the streets, the labyrinth of windows and arched openings of the inner city. The lake reflected the glittering crystals, the view all the more vivid because of the danger.

"I'm not used to feeling fear," Light said, clinging to the bands of light that kept him attached to the spider legs.

"I suspect you'll feel more of it down here," Jeric said. "It will make you want to stop, to retreat, to shrink from what must be done. You cannot let it—"

A rock cracked and came free, and three of Jeric's spider legs slipped off. He sucked in his breath as the others scrambled to hold on, but they too slipped free, and Jeric dropped off the ceiling of the cavern.

Light reached a hand out, two of his spider legs stretching over his shoulder to catch Jeric's legs. Light's other spider legs shifted, and he experienced a surge of terror. But to his immense relief, they held.

28

Upside down, Jeric released a shaky laugh. "As I said, don't let fear stop you from acting."

Light grinned and directed his legs to lift Jeric back to the roof. His spider legs reattached, and the elf managed a shaky laugh, the sound tinged with relief. They exchanged a nod, and then began to creep forward once more, with more caution.

The two spiders carried them across the ceiling, up and down the crags and cracks, through patches of darkness and occasional sections of vines. Light found the sense of danger exhilarating, bringing an unfamiliar sense of focus.

As they crossed the ceiling of the cavern, Light watched the legs reach into the crevasses and wrap around knobby holds. Shadow liked to climb, but Light had never seen the appeal. Now he wished he'd learned to climb with his hands. It seemed like he would be less afraid if his hands weren't hanging over the drop.

The protrusion above the Order's tower drew painstakingly closer, and Light eyed the distance. The tower resembled a large tooth, the sides of which were rough and cracked, almost to the point of instability. Five hundred feet below, the roof of the Order's home lay unguarded, because who was mad enough to do what they were doing?

The two spiders reached the protrusion and swiveled, causing Light's stomach to leap like it wanted to grab the ceiling. Then they descended to the tip of the protrusion, the two spiders clinging to the surface.

"Well," Jeric said. "We made it. Now for the hard part."

Light heard the trace of excitement in his voice. "So *now* you enjoy this?"

"Maybe," Jeric said. "But let's make certain we survive the fall. What's your plan?"

"I *did* want to use wings," he said.

"And now?" Jeric pressed.

"I guess we'll use the spider legs," Light said.

He scanned the nearby ceiling. The patches of vines would provide some power, but not enough to craft wings of solidity, not strong enough to support both of them. The legs, however, were already strong, and if angled in the right direction they might not shatter . . .

"So you plan to use threads of light like spider's silk?" Jeric nodded his approval. "You're more clever than I gave you credit."

"Er, yes, that was my plan," Light said.

Jeric smiled knowingly, and Light resisted the urge to strike his smug face. Just because his idea was better did not mean he could gloat. But it was better, so Light gathered the light from the nearby vines, gradually draining the energy from the leaves, and fastened it to not one, but three crags in the toothlike protrusion. As with the legs, he focused the magic into the rope so it would not be visible from the city.

"Ready?" he asked.

Jeric nodded. "As I'll ever be."

"What about Willow?" he asked.

Jeric pointed to the dark patch of vines. "She would have seen the ceiling darken. She'll be ready."

Light nodded, and then hesitantly directed the spider legs to grasp the rope. One leg at a time, he transitioned from the comforting stone to the terrifyingly unstable rope. The legs cinched the strand and began to descend like a real spider, and a moment later it vibrated when Jeric joined him.

The strand swayed back and forth with their movement, bringing them over the street and back over the roof of the Order tower. Light's stomach lurched in fear and he clung to the harness as they gradually descended from the ceiling. Five hundred feet became four hundred, and then three hundred, then two. And then the strand came to an end.

Light swallowed when he realized they'd gone as far as they could. From a few feet above, Jeric lowered his voice.

"You think these legs can manage a landing?"

"I think so," he said.

"Your lack of confidence is disturbing."

Light smiled faintly and looked up. "I'll go first? I'll probably survive an impact, and then I can try to help soften your landing."

"Clever and self-sacrificing," Jeric said. "You might actually become my favorite."

Light grinned, and then faced downward, eyeing the two hundred-foot fall. The strand continued to sway, swinging them away from the roof and over the street. He swallowed his fear and recalled Jeric's words.

A pinprick of light flashed into view from the opposite side of the cavern, where an abandoned arena was just visible. Light recognized it as Willow's signal that she was ready, so he gathered himself for the fall, timed the drop, and then willed the spider legs to come free. One by one they detached, until he dangled at the end by a single arch of light. Then he sucked in his breath and released.

Chapter 4: Hall of the Order

Light knew instantly that his aim was off, and he fell towards the edge of the roof rather than the center. He sucked in his breath as the roof filled his vision, the air snapping at his clothing, pulling at his cloak.

He sought to cast wings, but the effort only succeeded in getting in the way of his spider legs. Instead, he reached to his back and rotated the spider legs to his feet, attaching them to his boots. The legs reached down, extending to their fullest.

In his peripheral vision a blast of light blazed to life. Like a miniature sun, it exploded in the abandoned arena, filling the breadth of the great cavern in white light. The sounds of the city stilled and all eyes turned toward the light, dark elves raising their hands against the glare.

Light used the distraction to draw on the light, extending the legs of his spider. His fear spiked and he angled his body, desperately trying to catch the edge of the roof. He landed at the edge of the roof, the spider legs bending and folding, cushioning his fall. They took the brunt of the fall but he landed hard, his body flattening on the stone roof. The impact dislodged three of the legs and they slipped off the edge.

For a single, terrifying moment, he slid over the side, and then the spider legs dragged him downward, into the street. His fingers slid across the stone and caught the edge of the roof, his body coming to a jarring halt.

Hanging by his fingertips in a tangle of giant spider legs, he fought to pull himself upward, but the legs were bound and twisted, making the effort difficult. He glanced over his shoulder and saw the drop looming. A deragoth prowled at the limit of its chain, snarling in the direction of the arena.

A door opened next to the beast and a pair of dark elves came out. They stood clear of the chained predator and squinted towards the arena, unaware that Light hung from the roof above their heads. And the sunspot in the arena was beginning to fade.

Light struggled to disentangle the spider legs but failed, so he dismissed all but two, the magic disintegrating into sparks. The last two were on the ledge, and with their aid, he pulled himself up, shoving himself over the edge and dragging his legs after.

He flopped onto his back and raised his hands in victory. Then he saw Jeric plummeting towards the roof. He too had attached the spider legs to his feet and he dropped downward like a knife, the legs straight, ready to cushion his landing. He struck near the center of the roof, the legs folding outward, lowering him to the stone.

Jeric landed easily and hopped out of the spider legs, alighting on his feet. He laughed quietly, the sound tinged with delight, before strolling to Light with a smile on his face. The elf looked down at Light, raising an eyebrow.

"Are you well?"

"My bones seem intact."

"Then you're well," he said.

Light rose to his feet, his gaze settling on the broken spider legs scattered across the roof. They'd cushioned their landings, but they were ruined, the broken enchantments spitting sparks of light from the cracks.

"A tale for the ages," Jeric said, lifting his eyes to the ceiling, which now seemed disturbingly distant.

Light squinted to see the protrusion, pleased that he hadn't gotten them killed. And happy that his idea had worked. Still, he found he disliked the prospect of providing the plan, for he didn't care for the weight of responsibility that came attached.

"What now?" Light asked.

"Now you become Serak," Jeric said.

33

Light recalled Serak's dark eyes and cruel lips. His hair was easy, as was his build, and Light bent the light to his will, shaping the features so anyone who looked would see the Father of Guardians.

"Better?"

"Not really." Jeric circled him, examining the illusion. "But I think that's the point. Once you remove the charm on my face we're ready."

"Are you certain you do not wish me to give you another face?" Light asked. "I promise it won't have an oversized feature."

Jeric grinned. "I've never cared to don the persona of another. Besides, my reputation is colorful enough that the Order will accept me as a potential ally—if you are the one to give support."

Light inclined his head and reached up, dismissing the magic over Jeric's features, returning him to his elven skin and blue eyes. Then he strode to the back corner of the roof. Peering over the edge, he eyed the drop. The light from Willow's blast had faded, but the deragoths were still pacing, their unease apparent as they prowled the summit of the rocky hill, patrolling the exterior of the tower as if their lives depended on it. He wondered if they could be befriended, and if Mind would let him keep one as a pet. They looked dangerous, which would make Fire happy.

"Light?"

"Sorry."

Light clambered over the edge and used the artistic curves around the windows to brace himself. After the sobering experience on the cavern roof, he found a healthy measure of caution, and frequently looked down. The tower atop the fistlike hill put him at five hundred feet off the street, more than enough to kill him. Or could he be killed from a fall? He tapped his chin, wondering just how much it would hurt.

Jeric easily descended the slope and caught the top of a window, swinging himself into the space between glass and exterior. Then he withdrew a tiny black knife, which he passed around the edge of the window. Several times sparks burst from hidden traps, and then Jeric nodded to himself.

"Curses disabled."

Seized with excitement, Light followed the elf as he slipped into the room. With no walls or doors, the top floor of the tower extended for a distance, the walls stark and empty. Only one object resided in the room. The Gate. The mirror hung on the opposite side of the room, its silver surface reflecting the empty chamber. Facing the Gate, a wide set of stairs descended through the center of the floor.

"This is exciting!" he hissed.

Jeric flinched at Light's loud voice.

"Can you *try* to be quiet?"

"I'll try," Light said.

"We just need to wait for Willow to arrive." Jeric scanned the room. "But we need a place to hide."

"No problem," Light said.

The room may have been gloomy, but the lights of the city were bright—were they brighter than before? He vaguely recalled Willow talking about how the light dimmed and brightened each day, simulating the rise and fall of the sun. It seemed to be midday, now, but Light could be wrong. Still, he wondered if he could brighten the plants further and throw off their clock . . .

"Light."

Jeric's voice was nearly a groan, a sigh that revealed irritation and resignation. Light looked down and realized he was halfway out the window. He grinned sheepishly, an expression likely odd on Serak's face.

"Sorry."

"Is there something outside you need?"

"Just magic," Light said.

Drawing on the abundance of energy, he retreated into the room and shaped a wall around them, sealing off the illusion so anyone looking their way would see the wall. Nodding to himself, he yawned.

"We can hide here until Willow arrives," Jeric said.

"Then can I take a nap?" he asked. "The light and darkness shifting is making me tired."

Jeric waved to the floor. "Sadly there does not seem to be a bed—"

"Oh I can do that," Light said with a grunt of amusement. Drawing on more light from outside, he shaped a soft bed and flopped onto its surface. In the dark room, he was asleep in seconds.

He was poked awake from the dream of a beautiful sunrise, and he lurched upward. Jeric caught him and held him against the wall, covering his mouth. Light blinked at the irritating loss of sleep. His dream had been pleasant, but he was still in the blasted Deep.

"Mmphnifrunif."

"Someone's coming." Jeric's voice was barely audible. "Don't try to talk."

"Mphk."

Jeric cautiously released him, and Light peered around the elf. "How long was I asleep?" He was proud that he whispered.

Jeric's eyes were on the stairs. "Six minutes."

Light yawned, and Jeric covered his mouth. "Stop that. You're making me yawn, and it's not even nighttime."

"Darkness makes me tired," Light said.

The voices were coming from down the stairs and a door was opened, the creak of steel reverberating up into the Gate chamber. Light was equal parts enthralled and distracted by the scent of gorthon fish. How did it get up here? Then a lithe figure ascended the steps into view and Light veritably bounded forward when he recognized Willow. Jeric caught him and yanked him back when the second figure appeared.

Princess Melora.

"There was no need for you to accompany me," Willow said. "I was told to greet him alone."

"He always wishes to speak to his loyal acolytes," Princess Melora said haughtily.

Jeric caught Light's chin and forced him to focus. Then he pointed to the Gate on the opposite side of the room and made a motion of them circling the space, moving the illusion as they did.

Light nodded, and the two crept along the wall, working their way around the two dark elves. Willow's eyes flicked to the touch of movement and she shifted her feet. The princess shifted her feet as well, subconsciously moving to be opposite her, placing her back to Light and Jeric.

"As I said," Willow said. "I'm certain you are busy."

"Not so busy as to neglect greeting our master," the princess said, and then leaned in. "Your effort to gain his favor will not succeed."

Willow folded her arms and glared, an expression that caused Light to poke his face out of the illusion and make a rude gesture at Princess Melora's back. Willow's lips twitched, but she did not smile, and Jeric pulled him back behind the illusion wall. Princess Melora annoyed him, mostly because Willow did not like her. As second daughter to the queen of her nation, she was not bound for the throne. Unless the queen was absent and her sister killed. Light wondered what would happened if he killed Melora. It would be easy to cast a spear of light and hurl it into her back.

Jeric stabbed a finger at Light's face, reminding him of their purpose, and he reluctantly relinquished the idea. They continued to work their way around the room. Again Willow shifted, and again the princess did the same. As Light and Jeric reached the Gate, the princess leaned in to Willow.

"Serak has entrusted me with the knowledge of what he plans for you," she said. "And do not forget, I know how loyally you served the queen."

"I serve the seat of power," Willow said. "And we both know that power has shifted."

Jeric caught Light's sleeve and pointed to the Gate, spreading his hands wide as if it were opening. Light understood his meaning and the pair stepped in front of it. He again pulled from the illumination outside, pulling it into his palms and altering the color, siphoning off the other colors of light until only silver remained. Then he reached back and placed a hand on the stone beneath the Gate.

He hesitated, the magic crackling at his fingertips. What he was about to do, who he was about to become, sent a chill into his blood. This was Elenyr's plan, but he feared failure, of letting Jeric fall to his death, or Willow fall to hers. Then Jeric touched his arm and held his gaze.

The perpetually carefree elf had a surprisingly sober expression, his eyes set, his smile one of confidence. The elf nodded, and Light understood he was expressing his trust in their plan. Light bowed his head, glanced to Willow, and then released his magic.

Silver light blossomed in the Gate, shimmering into shape just as Light and Jeric stepped through the illusion wall, as if they'd simply appeared through the portal. Of course, they were a full two feet in front of the Gate, but who would notice? Princess Melora was not observant.

"Master," Princess Melora said. "It is good of you to come, but why have you brought a surface elf—"

"Silence," Light exclaimed, his voice haughty and forceful. "You will not look me in the eye for a full hour, that I may test your loyalty."

The princess looked between Willow and Serak, her expression shocked. Then her mouth snapped shut and anger tightened her features. Her eyes dropped to the floor and her voice burned with embarrassment.

"Master, if I have offended you—"

"You have," Light said. "And it is to your shame that you don't know your offense. Now, lead on, before I remind you."

Princess Melora scowled and descended the steps. Light grinned to Willow, raising a hand in victory. He hadn't thought it would be so

38

easy. Would all the Order members obey so quickly? He wondered what he could get them to do.

"And you were worried," Light whispered.

Jeric grunted in doubt, and murmured from behind. "Indeed."

Chapter 5: A False Serak

Light followed Princess Melora down the steps, pleased by the anger wafting off her rigid frame. The dark elf was royalty, disused to such a harsh rebuke. But she'd spoken to Willow with condescension, and Light couldn't let that be.

"Master," Melora said, "may I ask why you have the Ear in your midst.

Jeric groaned. "What does one have to do to shed a persona?"

"He is an ally," Light said.

Light was grateful they had talked about the purpose of Jeric's presence. The elf was well known by many, and the Order would be aware of his history. They would not trust him, but it was also believable that he would side with the Order, for a price. Of course, the Order had no idea of the attachment Jeric harbored for Elenyr.

"He was seen traveling with the fragments," Melora said, her eyes on the floor. "He is our enemy."

They reached the double doors at the end of the corridor, and as Melora reached for the handle, Light caught her neck and shoved her into the wood. Leaning close, he spoke into her ear.

"Are you questioning me?"

His voice was soft, dangerously so, and Melora shuddered. Light had no qualms about using rage, and against the princess it was an easy emotion to access. Willow had made it clear that unless the higher ranks of the Order thought him legitimate, the soldiers would never follow.

"No, Master," she said, fear in her voice.

Light released her, and then realized he had no idea where to go. "Then lead the way, Princess. I wish to see the queen."

Melora glanced his way, surprise overcoming her fear before she dropped her eyes once again. "You ordered her sent away," she said. "To keep her beyond the reach of rescue. Do you wish for me to recall her? It will take time for her to arrive."

Light noticed Willow give a warning shake of her head and realized that to demand such a request so quickly might lead to more suspicion. Light jerked his head in the negative, hoping his expression remained haughty.

"No," he said. "I will speak to her another time."

Melora nodded, and her eyes flicked to Willow. "Then do you wish to proceed with your previous request?"

Light hesitated, uncertain of how to proceed. Whatever Serak's previous request had been, it was likely not in their interest. But to refuse would seem out of character, and if the queen had been sent away, they needed time. With both Jeric and Willow attempting to signal an affirmative answer, such conclusions were easy to assume.

"Of course," Light said.

Melora's smile made his skin crawl, and her eyes again flicked to Willow. Turning on her heel, she opened the door and led them into the hall beyond. She strode with a purpose, down the corridor to the stairs at the end.

The interior of the tower was built in curves, matching the rounded exterior. Walls and rooms, even doors, were all without edges or points. The style did not resemble that of other structures in the city, and it seemed older, even ancient.

Instead of paintings, tapestries, or weapons, the walls were inscribed with a strange language. Runes and text, words and symbols, all unfamiliar to Light. He glanced to Jeric and saw him examining the walls with bright eyes. Their eyes met and Jeric mouthed a single word.

Krey.

It was the language of the ancients, and Light looked to the tower with renewed interest. The tower was not a building at all, rather it was an archive, a record that dated beyond The Age of Oracles, perhaps even to the Dawn of Magic.

The words glowed faintly, inscribed on the wall in long strings of symbols. The language was unlike any Light had seen, and contained swooping curls and arcs, artistic and flowing, a language of beauty. The choice of refuge by the Order could not be a coincidence, and suggested that the Order of Ancients had existed for a lot longer than Serak had been its head. They passed a room with an open door, the chamber beyond filled with krey relics. Light stared in wonder until Willow nudged him, and he managed to change his expression to cold apathy.

"Master," a guard murmured as they rounded a corner, his voice tinged with reverence.

Others spoke with similar fervor, and Light disliked their tone. In a testament to their faith in Serak, none questioned Jeric's presence, and only looked on with suspicion as the elf passed. They clenched the hilt of their swords, but Jeric merely smiled.

"It will take time to set everything," Melora said. "We thought you were still in Mistkeep."

"Are you displeased with my arrival?" Light asked.

"We are always grateful for your arrival," Melora said. "But if we'd had some warning we might have been better prepared—"

"I do not care for your incessant questioning," Light said. "Perhaps a week as a common guard would remind you of your place, or maybe you'd like to clean the floor . . . with your crown."

The woman glanced his way, a red flush lighting her grey skin. She bowed low and motioned to a guard, the dark elf taking the lead. Murmuring an order that Light could not hear, she cast Willow a baleful look.

"I will gather the senior acolytes," she said. "Then the truth will be revealed."

She turned and departed, and the guard took her place, guiding them deep into the tower. Jeric's expression gained a trace of worry, and Willow's features were rigid. Light hardly noticed, his attention on the script inscribed on the walls.

What did they say? Had they been written by the krey? Or the first Order members? Did Elenyr speak the krey language? He watched it all, fascinated by the ancient script. It covered the walls on every level, continuing as they descended into the bowels of the tower.

The outcropping of rock that supported the tower contained more of the structure, but the architecture remained the same. And still the text lined the walls, a single row of words, only broken by doors and hallways. Their guide led them deeper, and Light turned to Willow.

She jerked her head, motioning him to silence. He frowned, but her features were hard, and she kept looking to Jeric. Light raised an eyebrow when he noticed that one of the enchanted hilts he used for weapons was absent from its sheath. Willow's hand rested casually on her hip, where the hilt of her inksword ran down her leg.

"Willow—"

"Master Serak," Willow cut him off. "I'm certain you are hungry, perhaps you'd like to eat?"

The dark elf glanced back. "I will send a meal to the viewing room."

Willow nodded in agreement. "That will be well."

Light thought of the gorthon fish and his features brightened. "What's the—"

Willow elbowed him in the side, and he realized he'd completely forgotten that he was Serak. The dark elf glanced back curiously, waiting for him to finish the statement, and he coughed.

"—food you'll bring?"

"Your favorite," the dark elf said.

"That will be well," Light said, and hoped it wasn't broccoli.

He hated broccoli, the cursed vegetable that Elenyr always insisted he eat. Why did he have to eat food meant for rabbits? It never made him stronger, or smarter. And why did Elenyr have to be ethereal? With her ability, she'd often reached through his foot to find where he'd hiden the broccoli under his boot.

They came to the end of a corridor, where an ironbound door was flanked by two guards. They nodded to Serak and the door was opened, allowing them entry. The elf swept a hand to the darkened interior.

"I'll have your meal sent up."

"Some nice roast bird would be nice for me," Jeric said with a smile.

The dark elf scowled and left, and Willow followed Jeric into the room. Light stepped inside and the door creaked shut behind them, leaving them alone in a small, circular chamber. A window allowed light to spill inside, and he stepped to it, looking down into the spacious chamber below.

"Do you think Serak eats broccoli?" he asked.

"That's the least of our problems," Willow said, her voice tense as she stepped in. "I think they suspect Light. He hasn't been very subtle."

Jeric nodded. "Melora did seem rather surprised when Light threatened her."

"You didn't help." Willow rounded on Jeric. "Did you have to ask for your favorite meal?"

"I'm maintaining my persona," Jeric said.

"What's the problem?" Light asked, mystified by the conflict.

"The problem is that you are not a very good Serak," Willow said. "Did you listen to *anything* we said on our way down here?"

Light grimaced. "I thought I did."

"Where are we?" Jeric asked.

44

"This is the viewing room for the acolyte test," she said. "There's only one reason we'd be here, and that's if the Order wants to test the loyalty of one of its members."

"What do you mean, test?" Light asked.

"It's different for everyone," Willow said. "Only the senior acolytes are given the truth about Serak's identity and know the full history of the Order."

"Then who's going to be tested?" Light examined the amphitheatre, wondering if they would get to see a juggler. He loved juggling, especially with detonation spheres.

"*You* are going to be tested," Willow said. "Don't you understand? This is exactly the type of thing Serak plans for. And if they test you, there's no way you'll pass."

"I might—"

"You won't," Willow said. "We need to escape, quickly."

"But it was hard enough to get in here," Light complained. "And you already want to leave?"

"You want to be buried here?" Willow challenged.

"Too late," Jeric said.

He was standing at the window and looking down into the room beyond. Robed figures were filling the benches that surrounded the pit, each carrying a torch. The fires danced around the chamber, illuminating smaller viewing chambers on the same level as theirs, each containing more robed figures.

"The senior acolytes are arriving," Willow said, obviously dismayed. "That means Melora will return at any moment."

Light watched the rest of the Order file into place as Jeric and Willow argued in hushed tones. The Order members wore dark robes, occasionally interspersed with red, probably suggesting higher ranks. The ones in the other viewing chambers wore grey robes, each emblazoned with a symbol from the krey language. The senior members were masked, obscuring their identities.

The door clicked and swung open, and Willow and Jeric feigned neutral expressions. Then Melora entered with a pair of guards. Unlike the rest of the guards, these wore expensive silver armor, and each wore a mask of pure white, marked with jagged lines, like claws across the features. One had four claw marks, the other five.

Light's eyes widened in excitement before he recalled his persona and stifled the emotion. The Queen's Hand, five legendary warriors that served the queen of the dark elves, reportedly turned traitor and joined the Order. He wondered if they would consent to a memory orb so Light could remember the moment.

"As you requested," Melora said, motioning to the pair. "I brought Cutter and Black for this trial." Her smile was malicious as she looked to Jeric and Willow.

Light realized that their infiltration might very well be over, and the Order was set to destroy them. He gathered his magic, subtly drawing it into his flesh until his fingers veritably sang with the desire to strike. He glanced to Jeric and Willow, and found both to be tense, their hands already on weapons.

"Princess," Light said, attempting cool indifference. "Are the details of the trial ready to commence?"

"They are," she said.

Light expected the woman to strike, but the princess rotated to face Willow, her smile turning malicious. She motioned to the Hand and they stepped to flank Willow, placing hands on her elbows, anti-magic flowing from their gauntlets to wrap around her wrists.

"Willow," she said. "Serak has suspected you for some time, and now you will be tested."

Chapter 6: The Inkmage

Willow recognized what was coming the moment the Hand moved to flank her and used the precious seconds to consider her options. A glance at Light revealed his bewilderment, his features frozen as if he'd been on the verge of attacking Melora.

She could fight, of course, but in the confines of the viewing chamber and surrounded by hundreds of senior acolytes, she would not survive. Jeric probably wouldn't either, regardless of his skill with survival. Would they kill Light? Or seek to trap him? Probably the latter, but his childlike rage would not be bound, and they would probably be forced to kill him.

Or she could face the trial.

As the two members of the Queen's Hand caught her elbows, she considered what she'd seen in the trials she'd attended. The potential acolyte always faced a fight to prove their worth in combat, followed by a test of loyalty. Of the six she'd witnessed, only one had survived. Three had failed in the test of combat, while the other two had failed in the test of loyalty. Both had been members of other organizations, seeking to gain a foothold in the Order. Serak possessed an uncanny ability to identify traitors.

She didn't move as the anti-magic bonds flowed out of their gauntlets, wrapping around her wrists, a precaution extended to all the acolytes taking the trial, because loyalty was not assured until after.

She realized Serak had obviously intended for her to take the trial on his next return to the Deep, and fate had intervened so Light and Jeric were present. She met Light's gaze and saw the tension to his jaw. Melora would interpret it as an expectation of Willow's failure, but Willow recognized Light's mounting rage. If she did die, Light would fall to bloodlust, a rage she could see in his eyes.

"Master Serak," she said, drawing his attention. "I know you do not think me loyal, but I am grateful for the chance to prove it this day."

"Willow," Light said.

He twitched like he wanted to reach for her, but he held his arm in check. Inwardly she smiled, pleased that he managed to restrain himself. If Serak reached out and kissed her prior to her test of loyalty, it would probably lead to all their deaths, even if the shock on Melora's face might be worth it.

"Traitors," Jeric said, shaking his head as if lamenting the word. "I hate traitors."

"Do you have *anyone* you're loyal to?" Melora asked.

"Of course," Jeric said. "But it isn't you."

"Master," Melora said. "Permit me to throw Jeric in with Willow."

Those present looked to Serak, and Willow held her breath. His next words could maintain the persona or doom them all. He regarded Melora with veiled hatred, and then noticed Willow. She gave a tiny shake of her head, and then subtly traced her hand in the air, the symbol of peace.

"Willow will be tested alone," Light said.

Melora smiled and motioned the two members of the Hand to follow her out of the viewing room. Willow made no move to resist, or even reach for her tattoos, and allowed herself to be led into the corridor. As they descended the stairs to the bottom level of the tower, the princess slowed to walk closer to Willow, and her expression became a haughty sneer.

"I've suspected you since the day you accepted the Order's invitation," she said. "But Serak insisted you would be an invaluable ally. He was blinded by your unique magic and thought to turn you to our cause."

"He is ever intelligent," Willow said.

Melora turned and came to a halt, forcing Willow to stop and face her. "But I know you, Willow. You would never betray the elves or the crown. I would wager everything I possess that you joined the Order on my mother's order."

It was the truth, but Willow had a great deal of practice keeping her features fixed. She held the princess's gaze, unflinching, unmoving. Willow was a soldier sworn to protect the queen of her people. The queen may have lost her daughter, while her greatest soldiers, the Hand, had delivered her into the hands of the Order, but Willow would never yield.

Willow offered a faint smile. "When I succeed, you'll have to eat your words. Senior acolytes are above suspicion."

"You won't," she said. "Because you are a crusader, and you already have a cause. The good ones are always so easy to break, because there are certain lines they refuse to cross. I'd wish you luck, but I'd rather watch you die."

"I live to disappoint," Willow said.

Melora scowled, and then stepped aside, allowing the Hand to guide her to the steelbound door at the end of the hall. Her expression smug, the princess motioned the door to be opened, and Willow was led into the base of the pit.

The members of the Hand relinquished their grip and the anti-magic flowed back into their gauntlets. Then they retreated, the steel door shutting in a clang of steel on stone. Alone in the pit, Willow looked up and turned a circle.

Twenty-foot walls bordered the large pit. At three times that across, the pit was large enough for fifty to battle, and Willow had seen men and women flee before beasts and killers, or die when they were asked to kill their own mother.

Hundreds of Order members ringed the viewing space, all dressed in ceremonial robes. The senior acolytes were in their viewing booths, the krey letters on their robes shining. The multitude of torches flickered and danced, casting the pit into shifting light.

49

Princess Melora appeared in the viewing chamber beside Serak and spoke to him in low tones. Serak did not look pleased, a fact Melora and the other Order members would likely assume was indicative of his doubt in Willow's loyalty. Willow knew the truth, and realized that only Jeric's steady hand, lightly touching his side, kept him from leaping out of the booth and hurling himself on the Order members.

"Initiates and senior acolytes," Princess Melora began. "Today we have the privilege of witnessing the advancement—or demise—of a new member in our ranks. I'm sure you all know Willow. Her magic is recognizable across our nation, yet few know that she joined our number some time ago. To test her loyalty, Master Serak has crafted a special trial, one I think will endure in the halls of our memory."

She inclined her head to an acolyte standing at the edge of the pit across from her, and he pulled a lever. A grinding of stone echoed in the pit, punctuated by a faint snarl. A door gradually opened, lifting upward to reveal a darkened corridor beyond. Then the beast stalked into the open, and a murmur swept the crowd.

Melora's voice bordered on giddy. "I give you . . . a deragoth."

At just four feet long, the beast was not large, but menace seeped from every pore. The red scales lined the catlike body, glittering with its paralytic poison, capable of leaving her helpless as the beast began to feed on her live flesh. This close, Willow could see the luminescent white eyes and the wide maw filled with sharp teeth.

The deragoth came to the end of its chain where it prowled, yearning to be set free. Its eyes never left Willow, and she sensed its hunger. Willow caught the hilt of her chakram and pulled the weapon from her flesh. The ink coming free of her skin felt like a finger caressing her stomach, the ink stretching and pulling around her body, pouring into her hand and turning solid, the circular weapon falling free. It landed at her side.

"But this is Willow," Princess Melora continued, "the renowned inkmage, and a deragoth may be fearsome, but in his infinite wisdom, Serak has decided on a greater challenge."

She motioned to the door where Willow had entered, and it swung open a second time. Both Hand members entered and stepped to either side, drawing their unique weapons. Willow's heart sank. The Queen's Hand, five lethal soldiers, all gifted in every facet of combat, all sworn to protect the queen, to carry out her bidding of assassination or intimidation. The people feared the queen's wrath. The nobles feared the Queen's Hand.

The deragoth retreated a step and snarled, the sound reverberating in the pit, but Willow knew the cat had nothing to fear. The Hand took up positions behind Willow, their tactic obvious. If they drove her towards the cat, she would be surrounded, and once paralyzed . . .

She shuddered, the prospect of being devoured alive causing her hand to tighten on the handle of her weapon. She rotated in place, turning to face the two Hand members, with their fearsome clawed masks, and then the deragoth, which had begun to prowl again, pacing at the limit of its chain. It bared its teeth as if sensing the coming meal.

The initiates and acolytes shifted their feet, and a murmur of anticipation rustled their ranks. Willow had never seen such a trial and recognized Princess Melora's influence. The woman had wanted Willow to be killed, publicly, where it would be obvious she was not suited for serving the Order. But her very influence spoke to jealousy, an emotion to be exploited.

"Princess Melora," Willow called, raising her voice, "it seems you have assisted in planning this trial."

"Our Master wisely consulted me on how best to prove your loyalty," Melora said.

"And you have tasked me with fighting not one—but three impossible foes."

"If you are loyal to the cause, you will prove it this day."

"And if they do not survive?"

Serak spoke first. "Then they prove their failure."

Another murmur in the initiates, and Willow permitted a faint smile. She loved Light. He might be a deadly battlemage, but he had a child's sense of duty, and he spoke to protect her as a youth would a treasured friend.

51

"Then one more thing I ask," Willow said. "If I should be victorious, I ask that I take Princess Melora's place, at your side."

This time shock rippled among the initiates, and Melora seemed stunned. The request of such a high position would be unheard of in any setting, and if it were actually Serak, he probably would have laughed. Fortunately for her, it wasn't, and Light smiled.

"Upon victory may your reward be given."

Melora rounded on him, but the look he gave her would have caused a dragon to recoil, and she flinched, instinctively retreating a step before the rage in his eyes. Willow kept her surge of gratitude from showing on her face. Light would always fight for her.

"Those gathered to bear witness," Melora said, her voice significantly more subdued than before. "Does anyone wish to speak any words before the trial begins?"

"Are we allowed to wager on the trial?" Jeric asked.

All eyes shifted to him, and although hatred was evident, much laughter was stifled. Light even smiled, and Willow recognized the statement as an effort to calm Light, before he leapt into the arena to fight at Willow's side.

Melora motioned to the two members of the Hand. "Then let the trial begin . . ."

Chapter 7: Acolyte

Willow turned her back on the deragoth and faced the two members of the Hand, who moved to flank her. The one on her left possessed four claw marks across his mask, revealing his identity as Cutter. He pressed the rune embedded on the pommel of his sword, and the blade glowed bright blue. A sharpening augmentation. Extremely rare and notoriously difficult to cast, the magic constantly sharpened the weapon until it could slice through armor with ease, and even cut stone.

The other Hand member had five claw marks across his mask. Black, the Mage Killer. He touched the rune on his weapon as well, causing his blade to darken, the reflective steel the color of her ink. An anti-magic blade.

Both weapons were gifts from the queen, given to the Hand members when they forsook their name, their history, even their heritage to become a member of the Hand. None knew their real identities except each other, and the queen.

Willow set her chakram spinning, gradually lengthening the string until it became a blur at her side. At her back the deragoth snarled and leapt to the length of its chain, fighting to reach her flesh.

Unwilling to wait until they flanked her completely, Willow charged Black. At the same time, she redirected the chakram so it hurtled at Cutter, forcing him to evade. With her free hand, she caught the ink of a small crossbow on her bicep and yanked it free.

Black darted in, and Willow fired. He deflected the bolt with ease, and Willow dived to the ground, rolling beneath the flashing blade, yanking the chakram back into her skin. The weapon sank into her flesh as she came to her feet and spun. In the same motion she drew the dagger from her forearm and stabbed at Black's chest. She also pointed her crossbow at the white mask.

Black tilted his head to the side, allowing the bolt to fire over his shoulder. But the bolt had not been aimed at him, and it streaked across the chamber, sliding across Cutter's shoulder, cutting his tunic and drawing blood.

Willow retreated as Black unleashed a blistering assault. Releasing her crossbow, it sank back into her flesh, and she grabbed the handle of the chakram, yanking it back into her hand. It began to spin, the head whirling as it came at Black's spine.

The warrior sidestepped, and Willow wrapped the cord around her back, sending it spinning at Cutter, again forcing him back, driving him toward the wall. But Cutter swiveled and brought his sword down on the cord, the sharpening augmentation striking the thread of ink.

Willow hissed as the ink brightened, and a line cut into her back where the tattoo normally resided. Yanking the weapon back to her before he could strike again, she retreated from the flashing sword of Black—but the retreat was a feint.

Now with a sword and dagger, she struck left and whirled right, driving her sword into his side, and then lunging into a stab, her dagger driving for his gut. He parried the first and then slid to the side, allowing the dagger to slide in front of his stomach. Then he reached out with his free hand and struck Willow across the cheek.

Willow's head rocked back. The blow could have been with a fist, but the open palm was meant to send a message. That she was not worthy to fight the Hand, that her skill was beneath them. A surge of defiance welled within her and she spit the blood from her lip, and then sheathed both the dagger and the sword, allowing them to sink back into tattoos. Drawing the crossbow from over her shoulder, she leveled the large weapon at the two foes and unleashed a volley.

The automatically reloading weapon fired with shocking speed, filling the pit with sharp bolts. Both were forced to retreat, driven backward to evade the volley of bolts. They expertly veered apart, providing two targets. She maintained her attack on Black, while Cutter charged.

Willow placed her crossbow on her shoulder and it sank into her flesh. She had just enough time to draw her sword and dagger before

Cutter's flashing blade came for her throat. She ducked and knocked his weapon high. She spun, attempting to evade, but Black appeared, closing her chance at escape.

She desperately sought to parry both swords, but was driven backward, toward the snarling deragoth. Its claws slashed across her cloak, tearing the material and nearly reaching her skin. With nowhere to go, she dropped both weapons and caught Cutter's wrist. Twisting her body, she redirected his blow to come down on the chain binding the deragoth.

The augmented weapon sliced through the chain like it was made of cheese and cut deep into the floor. Already straining against the collar, the cat lunged for the nearest body, which happened to be Cutter.

The Hand member recoiled, slashing his sword in an attempt to fend off the beast, but the cat parried and attacked, forcing him to retreat further. The two combatants fell away as Willow battled Black.

"Well played," Black said, speaking for the first time.

"I do what I must," Willow said.

She deflected his sword high, but he used the parry to spin and strike again. She blocked, but the attack had been a ploy, and he kicked her in the chest. She tumbled backward, losing her grip on her sword. It fell onto her side and returned to ink. Landing hard, Willow rolled away and drew her dagger, raising it just as Black pounced.

His dark sword came down on her throat and struck her dagger. He leaned into the blow, the anti-magic slicing into her blade, only the magic of her tattoo holding the weapon together. On the floor and trapped, Willow felt the flesh of her upper arm split as the sword cut deep into the location of the tattoo. Blood dripped onto the floor and she hissed in pain.

"Too bad," Black said, his voice hard as he put his whole weight into driving his sword through her dagger. "You could have been a member of the Hand."

She leaned to the side and let the sword slide off her dagger, the blade just missing her throat and striking the stone floor. The tactic had a cost, and it cut deep into her arm. But doing so gave her a free hand, and she pulled the small knife from her opposite wrist. With a quick jab, she stabbed Black in the stomach.

He grunted in surprise and pain, and was forced to roll away. Unfortunately, the only route of escape took him toward the deragoth, and the beast rounded on him. Leaping away from Cutter, it pounced on Black, raking its claws across his shoulder. Black rolled to his feet and tossed the cat away, but the damage had been done, and the paralytic poison seeped into his body.

"Cursed beast," he growled, and stumbled backward.

Cutter leapt in front of his companion, engaging the cat before it could strike again. Doing so gave Willow time to rise to her feet. Before she could dispatch Black, Cutter rotated and slashed at the deragoth's flank, driving it toward Willow.

She drew her dagger and caught the handle of her whip. With a tug, she pulled the tattoo free and snapped it at the beast, keeping it at bay. It recoiled, but Cutter used the time to grab his companion by the shoulder and drag him to the edge of the pit, temporarily out of harm's way.

"Well done!" praised Serak.

Willow looked up in time to see Jeric subtly catch Serak's arm before he could clap. As Melora looked at him in surprise, he modified his expression to the haughty demeanor more common on Serak's features.

"Could you do as well?" Serak challenged Melora.

She scowled and stabbed a finger to Cutter. "Will you just kill her?"

The soldier inclined his head and charged Willow, so she snapped the whip at him. Instead of avoiding it, he put his arm up and let the whip coil around his arm. Then he yanked Willow from her feet. He raised his sword, intent on striking her when she was off balance, but Willow rolled up the blade, closing the gap.

Cutter dropped to the ground to avoid Willow's dagger and a knife erupted from his gauntlet, the spring inside, driving the blade out. Cutter struck once, the blade driving into her leg and forcing her to retreat again.

But the attack put him close to the beast, and the deragoth now came for him. He spun and sprinted for his companion. Leaping to the wall, he jumped into a flip that carried him over the deragoth. Without his intended target, the cat lunged for the paralyzed Black.

Cutter landed behind the deragoth and brought the blue sword down, plunging it into the floor of the pit. The blade passed through the final link in the chain and sank into the stone. The section of chain went taut, and the beast came to a halt, just inches from Black's body. It snarled and snapped, but in vain.

Turning away, Cutter strode to the center of the ring, where Willow waited. He scooped up Black's discarded sword. With blood dripping from her wounds, Willow would not let him gain the satisfaction of her retreat, and so she stayed firm, her sword in one hand, a dagger in the other.

Cutter came to a halt, and to Willow's surprise, inclined his head. The mark of respect brought a surprised whisper from the viewing initiates, and then he sheathed his sword and turned to Serak.

"Her skill has been proven."

"The contest is not yet finished," Melora protested.

"Only a fool would wish to see such a warrior die in the home of her friends," Cutter said.

Melora flushed, and Willow looked to her. Cutter had forced the princess into a difficult position. She could press for a kill, but doing so would lose the respect of many. Or she could let Willow live. However, it was not up to her.

"Her skill has been proven," Serak said, his tone pleased. "But, of course, her skill was never in doubt."

Willow allowed a small smile and struggled to retain her feet as the blood seeped from her wounds. Melora scowled but waved a hand in dismissal, and Cutter turned away. Skirting the reach of the deragoth, he retrieved his paralyzed companion.

"I hope you win the day," Cutter murmured as he passed.

A pair of guards entered, and with long poles, caught the deragoth and guided it back into its cage. When she was alone in the pit, another door was opened, and a new figure entered the chamber.

A young girl.

No more than ten years of age, the human child trembled, and looked up to the tattooed and bloodied Willow, her eyes dark with terror. She sought to flee, but spears were held at her back, and she was forced to turn and face Willow.

Willow looked up to find Melora's malicious smile. "Obedience to Serak must be absolute, even when the task is difficult. Kill the girl and prove your loyalty to the cause."

The child began to cry, weeping silent tears as she fell to her knees, crumpling in shock and fear. Her hands fell on the spot the deragoth had paced, and the paralytic touched her flesh. Her whimpering quickly slowed, and she slumped, only her bright blue eyes still moving.

"Such an easy task," Melora taunted. "A single stroke, a single life, and you will be granted unquestioned loyalty among the Order."

Willow stared at the frozen girl and heard the click as hundreds of crossbows were pointed at her. All the initiates leveled their weapons at her, the barbed shafts too many to avoid. If she failed to kill the child, her own life would be forfeit. But Willow could never commit such an atrocity.

She looked to Light, an apology on her tongue. But he had a sly smile on her face, and he inclined his head, an unspoken order to continue. She recognized the glint in his eyes, and the touch of his magic on her hand. She looked down at the blade, and then back to him. He nodded again. Steeling herself for what was to come, she set her gaze on the captive. Then she advanced upon the frozen girl, knelt, and stabbed her in the heart.

Chapter 8: Serak's Office

Melora stared in shock, and the spectators fell silent. From the viewing booth, Light watched Willow withdraw the knife. Then she leaned over the child and shut the girl's eyes. In the stillness, she got to her feet, grimacing as the act forced her to use her leg.

Light wanted to cheer, to shout his pleasure that Willow had survived, to taunt Melora for her failure. But even he recognized the somber moment, so Light kept his features controlled—or as controlled as he could.

"You killed her," Melora's voice was still tinged with disbelief. "An innocent child."

"I serve our master," Willow said coldly. "And now I claim my reward . . . at Serak's side."

Melora recoiled as if she'd been struck. Her gambit to destroy Willow had been for naught, because Willow had done what she never would have believed possible and killed an innocent. She stared in disbelief at the corpse.

"Melora," Light said, and tried to keep the pleasure from his voice. "You may depart. Willow, take her place."

Willow inclined her head, and Melora abruptly whirled and exited the viewing chamber. As her footfalls faded into silence, Light fought to keep still, excitement spilling into his veins. The guards moved to retrieve the body of the girl, but Willow shook her head.

"I will care for the body."

The guards inclined their heads, and Willow again knelt. As she gently lifted the slain child into her arms, Light and Jeric exited the viewing chamber and Light all but sprinted down the stairs to the door of the pit.

Willow appeared and stepped into the hall. Her expression was as sober as Light had ever seen, and it took all his restraint to keep himself in check. Willow took the lead and led them down a secondary corridor. When they rounded the corner and were alone, Light burst into a smile.

"You were *brilliant*," he breathed.

"Indeed," Jeric said.

Light was bouncing on his feet, unable to contain his excitement. "That duel was epic, like when you swung your dagger—or when you pulled your knife from your wrist—or cut the deragoth chain with Cutter's own blade—"

"Light," Willow admonished, her voice strained. "Do try to keep your voice down. Let's not get caught now."

Light, smiling so wide he thought his face would split, managed to stop moving. "Why are you so worried? My magic was perfect."

He passed a hand above the girl's body, removing the illusion charm he'd placed. The blood from the wound, the stillness to her body, even her closed eyes, all evaporated, revealing a very scared, still paralyzed, young girl.

"Rest easy, little one," Jeric said. "I know you can't move, but all is well. It will pass." He looked up to Willow. "I have a few connections in the city. I'll find a way to get her home and then return."

Willow nodded. "I'll let the guards know to permit you entry. And Light . . .?"

She motioned expectantly to the girl, and Light started. "Right, she's supposed to be dead."

He recast the illusion, and the very alive girl returned to being dead. Jeric gently picked her up and hummed a soft tune as Willow pointed the way to an exit. When he was gone, Light abruptly wrapped his arms around Willow, crushing her to his chest.

"I've never been more terrified," he said. Willow flinched, and he immediately withdrew. "Sorry."

60

"Your exuberance is appreciated," Willow said softly, and leaned up to kiss him. "But perhaps we can wait until I've seen a healer?"

"Done," Light said.

He leapt away, intent on finding a healer. Then he noticed Willow was not at his side and looked back to see her limping down the hall. He returned to her side and she offered a faint smile.

"Perhaps a little slower."

Fighting the urge to run, he plodded at her side, and they gradually ascended two levels. Dark elf guards and Order members, some in armor, others in robes, all inclined their head to Serak, and to Willow.

The motions seemed normal, but a current of tension had seeped into the halls of the Order, with many looks cast between guards, and hissed conversations. Light noticed the tension but did not feel it, his thoughts dominated by Willow's injuries.

"Send for a healer," Light said to one guard.

"To Serak's office," Willow added.

"Of course," he said.

When he had departed, Light whispered to Willow. "Where's my office?"

Willow pointed to a set of stairs, and they made their way up the steps to a large set of ironbound doors. The two guards nodded to him and opened the doors, permitting them entry into Serak's office.

Light stepped into the room and turned to Willow, but she warned him to silence. When the door was shut, she sighed and sank against the wall. He darted to her and reached to the wounds, but she waved him away.

"I am well," she said. "Nothing a healer won't be able to fix."

He lifted her bloody sleeve. The gash across her dagger was deep, and blood seeped into her tunic. The wound in her leg was deeper. He grimaced, a surge of anger driving him to his feet, where he started to pace.

"I'll kill the Hand for what they've done."

"They could have killed me," she said. "Yet they did not. We need to know why."

He came to a halt. "So I can't kill them?"

"Not yet," she said, smiling faintly.

She closed her eyes, and he darted to her. "Don't die!" he cried.

"I'm not dying," she said. "I'm just tired."

"Oh."

She chuckled and reached up to put her hand on his cheek. "Thank you for saving my life."

"When did I do that?" he asked, confused.

"I wasn't about to kill that girl," Willow said. "And if you hadn't cast that illusion, they would have killed me."

Light stared at her, recalling the moment the captive had entered the arena. He hadn't wanted her to die but hadn't realized Willow would perish for failure. Then Jeric had leaned over and murmured in his ear.

"Time for an illusion."

"It was Jeric's idea," Light admitted.

"You were still the one to save my life," she said. "As you have many times before."

"I love you," he said.

"And I you," Willow said.

A knock came at the door and Light stood, calling for it to be opened. The healer stepped in and spotted Willow. She moved to Willow and examined her wounds, and Light hovered behind her.

"Will she be well?"

"Serak," Willow said wearily. "You mentioned an archive you wished to share?"

Remembering that he was Serak, Light gave an apologetic look, and then turned away from the healer and Willow, examining the office for the first time. Like the rest of the tower, the wall contained script, the line of text surrounding the wall. But that was where the similarity ended.

The room was not square, but a dome, the curved ceiling lacking any point or edge. The floor was partially transparent, solid to the touch, like clouds frozen in glass. The murky liquid swirled about, the current drifting beneath his boots.

Orbs of light hung from brackets in the ceiling. The script extended to the floor, cutting off as if it extended to a room beneath. The office contained only four pedestals at the center, each supporting a single object. Four memory orbs sparkled with light, illuminating the room, as did the glowing text in the ancient language.

"You will be fine," the healer said. "But you should rest for a day or two."

Light turned back, and managed to hide his wonder at the room, and the subsequent grin. What would the woman do if she found her supposed Master marveling at his own quarters? Stifling his amusement, he inclined his head to the healer.

"That will be all."

She inclined her head and departed, and Willow eased herself to her feet. The healing magic had closed her wounds, but it had sapped her energy, and she would be sore for some time. She sighed in relief and then motioned to the office.

"We need to discover the queen's location, quickly."

"Why hurry?" he asked, marveling at the strange chamber. "You're now a senior acolyte, and I'm Serak."

"It's only a matter of time until they figure out your identity," she said.

"Am I not doing well?"

"I love you, but no."

"Hey!"

"It's true," she said, patting him on the chest. "But I would be worried if you *were* good at being a cold, calculating murderer."

Light couldn't argue with that, so he swept a hand to the chamber. "So where are his records?"

"I don't know," she replied. "I've only been here a few times, and it always looks like this."

Light scanned the room again, but there was nothing to see except the pedestals and the domed ceiling. No doors, no archives, nothing. Light frowned and searched the room with his magic, hoping to illuminate a hidden crevasse. But nothing revealed itself.

"What now?" he asked with a shrug.

Willow limped her way to the four pedestals. "It must have something to do with these," she said.

Light approached the nearest and peered into its depths. Most kept memory orbs to remember events or people, but these were not orbs of memory. Instead they pulsed with faint power. He reached up and touched one.

"Wait!"

He yanked his hand back but it was too late, and his finger slid across its surface. He blinked in surprise when the domed ceiling turned a few feet, the entire room shifting, the script of the ancients sliding into the floor. The door remained where it was, the walls gliding around it, reshaping on the opposite side.

"It's not a dome," Light exclaimed in awe. "It's a sphere."

She reached for another orb and turned it, and the chamber rotated in a different direction, a faint grinding emanating as the sphere rotated on a different axis. She then reached for the third orb, rotating it in another direction.

Light caught the fourth orb and eagerly turned it, but instead, the entire chamber spun in a variety of directions, the text rising and falling before swirling to the side. Confused, he looked to Willow to find her nodding.

"Three orbs to turn the lock, one to reset."

"Reset what?"

"It's a vault," she said, sweeping a hand to the chamber.

Dubious, Light pointed to the empty room. "A vault for what?"

"I don't know," she said. "But I'm guessing only Serak himself knows the key. Perhaps with my newfound rank I'll be able to—"

"It repeats," Light exclaimed.

"What?"

"The ancient language," Light said, stepping to the wall and spreading a hand across the symbols. "It repeats everywhere in the tower—except for this room."

"Light," she said gently. "We need to focus on the vault. We cannot leave until we have discovered where Serak sent the queen."

"Then we stay," Light said, shrugging as he continued to examine the text. Why was it different here? He hadn't realized it before, but the text and symbols were the same on every level he'd seen, the sole exception being this room. The mystery was maddening, and he wished Mind were present. He would know how to solve the vault.

A knock at the door sounded and Willow hissed for him to become Serak. Reluctantly, he turned away from the script on the wall and stood with Willow as a quartet of senior acolytes entered with a set of robes.

"Willow," the leader said, "I am certain Serak has been informing you of your new duties as an acolyte, but it falls to us to grant you the robes of your new office."

Already bored, Light tried to pay attention, but his eyes wandered to the ancient script, and he wondered what it meant. They gave Willow grey robes and droned on before whisking her away. Willow cast him a worried look, but he was already staring at the ancient script again, his persona all but forgotten.

Chapter 9: Light's Command

Light expected the chamber's lock to be easy to solve, but no amount of turning made the room do anything but spin. Light's frustration mounted, but a distraction came soon after, when a handful of dark elves appeared, wanting instruction on previous orders. He responded with irritation and they departed quickly.

Throughout the rest of the day, Serak dealt with issues of the Order, quickly regretting the plan to become the head of a shadowy organization. He hadn't realized it would be so laden with administrative tasks.

Members of the Order arrived and departed. Most were dark elves, but a handful were human or elven. Light issued orders without any understanding of the real Serak's plans, frequently receiving strange looks in return.

"Lord Horus in the elven kingdom has joined our ranks," one elf said, offering a bow. "He wants to know your desires for him."

"Inform him to sell everything he possesses," Light said.

The elf's eyes widened. "You want him to relinquish his birthright?"

"Yes," Light said, hoping he sounded certain. "And if he refuses, give evidence to the elven queen that shows he is a traitor."

"As you will, Master Serak," the elf said, departing with a confused look on his face.

On and on it went, each requesting direction or information. Guard rotations, new acquisitions, secret treaties. Light answered them all, even sending soldiers to the snowy north to await the winter solstice. When the captain departed, Light released a light laugh, imagining a score of dark elves huddling in the snow, wondering why Serak had sent them to the distant north.

His favorite was when Princess Melora returned. She tried to act with understanding, but it was obvious she was seething from being replaced. Light listened to her not-so-subtly asking for her position back, and then interrupted.

"You are a princess," Serak said. "And you deserve a position of respect."

Taken aback, the woman nodded vigorously. "I'm glad you understand, Master Serak. I had thought that—"

"And I know just the position for you," Light said. "With all the losses from the fragments, we need a full inventory of our assets."

"You want me to count our coin?" she asked.

"It's an important assignment," Light said. "One I can only trust to you."

Disbelief, and then anger washed across her features. It was a menial task, one the princess had likely never done, and it sparked a touch of hatred in her gaze. Light kept the smile from his face with difficulty and relished the discord he was causing.

It dawned on him that the Order members were following his orders because they had such trust in Serak, a leader that had lived for thousands of years. How far could he push them before they become suspicious?

"One more thing," Light said. "Loyalty must be proven, to regain your rightful place at my side."

She brightened but was obviously still confused. Light smiled, pleased that he'd managed to salvage the situation. Regardless, the talk would likely keep the traitorous princess occupied long enough for Light to figure out the key to the chamber lock, which absorbed his attention as few tasks ever had, making all other interruptions an annoyance.

The next several requests he actually tried to answer like Serak, but as evening came, he grew bored, and his interest in the krey script only intensified. By the time Willow returned, he'd all but dismissed everyone so he could attempt to discern the meaning of the ancient language.

Willow returned with members of the Hand, Black and Cutter, and although it was obvious she wanted to speak freely, the presence of others prevented her from doing so. The Hand members wanted to test her abilities, and Light waved in dismissal. Willow cast him a shocked look before departing, and Light turned his attention back to the ancient script.

Jeric returned shortly after, and Light vaguely recalled answering his requests, but when a dark elf entered to request information regarding a shipment to the Ravens Guild, he sent Jeric to help.

"But Master Serak," he said, a touch of urgency in his voice as he glanced to the dark elf at his side. "Did you not ask that I assist you in another matter?"

"No," Light said without turning. "I can handle it."

Jeric's worry went unnoticed, and he departed as well, casting several glances over his shoulder. With his attention on the script, Light didn't notice, and mumbled to himself as he examined the wall.

Time slipped by, and he vaguely recalled a number of visitors, but their requests were a nuisance. He turned the chamber in every direction, examining and re-examining the ancient text, parsing out a word here, a meaning there. In his youth he'd found a handful of books in the krey language in Elenyr's library, and loved the swirls and dots, the ornate script that begged to be solved. Now he got to solve text written in such beautiful, shimmering light.

Jeric and Willow were frequent visitors, and he spoke to them with excitement, but when he looked up, they were gone. Annoyed, he returned his attention to his task, and turned the chamber anew.

"Light."

He looked up and found Willow at his side. He hadn't even heard the door open, and he beamed at her appearance. "You have to see what I learned," he said, catching her arm and dragging her to a section of the script.

"Light," she repeated wearily. "Do you have any idea what you have done?"

"Of course not," he scoffed. "What made you think I knew how to be Serak?"

"The Order is in chaos," she said. "And there are whispers that you've lost your wits."

"Isn't that what we want?" he asked, mystified.

"No," she said. "We want to know where the queen is."

"Right," he said, and dragged her to the side. "Look at this."

He pointed to the script. He'd turned the orbs until the script wrapped around the room, half above the floor, and half beneath. He pointed to it proudly, and she shook her head, pointing to the door.

"Don't you see? There's no way we have time to figure out the lock now."

Her tone was frustrated and angry, but Light didn't notice. "The symbols repeat themselves, but only half are visible, the rest is below—on the opposite side of the room. I think they—"

"*Light*," she said. "I didn't come to crack the lock, I came to get you out, before they come for you."

"What did I do?"

"What *didn't* you do?" she asked. "You sent a princess to count coins, a captain into the northern snows, and don't even mention what you told others to wash. Do you truly not know what you've done? There are three dark elves out in the street, singing, while a fourth tries to light their shoes on fire."

Light laughed to himself. "I'd forgotten about that."

70

Willow wiped her face with her hand. "You sent a human man to stand over a rock like he was hatching an egg. Another is squatting over another rock, growling, 'I caught you.' The city guards have taken notice and are starting to detain the Order members."

Light beamed in pride. "Just as I planned."

Jeric opened the door and entered, and shut the door before darting to them. "We don't have much time. The princess is gathering the senior acolytes that suspect you. I think Light forcing her to wash the floor tipped her over the edge."

"What do you mean?" Light asked, bending and spreading a hand across the text. "We've only been here a few hours. Surely they do not suspect us already."

"Light," Willow said softly. "Do you know how long we've been here?"

Light didn't take his eyes off the symbols. "We got here earlier today."

"Really?" Jeric shook his head in disbelief. "I knew you'd been obsessed with the ancient words, but not to this extent."

Light heard the dismay in his voice and finally focused on him. Turning, he noticed Willow's tension, and Jeric stood at the door as if he were expecting a fight. Confused, Light motioned to them.

"Why are you behaving in such a fashion? I only answered a few orders."

Willow jerked her head. "It's been four days."

Light burst into a laugh. "That's absurd. I just answered a few requests . . ."

His voice failed when he spotted Willow's wounds from the testing. They were gone, the skin smooth and fresh. Even if healing magic had been used, it would have taken a few days for such extensive wounds to heal completely . . .

He recalled a flurry of visits, of dark elves and others. Some he answered, others he simply ignored. Willow and Jeric returned and departed, unable to stay without arousing suspicion. Light recalled hissed conversations as they sought to convince him to be Serak, and all he talked about was the ancient language.

"Has it really been four days?" he asked in a small voice.

"You really didn't know?" Jeric asked. "Because we've been trying to get your attention since the moment you saw this room."

"We're wasting time," Willow said. "We need to leave before it's too late."

A clanking came at the door, followed by Princess Melora's voice, an overly sweet tone. "Master Serak? I have an urgent matter that requires your attention."

"Have you finished cleaning the floor?"

There was a weighty pause.

"Yes."

"You do not sound certain."

Another pause, and Light thought he heard a whisper of conversation, as if several individuals were trying to decide what to do. Willow and Serak exchanged a look, and Serak shrugged.

"They aren't sure if he's the real Serak or not."

"That gives us time," Willow said.

"Only until they realize I barred the door," Jeric said.

The clanking sounded again, and Melora called to Serak. "We fear a traitor has infiltrated our ranks. We must speak immediately."

"We'll have to fight our way through," Willow said.

"It's really been four days?" Light asked.

The both turned to him, and Willow reached up to touch his cheek. "I need you to focus now," she said. "If we don't act quickly, they're going to discover your identity, and I won't be able to protect—"

"But I can unlock the chamber," Light protested.

Jeric swiveled to face him and shook his head. "I spent hours in here and saw nothing but the blank walls."

"But the ancient language—"

"There *is* no ancient language on the walls," Willow snapped.

Light stared at them. Then he stared at the glowing text, the shimmering lights, the vibrant colors. Then he began to laugh. He'd been so occupied with solving the puzzle, he'd never realized the truth about the fascinating language. The spectrum of light was not one they could see.

"Master Serak?" Melora's voice came through the door, and then softer to someone else. "Break the door."

"Are you certain?" someone asked.

"I am," she said.

A fire lance struck the steel door, spitting sparks as the magic began to carve through the metal. Jeric pulled the hilts free and activated two swords of aquaglass. He retreated from the door and pointed to the breach.

"We need a plan," he said.

"You need to see the message," Light asked.

Willow rubbed her forehead. "There is no message."

"Of course there is," he said.

He pointed to the words, bending the light in the room to shape the letters and the symbols, showing the words that had dominated his attention for four days. The strange symbols and runes appeared, glowing on the stone, a shimmering iridescent blue, sparkling with silver and gold. Other letters were like fire, still others like dark embers.

Willow sucked in her breath, her eyes wide as the lettering appeared around the room, filling the breadth of the chamber in shining text. The magic brought the text into a spectrum they could see and Light stepped to the orbs, rotating the chamber to show the symbols sliding into view, those across the room gliding from sight. Then he reset the lock by touching the last and stood proudly in the now glowing chamber.

Chapter 10: Serak's Vault

"He was right," Jeric said, dumbfounded.

"I thought you'd gone mad," Willow breathed.

"What did you think I was doing?" Light asked.

Jeric chuckled and motioned to the shimmering language. "It looked like you were talking to the blank wall."

"That would just be stupid," Light scoffed.

Willow looked to the door, where the lance of fire had cut through half the door. "We're out of time. Can you really unlock the chamber?"

"I can read it," Light said. "Doesn't mean I know what it means."

"Then read it," Willow said. "And quickly."

"Ero and Skorn, God and Devil, Devil and God."

"That's it?" Willow asked.

"That's all I understand," Light said. "There's more but I don't know those words."

"The Dark Gate must not be opened," Jeric murmured.

Both turned to him, and Light raised an eyebrow in surprise. "You can read the krey language?"

"When you're as old as I am, you pick up a few things," Jeric said.

The door clanged again.

"How does this unlock his records?" Willow asked.

"Because the letters are all wrong," Light said. "They are all cut in half unless I do this . . ."

He rotated the spheres, turning the glowing letters until the words lined up. Both Jeric and Willow blinked in surprise, their eyes dropping to their feet. Light looked to his feet as well, but the cloudy floor had not changed.

"Did you hear it?" Willow asked.

"I did indeed," Jeric asked.

"Blasted elven hearing," Light complained.

"We should have done this together," Willow said. "We would have figured it out days ago."

"Doesn't matter now," Jeric said, searching the floor. "But something unlocked."

"A hidden door?" Light asked, growing excited.

The fire lance in the door continued to cut, severing nearly the whole of the door from its moorings. Jeric and Willow, on their hands, sought a hidden catch, both glancing to the door that was about to fall.

"Here!" Jeric called.

He lifted a hidden ring that blended seamlessly with the floor, and pulled. A trapdoor appeared and he motioned Light and Willow inside. Just as they shut the door, Jeric caught Light's shoulder and stabbed a finger toward the room.

"Don't let them see the writing," Jeric said.

"Right," he said.

Light clenched a fist, extinguishing the magic. Jeric shut the door, just as a rending of steel signified the room had been breached. On the hidden stairs beneath, Light looked upward, a wild grin on his face.

Footfalls echoed from above, and through the clouded floor Light watched the faint outline of two dozen soldiers search the empty chamber. Melora shouted in dismay, demanding answers, but empty walls greeted her.

"I know you are not Serak!" she shouted. "Which means you must be the fragment of Light. Only he has the power to become another."

"We can hear them," Jeric whispered.

"Which means they can hear us," Willow murmured.

They motioned Light to silence, and then crept down the stairs. Enthralled by the hidden chamber, he remained at the top of the stairs, listening and trying not to giggle at those trying to find them.

"Light!" Melora bellowed. "You think I will not find you?"

"We're not here!" Light called.

Silence from above, and Light turned to find Willow and Jeric staring at him. Jeric raised his hands wide as if to say *why would you do that?* Willow merely sighed. Then Light realized what he'd done.

"Sorry," he said.

"Cut the floor!" Melora shouted. "don't let them escape!"

"Don't worry, Light," Willow said. "You got us down here. Now let's see what we find."

For the first time Light examined the bottom half of the spherical room. Like the upper half, it contained the string of krey words glowing on the walls, but they were not what caught his attention. Instead of four orbs, as there had been above, this half of the chamber contained one, a sphere as large as his head, floating off the base of the curved floor.

"I found the records," Willow exclaimed.

Light spared her a glance and found her standing next to a collection of tomes set on a small desk. She had one open, and read the script written in Serak's own hand. Jeric joined her and flipped open another.

"It's his journals," Light cast over his shoulder.

"What about that?" Light asked, pointing to the floating orb.

"Let's just get what we came for," Willow said. "Then we can escape."

A shard of fire pierced the floor above, and a moment later a second one plunged into view. Both began to cut, curving towards each other where they would make a hole. Willow and Jeric exchanged a look.

"Better hurry," Jeric said.

Light stepped to the floating orb and examined the clear ball. He reached up and touched it, his finger sending ripples of purple light. Delighted, he touched another, and watched the ripples cascade away.

"Do you have any idea the damage you have caused?" Melora shouted.

"I hope it was a lot," Light called back.

"Will you stop talking to her?" Jeric asked, exasperated.

"Why?" Light asked. "She already knows we're down here."

Light touched the orb again, running his finger across the surface, and watched the ripples cascade away. He'd never seen magic act in such a manner, and purple was the color of the fragment of Mind. What did that mean?

The orb hovered above a small platform, which also hovered above the floor. He passed a hand beneath and around the purple orb but felt nothing holding it aloft, creating no small amount of excitement.

"I think the chamber was built by a krey," Light said. "Someone afterward added the floor and locking mechanism." He pointed to the floor above their heads.

"Probably to hide that thing," Willow said, pointing to the floating orb without taking her eyes from the book.

"But why?" Light asked. "What does it do?"

"I've sent a message to the surface," Melora had to shout over the fire slicing through the floor. "It won't be long before the real Serak arrives. I do look forward to seeing what he will do to you."

"Did you clean the deragoth cages yet?"

"*You* ordered me to do that!"

"But is it done?" Light asked. "Because those animals smell terrible. When's the last time they had a bath?"

"When I get my hands on you I'll—"

"Look!" Light shouted. "I think I just activated it."

He'd put both hands on the orb, and instead of ripples, the entire sphere brightened with purple light. His fingers tingled with power until he removed them, and he watched with wide eyes as tiny sparks of purple power arced between his fingers.

"Epic," he breathed.

"Light," Willow called. "Will you leave that alone and come over here? There's thousands of years of records."

"And they're not sorted by era?" Light asked.

"Of course they are," Jeric said. "But there are two books just from this year."

Light removed his hands from the floating sphere and then walked around it, fascinated by the colors and magic. But was it magic? Elenyr had always said that the krey could not wield magic, that their bodies lacked the capacity to do so. So had the sphere been crafted by them?

The hole widened in the ceiling, and Order members sought to enter. Annoyed by the distraction, Light reached to the illumination in the room and cast a spike, the blade rising and piercing the hole, passing into the room above. Shouts erupted above, and Melora shrieked an order. Moments later, another hole began to be cut, this time further away.

"Do you have to be so *loud?*" Light called.

He shattered the spike of light into a hundred birds. The animals burst through the hole and flooded the upper chamber. Instead of striking to wound, they dove for faces, and latched onto their mouths. Their wings wrapped around the Order members heads, closing off their ability to speak. Shouts died as the dark elves struggled to dislodge the gags. Their feet stomped and there was much grunting as they ripped at the gags.

"Much better," Light exclaimed. "Thank you."

"Light," Willow called. "Although I appreciate you keeping them out, do you think you can stop dimming the room?"

He looked up, and realized he'd drawn away much of the light in the chamber, leaving the room dim. Both Jeric and Willow stood against the outer wall, using the illumination from the krey script to read.

"Sorry," he said.

Light stepped to the hole and leapt upward, not hearing Jeric's shout. Catching the edge, he levered himself into the upper half of the sphere. Picking his way through the dark elves struggling to release the gags, he came to Melora, who tore at the gag with her fingernails.

"What do you know of this chamber?" he asked, his tone curious.

She glared at him and pointed to the gag that prevented her from speaking. Light blinked in understanding, and pointed to the gag, but he stopped short of ending the charm, his eyes widening with delight at the sudden realization.

"What if it was built by Ero or Skorn? That would explain the message—the text is so flawless, so detailed. It must have been written by them. Don't you think?"

A pair of dark elves abandoned their efforts to dislodge the gags and crept toward Light, but the birds went mad, yanking the two to the floor, battering them with their wings even as they continued to cover their mouths. Other birds did the same, and the entire room dissolved into a silent struggle to defeat the birds.

Swords and daggers fell to the floor as the men and women ripped at the birds. Some came free, but another quickly took its place, sealing their mouths before they could shout or scream. Oblivious to the pandemonium, Light's excitement continued to grow, and he began to pace in front of Melora, words tumbling from his lips.

"I've met Ero, you know—but I don't think he's the sort to build something like this. Krey architecture is so angular, so rigid—so why this sphere? Is it a home? Or a maybe a toy?" he shook his head. "No, not a toy. Maybe it's a . . ."

He whirled to find Melora on the ground, clawing at the gag preventing her from speaking. The wings of the bird flapped and spun, turning Melora over and over. One dark elf was smashing his face on the wall, while another was carefully trying to cut his gag with a dagger, a task made difficult by the furious flapping of wings.

Light clapped his hands together. "Do you know what this means?"

Threading his way through the melee, he dropped through the hole and hurried to the sphere, eager to test his idea. Willow and Jeric were pouring over a book, both reading aloud, but Light only had eyes for the floating sphere.

"Light!" Willow called. "We found it, although the record is incomplete. Serak either sent the queen to Mistkeep to be guarded by the Bloodsworn, or to the north, to be guarded by Bartoth, an exiled rock troll with body magic."

Light reached up to the sphere and put his hands on both sides. Again magic tingled into his flesh, arcing into his fingers and up his arm. He shivered in delight, and distantly heard a shout from above, followed by another. The birds were being destroyed, and in seconds the Order guards would flood through the open hole.

Abruptly the entire spherical chamber trembled, drawing a stilled silence as those above and below looked upward. Then Willow looked to Light, her eyes widening when she saw Light standing over a sphere that was no longer a sphere.

It had become a wheel.

"Light . . .?" she called.

Light heard Willow's voice and looked over his shoulder, his voice filled with excitement. "Don't you see?" he called. "There's only one reason to have a sphere—so it can *move*. It's a vehicle!"

She shouted a warning that Light did not hear, and he pressed a rune on the handle. The floor separating the two levels of the sphere disintegrated, and dark elves rained down upon them, shouting in shock as they landed in heaps around Light. Then Light caught the wheel and proudly spun the mechanism . . .

Chapter 11: The Ancient Sphere

The response was instant and violent. The entire chamber rotated like a ball spun on the ground. Order members, Jeric, and Willow crashed into the outer wall as the sphere turned, their bodies sliding across the exterior as the sphere spun. Trapped inside the Order's tower, it spun in place, a grinding of stone echoing as the fifty-foot sphere rotated against the surrounding stone.

The floating platform had lifted Light off the base of the sphere, holding him free of the spinning. Delighted by the results, he looked to Willow as the sphere slowed to a halt. She groaned and slid down the curved base of the sphere.

"Light," she said, her tone exasperated. "Do you have to touch *everything?*"

"Yes," he said, like it was absurd question.

One of the dark elves rolled onto his knees and vomited, retching from the spin. The others struggled to stand, with only Jeric recovering quickly. He caught Willow about the waist and dragged her to the platform where Light stood. She clung tightly to Serak's archive.

"What's wrong?" Light asked, concerned.

Willow held her stomach as another dark elf in the sphere failed to keep his meal down. "Motion makes me sick," she said.

Light took his hands off the wheel and reached for her, but Jeric jerked his head. "No, you've got the right idea. We need a way to escape and you've given us an exit."

"You can't mean to use this to escape," Willow said.

"Why not?" Jeric asked, his eyes gleaming. "When it spun, the stone supports shuddered. A few more turns and we should be able to break free."

"And then what?" Willow asked. "Blast through the tower and roll through the streets?"

"It's the middle of the night," Jeric said. "The streets are empty."

"Great idea," Light exclaimed.

"Get them!" Melora growled, but her face was also green, and she held the wall like the stone would settle her stomach.

Light reached for the wheel and spun it again. The dark elves, in the midst of staggering towards the floating platform, were hurled against the wall as it whirled about. Faster and faster it spun, the grinding of stone audible, followed by a cracking—and suddenly they rolled sideways, the great sphere crashing through a wall and rolling into the entrance hall of the Order tower. It flattened several of the trees in the room before colliding with the outside wall, sending cracks arcing outward.

***

Hendor, a dark elf child, looked up. Because his mother had taken his toys, he'd slipped out the window into the empty streets of Kordune. Thrilled at the prospect of wandering alone, he'd made his way to the towers at the heart of the city and was busy playing when the ground began to vibrate. He retreated into the shadows, his eyes lifting to the tower at his right. The shuddering continued to rise, and the cracking of stone heralded danger.

"Hendor!"

He whirled and spotted his mother striding forward, her expression one of fury. "Do you have any idea how worried—"

A giant ball exploded through a wall inside the tower, shattering rooms as it rolled through the trees lining the entrance hall. It collided with the outside wall, hard enough to crack the stone all the way to the roof. Then it began to spin again, faster and faster, rotating in place like

84

it wanted to roll right through the wall and down the street. Panicked screams came from within.

Hendor retreated to his mother, a wild grin on his face. He glanced to her, but she stood agape as the wall cracked, and cracked again. She sought to drag him away, but Hendor stood his ground, wanting to see what he knew was coming . . .

The wall shattered, the sphere bursting forward and rolling down the street, so large it scraped the two towers to either side. A cart had been left outside a structure and it was flattened. The screaming from the interior of the ball echoed briefly, as if someone was rolling up to the top and then back down.

"Can I ride it mother? Please?"

But she stood frozen, staring in astonishment as the enormous, glowing sphere barreled down the street, bouncing off buildings and careening towards the water. Shouts of alarm went up in the city, and many dark elves leaned out of windows, staring in astonishment at the gaping hole in the base of the tower. Hendor tossed his toy away. He knew what he wanted now. But where to get one in his size?

***

Inside the sphere, Light's laughter reverberated off the walls, contrasting sharply with the screams of the dark elves caught on the wall. The ball rolled forward, so fast that the Order members were swept upward and then downward, and back upward.

The sphere slammed into a rock outcropping at the end of the street, knocking everyone sideways. Jeric and Willow were sent tumbling off the platform, and Light yelped as Melora crashed into him. He tried to catch the wheel as he went by but that only sent it spinning, and he too went falling into the pile of bodies.

The sphere spun sideways, careening down another street and bouncing off a building farther down. The streets were empty except for a handful of dark elf patrols, and they dived to safety, staring in disbelief as the glowing sphere ricocheted off towers and hills.

"Light!" Willow shouted desperately. "We have to stop!"

She pulled her whip from her body, the tattoo turning solid as she flew up and then down. She lashed out, just managing to catch the platform beneath the wheel. Jeric rolled by and shoved her in the direction of the platform.

Light managed to get to his feet and ran down the base of the bowl, his sheer speed keeping him on his feet. A dark elf fell in front of him and he jumped, accidently landing on Melora's side. She grunted in pain and anger.

"Sorry!" Light called as he sprinted away, but she appeared a second later, rolling past him anew. "Are you okay?"

"NO, I'M NOT OKAY!!" Melora screamed.

Light slipped on what looked suspiciously like vomit and tumbled into a pair of dark elves. Both had their blades out but could barely wield them in the rolling sphere. One of their swords nicked his back, another his side, and he hissed in pain.

Willow managed to get to the platform and dragged herself above. She caught the wheel, slowed them to a halt. Light kept his feet and hurried to join her, picking his way through the groaning Order members. He stepped onto the platform from the side and noticed several runes across the side of the wheel.

"Look at these," he said. "What do you suppose they do . . ."

Willow saw his intention and reached to stop him. "Don't!"

Too late.

He touched a rune. At first nothing happened, and then the exterior of the wheel turned transparent. Light grinned, pleased to see the view all around them. They'd come to a stop in a square between a group of structures. Dark elves stared at the sphere in surprise, clogging the windows of the nearby buildings.

Dark elf soldiers rushed to the sphere, forming ranks but keeping their distance. When the exterior of the sphere turned transparent, they hastily retreated, and then one blinked in surprise, peering at Melora. The princess lay on her stomach, halfway up the curve, two Order members on top of her, squishing her face into the wall.

"Princess Melora?" he called hesitantly. "Is that you?"

Willow reached out and touched the rune, and the sphere went solid again. "Why did you do that?" Light asked.

"Because we don't want them to see *us*," she hissed, motioning to Jeric and herself.

"Right." He winked in agreement. "Let's try another one."

He reached for a rune, but she caught his hand. "Light," she said, her voice tight with warning, "you've done enough for the moment."

"He's going to need to do more," Jeric said.

The dark elves were getting to their feet, but they were a sorry group of soldiers. Several were on their knees, fighting not to retch. Others had lost their swords and stumbled about, searching for them. Melora freed herself and turned to Light, her eyes flicking to the wheel.

Jeric pointed to the door, tilted sideways a few feet up the curve nearby. "If you tell us where the queen is, we'll let you go."

"Never," Melora spat.

Jeric stepped to the wheel, taking Willow's place. "Then shall we continue?"

He spun the wheel sideways, causing it to spin in place, slow at first. The dark elves scrambled forward, desperately trying to keep their feet, to reach the platform before the sphere accelerated.

One got close, and Willow drew her sword from her skin. She deflected his attacked and kicked the elf in the face, sending him tumbling backward. Another approached the opposite side and Jeric pressed the wheel, causing it to accelerate. The motion was a warning the others wisely obeyed, and they retreated from the platform.

"Are you going to kill us all?" Melora asked.

"I think I'll just make you spin until you give up," Jeric said, easing the wheel a little further.

Melora scowled and held the wall as it rotated around the center axis. "The city guard will stop this thing," she said. "And when they do, they will see you with a kidnapped princess. You'll be executed in hours."

Jeric's smile was confident. "Not if we—"

The sphere leapt into the air, soaring over the city, clipping the top of a building and setting it spinning sideways, sending it hurtling towards the lake. Order members were flung in all directions, and Jeric looked daggers at Light. He took his hand off the second rune.

"Sorry."

She reached out and pressed the rune that made the sphere transparent. Light faced forward and realized where they were headed. He instinctively ducked and grabbed the platform, Willow and Jeric doing the same as they fell towards the lake.

They struck the surface of the water in a tremendous splash, their momentum carrying them under. But the air in the sphere was enough to send them back to the surface, and they bobbed and spun lazily.

"I think I'm done now," Light said, catching the platform as the sphere rotated. "Can we get off now?"

To his surprise, Jeric reached for the last rune and locked eyes with Melora. "I don't know much of the krey language, but this symbol is for open. If I press it, I suspect doors will open and you'll end up in the water."

She glanced through the transparent floor and spotted large shapes moving upward. Drawn to the splash, gorthon fish surfaced and circled the sphere, their fins appearing before they dived and drifted about. Melora glanced toward the shore, but the distance was too great for them to survive.

"I cannot tell you where the queen is," she said.

"I hope they enjoy the meal," Jeric said, reaching for the rune.

"But I can tell you about Elenyr."

88

Jeric's hand froze. "What about her?"

She smiled. "Take us to shore and I'll tell you. I swear it."

"What about the queen?" Willow asked.

"Done," Jeric said.

He turned the wheel, and it spun forward, gradually picking up speed as it rotated on the water. The dark elves pushed their way up the sides, where the axis wasn't spinning so much, and the ball rolled across the surface of the water towards the outer bank.

"That's far enough," Jeric said, spinning the wheel backwards to bring them to a halt. "Talk fast, before the fish get close."

Melora scowled and then relented. "Serak intends to kill her."

"Many have tried," Light said with a laugh.

"None have tried with a lightning mage."

Her expression was triumphant, and Light's gut tightened with dread. Lightning magic was Elenyr's weakness, and even in ethereal form, it could kill her. Melora's sneer elicited a surge of anger, and Light's hand clenched into a fist.

"When?"

"We had a deal," Melora said, glancing to the gorthon fish that were approaching again.

"Where?" Jeric asked.

Melora shook her head. "I have told you what you wish to know."

"You have told me *nothing*," Jeric snapped.

"Perhaps this will get her to talk," Light said, and pressed the rune that said *open*.

Chapter 12: Melora's Truth

The krey sphere stopped rotating, and a chunk of the wall broke free. It collapsed inward and collided with the wheel, which had lost its handles. The section of wall shrank, compressing in size until it covered a piece of the purple sphere. Another broke free, and then another, then the entire sphere began to disintegrate.

Chunks fell and shrank, covering what had once been the wheel, aligning with their former location on the outside. Melora was forced to leap aside when a hole opened beneath her, and then another nearby.

A chunk rose from the bottom, and water spilled into the sphere. More chunks broke free only to shrink and collapse onto the guiding sphere, which had grown dim, the light fading. A large piece broke free and a dark elf fell into the water beyond. He surfaced and raised a hand, just as a gorthon fish burst into view. A large mouth appeared, swallowing the dark elf and carrying him under. The shocking kill galvanized everyone to action, and they climbed the walls.

Light jumped from the platform and sprinted to Melora, but Jeric surprisingly got there first. He kicked her hand before she could pick up a sword and leaned onto her arm. When he spoke, it was the darkest Light had ever heard.

"Where will she attack Elenyr?" he growled.

"Are you mad?" Melora growled. "Stay here and you'll perish as well."

A section of wall beneath Melora's shoulder came free and she tilted outward. She struggled to move, but Jeric grabbed her free hand and held her in place, leaning closer. His eyes gave no room for argument.

"Where?"

He ground the word out, ignoring the scream as a dark elf was snatched from an opening, the gorthon fish catching his arm as he sought to climb on the outside. It dragged him into the water.

Willow pulled her whip free and sent it towards a hole at the top, allowing her to ascend. Then she lowered the whip like a rope and called out to Jeric and Light. Torn, Light remained at Jeric's side.

Panic touched Melora's features and she cast about, but her soldiers were abandoning her, climbing the edges of the sphere using the many holes. She fought Jeric's grip, but the elf would not be moved.

"Cloudy Vale!" she cried. "He will kill her in Cloudy Vale!"

"And the queen?"

Melora shook her head, just as another section shifted beneath her head. It rose up and struck Jeric, loosening his grip. Melora yanked her arm free and rolled away before scaling the exterior of the sphere.

Fishing vessels had approached, sailors offering aid. Melora shoved a dark elf out of her way and jumped, catching the edge of a railing, where she was pulled upward. Light and Jeric jumped to Willow's rope and used it to climb to the top of the sinking sphere.

The krey sphere was sinking fast. This far from the city and walls, it was too dark to cast wings, so Light did the next best thing. Drawing on the illumination, he shaped a small boat. As they climbed aboard, the sphere collapsed, dropping them into the water. Order members leapt, desperately seeking to reach the fishing boats before the gorthons caught them.

Light leaned over the edge of their small craft and watched the sphere collapse inward, sealing the operating mechanism in a casing. On impulse, he sent a thread of light into the water, catching the ball before it disappeared into the depths. Drawing it upward, he found that it had shrunk considerably, and now fit comfortably into his hand. Slipping it into a fold of his cloak, he patted the ball and smiled.

"They are enemies of our people!" Melora shouted.

Light, his action going unnoticed by Willow and Jeric, turned to see where they were looking, and spotted an army of soldiers rushing across the bridge. Jeric looked to Light and pointed to the bank.

"Time to leave."

Light turned and tapped the boat, casting a pair of oars that began to row, driving them forward. Sailing away from the charging army, they reached the shore and jumped free. Willow took the lead and raced toward an exit, Light and Jeric close behind.

The trio sprinted across the shore and ducked into a cave. Willow led them into the darkness, and Light immediately felt tired. Yawning, he struggled to keep up as Willow took them away from the shouts of pursuit. She did not stop until Light groaned.

"Do we *have* to run?"

Willow slowed and came to a halt, panting from their flight. Jeric too, was breathing hard, but his jaw was set in a determined line. Light had never seen him look so forceful. Then he stabbed a finger towards the ceiling.

"We must return to the surface."

"We don't know where the queen is yet," Willow said.

"Doesn't matter," Jeric said. "They're going to kill Elenyr."

Light chuckled wearily. "Do you have any idea how many have tried to do that?"

"Not one like Serak," Jeric said. "He's cunning and patient. He would not strike unless he could kill."

"An assassin tried to kill her a few years ago," Light said.

"I know," Jeric replied. "And the man used a sword with lightning magic."

"It failed," Willow said.

"I believe it was supposed to," Jeric said. "Serak has studied the fragments for ages, remember? He would have studied Elenyr as well—and sought a weakness. If he intends to strike, it will be lethal."

"And the queen?" Willow asked. "We cannot abandon her. The Order knows about Light, now. He won't be able to assume the persona a second time."

"I'm not leaving Elenyr to die." Jeric began walking again, forcing them to join him.

Light shook his head. "She's the Hauntress. She can take care of herself."

"She's more vulnerable than you think," Jeric said.

Light cocked his head to the side, confused by the sudden shift in Jeric's voice. Elenyr and Jeric had shared a relationship some time ago, but as far as Light knew, it had ended poorly. Elenyr had gone to meet him one day, and returned alone, and angry.

An echo came from behind, and Willow motioned to the tunnel ahead. "We should hasten."

The trio worked their way through the Deep, gradually ascending toward the surface. Light's fatigue quickly set in, and he shuffled after his companions, his weariness turning to anger every time Jeric urged them faster.

Unwilling to stop, Jeric drove them for three days, the endless caverns, tunnels, and crevasses becoming a blur interspersed by patches of blissful sleep. Jeric's tension never faded, and the group spoke little. Light did notice that Willow walked a short distance from him, and he wondered if she were angry with their failure in Kordune.

The stone beneath their feet gradually gave way to soil, the luminescent plants of the Deep growing in smaller and smaller patches, until finally they reached the mouth of a cave. Excitement spilled into Light's blood and he darted past the others, stepping into the open. He breathed deep of the night air, relishing the tinge of pine to the scent.

A gurgling brook trickled nearby, the sound a welcoming song that Light wanted to answer. Stars twinkled in the heavens, and a partial moon compelled Light to gaze into the sky and release a shout of joy.

"Where are we?" Jeric asked.

"Western Talinor, I think," Willow said, pointing to the stone around the cave. "This is the only region with stone bearing this type of striation."

Jeric nodded in satisfaction and motioned east. "It will take me a week to reach Cloudy Vale."

"You're not coming to Mistkeep?" Light asked.

Jeric jerked his head. "Elenyr is in trouble."

"I could send a lightcast bird as a messenger," Light said.

"Too unreliable." Jeric knelt and checked his pack. "It might not find her in time."

"She is the Hauntress," Willow said. "Are you certain she cannot handle a lightning mage?"

"Not if she doesn't know he's coming," Jeric said. "There hasn't been a lightning mage in a century, and if Serak truly has one at his side, Elenyr won't know the trap she is stepping into. I must warn her what is coming."

Willow inclined her head. "We will journey to Mistkeep and see what we may learn of the queen."

"I hate Mistkeep," Light said with a sigh. "So dark and creepy. I wish we had Shadow with us. He loves that place."

"It is probably not like you remember," Willow said. "Unless you have been there in recent years."

"I've avoided it," he said. "You really think the queen is there?"

"We will find out soon enough," Willow said, and then turned to Jeric. "I hope you find her well."

94

"Travel safe." Jeric rose and departed.

"You're not going to stay until morning?" Light asked, and then yawned.

"Goodbye, Light," Jeric cast over his shoulder. "Try not to destroy everything you encounter."

He cast a tight smile over his shoulder before disappearing into the trees. Confused, Light waved farewell, and then faced Willow. The dark elf had a frown on her face as she stared at the empty trail.

"Do I really destroy everything I encounter?" Light asked.

"Usually," Willow said.

"But I thought Jeric enjoyed what we did in Kordune."

"He would," she said. "But right now he has a more pressing concern."

"Elenyr?"

She rotated to face him. "He still loves her."

Light blinked in surprise. "*Oh*."

She chuckled softly and leaned up, kissing him on the lips. The contact was soft and tender, and his heart stirred. When they parted he regarded her with curiosity.

"What was that for?"

"For getting us out alive," she said. "And finding the archive."

"I thought you were angry with me," he said, motioning to the cave.

"I was," she admitted. "But I was more angry with myself. I should have trusted you."

"No," he said, recalling how many times in the last few days he'd failed. His voice turned sad. "I think I've proven I cannot be trusted."

95

She reached up and caught his cheek, forcing him to meet her gaze. "Our world is a dark place, but you see brightness. You may not notice everything, and destroy a great deal with your impulsivity, but you always find a way—even if it's not the way I expect."

"I'm sorry," he said.

"Don't apologize for the reason I love you."

He finally smiled and pointed to the dark trees. "Are we going to travel now, too?"

"No," she said, chuckling at the obvious reluctance in his voice. "With your magic, we'll travel much faster during daylight."

Pleased by her answer, he followed her into the cave, where they laid out their bedrolls. Normally Light would have been asleep in seconds, but he found his thoughts dwelling on Elenyr.

The Hauntress was formidable in combat, always seeming to escape death—to the extent that Light had begun to think she was invulnerable. But Jeric, an adventurer that enjoyed fun as much as Shadow, had been worried, even afraid.

A cold knot settled into his stomach as he imagined losing Elenyr. The woman was the only family he'd ever had, aside from the other fragments, and losing her would be catastrophic. Light's hand tightened into a fist, the spark of rage sudden and powerful. If someone really did kill Elenyr, he would hunt them down like a rabid dog, tear them asunder as they screamed for—

"Light," Willow asked. "Are you well? Your hand is glowing."

Light opened his eyes to find his fist glowing bright, reflecting the rising rage. But the emotion faded as quickly as it had come, and his hand darkened. With a sigh, he rolled over and tried to sleep, annoyed that his worry would not be so easily extinguished.

Chapter 13: Above the Mist

Willow woke at dawn to Light's shout of joy. She smiled and sat up, her gaze drawn to the fragment as he cavorted outside the mouth of the cave like he'd just discovered presents on his birthing day.

She watched him, unable to resist a small smile. Light's joy was as forceful as his rage and was even more pronounced in the full light of day. The magic bleeding off his frame ignited dead leaves, and he panicked, but managed to extinguish the fire before it spread.

Her thoughts turned to the events in the Deep. Light had utterly failed at being Serak, but he had succeeded in getting the information they desired, even helping them escape in his typical, chaotic manner.

He noticed she was awake and bounded into the cave. "Is this not the most glorious morning you've ever seen in your life?"

"You say that every morning."

He burst into a laugh and kissed her—before leaping outside again, sprinting around like a child running circles around his parents. He spotted a bird's nest and leapt into the trees, driving the screeching bird away.

She smiled at his antics and rose to gather her bedroll. With some prompting, she got him to gather his things and then he cast a pair of wolfsteeds. The strange animals were Light's favorite, and had the body of a horse but the head of a wolf. More importantly, they were fast.

They mounted the animals and the steeds leapt away, threading through the forest at shocking speed, kicking up the leaves that had fallen. Gold, brown, and red fluttered around them, drifting to the ground and swirling in their wake. Despite their need to hasten, she smiled at the beauty.

"We're going almost as fast as the krey sphere," Light called, his features a mixture of excitement, curiosity, and wonder. "I've never gone so fast before—except when I fell down a mountain—because falling is faster. Have I ever given you wings before? Flying is even more exhilarating than riding—but of course you know that." His eyes glowed with excitement. "Why don't we give wings to the *horses*?"

He pointed to her steed, but she raised a warning hand. "Don't. We're going fast enough, and I really don't want to draw undue attention. We made quite a mess in the Deep, and the Order will be out for blood."

Light giggled and pointed downward. "Did you see Princess Melora's face? She was so angry."

"You did gag her."

"I wish the Queen's Hand had been there," he said, his features darkening in an instant. "I would have liked to punish them for what they did to you."

Willow grinned at the image of Light battling Black and Cutter. They were formidable, but Light was a fragment of Draeken, and they would not likely survive such a duel. Still, Black's sword could do significant damage to one born of magic. Then her smile faded as a question came to mind.

"Why did Melora not bring the Hand with her?" she wondered aloud.

"What?"

Light was no longer listening. He stood on his horse, holding a squirrel he'd caught as they raced beneath a tree branch. The animal struggled to escape while Light petted its back, and scolded it for scratching.

"You are adorable," Light exclaimed. "I think I'll call you Epic Furry." He chuckled to himself.

Willow's thoughts were on the battle in the sphere. If Melora had suspected Serak, why bring just twenty soldiers? Why not bring Black and Cutter? The obvious answer was that they had not been present, but

Willow wondered if there was another reason. Was it possible the Hand was still loyal to the queen?

In the months leading up to the queen's kidnapping, the Hand had been dispatched to infiltrate the Order of Ancients. None had returned, and Crown Princess Arane had received information that they had betrayed the crown and joined the Order. But if that were the case, why had Black and Cutter spared her life in the testing? And then not been present when Serak needed to be confronted?

Her lips tightened when she thought of her trial. Cutter and Black had used attacks meant to kill, every swing intended to be lethal. Trusting them as allies could get her killed, especially if she was seeing hope where there was none.

"Epic Furry bit me," Light said, his voice so forlorn that Willow chuckled.

"I think it's time to let him go."

Light sighed in regret, and then tossed the struggling squirrel into the trees. It caught a branch and skittered away, chittering its fury. The miles slipped by, the two horses running without growing tired, without slowing. They passed a woodsman, who cried out and leapt off the trail. Light swiveled in his saddle and raised a hand in apology.

"Sorry!"

They came upon a village and galloped through, scaring the children playing in the street. They huddled behind a statue of a black dragon, and one of the women called to the statue, praying to it for salvation as if it were a god.

"Should I have given Jeric a horse?" Light asked, pulling her from her thoughts.

"He wouldn't have wanted a mount he could not control," she said. "And besides, he prefers a more subtle means of travel."

"Even when Elenyr is in danger?"

Although it was evident he tried to hide it, a trace of worry crept into his voice, and she cast him a measuring look. Light rarely expressed worry for the fragments or Elenyr, of whom he had complete confidence.

"So you think he was right?" she asked. "You think she is in danger?"

"I don't want to lose Elenyr."

It was the most sober expression Willow had ever seen on Light, so she smiled reassuringly. "I'm sure she will be well. As you said, she is the Hauntress, and few are capable of standing against an ethereal warrior."

"Really?" he asked earnestly.

She managed to keep her worry from showing in her features. "Trust the Hauntress."

He smiled, and all the worry evaporated from his face. Willow smiled faintly, wondering what it would be like to extinguish worries so easily. Light was always unfettered, his smile bright and open, except when someone provoked his slumbering fury.

She'd often wondered about Draeken, and the fragments that formed the guardian. She'd only ever seen Draeken once, and it had been terrifying. She'd thought he would be a combination of all the fragments, but he'd been entirely different.

"What is the purpose of your frown?" Light asked.

"Just thinking about the first time I met Draeken," she said. "Do you remember?"

"Mind, Shadow, and I became Draeken to fight a black dragon," Light said. "I think Shadow called it a delightful conflict."

The black dragon had been pillaging dark elf cities for months, and the queen had requested Elenyr's aid. After a week of hunting, they cornered the dragon in an underground canyon, where the three fragments had become Draeken. Recalling that moment made her wonder as to Serak's purpose.

"What do you suppose Serak wants with you?" Willow asked.

Light shrugged. "Does it matter? It's not like he's going to get it."

Light spotted a deer and leapt out of his saddle. It was close to night and the wolfsteeds had begun to slow. Willow reined in her mount and watched Light chase—and catch—the deer. But her thoughts remained on the murky loyalties and mysterious purposes of her foes.

They ate roast deer that night, and smoked venison for the morning. Throughout the next day they skirted the southern border of Talinor, following the edge of the Evermist eastward. At home in the stone and warmth of the Deep, Willow hated the swamp.

Steeped in greenish mist, the swamp carried the stench of death and decay. Quicksand, ravenous beasts, and the ease of getting lost made the bog a danger to all. Fortunately, Light was her companion, and four days after departing the cave, he cast a pair of wings and fastened them to her back.

"I am uncomfortable with heights," she said uneasily.

He laughed like the comment was absurd. "Everyone likes heights."

"I live *underground*."

"Then you'll love the air," he said.

He cast his own wings and then launched himself into the air, banking to swerve around her. She remained on the ground, eyeing the swamp, wondering which she preferred. At the least, the swamp had solid ground. Most of the time.

She'd flown with Light before, when he'd talked her into trying, but now as she gazed on the swamp, she realized she would not be crashing into a nice, bright lake. She'd be crashing into a swamp that liked to devour intruders.

"Are you afraid?" he asked, swooping lower.

"Yes!" she said with an uneasy laugh.

"You are the inkmage," he said. "I thought you did not know fear."

"Anyone who has fallen from the sky has felt their insides clench," she said.

"That only happened once."

"You are a fragment of a person," she said. "One of the others must have gotten the fear of heights."

He chuckled. "That would be Water."

"See?" Willow exclaimed. "I have all my fragments inside of me, so I don't have the luxury of my fear being with another."

He alighted on a branch at the edge of the swamp, looking like a giant bird. "You're the one who said we should hasten," he said. "And the longer you wait, the more daylight we lose . . ."

She clenched her jaw, realizing what his teasing tone meant. If they didn't find the fortress by the time the sun set, they would have to camp in the Evermist, a prospect she disliked. She sighed, and then willed her wings to flap.

The wings fluttered, and her feet came off the ground. Panic gripped her, the motion ignored by the wings as they continued to lift her into the sky. Her stomach clenched like her tattoos had constricted her waist, and she fought for breath as the ground receded.

"Isn't this exciting?"

"No!" she cried.

He laughed and soared south. Her wings pulled her forward, and she sucked in her breath as they passed through the mist wafting up from the dark trees. She yearned to return to the earth, to feel the stone beneath her feet, but she was also loath to land in the swamp.

Light soared around her, swooping so the mist curled off his wings. He ducked into the mist, briefly disappearing in the trees of the swamp. Her fear spiked but he burst into view a moment later with a rusted sword.

"I found a sword!"

"Where's its owner?"

"Just bones," he said, swinging his new discovery with abandon.

"Can we focus on finding the fortress?" she asked. "Before we end up like him?"

"This way," he called, and swerved east.

For the next several hours they flew above the swamp, and after a while her fear gradually diminished—not enough to enjoy the view, but enough so her stomach stopped flipping. But as time passed her shoulders began to ache, as did her body from attempting to hold herself aloft.

"Are we lost?" she finally asked.

"Of course not," Light said. "It just looks different from up here."

They flew south and east. Then south. Then east. Then north and west. When the sun began to set, Light came to a stop and turned about, scanning the horizon. But there was only the endless swamp stretching in all directions.

"I think we're lost," he admitted.

Their wings began to wilt as the sun continued to decline, and Light began to hurry. Willow followed and kept glancing at the sun. Like many dark elves, she found the sun far too bright, but this time she wished it would not disappear.

The seconds passed until they were forced to drop into the swamp, their wings fading. Willow and Light passed through the trees and landed on a fallen tree. Willow's wings faded and she turned, watching the dark swamp grow darker. Insects buzzed and the fetid air seeped into her clothes and nose. A beast coughed nearby, the sound ominous and threatening.

"At least we aren't flying," he said.

"We're lost and we have no idea how to reach Mistkeep," she said.

"We can find it in the morning," he replied with a yawn.

"Don't fall asleep on me now," she warned. "I need you to stay awake."

"But it's so dark," he complained. "And you can—"

"Quiet," she hissed.

"What?"

"Listen," she said.

She closed her eyes, listening for what she'd heard before. It could have been a beast or a snapping of wood, but she was certain it had been a clang of steel. She knew that sound, the sound of swordplay. She smiled when she heard it again and pointed south.

"This way," she said, darting forward. "We're close."

Chapter 14: Mistkeep

Willow pushed her way through the trees, hissing for Light to illuminate the way. He managed to draw from the vestiges of daylight to cast a beacon above their heads. Although dim, it shined ahead, helping Willow avoid the pitfalls of the swamp.

"What do you hear?" Light asked.

"Swordplay," she said.

"Could be anything," Light said.

He rubbed his face as if it would wake him, and she was grateful for the effort. In the Deep, she'd seen him push himself in the darkness, seen a determination that had been absent before. It made him seem older.

"No beast makes the sound of steel on steel," she said. "And don't doubt elven hearing."

He grinned and pointed ahead. "You think it's Mistkeep? Someone training?"

"We'll find out soon enough."

She ducked under a low branch and threaded her way between two cypress trees. Jumping over a patch of mud, she found a path and followed it, working her way south, toward the sound she'd heard.

For several minutes there was only the sound of insects, the buzzing of the swamp. She pushed forward, following her instincts, hoping she was right. The seconds passed and sweat beaded her forehead, trickling down her back and bare skin. She glanced at Light and found him with his lips clenched.

"Are you well?" she asked.

"Trying not to speak," Light whispered.

She grinned and thanked him with a nod. Jumping over a dead tree, she froze when a creature passed into view of the light, but it was too small to be dangerous, and it skittered away. A moment later she nearly stepped on a snake, but Light snatched it up and held it aloft, grinning like he'd just found a lost toy.

"Can I keep it?"

"No."

His expression turned sad and he tossed it away.

Clash

The sound was louder than before, and she accelerated in that direction, running as fast as she dared in the gloom. Then another clash, and shouted orders. Light perked up, indicating he'd also heard the sounds of battle.

"We're close," he said, and his tone became one of admiration. "You have beautiful ears."

"Is that what you find attractive on me?"

"And other things," he said, flushing bright red.

She stifled a laugh and threaded a gap between a stone and a tree, using one of the branches to cross a stretch of murky water. A shape moved in the liquid, and they were past before it revealed itself. Ten steps later the bog came to an abrupt halt on the bank of a large lake.

Steeped in mist, the lake was difficult to discern, but the fortress rose above, the spires tall and proud. Fire burned in a window, and the sounds of swordplay echoed over the water. She exchanged a look with Light and the two sprinted forward, following the bank of the lake to the bridge.

Light pointed upward, bending the moonlight to warp around them. "Who's fighting?"

"Doesn't matter," she said. "We can use the distraction to sneak in."

They reached the bridge and sprinted across. The portcullis at the end was manned by two soldiers, both looking inward rather than outward. They craned their necks towards the courtyard beyond, calling for answers.

"The prisoners escaped!" someone shouted. "We need reinforcements."

"Go," one man said to the other, and the second sprinted away, crossing the courtyard and diving into an opening. In the silence, the remaining guard smiled to himself. "I'm not fool enough to hunt the Angel of Death and—"

He'd turned to the portcullis, just as Willow reached through a gap in the bars. She caught his tunic and yanked him into the steel, placing a dagger at his eye. He stared in shock at the inkblade.

"Who are you?" Willow demanded.

"The Bloodsworn," he said hastily. "We serve Gendor."

"An assassin of the guild," Light exclaimed, examining the portcullis with interest. "They call him the Blade Ghost."

"And a member of the Order of Ancients?" Willow asked.

The man recoiled, but Willow tightened her grip and poked him in the forehead with her dagger. Fear washed over his features and he glanced to Light before his eyes returned to the black dagger.

"Would you rather speak now?" Willow asked. "Or after you are bleeding?"

"A member of the Order," the guard said hastily.

"Who are you fighting?" Willow demanded.

"Lorica and the fragment of Shadow," he said.

"Shadow is here?" Light exclaimed, excitement tingeing his voice. "Where?"

The man jerked a thumb back towards the fortress—and then yanked his sword free, slashing at Willow's hand. She released him and he turned to run, but she dropped the dagger back onto her forearm and drew her crossbow. He took four steps and shouted a single word before the bolt pierced his heart and he fell.

"Let's get the gate open," Willow said.

She turned to find Light crouched, his hands on the bars. He was lifting with all his might, straining to lift the iron portcullis. She hid a smile as his face began to turn red, and then pointed her crossbow at the lever beyond the portcullis.

She fired, and the bolt struck the lever, releasing the mechanism and sending the portcullis upward. Light squeaked in surprise as the portcullis lifted, and looked up to Willow, but she'd already returned the crossbow to her skin.

"Did you see how strong I was?" Light exclaimed.

"Well done," she said, hiding a smile. "Now let's go find your brother."

He wiped the sweat from his brow and stepped under the portcullis. "I didn't know I was so strong," he said.

"You do now," she replied.

They crossed the misty courtyard and entered the keep. Light did not seem concerned that they were entering an enemy fortress, so Willow pulled him aside when a group of guards rushed by.

"Perhaps we should look like them," Willow said.

"Why?"

"Let's not cause more of a conflict until we know what is happening."

He shrugged and warped the light, reshaping their identities until they both resembled guards. She looked down and found a beard on her face and glared at Light. He shrugged in resignation.

"We haven't seen a woman here yet. I don't know what they look like."

"They probably don't have beards," she said.

He flashed a contagious smile and then stepped into the hall. Willow again took the lead, taking him down the hall and around the corner. She walked with purpose, her gait rushed, but not running.

The walls of the fortress were pristine polished granite. Brackets for light orbs hung from beams across the hallway, illuminating the many banners placed along the walls. Light looked about in wonder.

"It's cleaner than I expected," Willow said.

"It doesn't look like it did before," he said. "There used to be vines and moss all over the walls, and the floor was covered in mud and animal tracks." He shuddered. "It was as dark as the Deep."

Willow peeked around a door that was partially open. The room beyond was a bedchamber for a guard, probably an officer by the lavish furnishings. He had a fondness for horses, and figurines of various steeds lined the shelves. The bed was large and fashioned from Talinorian oak, the dark wood beautiful, the carvings intricate.

"Someone spent a fortune repairing Mistkeep," she said.

"Shadow wouldn't like it as much anymore," he said.

A set of hurried footsteps heralded the arrival of a woman. Dressed as the other Bloodsworn, in dark clothing and a sword, she skidded to a halt, nearly colliding with Light before righting herself.

"What are you doing?" she demanded. "Join your command and start hunting."

"What's happening?" Willow asked smoothly. "We were standing guard on the outer wall."

"And abandoned your post?" She sneered at them. "Gendor will hear of this."

The clash of blades and a shout came from above, and the woman looked to the ceiling. Light motioned upward, a trace of excitement creeping into his voice.

"Did they really escape?"

"What do you think?" she asked. "Serak's cage was supposed to hold Shadow forever, and it lasted only a few hours."

"Is the queen safe?" Willow asked.

"The queen?" Her voice turned haughty. "Only the higher ranks are permitted to know of her location. And you are just first level initiates." She reached out and poked the insignia on Light's chest.

His features darkened, and Willow subtly stepped in front of him before he burned the hair from her head. The woman ignored her, and stepped around Willow, poking him in the chest again.

"Are you stupid?" she demanded. "You leave your post, and wander around here like a fool. I'll have you whipped for this, and your wages garnished for a month. Here we are in the midst of a battle and you behave like a lumbering ox—"

"You aren't at the conflict either," Light growled. "What are you doing wandering the halls like a frightened monkey?"

Willow sought to stop the woman before it was too late. "Perhaps it's best we—"

"You dare to insult me?" the woman barked. "I am a senior acolyte, and I will make certain Serak hears of this incident. When he finds out I'm sure he'll tear you apart and string you up so the other Bloodsworn know the fate of the disobedient."

Light raised a hand and wiped his face, changing his features. "I *am* Serak."

The woman blanched, fear replacing her arrogance. "My apologies, Master Serak. I thought you went to the Deep to seek an imposter . . ."

Light stepped close. "Perhaps we should tear you apart and string *you* up, so others can know the fate of the disobedient."

110

She swallowed at the coldness to his tone, and Willow mentally applauded Light's resolve. The woman glanced to Willow, still in the guise of a Bloodsworn with a beard, and then her eyes flicked back to Serak.

"The Fragment of Shadow and The Angel of Death just escaped. We are hunting them now."

"Find Gendora and inform him of my return."

"You mean Gendor?"

"Er . . . yes?"

Doubt washed over the woman's face and then she reached for her sword. Willow was faster, and darted in, the blow sending the woman to the floor. Then Willow looked to Light and the fragment raised his hands apologetically.

"I forgot his name."

"Not something you can do," Willow said. "But too late now. Turn me back to Willow. We'll have to see if we can keep up the ruse if we meet anyone."

He did as requested and the illusion over her features faded. Then she led him to the curving stairs in a turret. They rounded a corner and Willow came to a halt when two individuals whirled to face them. She recognized Shadow instantly, but the woman at his side was unfamiliar.

"Willow?" Shadow asked, stepping into the open and pointing his sword at Light. "What are you doing with him?"

Light brightened and he rushed up the steps, avoiding the blade with ease to engulf Shadow in an embrace. Startled, Shadow fought to release himself from Serak's grip, but Light gushed into his ear.

"Shadow!" he cried. "I've missed you so much, and there is so much for me to tell you. You wouldn't *believe* what I've seen in the Deep."

Shadow finally disentangled himself and put his sword between them. "A few hours ago you wanted me dead. Now you act like you love me?"

Light giggled, and then passed a hand over his face, his features returning to those of Draeken. Shadow blinked in surprise, and then grinned, the expression exactly that of a brother greeting a brother.

"I bet you have a tale to tell," Shadow said.

"You have no idea," Light said fervently.

Chapter 15: First of the Hand

Excited that he'd found his brother in such a place, Light beamed at his brother, pleased that he was with Lorica, the Angel of Death. He wanted to gush and share everything they'd encountered in the Deep, but Shadow spoke first.

"Light? What are you doing here?" Shadow asked.

"Looking for—"

"We should get out of sight," Willow exclaimed.

They ducked into a storeroom, where barrels and crates were stacked in neat rows. Light craned his head, wondering if there was a fort beneath the crates. It reminded him of playing with his brothers when they were young. Or was it him playing, and the others told him not to play?

"I thought you were with Water and Lira," Shadow said.

"I was," Light replied, speaking in a delighted rush. "Then I met up with Elenyr and she sent me into the Deep with Willow. And who is your companion?"

"We don't have time for tales," Lorica said. "And I'd rather not be inside when that trap explodes."

"Right," Shadow said, and pointed to Lorica. "Assassin. Dead sister. Betrayed. Revenge. Fun. More fun. Wants to kill Gendor." He raised an eyebrow to Lorica.

She snorted a laugh. "I think that covers it."

Light grinned, enjoying the game. "Became Serak. The Deep. Tired. The Queen's Hand. Battle. Willow is beautiful. Kiss. Another kiss. Searching. See Shadow."

He beamed at the game, wondering if he'd won. What were the rules? Then he noticed Shadow's companion. She conveyed an intimidating air, and her cloak rippled in odd patterns. Just when he was about to ask what sort of magic it contained, Shadow motioned to him.

"What do you need?" Shadow asked.

"We're hoping the queen of the dark elves is here," Willow said. "She was taken by the Order."

Shadow grimaced. "It's on the east side," he said. "But in a few minutes that entire wing is going to explode."

Light and Willow exchanged a look. "Then we'll hurry," Light said.

Willow swung the door open. A roving patrol appeared on the stairs at the same moment, the three men looking up to see Willow framed in the opening. All three reached for their weapons.

Willow grabbed her bare shoulder, where the hilt of a crossbow was tattooed. The weapon seeped into her hands and turned solid. She pulled the trigger three times, the bow thrumming and sending bolts to pierce the Bloodsworn armor, knocking them down the stairs in a clatter of metal. Nodding in satisfaction, she returned the crossbow to her shoulder, the ink sinking into her flesh and returning to a tattoo.

"Let's go," she said to Light, and then darted into the corridor.

"Isn't she incredible?" Light whispered to Shadow, his voice awed as he slipped out the door and followed her out of sight. "Good luck!" he called back to Shadow.

Willow nudged Light. "You should be Serak for this."

"Right," he said with a wink. When he'd changed his features, he asked, "Who do you think is guarding the queen?"

"First of the Hand," she replied evenly. "And she is the most lethal dark elf in our nation."

"What makes her so dangerous?" he asked.

"Because she has her own unique magic," Willow replied.

114

"Like you?"

"Not like me," she said, her tone dark. "They call her Mimic, because she can duplicate the magic of another."

"Even me?" Light asked.

"We'll find out soon enough," Willow said. "Keep your Serak persona up as long as you can. I'd like to avoid fighting her."

Light imagined a person capable of mimicking the magic of another person, and it sent a chill down his back. Could she duplicate the magic of the fragments? Gain their power? It made him nervous to think of—

"What. Is. That?"

He stood in awe, staring up at a statue of a giant. At twenty feet tall, the stone figure filled the breadth of an alcove, his features fearsome. Although stone, the statue held a seven-foot sword, the black sword as sharp as the day it was forged, the dark metal matching the fearsome helmet.

"Light," Willow said. "We don't have time for this."

Light didn't hear her, and stepped to the statue, lifting his gaze to the helmet and sword. It was obvious they were real, and had been owned by a tremendous warrior, probably the giant the statue depicted. Then he noticed the name inscribed at the base.

"Beragemnan," Light read aloud. "Never heard of him."

"Light," Willow said urgently. "An entire side of the fortress is going to explode soon. We must hasten."

Light allowed her to drag him down the hall but continued to watch the statue until it was out of sight. He'd never seen such an effigy and was eager to know more of a giant bearing such armament.

"His helm had power," Light said. "Did you feel it?"

He shuddered as he recalled the emanations from the artifact. The helm had been pure black, the energy from within sending a tingling into Light's body, as if it wanted to be wielded, as if it were alive . . .

"Light," Willow pleaded. "Ask Elenyr about him later. We must hurry."

He nodded firmly. "She will certainly know."

He felt a pang of worry as he thought of Elenyr and wondered if Jeric had managed to find her. Had he found her in Cloudy Vale? Or was he still waiting? Willow caught his elbow and turned him against the wall, planting a kiss on his lips that robbed him of breath.

"What was that for?" he asked.

"I need you to focus, now," she said, "or we're going to die in the next few minutes. Mimic will punish distraction with death. I need you to stand with me, to protect me."

Her voice carried a trace of desperation that he could not refuse. "I'm with you."

She pointed to the corridor just beyond them. "We're here. Are you ready?"

"Promise we can ask Elenyr about the giant?"

"I promise," she said. "Now *be* Serak."

He drew in a breath and straightened. Willow was counting on him, and he was not about to let her die. Recognizing his readiness, Willow turned the corner and led him down a long hallway.

At the end, a single dark elf stood, her features obscured by a disturbing silver mask, with a single claw mark across the nose, like a talon had cut deep into the flesh. It was so visceral it looked like it should be bleeding.

Dressed in dark armor that covered her upper body and legs, she had her arms bare, revealing a faint mottling of color, as if she carried an illness. From what Elenyr had said of magic, such illness sometimes warped magic, likely granting her the mimicking ability.

Her pose languid, unworried, Mimic waited for them at the end of the hall. Shouts echoed from within the fortress, punctuated by a growl and then a *clang* of swords. Aside from her disturbing appearance,

116

Mimic could have been standing at a fall festival, watching the sun set over the entertainment.

Light came to a halt. "Mimic," he said, doing his best to imitate Serak's voice. "Shadow has placed a trap that will destroy this entire wing. We must move the queen before she is killed."

Mimic simply stared at him, or at least that was what he assumed. The mask was opaque over the eyes, and he sensed a charm allowing her to see through the barrier. She made no move to attack, but neither did she speak. Guessing Serak would be angry, he scowled.

"I gave you an order," he said. "Move, before I force you."

She held her hand upward and a ball of light flowed across her fingers, trickling over her knuckles and swirling above her palm. Willow subtly reached for the sword on her hip, but Light stood still, fascinated by the display.

"Master Serak," she said, a trace of mocking in her melodic voice. "At our previous encounters you possessed earth and water magics. Now you have the magic of light. I must say the change looks good on you."

She reached forward, and lazily swept a hand across Light's face. The charm turning him into Serak was stripped away as easily as if it were a real mask, and Mimic tossed the sparks of magic aside. Willow drew her sword and dagger.

"Your talent is beautiful," Light said, his tone awed. "I've never met anyone who could do that so easily."

"And Willow," Mimic said, turning to the dark elf. "It is always a pleasure to encounter another unique. Although I admit a touch of jealousy. Your ability did not require a cancer in your flesh, eating away at your body and mind."

There was a smile in Mimic's voice, but her words carried too much rancor to be pleasant. Light's smile faded as he heard the trace of anticipation, as if the woman *wanted* to fight them, to defeat them. He'd heard that voice in Shadow before.

"Is the queen even here?" Willow asked.

Mimic laughed lightly and drew on the light to cast a shimmering sword. She morphed the weapon into an axe, and then a hammer. The head tapered and spikes appeared, suggesting she wished to maim rather than kill.

"The queen was moved to another refuge," Mimic said. "I'm afraid you are too late . . ."

"Then why are you here?" Light asked.

"Relgor's order," she said.

Light blinked in surprise. "So you serve the krey?"

"They made me an offer I could not refuse," Mimic replied. She reached to her side and lovingly shaped a tigron out of light, dimming the corridor to conjure the steed. She mounted the huge beast and patted it on the flank.

"What could they offer that would make you abandon your oath to the queen?" Willow demanded, pulling on Light's arm.

Mimic swished the hammer experimentally, and then nodded to herself. Obviously liking the hammer, she cast a second weapon, the two hammers filling her hands. Willow pulled harder and the two retreated down the hall, but Mimic did not attack.

"As I said, you have your magic and your beauty. Can you fault me for wanting the same?"

"So that is the price of your loyalty?" Willow asked.

"It is," Mimic said. "And the krey have the ability to deliver. But now I fear I must take your lives."

"I am a fragment of Draeken," Light said, disliking the trickle of fear in his blood. "You will not kill me."

Her laugh matched her way of speaking, detached and cold, almost scornfully apologetic. It made Light shudder and he glanced to Willow uncertainly. She dragged him further from Mimic, who placed one hammer on her back and hefted the second.

118

"Oh my dear little fragment," Mimic mocked. "I know exactly who you are, and you are no match for me. What you possess, I possess, and we both know I'm far more intelligent than the fragment of chaos."

Light cocked his head to the side. "Is that what they call me? I'm still a guardian."

The tigron began to stalk forward, its soft footfalls advancing step by step. Mimic settled into the saddle and positioned the hammer low and ready. Then she set the weapon into a deadly spin.

"You aren't the first guardian I have slain," she said. "And you will not be the last."

The tigron charged, and Light and Willow fled.

Chapter 16: Mimic

Light and Willow sprinted down the corridor, with Light easily outstripping the dark elf. Catching her hand, he came to a halt and transferred his momentum, swinging her around the corner to safety. Then he cast his favorite curved sword and whirled, striking the spiked hammer as it came for his face.

Mimic's weapon bounced upward, and Light ducked the second hammer. The woman smoothly leapt off her tigron and the animal surged after Willow, while Mimic turned to face him.

"How will it feel to die by your own magic?" she wondered aloud.

"I don't know." Confused, he scrunched up his face. "Will you tell me? Oh, sorry, you don't have a magic of your own."

The woman did not speak, but the tilt of her head indicated Light had struck a chord. She charged, swinging her two mauls, one coming for his head, the next at his waist. He deflected the first and then leapt to the wall, attaching his feet to the light on its surface.

Sprinting along sideways, he raced the length of the hall and followed Willow, casting over his shoulder, "I'd love to stay and fight, but I prefer to fight with Willow."

As the woman gave chase, Light sprinted the length of the hall, following Willow by the sounds of her flight. He entered a darkened hallway filled with bound and gagged Bloodsworn. He hurried through, gently pushing the swinging men and women out of the way.

"Sorry. Sorry. Ouch, that looks like it hurt. Don't let that get infected."

He reached the other end and turned to find Willow battling the tigron in a small antechamber. With her whip in one hand and her sword in the other, she slashed and flicked her whip, keeping the animal at bay.

Light lunged for the cat and caught its tail. It spun to face him but he leaned back and hurled it backwards, where it collided with the wall behind him and slumped to the floor before rising with a snarl.

Mimic appeared and leapt onto her mount. One of the hammers was on her back, and in her free hand she held a glowing ball of fire. Her smile was evident in her voice as she again stalked forward.

"Look what I picked up from a dwarf in the hall."

She tossed the ball towards Light and it bounced along the floor. Recognizing the detonation spell, Light dived through an open door and sprinted onto the bed. He grinned as he bounced, recalling all the joys of jumping on the bed when Elenyr wasn't looking. Why did she always tell him to stop—?

The sphere detonated in the hall, shredding the door and sending Light hurtling into the wall. He bounced and landed on the bed, dazed from the impact. Coughing in the smoke, he rose and saw Mimic appear in the smog and toss a second sphere into the room.

"Goodbye, Light."

He scrambled backward but the sphere detonated, the force of the blast destroying the wall behind Light and sending him tumbling into the great hall beyond. He rose to his feet and dusted himself off—and then spotted the giant shape behind him.

The reaver of light was obviously a sentient, cast over many years to have a single purpose. Taller than a horse, and three times as long, the scaled reaver was a thing of beauty, and Light thanked his good fortune. Its jaws were long like a wolf's, with hundreds of teeth visible. Its body was scaled, small fins extending from the powerful legs, granting the reaver speed when underwater. The long tail contained a barbed tip, the barbs flattening and straightening. It rumbled a growl, its lips lifting to reveal teeth like needles.

"You shall do nicely," he said.

121

Ignoring its growl, Light leapt to its flank and touched its head. Its purpose was obvious, *Obey Serak*. The command had been inscribed on the magical flesh until it had gained a semblance of consciousness. Unfortunately for its creators, Light was better at such magic.

Obey Me.

The reaver's demeanor shifted in an instant, and it dipped its head, allowing Light to climb onto its back. Delighted with his new mount, he turned and the reaver streaked through the gaping hole in the wall.

"Willow!" he shouted. "Look what I found!"

The reaver was so large it barely fit through the hole, and Light had to duck. As he did, he caught a glimpse of the people in the room, and he hoped he hadn't stolen the reaver from someone else. But it wouldn't have been Shadow's, he would have hated such a powerful creature of light.

Shrugging, Light directed his newfound friend down the corridor after Mimic. The beast was enormous, barely fitting in the corridor. A guard stepped into view, squeaked in surprise, and dived back into the room from which he'd come.

The beast reached a narrow point between a case of weapons and a painting of Serak. The reaver hurtled past, its sheer bulk shattering the case and removing the head from the painting. Then the light reaver banked to the side and Light caught a glimpse of Mimic astride her now much smaller tigron. The leader of the Queen's Hand had maneuvered Willow into a corner and was stalking toward her.

Light raised a hand to catch Willow's eye. "Willow! You think this will help?"

Both Mimic and Willow turned, and for a moment neither moved. Then the reaver surged forward, a blood curdling snarl erupting from its lips. Mimic yanked on the reins and the tigron leapt down a side corridor. Light called out to Willow but the reaver swerved to follow Mimic.

"Isn't she beautiful?" Light called, his voice echoing in the corridors of Mistkeep as the giant beast charged after Mimic.

Tigrons were known for strength and speed, easily able to bring down mounted cavalry. The beast of magic matched its flesh counterpart. But a scaled reaver was a greater beast, and it surged down the corridor, closing the gap.

Mimic slid to a halt and dived through an open door. The door was too small to permit a reaver. Light hesitated, but the beast of magic followed the purpose Light had given, and it charged the gap. Light ducked as the reaver plowed through the opening, stones bouncing off the reaver's head and filling the corridor.

The room was an armory, with stacks of weapons spaced in neat rows. Several soldiers were present, gathering crossbow bolts from barrels on the far wall. They recoiled when Light blasted through the doorway.

"I love this thing!" Light cried.

Mimic had circled the outside wall and burst through the smoke, the tigron's claws reaching for Light. The reaver whirled, its barbed tale knocking weapon racks askew, scattering weapons in a great clattering of steel.

"Sorry!" Light called to the soldiers.

Mimic's tigron landed and began to circle about the back of the room. One soldier hastily armed a crossbow and took aim at the reaver, but its tail lashed out, bashing him into a statue holding a spear. Both were knocked sprawling, with the statue breaking on impact. The other soldiers retreated and huddled behind barrels and crates.

"Do you like my mount?" Light asked proudly. "I found him outside, but his owner seemed to be missing. I hope they don't mind."

"That sentry belongs to Serak," Mimic said.

"Now it belongs to him," Willow said, stepping over the pile of rubble that had once been the door. "Where's the queen?"

Behind her mask, Mimic's laugh was low and mocking. "I'm afraid she is beyond your reach now."

"Blast," Light said, and then brightened. "Where did she go?"

"You are as impulsive as Serak said," Mimic said. "But impulsivity gets you killed, especially against someone with your own magic."

"You're talented," Willow said, glancing to the Bloodsworn, but they had found a small back door and retreated. "But even you cannot cast a reaver."

"I do not need to," she said.

Mimic reached to her shirt and raised it to reveal her bare stomach. A large tattoo marked her side, the image of a krey explosive, a detonation sphere. She reached to the sphere, and the ink spilled into her hand.

"I had this inscribed on my flesh just for you," she said. "Did you know the queen considered asking you to join the Queen's Hand? I must say you are worthy to fight at my side, but unfortunately you chose loyalty over wisdom."

Light stared in awe as the woman hefted the sphere, and then threw it. Willow shouted a warning but the ball was not aimed at them. Instead it struck the side wall, where it detonated in a plume of smoke and dust. Mimic darted towards the opening and disappeared into the misty courtyard beyond.

"Go!" Light shouted to his mount.

The mist obscured his vision, but he caught a glimpse of Mimic riding ahead, leaping about as if avoiding large objects . . .

Rising from the gloom, a large ballista appeared. Light would have swerved, but the light reaver did not, and plowed through the large beams, knocking the war machine aside and sending it skidding into its neighbor. Light laughed as his reaver streaked through the courtyard filled with green mist, crashing through the weapons like they were toys. They were halfway through the hole before he realized he'd left Willow behind. Again. He grimaced.

"Sorry!" he called back as he disappeared.

He caught a glimpse of Willow sprinting in pursuit and then he followed Mimic through another corridor and down stairs to a lower level. He thought she would flee, but instead she led him further and further down the tunnel.

Water dripped around them, murky and dank, suggesting they had passed beyond the walls of the fortress and were traveling beneath the lake. In the gloom Light squinted ahead, and even with the brilliance from the reaver he struggled to see the fleeing tigron.

"Mimic?" he called. "Where are you even going? We've got plenty of space to fight back in the fortress unless you—"

A body fell from above, and Light caught a glimpse of Mimic's form as the illusion faded. She'd sent the tigron ahead, allowing her to ascend to the top of the tunnel and drop when he passed. She knocked him from his perch and the two tumbled to the ground. She wrapped an arm around his throat, the other hand placing a blade at his stomach.

The reaver spun but the tigron leapt onto his back, and the two creatures of light snapped at each other, snarling and biting, tumbling down the corridor. Light laughed in delight and pointed to the ceiling.

"How very clever!" he praised.

"I would let him go if I were you," Willow called, panting as she came to a halt.

Mimic turned, keeping Light between them. "And why is that?" she asked.

"Because you've seen his impulsive side," she said. "It's the fury side you have to watch out for."

"Don't try to trick me," Mimic said. "I know that Fire has the anger."

She poked the dagger into Light's back. "Light is nothing but a reckless child, the weakest of the fragments, the most foolish."

Willow had her sword in hand but she did not advance. "Light," she warned, "we still need answers, so please *try* not to kill her."

"It is *I* that will kill *him*," Mimic said, and plunged her dagger into his back.

125

Chapter 17: Flooded

Light cried out as the blade pierced his back, the tip of the blade poking through his chest. Pain lanced through his body, followed quickly by a burgeoning rage. He spun and struck Mimic in the chest, sending her tumbling backward.

"That hurt!" he spat.

"I was trying to kill you," Mimic said, rising to her feet. "It was *supposed* to hurt."

Light reached to his back but could not reach the handle, every motion sending pain spiking through his body, fueling his anger, the fury darkening his flesh. He fixed his gaze on Mimic, the cause of his pain. He lashed out, sending a spear of light at the aggressor.

Mimic sidestepped, the bolt blasting into the wall. Stone cracked and spilled downward, and water gushed into the opening, splashing across them both. Mimic retreated, but Light leapt the rocks and struck the woman in the face, the blow sudden and hard, shattering the mask and sending her rolling backward.

She rose to her feet and glared at Light, revealing her torn features. Her disease had spread into her cheeks and forehead, leaving mottled flesh and blackened sores. Her black eyes flared with anger and she drew on Light's magic to cast an illusion of a mask, obscuring her face.

"I will kill you both for—"

"Why would you stab me?" Light shouted.

He cast another spear of light, the weapon pulsing with power until he hurtled it at her. She ducked and spun, the spear passing over her shoulder to strike the opposite wall. When it detonated, debris filled the corridor, and more water poured into the tunnel, spreading in both directions, lapping at Light's ankles.

He drew on the flickering light from the orbs, the light swelling around his arms to create giant fists. The fingers came together and he struck Mimic, the blow rocking her into the wall. With his other enormous hand he pointed a finger at Mimic's face, the fingertip elongating and turning into a blade that touched her forehead.

"Let's see how you like being stabbed," he growled.

He was distantly aware of someone pulling on his arm, shouting for him to stop, but as he leaned into the killing blow, a large body crashed into his and sent him into the water. The tigron drove him into the water, causing the dagger to strike the ground. He screamed and caught the head of the tigron with his inflated hand, and then grabbed his hind legs with the other. Rising, he looked to Mimic as he held the tigron over his head.

"This is what I'm going to do to you."

He began to pull, ripping the tigron apart, tearing it in half. The beast opened its mouth in a silent scream as he tore it asunder. He hurled the top half at Mimic, knocking her backwards, and then the hind legs, knocked her backward again.

Mimic shoved the sparking halves away and retreated, but the corridor filled with light as the reaver returned, claw marks across its face and neck. It blocked the way of escape, and it lowered its head, snarling. Trapped between the reaver and Light's advance, Mimic appeared uncertain for the first time.

"Where's the queen?" Willow shouted. "I can stop him, but you must tell me first."

Light reached for the reaver, drawing on the decades of magic in its flesh, siphoning off the power, breathing it in until his whole body brightened. He stalked forward, rising as the magic encased him with yellow flesh.

"I'LL TEAR YOU APART!" he bellowed.

"Our queen is caged among thieves and brigands," Mimic said as she pulled on the same magic. "You will never find her."

Mimic spread her arms wide and a dozen Mimics appeared. The illusions filled the corridor and charged in both directions. He picked one up and smashed it against the wall like it was a doll, removing its head. Then he picked up a second and stabbed it through the heart. Both enchantments burst into sparks of light, but the others swarmed him.

Light smashed them into the wall and into the water, stomping on them until they detonated. Others he cut in half, and hurled the partial body into another, where the explosion ripped them apart. One of them was Mimic, and he *wanted* to rip her to shreds.

The water was to their knees now and rising fast. Behind him, Willow fought three at once. By dagger and sword she deflected their weapons and dealt lethal blows. On the opposite end, the reaver devoured two. Even after Light had stolen some of its magic, it was still deadly, and it ripped into the mirages.

Light caught a glimpse of a figure sprinting back towards the castle and whirled. He sent a burst of light so bright it boiled the water at his waist, and streaked down the corridor. Enshrouded by a mirage that negated light, the real Mimic dived into the water, narrowly avoiding losing her head to the blast. She rose and turned to find the reaver plowing through the water, splashing the walls as it charged the woman.

A great groan came from Mimic's end of the corridor, and the entire corridor rocked violently. A gust of heated air blasted into Light as he waded towards Mimic, and he heard the concussive clap as a great explosion occurred in Mistkeep. The already weakened ceiling began to crumble, with great stones dropping into the flooding tunnel. Water gushed in like the entire lake wanted to devour them. One boulder came free and landed on the reaver, pinning the beast as others rained down.

"MIMIC!" Light shouted, fighting to advance. "YOU WILL NOT ESCAPE!"

Stone and water poured into the tunnel, which was now up to Light's shoulders. Still in his golem form, he struggled to stay afloat, and raised a hand to knock falling stones aside. Through the maelstrom he thought he spotted Mimic swimming towards Mistkeep and pushed after her.

"She went that way!" Willow cried, pointing away from fortress.

Light didn't question her and turned about. He was distantly aware of Willow grabbing his arm, clinging to him as he pushed through the water that had risen to his neck. Just two feet remained between them and the ceiling, but his eyes burned with rage, and he drove forward, searching for the one that had wounded him.

He cast a chain of light and sent it hurtling down the corridor. The end expanded into a spiked maul that caught on the wall, and Light yanked, pulling them down the shrinking tunnel, intent on reaching the end and wrapping his hands around Mimic's throat.

Two feet shrank to one, and Light struggled to keep his head above water. Waves lapped around him, covering the light orbs and plunging them into darkness. He tightened his grip on the chain and drew a breath as the water filled over his head. And still the chain pulled.

Mimic was going to get away, and Light pursued with all the fury of the wounded. Only seconds remained of his air but it didn't matter, and he took no thought for himself. There was only the aggressor, and the need to tear her apart.

Pressure built up in his lungs, the darkness near absolute. He hated the idea of Mimic drowning, for it would rob him of the pleasure of killing her. The desire to strike thudded in his skull, compelling him to hasten, to reach the end and save Mimic—so he could rip her legs off.

A light appeared in the gloom, and Light felt a touch of triumph, wondering why his lungs wanted to burst. The tunnel came to an abrupt end, culminating at a set of stairs that ascended into a dead tree. He released the chain and clawed his way up the steps, bursting through the surface of the water and crashing through the fallen log.

"Where is she!" he snapped, water dripping off his frame. "I must find her!"

"She's not here," Willow gasped. "She was on the other end of the tunnel."

It took several moments for the words to register, and then Light whirled. Willow was on her knees, coughing and gasping for breath. Beyond her the lake stretched for some distance, the mist failing to obscure the burning citadel.

129

"You *lied* to me?" The shock of the betrayal robbed him of his magic, and his golem melted away, the lightflesh disintegrating into sparks that dropped into the mud.

"We would have died trying to reach her," she said, wiping the moisture from her features. "And your rage wasn't going to stop."

"But you lied to me," he said. "You've never done that before."

"I'm sorry." She wiped at the water on her face. "But did you want to die?"

His suddenly saw the tunnel duel from her perspective, watched himself ignore her and nearly crush them both. He could have killed her, and himself, without even realizing it. Then he spoke in a small voice.

"I failed. Didn't I."

"Not entirely." She caught a section of the fallen tree and rose to her feet. "We learned the queen was not here, and we also know more about our adversary."

"Do you think she survived?" he asked.

"Probably," Willow said. "And I'm sure Shadow survived as well."

He'd forgotten entirely about his brother, and the vestiges of his rage disappeared. He'd been so focused on Mimic he hadn't thought of Shadow—or Willow. The thought of losing her left him with a pit in his stomach.

"I'm sorry."

"Don't be," she said. "Now turn around so I can take care of that."

He looked down and realized the dagger was still through his chest. The blade was longer than he'd expected, slicing his tunic and leaving his clothing stained in blood. He grimaced and retreated from Willow's searching hand.

"It's fine," he said. "I like it where it is."

"No, you don't," she said. "I need to take it out."

130

"But it's going to hurt."

"Of course it's going to hurt."

"I'll heal," he insisted, twisting. "Honest. It's just a flesh—"

He bumped into a tree, the hilt striking the wood. He cried out and spun, and Willow caught the handle and yanked it free. He shouted in pain and reached to the spot, whirling to level an accusing finger at Willow.

"Better?" she asked.

"*No*," he replied, rubbing the wound.

"You'll heal," she said, leaning up to kiss his cheek.

He immediately felt better, but the sting of the steel through his body would not be gone so easily. Elenyr had always made it clear the fragments could be killed, but aside from Mind, a blade through the chest would not be lethal for any of them.

"We need to get moving," she said. "We have a long way to go."

"We didn't learn anything," he said.

"We learned everything we needed," Willow said.

"She said the queen was among thieves and brigands." He swept a hand to the darkened swamp. "There are more thieves than trees in the Evermist."

"True," she said, but she said thieves *and* brigands. And there is only one group allied with the Order of Ancients that fits that description."

"Who?" he asked.

"The one led by Bartoth," she said. "The exiled rock troll."

His eyes widened, and then a surge of excitement evaporated the lingering pain. Bartoth was a formidable bandit, with hordes of allies among dozens of races, and if he had the queen, rescuing her would be no easy feat. But his territory was on the surface, meaning they would not have to travel to the Deep.

He clapped his hands together and started away. "What are we waiting for?" he demanded. "Let's go."

"Light," she called.

He turned around and she smiled. "I'm pretty sure north is that way."

"Right," he said, and then advanced in the dark swamp. "Without you I'd be lost."

"Or dead," she said.

He laughed and nodded in agreement. "Or dead."

Chapter 18: The Fallen

Lancing pain brought Elenyr awake, and she sucked in a shaky breath, her last thought a giant bolt of lightning striking above her head. She'd been underground when it had landed, and recalled a searing agony followed by blackness.

She blinked her eyes and cast about, guessing that she'd drifted downward, through the rock until she'd fallen into the crevasse. The chasm was dim, but partially lit from above. Squinting, she raised her arm but the motion ripped a cry from her lips, and she almost lost consciousness anew. Fearing to look but unable to stop herself, she examined her wounds.

Her clothing was rent and torn from the duel with the lightning wolf, his claws having dug into her leg and arm. Both had stopped bleeding, but the wounds were deep and raw. Although painful, that was not what brought the agony, and she found burns covering her arm and leg where Carn had landed his lightning bolt. The energy had passed through her body, narrowly missing her heart but scorching her ethereal flesh. Forcing herself to look away, she turned her attention to her predicament.

She lay on a boulder at the base of the crevasse. Clenching her jaw, she reached her whole arm up, and clawed at the stone. Her ethereal flesh passed through it, but she managed to get enough purchase to drag herself to a sitting position. She hissed in pain, fighting not to scream, hoping Serak and Carn had gone. By the state of her bloody wounds it had been hours, but Serak was an ageless, and more than patient. If Elenyr managed to escape the crevasse and Carn was still present, she would be killed.

But she needed to be flesh, to turn her body whole and tend to her wounds. If she could. With one hand she pulled at her leg. Her burned leg was half ethereal, her shin and foot still embedded into the boulder. She sought to withdraw the limb but the excruciating pain forced her to stop. The movement had reopened the gashes in her leg where the wolf's claws had cut her flesh.

She paused, fighting to breathe, to stay conscious. The fragments needed her, and she would not let Serak subvert their loyalty. She lifted her eyes to the walls of stone to either side. Injured as she was, she could not simply turn ethereal and ascend. Her body would not respond as normal, and her wounds would resist turning ethereal.

Willing herself to rise, she used a crack in the stone to pull herself into a standing position, gradually withdrawing her foot from the boulder. With great care, she put her weight on her good leg. Then she set her jaw in a determined line and began to climb.

Using her good arm and good leg, she gradually scaled the side of the crevasse. She fought for every inch, every grip. Determined to reach the surface, she caught a stone at the edge of the crevasse and placed her burned leg against it, the agony robbing her of consciousness . . .

Again pain woke her, and she groaned. She'd landed on her burned arm and eased the ragged limb out from under her. Gasping, she looked about herself, grateful to see that at least she'd stayed corporeal.

When ethereal, she could will herself through anything solid. But lightning forced her to become flesh, and the bolt had struck her underground, burning her from shoulder to leg. The wounds were raw and painful, the skin blackened and cracking.

She looked up and examined the crevasse again. At the top, it seemed a cave curved higher, and a glimmer of light suggested it led to the surface. A pattern of ledges and handholds would help her ascend, but not in her current condition.

She reached for a ledge and began to climb. Careful to only use her left arm and right leg, she worked her way upward, her pace agonizingly slow. The base of the crevasse was fifty feet into the earth, not so great a distance when she could rise by force of will. Now it seemed a mountain.

She climbed the wall of stone, using the ledges in the granite to hold her broken body. Breathing was a challenge, and she tasted the soil on her tongue. The climb brought her within twenty feet, but the rock curved over her head, and she could not press through it. She clung to the wall of the crevasse as she desperately cast about for a way to ascend.

She spotted a small ledge on her right, curving to the cave that would allow her to escape the pit. She could see light coming from above and new it was her only hope. But it would require her to jump. She gathered her might, braced her good leg, and jumped.

Her fingers fell short of the stone, and she cried out as she slipped away. She forced her hand to turn ethereal and dragged it through the stone, but the fall was impossible to stop. She fell toward the slab of granite and braced for the impact. Again she screamed. Again she lost consciousness.

She woke and climbed. And fell again, slipping before she could catch the lip that would take her to safety. Again she tried. Again she fell. She managed to catch the wall on her way down, but doing so brought her body against the stone, and the pain caused her to lose her grip. She tried to turn ethereal to soften the landing, but the impact was brutal, and she cried out upon hitting the boulder. Groaning, she dragged herself to the wall again.

She climbed.

And fell.

When she woke after her latest attempt the pain was worse, and she reluctantly looked to her foot, which she'd twisted in the last fall. She lay back on the stone and stared at the top of the crevasse, despair rising up like a spider, its legs brushing across her neck, its fangs reaching for her skin.

She brushed it aside and rose to her feet, limping to the wall that she'd grown to hate. The next time she fell, she was slower to rise, and tears welled in her cheeks. She'd never failed, never to such a degree. The fragments would probably never know her fate.

"I'm sorry," she said.

Her voice was raspy, the dirt in her throat making it raw. The weight of her worry pressed against her like a boulder, suffocating and

135

terrifying. Tears welled in her eyes, and fatigue overwhelmed her. This time she welcomed the darkness for it also dulled the fear.

When she awoke again she felt weak and thirsty, and turned her eyes to the stubborn wall. Unbidden, she thought of Alydian, and the prison built for her in the Age of Oracles. For the first time in history, an oracle had been caged, and her imprisonment had endured for long enough to leave a permanent scar.

Alydian had rarely spoken of her time in a cell, even to her husband. Elenyr knew the most of her daughter's captivity and had always sympathized. But she'd never really understood what her daughter had experienced, and now the creeping despair settled across her like an icy cloak.

She clenched her eyes shut and willed herself to fight, reminding herself of what was at stake. Serak would seek to subvert her sons, turn them evil, force them into servitude. After all his millennia of planning, she feared he had the power to accomplish his designs. But the fragments were her family, and she refused to let Serak be the victor.

She rose again, her pace slow and deliberate, and pushed herself to climb once more. Fatigue had set in and her muscles trembled. She sensed this would be her final attempt, and if she failed, she would die. Each step was measured, each motion calculated. Just as before, she reached the overhang of rock, where the stone curved up and over, keeping her trapped. She looked to the ledge that had defied her, its comforting hold just out of reach.

She could not reach for the crack, not without another foothold. And she would not survive another fall. Clinging to the grip with her good hand, her uninjured foot resting on a secure ledge, she realized she needed another foothold. She looked to her trembling, wounded leg, and knew what she had to do.

Sucking in her breath, she bent her hurt knee. Pain spiked up her leg and torso, into her throat, so bitter she could taste the agony. Her skull throbbed but she continued to bend her knee, lifting the injured leg until her foot rested against the smooth stone. Then she willed her foot to turn ethereal. Mangled and bloody, the limb was slow to respond, and the pain rippled up her flesh, each new stab a reminder of what was to come

136

if she failed. Her toes pressed into the stone. She hissed, her chest heaving from the effort to push against the scorching pain, against the defiant stone.

Her ethereal foot pressed into the wall and she turned it just solid enough to find purchase. Before she collapsed, she pulled herself upward. Each agonizing motion heightened the pain, until consciousness threatened to fade, darkness rimming her vision. But she saw the ledge drawing closer. She could feel the rough stone over her fingers, her muscles trembling as the higher ledge crept closer.

With her good hand occupied, she was forced to use her burned hand, and reached upward, higher and higher. Her raw fingertips passed over the ledge and tightened, the relief coming fast, mingling with desperation and fear. Two fingers passed over, and then a third, and then the last. She clung to the hold with all her might, sweat beading her forehead, dripping down her back. Afraid she would tumble free, she carefully released her other hand and reached up as well, catching the hold.

The pain did not abate, but the striking joy scattered the darkness, and she carefully extricated her foot and swung herself to the higher ledge. From there she stepped into the cave and collapsed in relief, cradling her burned arm, tears flowing freely down her dirty cheeks. Then she began to laugh, the relief bubbling up into insane amusement. She'd climbed fifty feet, yet it seemed like she'd ascended the mightiest mountain.

She leaned against the rock, partially out of relief, but mostly out of fear. The ledge she was on curved around and upward, but she did not know what lay in store for her above. Gathering herself, she used the wall to pull herself to her feet, and then limped her way up the ledge, following it into the cave.

It was obvious the ceiling had caved in, a handful of charred beams suggesting it had come from one of the structures in Cloudy Vale. It had created a gap in the ceiling that she hoped led to the surface.

Tearing a strip from her ruined tunic, she wrapped it around her arm to brace it, and then began another ascent. This time thirst plagued her, and the pain in her skull had mounted, beating like an orc war drum.

The beam of light led to a tiny crack between shards of stone. Too small for a body, it forced her to turn her good arm ethereal and reach through. With great care she wormed her way upward, using her ability to thread gaps too small for a person, but large enough for her to bring her injuries through.

She paused to rest often, and several times awoke, surprised to realize she'd fallen asleep. Weakness now assailed her—the early triumph fading in the face of a new barrier. She struggled on, recognizing that each motion had grown progressively slower, but her only choice lay in reaching the surface.

Dimly she recognized that if Carn lay in wait she would be dispatched like an insect, but it didn't matter. There was only the next hole, the next opening between two stones. The stone was gradually replaced by burned beams, and at one point she felt the surface of carved stone. She recognized the pattern as a symbol above Mind's home, and realized she was beneath his house.

She worked her way through another tiny gap, gasping as her leg squeezed through the opening. But the light from above continued to brighten. She could not remember why she was here, or where the pain had come from. There was only the climb.

Her hands were raw and blackened from the wood, slivers in her flesh, but she worked her way up a tilted section of flooring and crawled onto the threshold of Mind's home. She stumbled out the door and collapsed, her dim eyes rising to the evening sky. The wreckage of Cloudy Vale lay about her but she could not see it, her eyes filled with tears that could not come.

"Hauntress," a voice said. "You are one tough woman."

She sank onto her back and cast about, spotting a man striding towards her. It was not Carn, but another, one with a sword in his hand. He stood over Elenyr, regarding her with a look of admiration.

"Serak actually thought you dead," he said. "But I wanted to stay and see for myself. He will reward me for ensuring your end."

"Jeric?" she croaked.

The man shook his head. "You're nearly dead already, so I'll give you a choice. Die like this? Or by my sword?"

Elenyr stared up at him, unable to move, unable to comprehend his words. But she understood when he raised his sword above her body, the blade hovering over her heart. He smiled.

"I thought you might say—"

An aquaglass sword burst from his chest, and he cried out, his sword tumbling from his fingers. He fell to his knees, staring in shock at the instrument of his death before slumping next to Elenyr. Then a pair of strong hands reached for Elenyr and an elf's features resolved into focus.

"Elenyr," Jeric said, his voice breathless, as if he'd been running, but also terrified. "I've got you. Just stay with me. Please just stay with me . . ."

Chapter 19: An Old Friend

Time passed in a haze of pain and fatigue, and Elenyr caught glimpses like they were from a dream. Jeric was always present, but others appeared, some in the uniform of the Bladed, the legendary mercenary guild, or elven healers. One woman spoke dire warnings.

". . . not even sure how she has survived this long."

"There must be something you can do," Jeric murmured, his voice tense.

"Her flesh keeps turning ethereal," she said. "It's impossible to stitch her wounds . . ."

At first she thought she was in Cloudy Vale, but in several dreams she was traveling, held aloft as if by magic, a mattress of air drawn behind a horse. Her eyes opened and she found Jeric at her side, his hand in hers.

"Jeric . . ." she murmured.

"Sleep," he said. "I'm here."

"You came for me."

"I always will."

She smiled, wanting to stay, but the pain came quickly, and darkness again claimed her. A nightmare took Jeric's place, and she watched Draeken kneel to Serak, the fragments following his will.

They spoke in unison. "We will obey, Master Serak . . ."

She screamed, lashing out at the image of Serak's dark triumph, but her arm caught in a blanket. A tug on her arm caused her to grimace, like a thread had been sewn into her skin, and she blinked, fumbling for what held her bound.

140

"Don't," Jeric's voice was soft, his touch calming her.

"Where am I?" she asked, her speech slurred.

"We're almost to . . ."

Darkness claimed her again, and this time her sleep was calm. She woke as they passed through a gate and caught a glimpse of hundreds of soldiers, all standing in ranks, craning to get a look at her.

"The Hauntress," one whispered. "I did not think she could be killed."

"She's not dead," another said, his voice hopeful.

"She looks like she is," another said.

"Return to your posts," a female voice spoke with authority, and the soldiers nodded.

"Yes, my queen."

A beautiful elven woman stepped into view and a feathery hand settled on Elenyr's arm. "Rest now, ethereal warrior."

"My sons are threatened," Elenyr mumbled.

"I know," she replied, and then looked up to answer a question. "Take her to the castle. Quickly. We must hasten . . ."

Someone touched her neck and sleep overpowered her thoughts. Her dreams were filled with pain and injuries, before everything faded and she was left alone, watching the sky fill with krey vessels arriving to claim Lumineia.

She awoke with a start—and grimaced, reaching for her arm. She found a strange bandage fastened around her wounds. It sparked at her touch and she realized it had lightning magic. Fear flooded her veins and she began to tear it free, but a hand caught her own.

"Elenyr," Jeric said, rising from the chair next to her bed. "All is well."

"The bandage has lightning magic," she said. "It must have come from Carn."

"No," Jeric said. "It came from the queen. To help you, she sacrificed a lightning shroud enchanted by her ancestor."

"What?" she asked, confused as she looked about the room. "Why?"

"It was the only way we could keep you solid," he said. "They had to stitch your wounds and care for your burns."

She noticed the room, which appeared elven, the bed of fine oak, the linens of magically woven cloth, soft and luxurious. Walls contained two large tapestries, both depicting the creation of Ilumidora, the castle nestled in the mother of all trees.

"Where are we?" she asked. "I remember climbing into Cloudy Vale, and then a man was waiting for me."

"One of Serak's Bloodsworn," Jeric said, his jaw tightening. "I arrived in time to dissuade him of his quest."

She looked into his face, and spotted the lines on his cheeks, the shadows under his eyes. His clothes were disheveled, his hair in disarray. She instinctively reached for him, but the act pulled on the bandage on her arm and leg, causing both to twinge.

"If you can stay solid, we can remove those," Jeric said.

"I think so," she said.

"I'll find the healer." He rose to his feet but she called to him. "Wait. How long have I been unconsciousness?"

"In and out for a week now." He offered a faint smile. "I almost lost you, more than once."

He sat on the bed, and she noticed a trace of moisture in his gaze. She'd never seen him cry. She reached out to him and he seemed to wilt, his shoulders hunching. He looked away, wiping at his eyes.

"I thought you were dead," he murmured.

142

"I missed you," Elenyr said softly.

He looked back, his jaw working. Then he seemed to shake his head, dismissing what he was about to say. "I'll get the healer."

He reached the door and departed, and a moment later returned with an elf. The woman was dressed in a healer's robe, the insignia on her shoulder marking her as a master healer, the royal seal beneath indicating she was the healer that served the royal house.

"Yorina," Elenyr recalled, vaguely recognizing her.

The woman smiled and expertly ran her fingers over the bandage. "You look better than you have in days."

"You have my gratitude," Elenyr said.

The woman smiled, and carefully undid the trappings around the shroud. "First time I've ever had to use lightning in order to heal, but it's good to see you back in the flesh."

As the bandage came away, Elenyr saw the stitching holding her arm together, shocked to see the length. When Yorina removed the bandage on her leg the injuries were worse, the burns a patchwork of red and black.

"Your wounds look better," Yorina said, and motioned her assistant to bring clean bandages.

"This is *better*?" Elenyr exclaimed.

"Much," Jeric said fervently.

Yorina touched the burned flesh and sent a thread of magic into Elenyr's skin, the pink light easing the ache. Some of the burns lightened, while the long stitches healed a little as well. A wave of fatigue washed over Elenyr.

"Now that you're awake I can heal you much faster," Yorina said, rebandaging the wounds. "When you arrived, you didn't have much strength." She then called for food and drink. "I'm sure you're hungry."

"Famished," Elenyr said, abruptly feeling a giant cavity in her stomach.

Yorina smiled. "Eat. I'll be back in an hour."

Elenyr thanked her and the healer departed, her assistant taking the bloody bandages in a bowl. When the door shut again, Jeric sank into his chair with a sigh and flashed a weak smile that lit Elenyr's heart.

"I did not know if you would survive," he said.

"Was it really that bad?" she asked. She recalled looking at her wounds in the pit but it had been too dark to see much.

"I've sought danger across the kingdoms," he said. "But that was the first time I truly felt fear."

"You saved my life," she said, and touched his hand. His fingers folded into hers, and she tried not to think of the last time they had been close, when they'd planned to meet and he had never come.

"Always," he said, flashing his rakish smile. It was weak, but stronger than before.

"What news of the fragments?" Elenyr asked.

The door opened again and a regal woman entered. She motioned to her guards to remain outside and then strode to Elenyr's bed carrying a tray of food. Elenyr eased herself to a sitting position with Jeric's help.

"Queen Alosia," Elenyr said. "You did not need to—?"

"Serve you a meal?" Alosia placed the tray on the bed and sat. "Unless I am sorely mistaken, you have saved my bloodline on several occasions, so I am grateful for the chance to save yours."

Elenyr inclined her head in gratitude, humbled by the queen's kindness. Short for an elf, the woman was nevertheless known for an indomitable spirit. She'd negotiated hard treaties with both of the human kingdoms, and never flinched in conflict. Although not trained for combat, she had the heart of a warrior. Many mistook her kindness as a weakness, until she revealed her strength.

144

"I owe you my life," Elenyr said.

"Your life is your own," Alosia said. "That pit you climbed out of would have killed anyone else."

"You saw the cave?" she asked, glancing to Jeric.

"You didn't come up with your sword," Jeric said. "My friends followed the blood trail to find what you escaped from. They said no one should have survived."

He pointed to her sword, which lay on the table nearby. She sighed in relief, grateful it had not been lost. She'd had it since her time as oracle, and was fond of the blade, for it had been crafted by her husband during her time as an oracle.

"I find it difficult to express my gratitude," Elenyr said.

The queen motioned in dismissal. "I am sure you want news?"

"Indeed," Elenyr said eagerly.

"Mistkeep was destroyed," Jeric said. "And reports are that Relgor was killed."

"Relgor is dead?" She tried to sit up and regretted the motion. "How?"

"The fragment of Shadow," Jeric said. "Mind and Fire arrived in time to see the end."

"Where did the fragments go?" She tried to keep the worry from her voice. After nearly being killed, her desire to protect her sons was overly intense. Not that she could stop the emotion.

"Light was at Mistkeep, but we believe he is back in the Deep now. Shadow went to help him, while Mind and Fire followed some of the Bloodsworn. They are currently tracking the halls of the Order of Ancients, hoping to find Serak and Wylyn."

"They are alive," Elenyr breathed. "But if Serak knows I am here, he will come for me."

145

"Let him come," Alosia said. "I would prefer a straight fight to all his sneaking about. But I don't think it likely he will come to Ilumidora. The castle guard is loyal to me, and I employ a memory mage to ensure it. My generals insisted on protecting me, and since you are here, they just happen to be protecting you as well."

"Again," Elenyr said. "Thank you."

Her stomach rumbled, and all three grinned in unison. "Eat," the queen said, rising to her feet. "When you are better healed, we can talk."

Elenyr noticed her hesitation. "What have you heard?"

The queen paused at the door. "The queen of the dark elves has gone missing."

Elenyr had known that, but feigned surprise. "First King Numen of Erathan and now another? Two monarchs taken in the span of weeks?"

"Three," she said. "King Justin of Griffin appears to have been taken as well."

Elenyr straightened. "By whom?"

Jeric passed a hand over his face. "We all know the answer to that question. The larger question is, why is Wylyn taking thrones?"

Chapter 20: A Brewing Conflict

Light could barely contain his excitement. Astride his wolfsteed mount, he galloped north, relishing the wind in his hair, the sun on his face. At his side, Willow clung to the horse that flew across the earth.

"Any chance we can slow down?" she called.

"We were in the Deep *forever*," Light replied. "And you want to slow down?"

"It was little more than a week," Willow said. "And yes, I want to slow down. I do not think man or elf are meant to move at such speeds."

Light glanced her way and saw the green tinge to her grey features. For the first time since they left Mistkeep, he looked about, and noticed the other travelers and wagons on the road. Men and women cried out as the two wolfsteeds streaked by, some falling off their horses, others screaming in fear.

A pair of soldiers wrestled their mounts as they bucked, one tumbling into the brush at the side of the road. Children huddled inside a wagon, peering with wide eyes as Light and Willow sped by, the image fading in seconds.

"Sorry," he said, and slowed the steeds to a quick trot.

"Better," Willow said, but the green tinge remained on her features. "But I fear they don't like your horses."

Light reached out to pat the neck of his wolfsteed. Fashioned of glittering yellow light, the horse had a wolflike head, with a long tapered snout and rows of sharp teeth.

"Why do people thank they're scary? They're beautiful," Light exclaimed.

They'd passed through the elven forests and were well on their way into Griffin. Autumn was in full swing, with trees turning gold, brown, and red, the leaves carpeting the forest and the road. The air had a chill in the evening and morning, like the jaws of winter seeking to devour the day.

He shivered and savored the cold, wanting to see the breadth of the forest before it turned all stark and empty. Autumn was his favorite season, the beams of light threading through trees, all shades of color on his fingertips. They passed under a pair of great oaks and he changed his wolfsteed to bright red.

"See?" he said proudly. "Beautiful."

A woman screamed as they rounded a corner. "Demons!" she shrieked, diving behind her husband, who hastily turned his staff on them. The two children stared in wonder, and then began to clap.

"The kids understand," Light said with a smug nod.

"Light," Willow sighed.

"Yes?"

He was watching the light play across his arms, the patterns of leaves and—was that a fox? He leapt off his horse and sprinted into the trees, running alongside the fox, admiring the sleek animal as it sought to flee. Its coat was just beginning to turn white, leaving a beautiful pattern of colors. Light kept pace easily, weaving between the trunks of trees and the fluttering leaves, and reached out to pet the animal.

"Foxes are so beautiful," he lamented. "Why would anyone want their skin?"

"Light!"

"Sorry," Light called,

He darted back to the roadway, but his red horse and her yellow steed were far ahead. He grimaced as he realized the two mounts had accelerated. Again. Casting a pair of wings, he launched himself into the air and flew after the sprinting wolfsteeds before dropping back into his saddle.

"I think we need a break," Willow said.

"Why?" he asked.

"Because I'm going to throw up."

Concerned, he slowed their steeds. "Was our morning meal displeasing?"

"No, Light," she groaned. "These horses go twice as fast as a normal horse, and it's making me sick."

"Oh."

He brought their steeds to a halt and directed them into the trees. Elenyr had repeatedly warned him not to let people see his wolfsteeds for it would cause a panic, and he hid them behind a wall of brush. Willow dismounted on unsteady legs and stepped behind a tree. Light joined her where she deposited the remains of their morning meal on the roots.

"Light," she said weakly, "a little privacy would be appreciated."

"Sorry," he said, and returned to the wolfsteeds.

He listened to Willow retch, feeling bad. He loved speed and couldn't imagine why anyone else would find it unappealing. He spotted a mint plant and plucked a few leaves, offering them to Willow as she returned.

"Thank you," she said, sucking on a leaf.

"Ready to continue?"

She laughed weakly. "We've crossed half a continent in a day. I think we should camp early tonight."

"Perhaps you are right," he said. "And I have that roasted liver and egg we picked up at the last tavern—why are you behind the tree again?"

They camped a short distance from the road, and Light flitted into the woods and back, vacillating between exploring the forest and concern for Willow. She sat next to a small fire, leaning against a fallen tree, unmoving even as Light disappeared and reappeared. Only when the sun began to set did Light slow, and sank into a seat by the tree.

"What happened to my roast liver and—"

"It must have fallen out on the road," Willow said. "Perhaps you can enjoy a nice plate of greens."

He grimaced. "I hate greens. How about fried potatoes and a nice fiery ale?"

"Actually that sounds delicious," she said.

"I spotted a tavern up the road," he said, jumping to the wolfsteed.

"Maybe on foot," Willow suggested. "Frightened commoners tend to burn your meal."

Light nodded in agreement. "Right."

He threaded his way into the trees, hurrying north to the tavern he'd seen. Several horses were outside and there seemed to be an abnormally high level of shouting, but Light skipped inside and crossed to the counter.

The shouting stopped at his entrance, and Light vaguely noticed several men huddled close to the tavern owner, their blades out, crossbows pointed at the sweating man. One held his wife, while another held his daughter.

"Two plates of fried potatoes and fiery ale," he proclaimed.

"Now?" the tavern owner asked, quivering in fear. "You think you can help me?"

Mystified, Light shook his head. "I'm terrible in the kitchen."

"Be on your business, friend," one of the men with swords said. "Before we—"

"You smell terrible." Light sniffed and wrinkled his nose. "Like pigs. Oh, do you have a pet pig? Can I see him? Little pigs are so cute, and adult pigs are delicious." He turned to the tavern owner. "Can you add bacon to my plate?"

150

The men around the tavern owner stared in confusion at Light, and then the leader stepped forward, raising his sword. The blade was not bright, and obviously needing sharpening. Light shook his head in disapproval.

"That wouldn't cut anything, but I can sharpen it for you."

He reached up and slid a finger down the cutting edge. The steel brightened as Light used the light of sunset on the blade, turning it bright red. The man recoiled with a curse, and then stared in astonishment as his sword began to melt. Drops of molten metal dripped onto the floor, each one sizzling on the wood, until most of his blade was gone.

"Sorry," Light said apologetically. "The sun's going down and it was hard to balance the right amount of heat—where are you all going? I promise to do better on your other swords!"

The men scrambled out the door, tripping off the porch in their haste to flee. Confused, Light watched them depart, wondering if the sword had carried sentimental value. Then he shrugged and turned to the tavern owner, who stared at the steaming pile of cooling steel with wide eyes.

"Am I at the front of the line now?"

"Yes—yes of course." The man hurried into the kitchens, while the wife thanked him profusely.

"I didn't do anything," he said, shrugging.

"Bless your soul," the woman said, tears on her cheeks. "So humble."

"I didn't do anything," Light repeated, now very confused.

Willow stepped into the tavern. "Of course you did."

The woman trembled in fear at the appearance of the tattooed dark elf, and the daughter ducked behind her. The pair of travelers that had been huddled in the corner beat a hasty retreat, leaving through the kitchens.

"Will you protect us again, good sir?" the woman quavered.

"From what?" Light asked. "This is Willow, the most wonderful woman you'll ever meet."

"You are too kind," Willow said dryly. "How close is our meal?"

"Just a few moments," the woman said, still trembling.

"Excellent," Willow said. "Because I'm feeling rather hungry now."

Light brightened. "They're going to add bacon to our meal."

"I love bacon," she said.

"Me too," Light said fervently. "And a man that just left had a pet pig. I didn't get to see him, though."

His expression was so forlorn that the tavern owner's daughter took a hesitant step forward and pointed to the back. "Our sow just had a litter, if you'd like to see them."

"Really?" he asked.

Light looked to Willow and she nodded, taking a seat. "I'll be here when you get back. Don't go far this time."

"I'm glad you're feeling better," Light said, already turning the corner at the back of the tavern.

The girl led him outside, where a small stable had an assortment of animals. In one corner, a large sow lay, with a collection of small piglets sleeping around her bulk. Light, recognizing the need for quiet, crept up to them in wonder.

"Would you like to hold one?" the girl asked.

Light's smile would have illuminated a great hall, and the girl smiled in turn. Reaching down, she lifted the piglet and offered it to Light. He accepted the animal gingerly. It made soft sounds and he soothed it with a song Elenyr used to sing.

"Do you really not know what you did back there?" she asked softly.

"Did what?" he asked.

"You saved us from bandits," she said.

"Are piglets always this small?" Light held the small animal to his face, peering into his small eyes.

"Do you always travel with the dark elf?"

"When I can," he said with a laugh. "She's so beautiful."

"I can see why she likes to travel with you."

The comment surprised him, and he looked to the young woman. "Why?"

"She is obviously used to war," the girl said. "To battle, blood, and death. But you are like this piglet, innocent and unable to see the world as it is."

He turned to face her. "What does that mean?"

"It's just a guess," the girl said, a touch of fear appearing in her eyes. "Can I have the piglet back now?"

He looked down and realized he'd been squeezing the animal, making it squeak. Relinquishing the piglet, he watched her return it to her mother, and then followed the girl back into the tavern.

Their meal was ready, so he and Willow sat down in the empty tavern. Several times he cast glances at Willow, shocked to notice the litany of scars along with the tattoos. The woman had survived countless battles and had the legacy of war on her very flesh. She was fearsome and deadly, yet traveled with Light.

"Are you well?" she asked. "You're being rather quiet."

"Just tired," he said, glancing to the window.

"I got us a room," she said. "You can sleep in a bed instead of on the ground."

153

He nodded his gratitude but remained silent. He'd always thought Willow loved him for him, but as he retired to the bed in the quarters upstairs, he wondered if the elven warrior wanted him along because he softened the legacy of war.

The girl had said the men were bandits, and he imagined the events in the tavern from her eyes. Light hadn't realized the man was a threat, and if he had succeeded in sharpening his sword, he could very well have harmed the family while Light departed with his meal, oblivious to the danger the men posed. In the darkness he grimaced, wondering why Willow loved him.

Chapter 21: The Exiled Troll

For the rest of the journey north, Light brooded on what the girl had said. Several times Willow asked about his silence, but he avoided the issue, uncertain how to talk about his fear. They journeyed north, through the length of Griffin to the northern range of mountains that had once marked the border. But Griffin had been expanding for years, pushing the burgeoning populace into the unclaimed lands of the north with promises of riches, wealth, and open land. Unfortunately, the land was already occupied. Goblin tribes, giant clans, and other outcasts did not take kindly to the expansion.

Much of Griffin's army was currently stationed in the new villages of the north, and the castle was being built adjacent to a river. Named Heraldin, the fortress had already been attacked several times, slowing the construction of the defenses.

A large village sat on the banks of the river adjacent to the fortress, and as they passed through the streets, many cast uneasy looks at Willow. Confused as to why, Light pointed to a group of soldiers eyeing her suspiciously.

"Why do they look at you with such fear?"

"I am a dark elf," she said.

"So?"

Willow sighed. "The people fear the dark, and many on the surface fear my darker skin."

"That's stupid."

"Yes, it is," she said with a smile.

Her expression of gratitude reminded him of what the girl in the tavern had said, and he looked away, wondering anew why Willow favored him. He was not one to hold to a thought, but this doubt had found a root and would not be removed.

The patrolling guards cast Willow suspicious glares, with some sending messengers back to the fortress. Light might have been concerned, but the sights of the village were an exciting distraction.

Weapons were everywhere, as were an abundance of soldiers. Warriors from across the kingdoms had signed mercenary contracts with Griffin, earning coin for bolstering the ranks of the beleaguered army. Most were dwarves, but there was a smattering of elves, and even a contingent of the Bladed, the renowned mercenary guild that only allowed a hundred members.

What surprised Light the most were the rock trolls, of which there seemed to be quite a few. Grouped into their patrols of six, the towering trolls patrolled the muddy streets, always wary, always ready.

Light had always been fascinated by the rock trolls. They stood nine feet tall, with tattoos spiking across their chest, arms, neck, and face, showing every kill, and the power of the foe that had been killed. Called the Sundering, the pattern of tattoos showed the nature of every troll. Each had a unique weapon, one forged by their own hand. All were lethal.

"They're prepared for war," Willow murmured. "And do you see how everyone is on edge?"

Once she'd pointed it out, Light began to notice the current of tension prevalent among the populace. Soldiers were wary of anyone, while even commoners carried weapons. Many of the buildings were under construction but not all were new, with many obviously destroyed by fire or battle.

"The northern races do not take kindly to losing their land," Willow said.

"Why are there so many rock trolls?" Light asked.

Overhearing them, a woman leaned in. "Bartoth has gathered the goblin tribes, giants, and the bandits of the region into a single army, and the rock trolls want to end his reign before it begins."

"His reign?" Light asked.

The woman cast furtive glances up the northern hills, as if Bartoth were about to descend with his hordes. "He has promised the tribes he will repel the Griffin invaders and claims to be their new king."

Willow snorted in disapproval. "He is cast off the throne by his own people, so he creates a new kingdom."

The woman eyed Willow, apparently just realizing she was with Light. Then she turned and walked away with a disapproving look fixed on her features. Light raised a hand towards her back and magic gathered on his fingertips, but Willow caught his arm and shook her head.

"I appreciate your desire to defend my honor," she said. "But here, you will be fighting for quite some time."

She frowned and looked past Light. He turned and spotted a group of rock trolls approaching. The leader came to a halt in front of Light, the others continuing to circle them in a ring of hardened flesh. The leader motioned towards the partially built castle on the north side of the village.

"Your presence has been requested,"

"By whom?" Willow asked cautiously.

"The queen."

"Whose queen?"

"Ours," the second one said.

Light and Willow exchanged a look, but it didn't seem like they had an option. The host of other soldiers and commoners watching the exchange stood ready to join the conflict, some with drawn blades. Willow offered a faint smile.

"It would be a pleasure to meet her."

"This way," he said. "The battle is about to begin."

"Battle?" Light asked.

"Bartoth arrived last night," he said. "He has issued an ultimatum, depart or be slaughtered."

The trolls led them north, but not to the fortress. Instead they exited the village and ascended a slope to the hill beyond. As they crested the rise, a long valley appeared, a shallow depression with slopes on opposite sides. Both contained an army.

On the opposite side of the valley, hordes of goblins and giants stood in ranks, with a smattering of other races also present. Outcasts and bandits, the dregs of the races that had been exiled from other kingdoms, all had found a home under Bartoth's reign.

At ten feet tall, the rock troll standing at the head of the army hefted an enormous hammer, the weapon slung across his shoulders, as if he cared nothing for the battle about to commence. Even with the distance, the thousands of tattoos were visible on his flesh.

Griffin's army stood in organized ranks but was obviously smaller. Soldiers stood in the center, while mercenaries and other allies formed the flanks of the army. A knot of fifty rock trolls anchored the center of the Griffin contingent, and Light's captors turned towards their kindred.

Light and Willow were guided through the ranks of Griffin soldiers, their uniforms grey and red, the colors distinct for those serving in the northern regions. Many displayed fear at the impending battle, and nervously shifted their feet.

The trolls seemed oblivious to the aura of fear, their gait smooth, almost casual. Light looked up at them in awe, examining their weapons, their stance, their fearsome tattoos. Unwilling to resist, he gathered sunlight and cast it about himself, the lightcast flesh lifting him off the ground, covering his arms and legs in oversized muscles, until he stood as tall as the trolls. Hulking and powerful, he walked among them, feeling mighty.

"Light," Willow's voice was tinged with warning. "Can we *not* start a war with the rock trolls?"

"Rest easy, elf," one of the rock trolls said. "We know of your companion."

"You do?" Light asked.

"Your brother is here," the leader said.

Light blinked in surprise, but before he could ask, they reached the rock troll contingent. They were led to the front, to a towering female rock troll. She stood a head taller than her companions, her black hair hanging past her shoulders. She had not one sword, but two, both on her back.

She wore battle armor that went from neck to knee. Unlike the others of her kind, she did not have any tattoos. Their absence was not as commanding as the missing limb. From elbow to fingertip, her left arm was pure, liquid steel. Obviously dwarven made, obviously very expensive.

"Queen Rynda," the leader of the patrol said, offering a short bow. "As you requested, we brought the light mage and his dark elf companion."

The woman spared Light a look, eyeing his oversized muscles with a faint look of amusement. Then she looked to Willow, a touch of recognition appearing in her dark eyes before she looked back to Light.

"Why are you here?"

"My queen has been taken by the Order of Ancients," Willow said. "We have reason to believe Bartoth knows her location."

"He won't survive the day," Rynda said. "Bartoth has been stealing from caravans for some time and used the coin to prepare his army. He is a blight on our kind that we are honorbound to eradicate before—"

"Can I touch your hand?" Light asked.

She scowled and jerked her head. "No."

"That must have cost a fortune," Light said, reaching out to the limb anyway. A troll caught his hand, preventing him from doing so.

"Bartoth took my hand when I took his throne," she said. "My people were kind enough to pay for a replacement."

159

"Steelflesh is the most difficult of magical fleshes," Light said, glancing to Willow. "Dwarves have to cast the metal in perpetual heat to keep it from turning solid. It's supposed to be hot enough to cook eggs. Have you ever tried it?"

Rynda stared at him, and then began to laugh. "You are an amusing one, much unlike the other one."

"Which of my brothers is here?" Light asked.

"Water and Lira are present," Rynda said, waving east. "They are reinforcing the weak left flank."

"Water?" Light was delighted with the news and craned his head to see in that direction. "When did he arrive?"

"He came at the request of the Hauntress." Rynda sniffed, as if she did not care for Water's presence. "They wanted to convince me to prepare for some sort of invasion."

"The krey," Willow said. "They seek to reclaim what they have lost."

"I have my own war to fight," Rynda said. "And Water agreed to help me kill Bartoth. Apparently they have already dueled once, and Bartoth escaped."

Goblin drums began to beat, the sound reverberating up and down the valley, the hordes shouting and shrieking, working themselves into a frenzy. The giants hefted boulders, while the other races drew their weapons. Bartoth's army outnumbered the Griffin forces by two to one, and they seemed eager to fight.

"Where is the Griffin Duke?" Willow asked.

"He hides in the walls of his fortress," one of the other rock trolls said, sniffing in disdain. "He thinks it will save him from their numerous hosts."

"You did not know Bartoth had so many?" Willow said.

"Not until Bartoth arrived," Rynda said. "He has planned well, but we do not shrink from a fight. And I will kill him even if I must wade through thousands of goblins."

"But we need to talk to him first," Light protested.

Rynda shrugged. "Then you will have to do it before I kill him."

"I can do that."

He gathered more light and cast his wolfsteed—one twice the normal size because it needed to support his new giant muscles. The sudden appearance of a massive, demon horse caused even the rock trolls to retreat, and then Light urged his horse forward.

"I'll be back in a moment," he called over his shoulder.

He accelerated into the open, his enormous mount galloping across the valley. Shouts and curses were hurled at him, but he had his gaze fixed on Bartoth, the rock troll with body magic. The troll stared at him, surprise on his tattooed features.

"Bartoth!" Light shouted. "Can we talk for a moment?"

His voice was lost in the din as both armies saw his advance as a call to fight and charged the battlefield. In the ensuing shouts and *twang* of archer bows, Willow's voice somehow managed to reach his ears.

"Light!" she bellowed. "I told you not to start a war!"

He looked back, to see Willow in the midst of the running rock trolls. He'd thought to talk to Bartoth before the battle, but now both sides were surging the battlefield, all ranks in chaos. He grimaced, and realized he'd inadvertently been the catalyst.

"Too late!" he called and did the only thing he could think to do. He accelerated towards Bartoth.

Chapter 22: A Broken War

Light galloped across the valley as both armies flooded onto the battlefield, their ranks in chaos, contrasting orders sending the soldiers clashing together in confusion. Bartoth bellowed in rage but his voice was lost in the din, and the legendary warrior was forced to join the throng.

Rynda and her rock trolls held their line, sprinting in perfect formation as the rest of the allied forces raced about, some running ahead, others hesitating and falling back. Shouts and anger were everywhere, but one sound managed to reach Light's ears.

"LIGHT! WHAT ARE YOU DOING!"

He turned towards the voice and spotted Water and Lira on the right flank. Both were on horses crafted from water, the mounts outstripping the steeds on their sides as they raced toward Light's position. Delighted to see his brother, Light raised a hand in greeting.

"I'll see you after I talk to Bartoth!" he shouted.

He crossed the center of the field and boulders rained down around him, slamming into the ranks of soldiers at his back. His wolfsteed responded to his touch, veering one way and then the other, avoiding the great stones.

"Bartoth!" Light called. "Can we talk before they kill you? It will just take a moment!"

A boulder came down in his path and Light jumped, the stone shattering the wolfsteed. He landed in a run, while the boulder tumbled into Rynda's trolls. Rynda dropped to the ground and tilted her shield, the stone rolling up and over before she rose and continued her run.

"Bartoth!" Light waved in an attempt to get his attention. "I have a question for you!"

162

The rock troll had reached the front line of his charging army and raised his hammer, bellowing an order to his ranks. They released a ragged war cry, but the attempt to intimidate had been lost in the mad dash to reach the opposing forces.

Boulders rolled across the battlefield, evidently chosen for the slope that forced the Griffin army to ascend. Screams pierced the morning as those too slow were caught and crushed. Well ahead of the allied forces, Light dodged a falling boulder and closed the gap to Bartoth.

The rock troll sneered and swung his hammer, the blow meant to crush Light. But he stepped out of the giant muscular golem, allowing it to absorb the blow, and jumped to Bartoth's shoulders, alighting and clinging to the armor over his shoulder.

"Hey," Light said. "I'm looking for . . .

The hammer came at him and he swung to the opposite shoulder, holding the troll's neck.

"—the dark elf—"

Bartoth roared and reached for Light, but he grabbed the troll's hair and leaned back, causing him to cry out.

"—queen and I was told—"

"I'll flay your skin from your bones!" Bartoth bellowed and swung for Light again.

"—you would know—"

The hammer missed again.

"—where she is and—"

Bartoth clawed for Light, but he ducked and twisted, holding on to his shoulders, belt, or even his arm as he leapt about. Bartoth's army had passed him by and the battle begun, with shouts and cries echoing across the ground, but Bartoth twisted in place, furiously, desperately, attempting to dislodge Light.

The troll cast agility, strength, and speed, running and stomping the ground, tearing at Light with every twist, but Light flitted about, a continuous stream of questions bombarding the infuriated troll. Bartoth's face grew redder and redder as his army collided with the smaller allied force. Without his dominating presence the goblin tribes were already beginning to crumble, and even the giants seemed lost.

A pair of fire giants added fire to boulders and launched them, but their aim was off, and they landed in a goblin tribe, the flaming volley rolling towards Water, who extinguished them and galloped through the smoke. He and Lira cut the remaining goblins down as they sought to push through the throng to reach Light.

Bartoth came to a halt, his chest heaving, his eyes blazing. "You are *ruining* my war!"

"It isn't going very well," Light agreed, nodding from his perch on Bartoth's head. "But at least Rynda hasn't gotten to you yet. She *really* wants to kill you."

"If I tell you what you wish to know, will you leave this blasted place?"

"Of course!" Light said eagerly.

"She's at my—"

"Light!" Water cried, slipping through a knot of battling goblins and humans to reach him. "What in Skorn's name are you doing?"

"Hey Water!" Light said brightly. "How are you doing? I was just having a conversation with Bartoth here—"

Bartoth used Light's distraction to reach up, and his hand closed around Light's throat. With a shout of triumph he hurled him into the battle, to a spot where a boulder was about to land. Light landed with a grunt and bounced through a trio of human mercenaries, lifting his gaze just as the boulder filled his vision.

The boulder struck the ground with the sound of cracking glass. Sparks blasted outward, and despite the raging battle, many of those nearby recoiled and shielded their eyes. Bartoth sniffed and turned to Rynda arriving on his flank.

The boulder moved, rolling to the side as Light ascended the wall of the crater. Cracks appeared in his visage, and reddish light spilled from within. Gone was his smile, and he stalked Bartoth with a look of unbridled fury.

"Not again," Water breathed, and jumped in front of him.

"Light," he said. "Calm down. Everything will be fine if—"

Light struck him in the jaw, knocking him aside and surging into a sprint. Bartoth barked an order and goblins and giants stepped to intervene, but that only served to augment Light's fury, and he waded through them, casting them in every direction.

"All I wanted was to *talk!*"

Light cast a spear and hurled the weapon at a giant. The giant tried to swat the spear aside, but the weapon grazed his hand and his chest, sending him tumbling backwards. The spear detonated, tearing the nearby goblins apart. Another giant hefted a boulder above his head but Light jumped high, landing on the boulder and striking it from above.

The stone shattered, stones pelting the goblins and the giant, who now stared at his empty hands in confusion. Light cast a floating spear and carried it down, driving it into the giant's skull. He died with a look of confusion still on his face and flattened his companions when his bulk crashed to the ground.

"*One* question!" Light shouted. "I wanted *one* answer, but you tried to *crush* me!"

Bartoth, now locked in a duel with Rynda, spared a glance at Light, a touch of uncertainty in his gaze. Rynda punished the distraction, driving her sword at his belly. Even taller than Bartoth, Rynda was a match for Bartoth in skill, but not in magic, and brown light shimmered on his form as he cast agility.

Slipping past the sword, Bartoth struck another troll in the face and kicked a third before whirling back to Rynda, the tactic placing Rynda between him and Light. Light cast another spear and aimed it at Bartoth, heedless of the fact that it would strike Rynda. Water got there first, and a coil of liquid wrapped around Rynda's arm, pulling her off balance enough for the spear to pass over her shoulder.

Bartoth deflected the spear, sending it spinning into a group of goblins, where it detonated, filling the air with dust and smoke. Light felt a tug on his arm and shoved Willow away, his gaze fixed on Bartoth.

"Light!" Willow shouted. "You must stop!"

"*He tried to crush me!*" Light shouted, his voice gaining a disturbing timbre.

Allied forces and rebellion alike recoiled from the sparks and arcing power cascading off his frame, the retreat cascading through the chaotic battle as both forces thought they were supposed to withdraw. Less than twenty minutes after the battle began, soldiers on both sides flooded back to their respective camps, casting confused looks at the bright figure at the center of the battlefield.

"WILL YOU STOP MEDDLING IN MY WAR!" Bartoth's bellow was met by scornful laughter from Rynda.

"You were always such a fool," Rynda said. "You always fought for yourself, never depending on others or teaching others to rise to their strength."

"None are as strong as I," Bartoth sneered.

"We'll see soon enough," another rock troll said, darting in.

Rynda raised a hand, and he came to a halt. "He's mine," she said. "After what he took, I want to show him—"

The hammer of light smashed into Bartoth's back. He rolled twice before coming to a halt, and Light stalked after, the enormous hammer spinning in his grip. Rynda stepped between them and raised a hand to Light.

"I like you, but don't become my foe."

The hammer struck Rynda in the shield, sending her into the dirt. The other trolls surged forward but she came to her knees and spit blood. The trolls pounced on Light, but the large hammer knocked them aside.

Rynda rose and glanced to Bartoth. Then she stepped out of Light's path and raised a hand to her soldiers. "Leave him be."

Light didn't hear Willow, Lira, or Water shouting his name. His vision pulsed with anger, his face cracking with pain. He grimaced and reached up, touching the crack on his cheek, where illuminated blood dripped onto his chin.

"I just wanted an answer." His words were harsh, grating, deadly. "But you would rather let a boulder fall on me. Let's see how you like it."

He pointed to a nearby boulder, the surface of which was on fire, the flames licking off the handprint of a fire giant, where the magic still lingered. A giant shaft of light coalesced into shape and attached to the boulder. A hand gathered from the reddish light, sparking and spitting heat as Light grabbed the shaft and lifted the thirty-foot hammer, the boulder on the end rocking back and forth.

Bartoth got to his feet and looked up at the makeshift hammer, his eyes wide with surprise. With speed active he leapt aside, and the boulder-hammer thudded into the earth where he'd stood. Bartoth wisely fled, but Light reached out, and threads of sunlight turned to ropes that entangled the rock troll's legs, bringing him down. His hammer tumbled from his grip and fell away.

"You think to escape?" Light snarled, stalking forward.

"Bartoth!" Water called, limping closer with Lira under his arm. "You must apologize."

Bartoth looked daggers at him. "I am a rock troll! I do not apologize!"

"Then he will kill you." Willow wiped the blood from her cheek and joining Water.

Oblivious to the exchange, Light stalked forward, his enlarged hand wielding the giant hammer at his side. The hand was taller than he was,

167

the fingers tightening on the shaft as he clenched a fist, the shadow of the hammer falling on Bartoth.

"You need to apologize!" Willow shouted.

"I'd rather die!" Bartoth snapped.

"You will," Light said.

Light came to a halt, the hammer looming over the bound rock troll. Both armies straggled across the battlefield, the goblins, humans, dwarves, giants, all craning to get a look at Bartoth. A hush fell over the two forces.

"You always thought you'd die in battle," Rynda said, absently wiping the blood from her shoulder where Light had struck her. "Is this really how you want to be remembered?"

"I am the mightiest of my kind," Bartoth snarled, squirming in the bonds. "I will not bow before an abomination. I will not yield to an inferior warrior or die like a bound animal."

"Your boulder cracked me," Light said, his voice so dark that fear touched the rock troll's eyes. "Mine will *break* you."

He lifted his hand and the hammer came down, just as the rock troll spit the words, "I'm sorry!"

The boulder came to a halt, inches from his face. For several seconds it hovered, and then it tipped to the side and Water's face appeared, his expression relieved. Water shook his head in disbelief.

"Sorry about that. It's not a good idea to anger him. Are you well?"

Chapter 23: Bartoth's Warning

"NO, I'M NOT WELL!" Bartoth roared.

The boulder thudded to the ground, the shaft and hand disintegrating. Light hurried close and stood next to the squirming rock troll. Indignant, he glared at the troll and scolded him like an errant child.

"It isn't kind to strike at someone you just met."

"He's not very kind to begin with," Rynda said, joining them. "But I'll take care of him."

"Set me free so I can fight," Bartoth snarled.

"As you will," Light said.

The bonds disappeared, and the astonished Bartoth rolled to his feet and leapt away. He took two steps before Rynda leaned down and murmured into Light's ear. He raised a hand towards the escaping rock troll.

Bonds appeared again, coiling about his body, locking his arms and legs together. With a curse on his lips, he again crashed into the dirt, his face embedding into soil just inches from his hammer. One of the trolls caught his shoulder and turned the sputtering troll onto his back.

"Sorry," Light said, his tone apologetic. "But I like her more than you."

The rock troll fixed Light with a baleful glare, but Light suddenly recalled why they had come, and hurried to his side. Kneeling, he repeated the question they had come to ask.

"Where is the queen of the dark elves?"

Bartoth glanced between Light, Willow, and Rynda, and then scowled. "The guards move her often," he said. "A week past, she was in my fortress. Who knows where she is now."

"Where's your refuge?" Willow asked.

"You think I'll tell you anything else?" Bartoth spat. "You've already taken my pride."

"A deep wound," Rynda said with a smile. She then turned to Bartoth's forces, those that hadn't already fled, and raised her voice. "Your leader has fallen. Those that remain will suffer the same fate."

The group beat a hasty retreat, with goblin tribes gathering their gear and weapons and sprinting for the hilltop. Giants lumbered away, disappearing into the barren ground of the Unclaimed Lands. Rynda gave a satisfied nod and then motioned to her trolls.

"Find anti-magic chains and bind him."

"You won't kill him here?"

She shook her head. "Now that he is imprisoned, our people deserve to witness his execution."

Bartoth scowled but fell silent, and a pair of trolls dragged him back toward the camp. Willow leaned over and suggested Light confirm the bonds would not be broken by the powerful troll.

"Right." He thickened the bonds around Bartoth. Then he turned to Water and smiled broadly. "I did not expect to see you and Lira in the north."

"We just arrived," Water said. "We were headed to Astaroth to speak to Queen Rynda when we learned she had come here to ally with Griffin."

"Not an ally," Rynda said, turning back to them. "We were here for Bartoth, not Griffin."

"I meant no offense," Water said.

"Griffin has been attempting to expand its borders for years." She folded her arms and glared at Water. "And we do not ally ourselves with them, or with the goblin tribes of the region."

"You did speak of your duty to the people of Lumineia," Lira said.

"Indeed," Rynda said, her voice noticeably less harsh. "Before the battle you spoke of an impending invasion. What makes you think I would risk my people in such a war?"

"You've heard of the return of the krey?" Lira asked.

"The ancient race." Rynda shrugged as if it did not matter. "Those are just rumors."

"We saw one just a week ago," Willow said. "In Mistkeep."

Rynda regarded the dark elf, and Light realized she looked tiny compared to the rock troll queen, whose sword probably weighed more than twice the dark elf's body. Light was proud that Willow did not seem intimidated.

"The inked one," Rynda said. "You are known to me, and you have my respect."

Willow glanced to Light in surprise, and he laughed, delighted with the revelation. "You know of her?"

"We are the flesh of war," Rynda said. "We know all warriors of renown, including Draeken. I rarely respect males of other races, but Light brings a smile to my face."

"He does that for us all," Willow said.

Her words reminded Light of the girl in the tavern, and his smile faded. Lira seemed to notice his crestfallen expression but a handful of rock trolls parted, and a newcomer arrived. He shouldered his way through surrounding trolls with a quartet of guards in pristine armor.

"You have our gratitude . . ." he eyed Light in confusion.

"Duke Hethion," Rynda said, disgust in her voice. "You missed the battle."

171

"I did not think it would be over so quickly," the portly man said, squinting to see the breadth of the halted battle. "You are nothing if not efficient."

"Unfortunately, the credit goes to our new friend." Rynda motioned to Light. "You have him to thank for the . . . victory."

"The light mage," the duke said, beaming in pride. "One of our own race. You must dine with me, of course—"

"I do not like you." Light frowned. "You should go."

The man stared in bewilderment, and Light noticed the wine on his expensive tunic. Light rarely disliked someone to such a degree, but the man made him cringe, like finding a crushed insect in an otherwise tasty meal.

The man seemed to settle on anger as an appropriate response, and he grabbed his belt and cinched it up over his rotund waist. "I do not care for your insolence. Hero of the battle or not, you will respect me or—"

"I think you need to leave," Water said, his tone becoming a warning as he glanced to Light.

"Bind him and cast him in irons," the duke sputtered, and then stabbed a finger to his quartet of guards. "I'll not depart before a single mage."

"How about now?" Rynda asked, stepping to Light's side.

"I knew I liked you," Light said.

The towering rock troll allowed a faint smile, and then stabbed a finger in the direction of the fortress. "Return to your halls, before I consider your effort to expand your kingdom as a threat to my race."

"Words of war, good queen," the duke said, but he didn't appear angry. Instead he appeared almost triumphant. "They may come back to haunt you."

"The only thing that haunts me is your face," she said.

The duke turned bright red. "The king will hear of this."

"Make sure he knows I stand with her," Light said, smiling broadly.

"I don't even know who you are," the duke spat, before whirling and stomping away, his honor guard in tow. One of the soldiers flashed an apologetic look as he left.

Rynda sighed in regret. "Griffin will not be satisfied with the unclaimed lands," she said. "In time, they will seek to claim the whole of the north."

"Their hunger has no end," Water agreed.

"Are we talking about food?" Light asked. "I'm rather hungry."

Lira grinned, while Water and Willow laughed. Rynda spread her hand back toward the rock troll camp. "Our fare may not be as sumptuous as the duke's, but at least there will not be a viper at your table."

"I do not care for vipers," Light said, and shuddered. "Their meat is chewy and tasteless . . . is something amusing?"

"I just missed you," Water said, clapping him on the back.

Confused, he nevertheless accompanied Willow, Lira, Water, and the rock trolls back to their camp. The battle had been brief and hasty, with only a handful of soldiers slain. Some of the rock trolls had been injured but none killed, a fact that seemed to please Rynda.

The rock troll camp was set apart from the Griffin army, on a ledge of stone a short distance off the ground. A plunging canyon on one side led to the river, and a slope on the other ensured it was well guarded by the landscape.

No tents were visible, but short battlements had been constructed, the barrier allowing the rock trolls a place to guard against attack. Even near allies, the trolls were always ready for combat.

Light gazed about in interest. He'd visited the troll nation before, but rarely seen them outside of Astaroth. Rynda ensured Bartoth was secured before joining them. Instead of a table, they sat on the warm stone, and ate a meal of seared kull meat, while Water and Lira explained the full truth of the Order of Ancients. Light noticed Lira did most of the talking.

"You say the dark elf queen was taken by the Order?" Rynda asked. "That is intriguing."

"How so?" Willow asked.

"Because King Meroosi of the gnomes, and the orc monarch, King Werin, have been taken," Rynda said.

Water and Lira exchanged a look. "On our journey north we learned the King Prolin of Talinor and King Justin of Griffin have been mysteriously absent."

"It appears that only three thrones remain, the queen of the surface elves, dwarves, and you." Willow pointed to Rynda.

Lira motioned to Rynda. "I do not envy the one that comes for you."

Light laughed at the image of the Order attempting to drag the queen from her home. He doubted even the dakorians would be a match for her, especially the males. He cocked his head to the side, the obvious question bursting from his lips.

"Why do you dislike men?"

One of the nearby rock trolls snorted but strode away before Rynda's gaze settled on him. Water and Lira seemed to hold their breath, while Willow continued to eat. Rynda regarded him with a strange look and then shrugged.

"Too often they speak with lies on their tongues."

"Like Bartoth?"

"Like Bartoth," she said. "But many others. I distrust men until they have proven their worth."

"A wise tactic," Light said, glancing about suspiciously.

She motioned to him. "What do you think of the krey?"

174

"My brother does not always speak with wisdom," Water said. "Perhaps I can—"

"I didn't ask you," Rynda said, without taking her eyes from Light.

"They are greedy." Light tapped his chin. "And they seem to be rather intelligent, but I do not like their arrogance." He brightened. "They remind me of Duke Hethion. The krey come to claim what is not theirs to possess."

Rynda inclined her head and turned to Lira. "If you have need, you may call."

She blinked in surprise. "You agreed because of what Light said?"

"You speak with eloquence. Light speaks with simplicity. And I do not take kindly to invaders thinking to claim what they do not own."

"You have our gratitude," Water said.

"I didn't do it for you," Rynda said coldly.

Light enjoyed Water's consternation. Water was the fragment with honor, and nearly everyone respected him. Seeing him out of sorts brought a smile to Light's lips. Then Rynda turned to Willow.

"Perhaps I can send a patrol to help you find Bartoth's refuge."

"You do not know its location?" Willow asked.

Rynda frowned and cast Bartoth a look, where he was bound by thick chains to a boulder even he could not lift. "No."

"I do," Water said, drawing all eyes to him. He winced under Rynda's glare. "I hunted him before and tracked him to his lair. I can find it again."

"Perhaps you are not entirely useless." Rynda rose to her feet. "Enjoy the meal. We depart in the morning. If you have need of us, don't send him." She pointed to Water.

When Rynda walked away, Light veritably crowed. "She *really* doesn't like you."

"But I didn't say anything mean," Water said, wiping the perspiration from his brow, as if he'd been nervous around the queen.

Lira grinned and leaned over to kiss him on the cheek. "It's not your words that offend," she said. "It's your gender."

"She likes *him*," Water said, motioning to Light.

"Because I'm likable," Light replied, feigning a haughty pose.

"Indeed," Willow said, and then turned to Water. "Now, tell me about Bartoth's fortress . . ."

Light yawned and glanced to the sky, which had begun to darken. Although he wanted to listen, fatigue settled in and his thoughts shifted to the monarchs. Why would their foes want the kings and queens? Forcing them to be Serak's friends didn't seem like a good option, but he yawned again, his thoughts scattering. He looked longingly at the warm stone. Perhaps a little nap would do him some good.

Chapter 24: An Empty Throne

Willow listened to Water talk of the fortress until deep into the night, long after Light had fallen asleep. As the fragment snored, Willow continued to press Water for more, until she had a full understanding of Bartoth's refuge. She hoped the dark elf queen lay hidden within, or would they find all the kidnapped monarchs? When she voiced her thoughts, Water looked to Lira.

"Have you ever seen the krey take leaders?"

Lira leaned back against the stone. "Never, but they usually sweep in and cart off everyone."

"Perhaps it is not the krey that are taking them," Water said.

Willow watched the exchange, curious about Lira. The woman was obviously close to Water, but Willow had never met her before. Who was she? And why did she know so much about the krey? It was obvious the woman kept herself guarded, and Willow did not perceive her as a threat. Still, she couldn't help wondering as to her identity.

"What do you mean?" Willow asked.

"Thorg took King Numen," Water said, "and Thorg works for the Order of Ancients."

"And the Order of Ancients is led by Serak," Lira said, her voice tinged with understanding. "But why would he want to take the leaders?"

They looked to Willow, but she remained silent. The prospect that Serak was kidnapping monarchs spoke to a broader plan, one that went beyond Wylyn and the krey. The man was a tactician with thousands of years of time to craft his design. But what did he want?

"Serak is all but worshiped by Order members," she said. "He knows more, plans bigger, and always has a purpose."

"Like Elenyr," Water said quietly.

"You think the Hauntress is like Serak?" Willow asked dubiously.

"She has a multitude of secrets," Water said. "And she too, always has a plan."

"Are you saying you don't trust her?"

"My faith in Elenyr is absolute," Water said. "It's just disturbing to discover one with her ability, but without her morals."

Light chose that moment to snore, the sound loud and sudden. Willow smiled softly and reached out to brush his hair from his cheek. He twitched and then relaxed in slumber. Noticing the motion, Lira pointed to Light.

"Do you ever fear he will hurt you?"

"He may lack restraint, but he has saved my life more times than I can count."

"He loves you," Water said.

"I know," Willow replied.

In the stillness of night, the camp had gone quiet, except for the shifting of feet as the guards kept watch. Bereft of clouds or moon, the night sky twinkled with stars, soft and peaceful. It was Willow's favorite part of the surface.

"We should get some sleep," Lira said. "We have a long journey to Bartoth's refuge."

"You're coming with us?" Willow asked, turning to face them.

"I think it would be for the best," Water said. "Rynda has agreed to help us if we have need, so we may as well join your assignment. Besides, infiltrating a fortress is not really Light's talent."

"Or yours," Lira said with a knowing smile.

Water grinned, and the fondness in the expression implied their relationship had grown beyond friendship. Willow wondered how it would affect the other fragments. As much as they behaved like they were separate beings, every choice they made affected Draeken, and not always for the better.

She recalled the year Fire had argued with Mind, and departed from the others, refusing to return. All had been on edge, and strangely weaker. Light's magic had been muted, and he'd been unable to cast his wings until Fire returned.

"You may join us," Willow said.

"You have our gratitude," Water replied.

Willow rose and stepped to the bedroll she'd laid out for herself. Reclining, she stared into the great expanse of stars, her thoughts on Serak and his designs. Her position in the Order was undeniably over, a fact for which she was grateful, but she disliked how little she'd managed to learn from her time in their ranks.

Serak had spent his entire life preparing to fight a war. The Bloodsworn had been positioned to take the place of the Assassin's Guild, the Ravens to replace the Thieves Guild. Both were now in shambles due to the fragments of Draeken. But what about the Order of Ancients? He'd built them up and trained them to the pinnacle of discipline, but who were they meant to replace? They obviously weren't meant to be kings. They behaved more like an army to a single king.

She frowned, disliking the prospect of Serak sitting on a throne. But even if he had taken the kings, would the people follow his rule? She jerked her head, dismissing that prospect. Her own people loved the queen, but they would not kneel before Serak, not for anything. So why take the monarchs? Wondering what role Draeken played in Serak's plans, she lapsed into slumber . . .

—A shout roused her awake. Tinged with alarm, the voice heralded combat and blood, bringing her to her feet in an instant. She caught her sword from her hip, pulling the inkblade free at the same moment she drew her small crossbow. Then she spun, looking for the threat.

Part of her mind registered that it was still night, the stars having moved but the sun not yet touching the horizon. Water and Lira were both on their feet, while Light snored blissfully between them.

Rock trolls rushed toward the back of camp, and a surge of panic gripped her. If Bartoth had escaped, he would be out for blood. And Light had nearly single handedly brought him down, making him the primary target. She took two steps to see Bartoth and sighed in relief.

Bartoth was still chained to the short cliff at the back of the camp. His dark hair hung about his face, his face bearing a strange smile. Confusion washed across Willow and then she spotted the source of the conflict.

The trolls were gathered around a spot nearby, their bulk preventing her from seeing what drew their attention. A rumble of doubt, of fear rippled among the trolls, the sound disturbing, for Willow had never known a rock troll to fear.

"What happened?" Water asked.

"I don't know," Willow said.

Lira shrugged and shook her head. "Isn't that where Rynda slept?"

Fear gripped her spine, and Willow darted into the pack of rock trolls, pushing her way through the muscled bodies to reach the center. Water and Lira joined her, all three coming to a halt when they found what the trolls had discovered.

In the spot where Rynda had slept, the ground was sunken, a shallow pool of water in the basin. A note floated on the surface of the liquid, the lettering large enough to see in the torchlight.

Two thrones remain.

Willow sucked in her breath. Rynda, the mightiest of rock trolls, had been kidnapped in the midst of her kind. Without a sound. Someone barked an order and the others raced to search the camp, rushing to find their queen.

"This is Serak's water magic." Water stooped and put his hand on the surface. "There's a cave beneath here that connects to the river. He must have dropped her beneath and sealed the stone after."

"She must have fought," Lira said.

"She would *always* fight," a troll said, his voice savage.

A shout of alarm rang out, drawing all to the edge of the stone, the side that overlooked the river. Willow crouched and began to descend the cliff to the river, following the rock trolls. Water and Lira brought up the rear.

Willow dropped into the water, her boots splashing. Others landed about her, all peering into a large opening, one obviously made by magic. A rock troll tossed a light orb inside. It bounced off the rocks and landed in the shallow water. Half submerged, it revealed a large cave directly beneath the rock troll camp.

"Blood!" a troll called.

"And Queen Rynda's oathsword!" another called, lifting the giant weapon from the water.

"She would not leave it behind," Willow said. "Trolls do not abandon their weapons unless they are unconscious or—"

"Dead," a troll snapped.

Water eyed the ceiling of the cave. "Serak has stone magic and water magic. He must have opened the cave and entombed her in stone to keep her from shouting a warning."

"You know a lot for one that just arrived," a troll said, pointing his axe at Water.

"Me?" Water exclaimed in surprise. "I don't know anything about this."

"I say we gut you and let the gods decide your innocence," he barked, taking a step forward.

181

Water raised his hands, and the liquid rose into a pair of spears pointed at the troll's chest. The other trolls leapt to support their brother, and in seconds Willow found herself facing two dozen enraged rock trolls.

"Perhaps we should depart," Lira said quietly.

Trolls moved to cut off the exit, but the one who had taken orders from Rynda jerked his head. "Let them go."

"But they—"

"Rynda trusted them," he barked. "Now spread out. Find her."

The trolls sullenly parted, and exited the cave to the river, hurrying to follow their kidnapped queen. The troll turned back to Willow, Water, and Lira. He stabbed a finger to the camp above, his features dark.

"Gather your things and go, before I change my mind."

"As you order," Willow said.

Willow, Lira, and Water departed the way they had come, ascending the rocks to the nearly abandoned camp. Only Bartoth, still bound to the cliff, and his guards, remained in the deserted plateau. As Willow strode to the sleeping Light, Bartoth called out to them.

"You won't find her."

"What do you know of it?" Water demanded.

Bartoth's chuckle was dark and menacing. "The Father of Guardians knows all, and soon every throne will be vacant."

"Is that what this battle was about?" Willow asked. "A ruse to draw Rynda from her seat in Astaroth?"

"Very clever, dark elf," Bartoth said. "Of course, I was supposed to be sitting at Duke Hethion's table, drinking ale while his corpse hung from the rafters."

"Serak left you here," Lira said. "He didn't save you. If you tell us what you know, perhaps we can help you."

"He will return," Bartoth said. "And when he does, I will reclaim what is rightfully mine. Not you, nor the other fragments of Draeken, not even Ero himself can stop Serak from raising the Shard of Midnight and ushering in the greatest era our world has ever seen."

"I've never known a troll to worship a man," Willow said.

Bartoth's eyes settled on her, and a sneer lit his expression. "I worship war, and there is no warrior greater than Serak. Run about, seek to save what you have lost, but in the end, you will find yourself his ally, for Draeken will be joined to Serak."

Water snorted in disbelief. "I would sooner die."

"I wasn't referring to you, *fragment*."

Willow looked between them, the fragment of Water and Bartoth, and then pointed east. "We should hasten before the trolls decide that we, too, should be in chains."

"I hope they execute you quickly," Water said.

"I will not die at their hand," Bartoth said, raising his voice as the trio turned and walked to the slumbering Light. "You will see soon enough!"

Willow listened to the troll's laughter, disturbed by the conversation. With Rynda gone, the promise Water and Lira had exacted from them would not stand, and now another throne lay empty. She scowled and knelt by Light's side.

"You must awaken," she urged, shaking him awake.

Light sat up and yawned, stretching before his eyes rose to the sky, which was still dark. "Why are we waking so early?"

Willow caught his hand and dragged him to his feet. "We must depart."

"Why?" Light asked. Then he seemed to notice the nearly empty campsite, and the trolls preparing to move Bartoth. He rubbed his eyes. "Did I miss a lot?"

"Yes," Water said. "But we'll tell you on the way."

The foursome exited the camp and began the hike north and east, all the while Bartoth's laughter echoed from the rock troll camp. Willow scowled as she realized the truth. She'd thought they were ahead of Serak. How had he gotten the better of them?

Chapter 25: Aurora

As they worked their way north, Willow listened to Water attempt to tell Light what had happened in the rock troll camp, but he yawned his way until sunrise. Willow kept to herself, pondering the ramifications of what they had learned, and what she knew of Serak.

She kept thinking there was something she was missing. The fragments spoke of Serak as an adversary, while Lira was obviously focused on Wylyn. It was the first time Willow had met the woman, and Lira was an enigma. Although it was clear they were allies, their language suggested the connection was recent.

Lira's words were also odd, a twist of speech here, a lyrical note there. Willow found her speech fascinating, especially because it did not come from any kingdom that Willow had visited. But Willow had heard such language before, in the hall of memories kept by the royal line.

"Why do you watch me?" Lira asked.

"Curiosity," Willow said. "Your language is not of elf or man."

"I grew up in a strange home," she said.

"Your weapon is also unusual," Willow said, pointing to the woman's thin sword. "But I suspect you have body magic?"

"Why would you say that?" Lira asked, a touch of amusement on her features.

"In the battle with Bartoth you fought with heightened agility," Willow said, recalling her leaping over a goblin dagger.

"You have a keen eye," Lira said, and pointed to her tattoos. "Your own magic is impressive."

185

"My magic merely allows me to carry my weapons," Willow replied.

"It's true," Water said. "But what she isn't saying is that she is a clever and forceful warrior."

Disliking the shift in attention to herself, Willow asked, "Where is your country of origin?"

Water and Lira exchanged a look, and then Lira shrugged. "I have lived many places. Few would be known to you."

"I have traveled far," Willow said, disliking her reluctance to speak the truth.

"She's an Eternal." A yawn muffled Light's voice. "She's been alive since the—"

"Light," Water hissed. "Stop telling the secrets of another."

"Right," Light said, and winked. "I won't tell Willow she's an Eternal."

"*Light*," Water groaned. "You have got to learn when to hold your tongue."

"It's early." Light cast Lira an apologetic look.

"You are forgiven," she said. "As long as your companion does not speak my identity."

"I know nothing of the Eternals," Willow lied with a faint smile.

In truth she knew a great deal, for the earliest memories contained in the hall of memories spoke of the Eternals, and their purpose. But Willow held her tongue and nudged the conversation in a different direction.

"Perhaps we should know of Bartoth's fortress."

"We've been talking about it for hours," Water said.

"Light?" Willow asked. "What does his fortress look like?"

186

Light groaned. "Why do you try and tell me things at night? You know I don't remember them."

"Indeed," Water said with a sigh, and then started again.

As Water described the strange citadel, Willow only gave half an ear. The presence of an Eternal in their midst, along with a krey and Serak, made her feel small, and she disliked the doubt they instilled. She suddenly realized that all three of her companions had lived for thousands of years, and she was hardly in her third century, young by her race, and a babe when compared to the fragments, or an Eternal.

For the first time she realized she was stepping into a war of much greater magnitude than she'd ever faced. She disliked the feeling of being insignificant, so she fell to silence. Light, too, seemed quieter than normal. Even when the sun rose, he did not exult as he normally did, and after a time they drifted behind Water and Lira.

The sloping hills and stunted trees gradually gave way to the tundra of the north. Winter had come early, and snow spotted the frozen earth, a dusting of white that made everything seem brighter. Instead of trees, stony outcroppings littered the landscape.

The terrain grew increasingly treacherous as they hiked into the mountains, and Water followed a narrow trail through a slim pass. At Lira's suggestion, Water cast a group of water horses, hastening their journey. On the other side, they were greeted with plunging canyons and frozen cliffs. Great peaks rose about them, and still Water pressed on.

They camped for the night under a small stand of hardy trees, the leaves having already fallen to the ground. The trunks afforded some resistance to the wind that managed to reach its clawed hand into the steps of the mountain.

Willow watching Light slip away from the group and disappear up the slope. Water and Lira were deep in conversation and hardly noticed. Curious, Willow followed, angling her soft footsteps to follow Light to the cliff's edge, where he'd taken a seat.

"Light," Willow said softly. "May I join you?"

"If you desire," he said distantly.

She took a seat at his side, and for several minutes they sat in silence. Light kept his gaze fixed on the northern horizon. They'd finally ascended above the lower peaks, granting a breathtaking view of the snowy north. The sun had set hours ago, and a stream of otherworldly colors flickered to life in the sky.

"I've never seen such beauty," Willow murmured.

"The goblins call them Aurora," Light said. "But I wager none see what I see."

"Tell me what you see."

"Do you love me because I am simple?"

The question tumbled from his lips, hurried and afraid and hopeful. She cast him a look, but his gaze remained fixed on Aurora. It was obvious he wanted to say more, the tremble to his jaw indicating he held a multitude of words in check.

"You are hardly simple," she said.

"I am," he replied. "I've heard Mind and Fire describe me as such. Shadow thinks the same, I wager."

"You are innocent," Willow said.

He finally met her gaze. "I have killed many, and hurt many more, especially when fury grips my body. I am hardly innocent."

"You lack the restraint of the other fragments," Willow said. "But you have an attribute they do not possess. You see the world—not as it is—but as it should be."

"And that's not simple?"

"Hope is not simple," she murmured, intertwining her cold fingers into his warm hand. "When all others would crumble to despair, or view the world for its realities, you look to others as they could become. Even me."

"You are already more beautiful than the Aurora," he said, shifting to face her. "Both inside and out."

She chuckled dryly. "Others fear me because I am a dark elf, and my own people see my tattoos and fear. When you look upon me, you see a woman, one who fights for what she believes in, one valiant and strong. It is the reflection I wish to see in the mirror."

"So you don't think I'm simple?"

"Of course not," Willow said, leaning her head on his shoulder. "To everyone else I am a soldier, a warrior, a killer. To you, I get to be me."

"Even when I create a mess?" Light pressed, his voice urgent, needing to understand. "Like with Bartoth's battle?"

She chuckled lightly. "You started a war, I'll give you that, but you also ended it quickly, and saved thousands of lives. Your lack of restraint may cause messes, but your luck gets you out of them."

"You think I'm lucky?"

She cocked her head to the side, and realized Light had never recognized the sheer complexity of his own fragment, or that of his brothers. She held aloft her hand, turning it so he could see her fingers.

"My hands were born to battle, but I also love music, dancing, and carving stone."

"I didn't know you carved."

She smiled at the revelation. "I have my own fragments. They just happen to be in a single body. You have luck and joy, innocence and hope. You may be a fragment, but you are also complete in your own way."

"*You* make me happy," Light said.

"You were happy before you met me," she replied, her smile fading as she thought of her long-lived companions.

"Did I say something amiss?"

"No," she said. "I just wonder about my place in this conflict."

"Your place is at my side," Light said.

"For how long?" she wondered aloud.

She realized the doubt had been simmering for some time, the recent events bringing it to the fore. She grimaced, unwilling to meet Light's gaze. Instead she looked to Aurora and thought of her family.

"I don't understand," Light said.

"Do you remember my mother and father?"

His features lit up with delight. "Your father is an excellent cook, while your mother is a warrior nearly equal to you."

"When I was a child my father taught me how to cook bread and roast meats. I spent days training with my mother, and nights cooking with my father. I remember laboring over a hot oven, cursing my family's lack of coin that required me to labor."

"A hard youth," Light said.

"When I began my schooling, the other students spoke of their fathers and mothers like they were distant figures, or they did not speak of them at all. My trainings with my mother continued, as did my time in the kitchens. In the heat of anger, I called myself a slave."

As Willow spoke, she imagined the heat from the oven, her father's kind voice directing her hands. The burn on her fingers, and the scent of roasted meat in her nose. Sweat trickled down her arms and neck. Laughter filled her ears and touched her lips.

"I do not know when," Willow said. "But the day came that I realized the duty was no longer onerous. The training hall and the kitchens had become my home, the time with my mother and father as precious as any jewel."

"I feel the same towards Elenyr," Light said.

"You must understand," Willow said. "That is the future I want, to teach my daughters and sons what it means to be family, to watch them learn at the stove with my father and learn the blade from my mother."

"Why do you speak of these things?"

190

"I travel with beings that have lived for ages, seen wondrous things. But I am simply a servant to the crown."

"Would you like to be ageless?" Light asked, growing excited. "I wager Elenyr knows how to change your flesh."

She jerked her head before his excitement prevented reason. "No," she said hastily. "I want a life and a family, to raise children, to teach them their place in this world. Walking with you, Water, and Lira reminds me that I do not have a place in their war."

"Even if it was to be with me?"

She reached up and touched his cheek. "I love you, but I do not want your life."

Willow had not planned the words, but they were true, and she did not attempt to take them back. Light stared at her, his obvious surprise binding his tongue. She smiled sadly and disentangled her hand from his.

"I'm sorry, Light. But you need one that can live as you do."

"What are you saying?" he mumbled.

"When this conflict is over, we part ways," she said.

She stood and walked away before her nerve failed her and strode back to the camp. She passed Water and Lira, who jerked away from each other as if they had just been kissing. Ignoring their hasty excuses, she reclined on her bedroll and wrapped herself in the blanket. Her position by the fire afforded heat, but she faced into the dark mountainside so they would not see her tears.

Light returned, silent and trudging. Water asked the reason for his sadness, but for once he did not speak, and merely reclined on his own bed. Water persisted, but Light remained silent, and after a time he gave up.

Willow stared into the snow, wishing she had not hurt Light, and wondering if she'd committed a fatal mistake. The others lapsed to slumber, but she remained awake, and told herself the ache in her chest would fade in time.

191

Chapter 26: Tired

Light didn't sleep. He stared at the night sky as the cold sank into his skin. His fragment brothers occasionally teased him for not understanding, but this conversation he understood. And that is what hurt. Willow loved him for who he was but could not be with him for the same reason.

The hours of night were dark and heavy, and after ages of sleeping with ease, he finally understood how others complained they didn't sleep well. Dawn came, but the usual burst of energy that came with sunrise was like a groan instead of a roar.

They rose and ate, and it didn't take long for Water and Lira to pick up on the silence. Water cast Light several searching looks and Light hoped his brother would be silent, for once, but he was never good at waiting.

"What's going on?"

"Just tired," Light mumbled.

"You never get tired during the day," Water said suspiciously, his eyes flicking to Willow and back. "What happened between you two?"

Silence.

Lira shook her head. "It's obvious something is wrong."

Silence.

"Light," Water said. "You've always been terrible at lying. Just tell us what—"

"I'M JUST TIRED!"

Light's voice echoed off the stones next to them but faded quickly, muffled by the snow. He jerked his hand in dismissal, and accidently

192

sent a burst of magic into the rock adjacent to the tree. Water leaned down and looked through the hole. Extending through the entire boulder, the hole leaked molten stone, steam rising as it touched the snow.

"I guess you're just tired," he said, eyeing the damage that could have been through his body.

Light gathered his bedroll and waited at the trail as the others gathered their things. As the foursome departed their tiny campsite, little was said. Light, still brooding on his conversation with Willow, trudged at the rear of the group, while Willow walked with Lira at the front.

The hours bled away, and Light stared at the rocky ground at his feet. Patches of snow were frequent, as was the occasional piece of ice in a hollow. The wind cut through his cloak but he was already numb, so he didn't feel its bite.

"Light."

He looked up and saw the annoyance on Water's face. "What?" he asked.

"We're here."

Light looked to the sky, surprised to find the sun was setting. He'd trudged all day without even realizing how far they'd gone. Then he noticed Water tugging on his shirt, attempting to pull him down.

"Will you stop touching me?" he asked, slapping his brother's hand away.

"They're going to spot you," Lira said.

Light looked to her and realized they stood at the top of a small cliff, where the rocky terrain allowed the other three to hide. Beyond the cliff, a short valley stretched to a squat hill. A wall surrounded the hill, turning it into a fortress.

"Will you get down here before they see you?" Water hissed.

Light reluctantly crouched behind a stone but continued to examine the citadel. Its outer wall was made of large boulders that had been rolled into place, makeshift battlements built across the top. A handful of giants stood inside the barrier, while goblins and humans patrolled the top of the uneven wall.

Beyond the outer fortifications, a wide staircase had been cut into the slope, winding its way up the hill to an opening near the summit. Light expected a keep of some kind, but the opening was just a door leading into ground near the top of the hill. He guessed the keep was just under the snow, since the top of the summit was flat, and extended into an overhang to the east.

"We need to get inside," Willow was saying. "Quietly."

Water eyed the staircase. "I agree. If they see us coming, they could just shut that door. Or even take the queen through a Gate and destroy it behind them."

"You think they have a Gate?" Light asked.

"We got a message from Mind when we were journeying to the northland," Water said. "He'd met up with Shadow after he destroyed Mistkeep. Shadow said he'd encountered a Gate chamber that had dozens of Gates, each to a different destination."

"It's how they are traveling so quickly," Lira said.

"Then we need to enter quietly," Willow agreed.

Water cast Light a look. "Why don't you two go in and we'll stay outside. I'm confident you can be more subtle than two fragments of Draeken."

"That's a good idea," Lira said, looking meaningfully at Light.

Light frowned in confusion that bordered on anger. "Are you saying I tend to destroy things?"

"You *do* tend to destroy things," Water said with a stifled laugh. "And that's great, most of the time."

"I'll remain here," Light said, sinking back against a stone, and getting a plop of snow down his tunic for the effort. He yelped and brushed furiously at the cold chunk, eliciting smiles from his companions. Irritated, he brushed it away and ignored them.

"If a battle begins," Water said. "We'll be through the front gate in less than a minute."

"Watch out for the giants," Willow said. "I'd rather not see either of you crushed."

She spared Light a faint smile, which he did not return. Her smile faded and then she turned and departed with Lira, the two retreating into the snowdrifts. Light remained in place, watching the odd fortress, grateful Willow was gone, yet wanting her to return.

"Do you want to talk about it?" Water asked.

"I'm just tired," Light said.

"Sometimes when people say that, they don't want to admit something is wrong, but they can't keep it from showing on their faces."

Light glanced to Water, annoyed that he'd seen through his ruse. He'd thought it clever. Water looked upon him with sadness in his gaze, and a clear desire to help. Light released an annoyed grunt.

"At least the woman you're falling for can live as long as you will."

"Lira?" he asked, feigning ignorance. "I'm not falling for her."

Light rolled his eyes. "I'm the least observant of the fragments, but even I can see the way you look at Lira."

Water seemed stunned, and then shook his head. "Don't change the subject. What happened between you and Willow?"

Light wanted to hold it in, to ignore it, to pretend it never—

"Willow said she wants a family," he began.

Before he could stop himself, the words tumbled from his lips in a rush of hurt. Several times the pain burst into anger, spilling hot magic from his fingers. Water did not interrupt, and only pulled him lower behind the stones so they would not be seen. It seemed like he'd talked

195

for hours, but in just minutes his voice failed him, and he noticed Water using snow to extinguish small fires from his cloak.

"I'm sorry," he mumbled.

"I've been your brother for a long time," Water said wryly, casually brushing the ash aside. "A few burns won't keep me from being here for you."

Gratitude swelled into tears that Light stifled. "I just don't know how I can be different."

"You can't be," Water said. "You can only be yourself."

"But I want Willow to love me."

"She does," Water said. "But loving another isn't enough. You have to want what they want, hope for the same future, or you are fated to be torn apart."

"Is that what it's like for you and Lira?" he asked.

Water's smile was soft. "I hope so."

A flicker of movement drew their eyes to the road below, where two figures crept towards the boulders. Although the fortifications circled the entire hill, the guards were not well trained, and frequent lapses in discipline provided an unseen approach.

"Without Bartoth present, they do not stay at their posts," Water murmured.

The two women approached a pair of giant stones. The boulders were placed next to each other but left a gap at the top where the rounded surfaces curved away from each other. The space had been filled with wooden panels, which Willow cut, and Lira carefully removed.

"Do you think she's thinking about me?" Light asked.

"They're probably talking about you," Water said with a smile.

Light wasn't sure if he liked that or hated it, but he leaned forward as if the few inches would allow him to hear. The distance didn't allow them to see their lips, and only glimpses of their features. He yearned for more.

Lira and Willow paused as a quartet of goblins ambled by, their boots on the wooden battlements directly above Willow's head. Light gripped the stone tightly, ignoring the freezing snow dripping down his sleeve as he watched, wishing he was there to fight at Willow's side.

"Am I still going to fight with her? I really don't want to lose that too—or does the end of a relationship mean you never get to see them again?"

Water shrugged. "It depends. Sometimes you just can't bear to be around someone you cared so much about, and the memories continue to hurt. Other times you manage to remain friends."

"Which will it be with Willow and I?"

"How should I know?"

"Your wisdom is admirable," Light said sourly.

Water grinned. "I'm hardly the expert Fire is."

Light couldn't argue with that. Of any of the fragments, Fire had by the far the most relationships, discovering and wooing women from most eras. Light could never understand why women gravitated to Fire, even when he stood next to another fragment bearing the same face. Water laughed when he asked.

"Fire exudes danger," he replied. "And women like that."

"If I was more dangerous, would Willow love me more?"

"I don't think that's how it works," Water said.

"Are you sure?" Light cocked his head to the side, liking the prospect. "Because I think I could do that."

"Please don't," Water said, a trace of alarm entering his voice.

Willow and Lira had entered the fortress and managed to procure two sets of goblin armor. Sufficiently garbed to pass a cursory inspection, they passed the host of openings at the base of the hill and ascended the steps towards the opening at the top of the hill.

"You're right," he said, rising to his feet to peer at the doorway. "I just need to be more dangerous and then Willow will realize she loves me more than anything."

"Light," Water said, his tone one of warning. "That's not what I'm saying. You're twisting my words into—"

"I can prove I'm dangerous right now," he said, nodding to himself. "There are giants and goblins down there—and I can defeat them. I'm a fragment of Draeken, after all. I'm as dangerous as they come."

"That's not really the best idea—"

Light began to pace. "These are Bartoth's bandits. They've been marauding and pillaging for years. Now that he's with the rock trolls, one of his officers will take his place—unless his fortress is destroyed by someone dangerous."

"Light!" Water called. "You can't just—"

"Thanks Water," Light said. "You're the greatest."

He embraced his brother, failing to notice his sputtering. For the first time since last night, he knew what he had to do, and it was all because of Water. The ache he'd felt since Willow walked away had vanished, and Light leaned back and smiled.

"I'll make sure everyone knows it was your idea."

"Please don't," Water pleaded.

Light turned and jumped the cliff, diving into the snow and riding it down to the road. Water growled and jumped after, the two careening down the snow-filled slope. Light distantly heard Water's voice, but he took it as encouragement.

He reached the road and surged into a spring, drawing on the fading light of day. Tinged with the red on the horizon, he crafted a wolfsteed the size of a wagon, and leapt onto its back. Goblins shouted as the enormous mount charged the Gate.

Excited at the prospect of rejoining with Willow, he called out to the scrambling bandits. "Welcome to the danger!"

Sprinting to reach him, Water growled under his breath. "Not again."

Chapter 27: Water's Idea

Light charged the gates as giants hurled stones in his direction. But his wolfsteed was too large and too fast, and the stones impacted the ground in his wake, causing Water to curse and dodge.

The wolfsteed hurtled towards the gates and the goblins leapt away from the impact. Light balanced on the steed's back, jumping as his mount struck the barrier. Fashioned of wood and reinforced with steel, the gates exploded open, the pieces of the steed clattering into the courtyard and detonating.

Flame filled the morning, sending mud and goblins flailing in all directions. Light landed in the midst of a crater and cast a ridiculously oversized sword. That's when he realized just how many goblins were flooding in his direction.

Thousands of goblins, giants, and humans poured out of small caves set against the base of the hill. They charged from around the hill, the giants picking up stones or large cauldrons of boiling oil. Many of the goblins carried short black spears, the metal seeming to absorb the sunlight. Water sprinted through the shattered gates and skidded to a halt next to Light.

"Did you listen to anything on our journey here?" he demanded. "I said he had an entire army of cutthroats."

"It's possible I wasn't listening," Light said.

"They stole shipments of gnome spears," Water said, casting his favorite staffblade. "The goblins use them to take down mages."

"That's why you wanted Lira and Willow to go in quietly," Light realized.

"Yes!" Water said.

"At least it's dangerous," Light reasoned. "Now I *know* Willow will notice me."

"Not if you're dead," Water said.

The horde converged upon them and spears were hurled, filling the air. Light cast a bubble of magic, but the spears passed through it and dug into the ground all around them. Annoyed, Light picked one up but hissed as the shaft burned his skin.

"We can't touch them," Water growled, pulling him towards the stairs leading to the keep. "We're *made* of magic, remember?"

"Right," he said.

They sprinted up the steps as thousands of voices shouted behind them. The entire hill seemed to vibrate with the pounding of feet. Light slowed when they passed a pair of poles on either side, with the bodies of dead Griffin soldiers hanging from them.

"That's what they'll do to us," Water exclaimed.

Light came to a halt, nearly yanking Water from his feet. "They've murdered thousands," he said stubbornly. "We shouldn't let them go unharmed."

Water regarded him for a moment and then inclined his head. "You're right. Are you sure you want to do this?"

Light looked to the army massing at the base of the stairs and nodded. "It is going to be dangerous."

Water chuckled and turned to one side of the stairs. Blue light coursed from his fingers, turning the snow to liquid. He held it bound, preventing it from flowing downhill, even as more snow joined the rising wave.

On his side, Light did the same, using bursts of light to melt the snow. More and more shifted, falling into the blinding light, turning into a wave of water that pressed against Water's magic.

A boulder came down beside them, bouncing off the stairs and rolling into the wave. Another fell on their heads, but Light cast a spike of magic that struck the stone, cracking it like an egg. Then the spears came at them.

"Ready?" Water asked, his voice strained.

Light reached for the two broken halves of the boulder and cast a rod between them, turning them into wheels. Stepping onto the axle, he collected the first boulder that had fallen and mounted it on the front, making it resemble a flat wagon with three wheels, the front of which was a seven-foot boulder. The horde of goblins surged up the stairs, closing the gap.

"Ready," Light said.

Water released his magic, and the wave dropped down the slope. Huge and forbidding, the wall of water crashed into the wall of flesh, carrying the army of goblins into the courtyard. Giants braced against the wave, most keeping their feet as it burst across their bodies.

In his makeshift vehicle, Light bounced down the hill and rode into their midst, rolling right over the sodden goblins. Urging the wheels to greater speeds, he used the great wheel at the front to do the damage, smashing through the goblins. Helmets and boots went flying as the unyielding stone sped through their ranks.

Anti-magic spears were hurled at him but most clattered off the stone wheels. One struck Light in the shoulder, stabbing deep. Crying out, he reached up to the wound, but just touching the spear sent bile into his mouth.

"That *hurt!*"

Another spear came, this time grazing his leg, drawing illuminated blood that dripped down his knee. He winced, and instinctively curved his wheeled machine back toward the stairs, where Water used the remaining wave to fight.

"Light!" he shouted. "Are you hurt?"

Light veered towards Water and stumbled off his machine, sending it careening into the thickest knot of foes. Water caught his arm and helped him up the stairs, conjuring a small wave that carried them up. He reached for the spear.

"Don't touch it!" Light shouted, flinching away.

"This is my fault," Water said.

"Of course it is," Light hissed. "It was your idea!"

"It was not," Water said.

They reached the top of the stairs and the wave crumbled. They braced to fight but the guards were gone, the opening in snow vacant and inviting. They hurried inside, down a short tunnel of earth until it suddenly connected with another door. Instead of leading to a great hall, the opening led to a wide, curved structure.

Light's eyes widened as they entered the long chamber that seemed to extend the entire breadth of the hill's summit. He'd expected a hall of some kind, but instead the room was long, the ceiling curving into the walls, which also curved into the floor. The end that extended into the overhang came to a point, the floor and ceiling coming together into a shape that resembled the tip of a sword.

The opposite end contained a giant sphere, easily fifty feet tall, that seemed to float off the ground. Purple light glowed around the sphere, emanating from the dark material. To either side of the sphere, a large opening extended to a smaller, pointed chamber.

The interior of the hall contained an assortment of recently built structures, most of stone and wood. The quality was much better than the makeshift fortifications of the fortress, and suggested they were used by the officers of the bandit army.

Sections of the broad floor were used for training circles, with one larger circle obviously reserved for Bartoth himself. The dark stains on the floor suggested he did not use it just for training.

"What a strange hall," Light said.

"Looks like all the captains went with Bartoth to the battle," Water said, scanning the interior.

"We did move rather quickly?" Light swept a hand at the strange hall. "Did he build this place?"

"We must have gotten here before they did," Water said.

"I've never seen anything like this," he said. "And it's so *warm*."

Water used the moisture outside to seal the opening, filling the breadth of the short tunnel leading into the keep. Then he turned and all but pushed Light into a nearby seat. Still marveling at the strange room, Light didn't notice Water grab a pair of tongs from a nearby forge until the tongs closed on the spear in Light's chest.

"Ouch, what are you—"

Water yanked the spear out, causing Light to shout and strike Water in the chest. He tumbled backward with the spear, landing hard and rolling several times. The spear clattered away.

"Light?"

He looked toward the front of the chamber, the tapered end that resembled a sword. The rooms there looked different than the captain's bedchambers, the material all white, with a faint glow. Sections were broken off, indicating that the hallways and various levels had at one time extended all the way to the sphere at the back of the hall. One figure was leaning out of a doorway in the topmost wall.

"Willow!" Light called, waving. "I was dangerous. You should have seen it!"

"You weren't supposed to—never mind. Just get up here."

Light grabbed Water and pulled him to his feet. "Come on, I think it worked."

Water muttered under his breath as they hurried to join Willow. Sections of metal and broken portions of wall protruded from the walls and ceiling, and occasional sparks appeared. Water stared at them while Light only had eyes for the opening ahead.

Just as they reached the corridor at the front, a thud reverberated from behind, followed by the cracking of glass. Water grimaced and pointed to the seal he'd made over the doorway.

"That's not going to last long."

"Do you think she saw me?" Light asked.

Water groaned and stepped into the short corridor at the end. Left intact, the corridor ended at a circular room with a hole in the ceiling. Ladders had been erected for climbing to the upper levels, and Light was quick to ascend. He ignored the sting in his shoulder where the wound was already knitting.

They reached the top, an oval room with a long roof that descended to the front. A desk curved around the front of the room, the surface covered in runes, symbols, and strange recesses. Light bent to examine them, wondering why the symbols looked familiar.

"Any sign of the queen?" Water asked.

"Some," Willow said. "Bartoth's chambers had a Gate, and he had a record saying he was keeping the dark elf queen at the Forge of Light."

"The Forge?" Water exclaimed, his eyes wide. "The same one that created magic?"

"The same," Lira said, her hands roving the symbols on the desk.

"Will Bartoth's Gate take us there?" Water asked.

Lira jerked her head. "It's been sealed, no doubt to stop the goblins from using it. We'll have to get to the Forge from the outside."

A great cracking of glass caused them all to look downward, and Water shook his head. "First we have to get out of this hall."

"It's not a hall," Lira said. "It's a ship. A krey ship."

Light began to laugh, the sound delighted and excited. He saw the hall with new eyes, the shape, the tapered front, the sphere at the back, a krey gravity sphere large enough to power a ship. They stood in the very vehicle the ancients had once used to fly the sky.

"Can it fly? How high? What's that do—or this?" He began poking the runes at random, his excitement boiling in action. But nothing happened, and he grunted in dismay. "Will it not do anything?"

"It has power," Lira said, leaning back from the controls. "And the gravity sphere is intact, even if most everything else has been stripped away."

"Could Wylyn use it to power a Gate?" Water asked.

"I doubt it," Lira said. "There's too much damage to the ship."

"So it won't fly?" Water asked, obviously disappointed.

Lira jerked her head. "This antiquated ship uses a command sphere to operate. It would look round and small, about the size of—"

"Like this?" Light dug the ancient sphere from Kordune from his pocket and held it upward.

"Of course you kept it," Willow said, her tone half exasperated, half admiring.

"Exactly like that," Lira said. "Where did you get it?"

Willow briefly detailed their escape from Kordune, relating their infiltration and subsequent trail. She glossed over the details of Light's distraction, a fact for which Light was grateful, and then finished by explaining the shrinking of the sphere.

"Why did it expand into a large sphere?" Light asked.

"Because that's how they perform maintenance," Lira said. "It grows in size so engineers can work on the machine from the inside. Think of it like a key that unlocks this ship."

Light raised it to her. "Let's fly!"

"Attempting to fly this pile of junk would be foolish," she said. "We should find another way out before Bartoth's army returns."

"They already did," Water said. "They've probably surrounded the hill by now."

"I'd rather not fight ten thousand bandits," Willow said, folding her arms.

"Then we have to find another way to—"

Light spotted a hollow at the center of the runes. Not unlike a dish, it seemed the perfect size for the sphere in his hand. He glanced to the other three, but they seemed very focused. Best not to interrupt. Reaching out, he placed the sphere into the hollow.

And the ship began to tremble . . .

Chapter 28: Bartoth's Keep

Snow cascaded off its silver hull and dropped on the goblins on the hill. Those attempting to breach the opening stopped, and a stillness fell across Bartoth's forces, those closest to the opening recoiling in shock. The ship trembled again, a dull hum mounting from the back of the ship.

"Light!" Water groaned. "Do you have to touch everything?"

"I'm trying to be dangerous, remember? You said it would help me win back Willow."

Both women glared at Water, who threw up his hands. "I did not say that!"

"Yes, you did," Light accused.

Lira stepped to the sphere and sought to withdraw the object, but it refused her efforts. She slammed her fist on a rune, but it remained dark. Cursing under her breath, she began touching runes across the surface.

"Half the controls are dead, but the ship is powering up. We need to get out before it—"

The ship lifted off the hill, the rear end rising. Snow and earth cascaded away, ages of dust falling off the ship that hadn't moved since the Dawn of Magic. Water's barrier at the door crumbled. The door sought to shut, but a clanking echoed inside the vessel, and the door failed. Then the front of the ship began to rise.

"Too late," Lira breathed.

"We're flying!" Light exclaimed.

"You can fly with wings," Water said caustically.

"This is *so* much better."

"Not when we crash!" Lira shouted.

She furiously touched runes, but only a few brightened. The ship lurched—and then dropped. It struck the hill and fell down the slope towards the fortress wall. Bandits dived away from the careening ship, but many were crushed beneath the hull.

Light ricocheted off the floor and the walls, laughing as the ship bounced up and down. Willow clung to a section of wall. Water did the same, while Lira fought to hold onto the desk of runes.

The ship slid down the slope like a giant sled and plowed through the boulders, several bouncing upward, striking the front of the ship with a muffled *thud*. One hit right in front of them, and suddenly the front curve of the ship turned transparent, allowing a full view of their ship coming to a halt, its nose just feet from a giant. It stared in awe at the giant vessel, and the foursome standing on the other side of the window.

"Can we do that again?" Light asked.

"No!" Lira barked. "We need to get out of here!"

She got to her feet and took one step towards the door before the hum gathered anew, and the rear of the ship lifted into the air. The front did not. Light's eyes widened when the ship began to flip.

"Is it supposed to do that?" Light asked, mystified as the chamber began to rotate forward.

"No!" Lira shouted.

She reached up and spun the command sphere, causing the front of the ship to lift. Like an enormous floating sword, it lifted over the terrified giant. But the stern was still moving too fast, and the prow lifted. Hanging from the walls, the four struggled to retain their grip as everything in Bartoth's chamber pulled free and crashed into the front of the ship.

"Look out for the cliff!" Willow cried.

"Nothing I can do!" Lira shouted, striking the controls in vain.

The prow of the ship dragged through the snow until it struck the cliff from which they had surveyed the fortress. The front stopped. The back did not. It continued to flip forward, causing all four of them to tumble about.

A keening of metal sounded, like the vessel wanted to shear apart. Then the top of the ship hit the cliff and teetered over, falling forward. Light jumped onto the ceiling as the ship fell, accelerated by the gravity sphere that still sought to lift the ship upward, which was now downward.

"Brace yourselves!" Lira shouted.

The ship struck hard. Light's fingers were torn free of their grip and he slammed into the window, his vision briefly blurring as the ship settled. He collided with Water and ended up entangled with Willow, and he instinctively held her as the ship began to slide.

"We're going into the canyon!" Water shouted.

Light recalled the ravine behind the ridge. Plunging for several thousand feet, the canyon cut into the earth between two mountains, carved by ages of runoff. Hundreds of feet across, it had looked impassible until Water crafted a bridge from melted snow. Light recalled squinting into its depths, wondering how cold the water was at the base.

Upside down and sliding backwards, the ship slid into the canyon. Lira leapt to the floor and grabbed the command sphere, spinning it as the ship accelerated, the front of the ship swinging violently upward as the back fell.

The back of the ship collided with the opposite wall, a jarring impact that knocked Light from his feet. Then the ship slid down the icy stone. Lira managed to activate the ship's power, and the hum from the back of the vessel mounted, gaining an ominous whine. The power in the gravity sphere climbed, slowing their descent, but only at the rear of the ship. Like a sword balancing on the hilt, it began to swing to the side. The front of the vessel accelerated, scraping across stones and ice on its way into the depths.

"The power isn't reaching the prow!" Lira shouted.

"Light!" Water cried. "If you don't brace us, the impact will kill us all!"

"I can do that!" Light called.

He pulled on the vestiges of sunlight streaming through the window and bent them around the chamber, shaping into a pile of pillows. More and more he crafted, his friends bouncing off the pillows as they rolled with the careening ship.

"I don't think that's what he meant!" Willow cried.

"How else would I cushion the landing?" Light shouted.

The back of the ship came to a halt as the front of the ship continued to accelerate. Lira pushed past the pillows, desperately trying to press symbols. Some seemed to work because they briefly slowed, lights igniting across the chamber. Then they sputtered and went dark, and like a pendulum, the front of the ship swung down into the canyon as the stern came to a halt.

The ship spun a circle, the blade falling into the canyon. The prow of the ship bounced off the canyon walls, hurtling towards the icy waters. Light caught a glimpse of the rocks as the swordlike prow cut across the river just inches below the surface. Light was pressed into the mountain of pillows as the prow of the ship swung upward, bouncing off a protrusion of rock on its way upward.

It slowed as it continued the spin, and Light experienced a moment of sheer bliss when the ship reached the apex of the arc. He, his friends, and the pillows floated up around them, all seeming to come free of the pull of the earth.

Willow's hair floated around her head, framing her beautiful features. They locked eyes and Light grinned, an expression she returned. He wanted to reach out to her, but the fleeting moment passed too quickly, and suddenly the gravity sphere gave out, and the entire ship—now sideways—dropped into the river.

They hit the water in a titanic splash, wetting the canyon walls. The stubby left wing dug into the water, dragging across the submerged stones as the current carried them downstream. Unable to right itself in the confines of the canyon, the ship remained on its side.

Through the window, Light spotted the beautiful sunset, and realized the river was headed for a waterfall. He pushed the pillows aside and smacked Water on the face. His brother glared at him, until Light pointed to the upcoming waterfall.

"Is that bad?"

"Yes, it's bad!" Water nursed a bruised arm. "Everything in this blasted ship is bad!"

"I'll try to stop us," Lira said, shoving her way through the pillows of light to reach the command sphere. The controls were on the side, but she managed to get a grip on a section and reach for a rune.

"Wait," Willow called.

"For what?" Lira asked.

"See the boulder on the left side?" She pointed to the protrusion of rock sticking out from the canyon wall. "If you can pulse the power, the ship will push out of the current and the wing will catch on that."

"As good a plan as any," Lira said, eyeing the approaching waterfall. "But it's going to be close."

Still on its side and half floating, half dragging, the krey ship scraped and scratched its way down the canyon, until the prow reached the waterfall and pushed into open air. Lira slammed her fist onto the rune. The gravity sphere whined and tried to rise, but the ship was on its side, so it slammed into the canyon wall. The left wing swung into the protrusion of rock just as the ship began to teeter over the waterfall.

Clang!

The water pushed the ship forward, but the wing had snagged on the boulder, swinging the prow against the canyon wall. With thirty feet of the ship extending into space, it ground to a halt, and water poured over the top. For several seconds none dared to breathe, and then Light thrust his hands into the air.

"Epic," he breathed.

"Anyone hurt?" Water groaned.

"Best. Flight. Ever."

"We crashed," Willow said.

"That's why it was the best," Light exclaimed, grinning from ear to ear.

"At least we aren't dead," Lira said.

"We aren't far from Bartoth's army," Water said, gingerly sitting up and rubbing his back. "They're certain to come looking for us."

"Probably," Willow said. "And goblins are excellent climbers." She leaned against the window and peered upward. "It won't take them long to get here."

"But how do we get out?" Lira asked.

"I could—"

"No!" all three said in unison, and Water shook his head. "Why don't you let us find a way out of the ship. You could go see the inside of the ship. Wouldn't you like to see that?"

"Are you certain that's wise?" Lira examined a shallow wound on her shoulder.

"Can he do any more damage?" Water asked.

Lira shook her head. "This ship will never move again."

"I would like to see it now that I know it's a ship," Light mused. Without waiting for permission, he bounded towards the opening.

"We don't have much time before they get to us," Water was saying, his voice tense. "We need an escape route."

Light barely heard their tense conversation, his excitement driving him through the sideways rooms to reach the main hall of the ship. The moment he stepped into the empty interior his eyes widened in awe.

Bartoth's buildings were devastated, little more than piles of rubble on the side of the ship. Nothing had been fastened securely, so everything had fallen. Much of the rubble was underwater, and the left wing was fully submerged. The gravity sphere floated above the water, purple light emanating from its surface.

The hull was rent and broken, with gaping holes in the surface. Water poured in through the lower ones, sending mist into the air. The higher breaches allowed a view of the canyon walls, and a few glimpses of the sky.

"Incredible," he breathed, and dived into the mess, hurrying to the gravity sphere to see it up close.

A distant *clang* sounded as giants threw boulders at the ship, but he only had eyes for the fifty-foot sphere. He'd never seen anything so lovely. He cast wings and flew to the top of the sphere. He stared in awe until he spotted purple light seeping from the edge of the sphere. Several feet above, a protrusion from the roof seemed to point at it, almost as if it had once been connected. And that's when Light had an idea . . .

Chapter 29: A Short Flight

Light stood on the gravity sphere and approached the broken connection. The tube extended from the outer hull to where it had been severed, the metal jagged at the breach. The interior of the tube was pure white, with marks only made by bursts of light.

Growing excited, he conjured an extension out of light and shaped the magic into a tube that connected the broken tube to the gravity sphere. The response was instant, and the purple light flowed up the tube, turning white as it entered the hull.

"Light!" Water called. "What are you doing?"

"Nothing," he said quickly.

"Just don't touch the gravity sphere," Lira called. "If you crack its shell the entire ship will implode."

"I won't," he said, annoyed.

He actually didn't know the meaning of *implode* but disliked showing his ignorance. Figuring it didn't matter, he returned his attention to the other broken tubes extending towards the gravity sphere. With great care he conjured more tubes, connecting each that had been severed to the sphere.

"They're almost here!" Willow called.

"I found the Gate," Lira said, pushing stones away from the glass surface. "It looks damaged, but intact."

"I thought you said it was sealed."

"Maybe I can get it to work," Lira called.

"Make it fast," Willow said. "Because the horde is descending upon us."

"Light," Water called. "Get over here and help me seal the opening."

"In a moment," Light said.

"Light!"

But he wasn't listening, and Willow snorted. "You did tell him to go play."

"Sometimes I wonder how we are part of the same being."

Water rubbed the back of his neck as if he were in pain. Light grunted in irritation and tuned out their conversation. Each time he connected a tube, he felt the energy course through the ship. Lira had said the gravity sphere powered the vessel, and the power was converted into an unusual type of light that passed through the tubes.

He cast spider legs and attached them to his body, allowing him to scale the sideways ship to reach the broken sections of tubing. Entire sections were missing, but it was obvious what they were intended for.

"What's he doing?" Water asked.

Lira spared him a look. "I'd say he's trying to repair the ship."

"Can he do that?"

"No," Lira said flatly.

Everyone but Light looked up when a face appeared in an opening. The goblin howled, and others followed the order, the diminutive creatures dropping through cracks in the exterior and sliding down the curved hull.

"Willow!" Water called, attempting to use the river to seal the openings.

"I'm on it," she said.

She drew her crossbow from her shoulder and took aim, firing bolt after bolt into the goblins trickling through the openings. Water sealed them as quickly as he could, but anti-magic spears were shoved into the aquaglass, causing it to disintegrate.

"This isn't working," Water called. "How's the Gate coming?"

"I need more time," she said urgently, pressing the runes embedded into the borders of the mirror.

"Light?" Water called. "We could really use your help."

"I'm busy."

Water scowled, but Light had found a diagram on the hull. It was embedded into the krey material, explaining why none had managed to tear it away. It detailed a diagram of lines with strange symbols. He tilted his head to the side and grinned when he realized it depicted the lines of tubes and their placement.

The spider legs carried him aloft and he continued to cast tubes to repair the gaps. Urgent calls for his help went unheeded, and he barely heard the sounds of battle. A spear clattered off the hull near his head and he absently swatted it away, his magic disintegrating from the attempt. Annoyed, he recast the tube, and was rewarded to see the channel of light continue to the next breach.

"*Light*," Water groaned. "I know you like puzzles, but I could use your help."

Water and Willow were being driven back, the sheer volume of goblins pushing them away from the hull and onto the piles of rubble. They streamed through the cracks like ants, descending and joining the swelling ranks. Lira cast strength and picked up the Gate, carrying it to the front of the ship. She placed it inside a room away from the volley of spears.

"How close?" Willow called, fending off dozens of attacks.

"I think I've got it," she said.

A door was ripped upward and a giant pushed into the opening, dropping into the water with a splash. A large maul and a shield were dropped to him, and he charged Water and Willow. Both exchanged a look and retreated, diving into the room where Lira frantically worked on the Gate. She cried out when the glass shimmered.

"I broke the seal!" she shouted.

217

"I got it!" Light shouted at the same time.

Excited, he used the spider legs to reach the helm chamber, dodging the annoying spears that were thrown in his direction. He heard a shout and then a shattering of glass, and then he entered the helm chamber. He allowed the legs to fall away and then leapt to the command sphere, activating it with a touch. He'd seen Lira's motions when she'd tried to fly the ship and sought to imitate her actions.

Water and Lira tumbled into the room, and Water used his magic to pull a section of wall to barricade the opening. More water flowed around the barrier, as spears pushed into the gaps, the magic causing its bindings to disintegrate.

"Light!" Water shouted. "Willow is—"

"I did it!" Light cried.

Lira rounded on him. "YOU ARE NEVER GOING TO FIX THE SHIP!"

Light finally looked up. "I was just solving the puzzle," he said in confusion. "See?"

He spun the sphere—and the ship began to rise. Water and Lira fell onto the pile of pillows, both shouting in surprise. But Light was too excited to notice. The ship lifted free of the river, the goblins screaming, the giants bellowing as the ship climbed, it's passage smooth as silk.

Abruptly irritated that the ship was sideways, Light spun the command sphere to the side—and the ships wings slammed into the canyon walls. Light was knocked into the pillows, and the goblins in the hull tumbled about like potatoes in a sack.

Laughing, Light rose to his feet. "Sorry," he said. "I forgot about the canyon."

Lira and Water fought to climb free of the pillows as Light reached for the sphere and spun it forward, sending the ship grinding out of the canyon. Then he turned it to the side and righted them. Floating forward, the ship seemed to glide like a feather on the breeze.

Water streamed from the cracks in the hull, and wind whistled into the interior. Many cracks were large enough for goblins to pass, and the creatures hurried to flee the openings. Light turned to Water and Lira, beaming.

"I solved the puzzle."

"You fixed the ship," Lira said, her voice tinged with awe. "I don't believe it."

"Light was always good at puzzles," Water said, pushing the pillows aside and gaining his feet.

"But he fixed the ship," Lira said. "It would have taken a hundred krey engineers a month to do that."

"We're not out of the woods yet," Water said, stepping to the doorway. "There's a horde of goblins in here with us."

"Really?" Light craned to look. "When did that happen?"

Water laughed, the sound tinged with disbelief. "Light, you are incredible."

"Thank you," he beamed.

"Do you mind if I fly the ship?" Lira asked.

Light stepped out of the way. As Lira claimed the command sphere, he craned his neck looking for Willow, but didn't see her. Confused, he turned to Water, but he was pointing to the opening at the rear of the chamber, the doorway leading to the sound of enraged goblins.

"I think we made them angry."

"I can't believe this thing is flying," Lira said. "You connected all the power lines. How did you know how to do it?"

A touch of red lit Light's cheeks. "It was nothing," he said.

"Lira?" Water called from the doorway. "There's a few hundred goblins gathering to storm this room."

Lira reached out and hesitantly touched a symbol. It sputtered and glowed to life, and a dull clanking came from the interior of the ship. Light jumped to the doorway in time to watch the entire bottom of the ship open. Rubble, goblins, giants, all plunged into the sudden gap, and fell into the frigid lake at the base of the waterfall.

They surfaced, sputtering and trembling, and clawed their way to the snowy banks. Many cast baleful glares at the now hovering ship. Others shook their anti-magic spears and hurled curses.

"Thanks for joining us!" Light called.

The doors clanked shut and the ship banked to the side. It accelerated, but the entire vessel began to tremble. Lira slowed the ship and they flew across the landscape. Delighted with the smooth vessel, Light craned his head to look out of the window.

"I still can't believe it," Lira said.

The admiration in her voice caused Light to blush. "It was just a puzzle."

"I'm sorry," Lira said. "I thought you . . . dimwitted and foolish. I was wrong."

"I'm childlike," Light said. "I'm not a child."

Water began to laugh, the amusement rolling off him as Lira joined in. Light grinned, pleased that his friends were happy, and that the ship was in the air. It wasn't as fun as the first flight, but the view was stunning. But where was Willow?

"Willow!" he called, stepping back to the door. "You really should see the view from up here!"

"Light," Water said, his smile fading.

"What?" Light asked, not catching the soberness to his tone. "Why isn't Willow coming?"

"I fixed the Gate," Lira said softly.

"That's wonderful," Light exclaimed. "We can Gate directly to the Forge of Light."

She shook her head and then grimaced. "A giant managed to get inside the ship and attacked us. Willow was—"

"—Dead?" Light cried and leapt through the door.

He dropped to the floor and dug through the rubble that had failed to fall out when Lira had opened the hole. He shouted Willow's name, again and again, unwilling to believe she had perished. He was terrified that he would find her body yet unable to stop his search.

A hand caught his shoulder and he shoved it off. "Willow!" he shouted. "Answer me!"

He spotted shards of silver and rushed to what had once been the Gate. He dug through the section of rubble, the shards cutting his hands but he refused to stop. Then suddenly it was like the sun had been extinguished, and he crumpled to his knees.

"Please," he pleaded. "Please answer me."

"Light," Water said urgently. "I don't think she's dead."

"What?" Light looked to his brother in hope.

"She was knocked through the Gate," Lira said.

The relief was bright and overwhelming, but then followed by a piercing sadness. Willow was alive, but she was gone. And he would not get the chance to repair the damage that had been done. He slowly came to his feet and looked to his brother.

"But I was dangerous."

Emotion welled in Water's eyes and he nodded. "I know. But it's going to be okay."

Light looked to the shattered pieces of the Gate, tears of golden light leaking from his eyes. He'd lost her, and by the time he found her again, it would be too late. Water placed a hand on his shoulder and guided him back to the helm chamber.

"Come on," he said. "Let's see what this ship can do."

Light trudged behind his brother, wishing he had Willow instead of a stupid flying ship.

Chapter 30: Secrets

"You sure you're ready to do this?" Jeric asked.

"I used to run miles through solid stone," Elenyr said irritably. "It shouldn't be hard to take a walk through the castle."

Jeric grinned and held the door for her. She thanked him with a glance and carefully walked through the portal, exiting her quarters for the first time since the attack. Each step hurt, and she shuffled her way toward the stairs, cursing her weakness.

Other guest quarters bordered hers, all vacant, while a long window lined the opposite side of the corridor. The window provided an unbroken view of the interior of the citadel. Suspended five hundred feet off the surface of the lake, the fortress was held aloft by the great tree.

Unlike traditional fortresses, the queen's castle at Ilumidora was segmented into three parts. One enormous limb held the queen's wing. Built of several levels, turrets, and sweeping exterior staircases, the wing was reserved for the queen and was the most heavily guarded. Aquaglass walls merged seamlessly with smaller branches.

The second wing contained the guest quarters, the soldier barracks, and the training halls. The last wing faced the main entrance to the city, and contained the great hall, the kitchens, and the servant quarters.

Stairs of aquaglass and curving corridors connected the three wings and provided access to the host of gardens, overlooks, and smaller turrets that interspersed the segmented fortress. All looked onto the open heart of the citadel, where a fountain cast water into the sky. The plume of water fed the floating streams that circled the fortress, the water cooling the air and providing defense.

The beauty was not lost on Elenyr as she worked her way down the corridor to the stairs. She caught the handle and gingerly stepped down, wincing as the action put weight on her injured leg. Jeric hovered behind like a nervous mother.

"How are you doing?"

"It hurts," she said, wincing again. "A lot."

"The healer said it would take weeks to fully heal," Jeric said. "Your flesh was burned all the way to the bone."

"It feels like it," she said, pausing to catch her breath.

"Do you want me to carry you?"

She laughed sourly. "I've had my share of injuries over the years, but I'd grown accustomed to being impervious."

"We can all be killed," Jeric said.

"And this has been a reminder," Elenyr said.

She resumed her agonizingly slow pace. The stairs led to a small garden, which boasted a tree sheltering a host of flowers. Benches were placed close to the tree, allowing a view over the balcony into the fountain.

Fatigue washed over her and she gritted her teeth, forcing her feet to carry her to the nearest bench. She held the railing of the balcony as she did and tried not to let it look like she required the support.

"You don't have to pretend you are well."

She sank into a seat with a sigh. "I have not felt such weakness since I was poisoned in my final days as oracle."

"Weakness reminds us that we're mortal." He leaned against the railing and watched the fountain.

"And what are your weaknesses?" Elenyr asked with a smile.

He grinned and rotated to face her. "You don't already know?"

"Perhaps," she said.

His smile widened. "It is the weakness of Serak we must discern."

"True," she said.

Neither spoke as both pondered the question. She breathed deep of the cool air, relishing the moisture and breeze after being caged in the guest quarters for so long. The thought brought a touch of anger at Serak and Carn.

"Have you discovered the identity of the lightning mage?" she asked.

He shook his head. "I searched the queen's records but haven't found anything yet."

"It doesn't make sense. Lightning magic is volatile and dangerous, making it challenging for a young child to control."

"Unless the magic was bound when they were a child," Jeric said.

"Indeed," she replied. "But such power is held in awe by many. Who would hold such a secret?"

"Someone with a darker purpose," Jeric said.

"Or someone who doesn't want to compromise their position."

Jeric cocked his head to the side. "Someone poor would make easy coin with such ability, but someone with wealth would not have the need."

She sensed the truth to the words, and absently rubbed her arm, soothing the ache. A gust of wind carried a sprinkle of water from the stream flowing above their heads. The approach of winter would eventually freeze the fountain and the streams, a sight she'd always enjoyed, for it made the fortress seem like an object out of a dream.

"Will you tell me one of your secrets?" she asked.

He raised his eyebrow at the turn in conversation. "Why?"

225

"We always kept so many secrets from each other," she said. "I just want to know something you kept from me."

She expected him to ask for a secret in turn, or maybe refuse outright. He remained silent for some time and she didn't intrude on his thoughts. Nearly dying had focused her on what mattered, and since she'd seen how much Jeric had worried over her, she wondered what had kept them apart.

"Secrets are dangerous," he finally said. "We both know that."

She looked away, wishing she had not asked. For a while there was only the sound of wind and water. A servant passed them, followed by a pair of guards talking about the kidnapped king of Griffin. When their voices faded Jeric sighed.

"I'm sorry," he said. "I've spent a lifetime guarding who I am. It's hard to show it to another."

"Even me?" she asked.

"You kept your own secrets."

She met his gaze and then looked away again, unable to bear the weight in his gaze. She recalled their relationship. She'd loved him, but for a long time since had felt only bitterness. Now that he was back in her life, she found regret in her heart. It made her wonder if love and happiness were possible for people like her and Jeric. Or were there just too many secrets?

"You should be out there," Elenyr finally said. "Finding Serak."

"Not Wylyn?"

Elenyr pointed to her bandages. "Serak is the greater threat, at least for now. If the Order were destroyed, Wylyn would be greatly weakened. The opposite is not necessarily true."

"I do not think Wylyn would appreciate being told she is weak."

"Nevertheless," Elenyr said, "we both know it is true."

"It is for now. But if she succeeds in opening the Gate, our fate is sealed."

She eased back onto the bench. "How is it that you always know so much about everything?"

"I just listen," he said with a smile.

She knew they were avoiding the issue but didn't want the disappointment of talking again. The ache in her leg and arm seemed to have increased, and she didn't want it to spread into her heart. But she still needed to know something about Jeric, a reason why they could not have worked.

"Say what you will to the masses," she said. "But you're not fooling me. You knew about me and the fragments before I ever arrived. You knew about Wylyn, the ancients, and the krey. You knew of rebellions and conflicts, everything before I ever told you. You knew of the outcast rock troll, Bartoth, and even who sought to kidnap the young King Numen so many years ago. How?"

"How about I tell you what Mind and Fire said when they sent word."

"They sent a message?" Elenyr asked. She straightened, and then immediately regretted the movement because it pulled on her stitches. "When did it arrive?"

"When you were sleeping," he said. "They insisted I not wake you."

She scowled, annoyed that they had come and she'd been asleep in bed. "What did it say?"

"They'd gone to Herosian to speak to the king, but he had already been taken. In all the chaos they spoke to the king's historian, who'd heard of the Shard of Midnight."

"What did they learn?"

"Nothing," he said. "They managed to infiltrate an Order location in Talon's Well, a village a day's ride north of Talinor."

"I've been there." She nodded, eager for more.

"They managed to interrogate Heres, a senior acolyte, but didn't want to speak in a message."

"That's all?"

"They also found a record of a very old tapestry depicting the Shard of Midnight."

"And they are searching for this tapestry?" She knew he'd deflected the question, but she could not resist the information about her fragments.

"I do not envy the ones Mind interrogates in his search," he said wryly.

She raised an eyebrow. "He always said he couldn't breach your mental shields."

"Doesn't mean I haven't felt battered," he said.

She grinned and recalled Mind in his youth. The young man had endlessly sought to catch her unawares and break into her thoughts. She'd had practice as an oracle, but Mind was gifted, and he'd inadvertently forced her to become stronger.

"Wylyn seeks the Shard of Midnight," she mused aloud. "Do you already know her purpose?" She smiled, her expression reminding him of her unanswered question.

"Of course," he said. "She wants to capture all the living races and enslave them."

"Will you stop teasing me with morsels of information?" she groaned. "I'm stuck here while my family is in danger. Tell me something real. Are Mind and Fire coming back?"

"This afternoon," he replied.

Her smile spread across her face as she thought of seeing the fragments. After everything she had endured, she yearned to make sure they were safe, to see them with her own eyes. Jeric grinned.

228

"That's the smile I was hoping to see."

"Did you have to hold that information for so long?" she asked irritably.

"Yes," he replied.

She frowned. "That's why you encouraged me to get out of the room."

"Maybe."

This time her smile was for him. In the morning he'd encouraged her to bathe and exit the bedchamber for a walk. He'd been rather insistent, and now she knew why. He didn't want the fragments to see Elenyr so damaged, guessing that she would not want to look so weak. It was a small kindness, but meaningful.

"Thank you."

He claimed the seat at her side. "I don't like seeing you like this either."

"So you do care."

"That's not one of my secrets."

With a tentative glance his way, she carefully placed her head on his shoulder. She hoped he would not withdraw, and after a moment his arm wrapped around her back. Then she spoke in a murmur.

"I've never been more scared."

"For you or your sons?"

"Both," she admitted.

"You're the strongest woman I've ever met," he said softly.

"I fear Serak is stronger than I," she whispered.

It wasn't her biggest secret, but it was the most haunting. She hadn't meant to speak it, but right now she felt raw and vulnerable, and she needed Jeric. She felt fear, more than she had in a long time, and she felt like her courage had abandoned her.

"The first time I saw you," he said, "I saw a woman of courage, one capable of conquering any foe, any injustice, all by force of will. It's your most attractive trait."

"You still believe that?"

"I will always believe that,' he said.

She shifted her arm to get more comfortable. She didn't believe it herself, not after what Carn had done to her. But it helped that Jeric believed in her. Her physical wounds were healing, but it was the ones beneath that hurt the worst. Despite everything, Jeric's faith in her had not wavered, and a tiny bit of that wound began to knit.

Chapter 31: Welcome Visitors

Elenyr and Jeric talked for the next few hours, but several times the conversation lapsed into silence. Both made her feel better. She rose and stretched and enjoyed the garden, relishing the fresh air. Shortly after, an elven guard appeared, and she recognized him as Kendel of the House of Runya.

"Captain," Elenyr said, rising to her feet.

"I believe these belong to you," he said.

Elenyr smiled, her eyes settling on her two oldest sons. "They do indeed."

She embraced Fire and then Mind, the contact strong yet timid, as if they were afraid to break her. Both lingered, and she saw worry in their eyes, despite their matching smiles. She then resumed her seat on the bench, wincing as it forced her to bend her leg.

"You can walk," Mind said. "That's an improvement."

"I walked thirty steps and I'm exhausted," Elenyr said with a sigh. "Hardly an accomplishment."

Fire pointed to the bandages on her arm. "You survived a lot of damage."

"I should remember not to play with wolves of lightning."

Jeric laughed, but he was the only one to do so. Mind and Fire both stared at her, shock and then anger tightening their features, followed by a spark of worry. Elenyr was surprised to see the expression on Mind, who rarely felt such an emotion.

"Has she been resting?" Mind asked.

"I haven't left her side," Jeric said. "She's doing much better."

Jeric's words were light, like he was commenting on the weather, or a particularly nice flower. She rotated in her seat to regard him. He'd reclaimed his spot on the rail, and she noticed he looked much less haggard than he had the day she'd awoken. At one point when he'd been resting, Elenyr had asked a nurse about him.

"He won't sleep and hardly eats," the healer had said. "He must care for you a great deal."

Elenyr had smiled, but inwardly balked at the statement. Jeric had shown his colors and loved adventure more than her. Or so she had supposed. But in the following days she'd looked at him in a different light.

"So you like Jeric now?" Fire asked, folding his arms.

"You are as blunt as ever," Jeric said with a laugh.

"He saved my life," Elenyr said.

Her eyes settled on Mind, who regarded her with worry in his gaze. In his early years he'd disagreed with her, the arguments frequently growing heated. But he had never doubted her ability. Now was the first time a foe had come close to killing her.

"Are you certain you are well?" Mind asked.

"I am healing," Elenyr said. "And that is enough . . . for now."

Fire chuckled. "That's the Elenyr I know. So when do we get to go after Serak?"

"First I want to know what is happening." She shot Jeric a look. "I have been kept in the dark by my healers."

"They said she needed rest," Jeric said defensively.

"I've rested enough," Elenyr said.

Fire grinned. "After leaving Mistkeep we managed to follow several of the members of the Bloodsworn."

"I picked out their locations and we've begun mapping the Order's halls," Mind said. "A challenge made difficult due to Serak's structure.

232

Each hall is isolated, with no knowledge of other halls. Only the senior acolytes understand, but they have been given pendants that block memory magic."

"Serak is prepared for you," Elenyr said, motioning to Mind.

His jaw tightened, betraying his irritation. "Despite his precautions, we've managed to identify a number of their locations. Would you like to see the map?"

There was a nudge at the corner of Elenyr's consciousness, and she allowed Mind to share the image of the map they had been building. Tinged with his insights and assumptions, it depicted small halls scattered throughout the southern lands. At Jeric's request, Mind shared the image with him as well.

"We haven't explored north yet," Fire said. "But we did learn a location."

"Have you ever heard of a place called Beldik?" Mind asked.

Elenyr frowned, wondering where she'd heard the name. It was not recent, of that she was certain. Somewhere in her archives? She winced as she realized her treasured books were probably nothing but ashes.

"I do not know the name," Elenyr said.

Mind regarded her with a strange look, bordering on distrust. She frowned, confused as to expression, but Mind shifted and the expression vanished. He swept a hand to Jeric, but the elf shook his head.

"I have never heard of it," he said.

"Wherever it is, Serak religiously guards the name." Fire absently sparked a flame in his hand extinguished it, a habit from his early years of training.

"It's important," Mind said. "That much is clear."

"You've learned a great deal," Elenyr said. "But what is most significant is what you have not discovered."

Fire extinguished the flame in his palm. "What do you mean?"

233

"The Order does not have a presence anywhere close to the Oracle's Refuge."

"He is cautious," Mind said. "He does not want Senia seeing his future, so he keeps his distance."

"Then that is exactly where we should go." Elenyr began to rise but Jeric placed a settling hand on her shoulder.

"You aren't going anywhere."

"Are you going to stop me?" Elenyr asked.

"A child could stop you," Jeric scoffed.

A wave of fatigue washed over her and she settled back onto the bench. "As much as I am loath to admit it, Jeric is right. You and Fire should visit her and learn what you can."

"And if she gives us someone to hunt?" Mind asked.

"Go where she indicates," Elenyr said. "But do what you can to send a message back to me."

"We will," Mind promised.

They spoke of other things, and she absorbed the information, relishing the view of the battlefield. In becoming the Hauntress, she had not set out to be a soldier, but that is what she became. Now she was forced to sit in a healer's tent while the war raged.

Eventually the sun began to set and Mind glanced to the sky. "We should go."

"Give my regards to Senia," Elenyr said, feeling weak after the day outside a bed.

They said their farewells and Elenyr watched them go, noticing the odd tinge to Mind's gaze, as if there were a chasm between them. The fragments had always looked up to her, respected her, and now they saw her as mortal. She hoped their worry wouldn't turn to a lack of faith.

She yearned to depart with them and hated the injuries she had sustained. But she had no choice. When they were gone, Jeric offered

234

her his hand, and she reluctantly accepted it. Even slower than before, she worked her way back to her quarters and to her bed. But instead of reclining, she rotated to face Jeric.

"Why did you not meet me at the inn?"

He chuckled wryly. "That was always something I loved about you. While other women speak many words, you only speak what matters."

"When you've lived as long as I have, you learn that time has a great deal of meaning. Now answer the question."

He sighed and looked away, his gaze on the city. "I did come."

Her forehead creased. "No. I was there. I waited for several days."

"I was in the trees outside," he said quietly.

She stared at him. "You came, but left me wanting? Why?"

He was quiet for several moments. She wanted to demand answers, but recognized the conflict written on his face, the worry, the doubt, and a trace of regret. Jeric was never serious, his features always bright with amusement. But not now.

"Did you really want to be married?" he asked.

"I showed up, didn't I?"

"When we talked about it, you were so excited," Jeric said. "You talked about surprising the fragments and wondered how they would react. I'd never seen you so happy."

"And you didn't feel the same?" she challenged.

It hurt to voice what she'd held for so many years, but the words escaped her lips like they'd pushed their way out. She wanted to take them back but it was too late, and Jeric regarded her with his arresting blue eyes.

"I did," he said. "Right up until the moment I saw you standing on the balcony, waiting for me."

"*That's* when you left?" she demanded. "I never took you to be *afraid*."

All the anger, regret, and betrayal seeped into the words, so harsh it seemed to grate across her teeth. She clenched a fist, willing the emotions back into the cavity from which they'd sprung, but they proved the stronger.

He looked down at his hands, and then out to the city. Then he grimaced and leaned in to take her hands. She wanted to pull away but there was a tremble in his fingers that held her fast. She waited.

"I *was* afraid," he admitted.

"You were afraid to be tied down," she said. "You thought all your adventures were going to end and saw me as a death knell to your wondrous life. Did you not know me? Did you not see how much I did with the fragments? Your adventures would not end. They would just be with me, but I suppose that was the truth. You were frightened to give up your freedoms."

"Do you have any idea what you looked like when I found you in Cloudy Vale?"

His question startled her from her anger. "What does that have to do with you departing?"

"Everything," he said. "I saw you there on the balcony and saw what lay ahead. I foresaw you and I battling with the fragments. I imagined adventure and conflict—all the greater because I was at your side."

"Then *why?*"

"Because that was not all I saw," Jeric said. "You fight with an iron will, but if you ever faced an enemy stronger than you, I knew you would not retreat."

"You were afraid of me dying?" She laughed at the notion. "I'm the Hauntress. I don't die easily . . ."

Her voice failed her and she looked down at her wounds, realizing that for all the conflicts she'd fought, all the foes she'd faced, she'd never really seen herself as mortal. Not anymore. But Jeric had seen her mortality, and feared.

"You were afraid for me," she said softly, her voice tinged with recognition.

"My love for you ran deep," he said, "and the prospect of watching you die in my arms was agony I could not describe. And so I remained outside the inn, afraid of entering, afraid of what the future would hold. I thought I was doing what was best for both of us. For years I clung to that belief, thinking that we were better on our own. But then I saw you in Cloudy Vale . . ."

His features twisted and he looked away, and Elenyr was highly conscious of the shouts of vendors in the city. She wanted to tear her eyes from Jeric but could not. She'd thought the worst of him for a lifetime, only to see the truth.

"You were so . . . broken," he finally said. "And I realized in that moment that regardless of our fates, I wanted to be with you. I *want* to be with you."

"I've lived for thousands of years," Elenyr said softly. "And you made me believe I could love again. I wish you had told me your fear."

"I'm not very good at that," he said with a wry laugh, as if trying to lighten the mood. "And there is a great deal about me that you do not understand."

She shifted on the edge of the bed, the act turning her leg. She sucked in her breath and Jeric rose to his feet. "I'll get the healer. It's time for her to check on you, anyway."

He strode to the door, but paused with his fingers on the handle. Then he looked back and met Elenyr's gaze. "Is there still a chance for a life of adventure together?"

She stared at him and finally shrugged helplessly. "I don't know."

"That's better than a no." He smiled, almost looking like his former self.

The door opened and shut and Elenyr was left alone. She wished she'd known the truth, but now she feared it was too late. Jeric was older and the threat they faced was even more dire. From the beginning Elenyr had worried that she wouldn't get much time with Jeric. He was over nine hundred years old, after all. But now she wondered if the season of their romance had come to an end.

Chapter 32: The Lost Soldier

Willow tumbled through the Gate and rolled to a halt. Her vision swimming, she forced herself to her feet and stumbled back towards the mirror, one thought on her mind. She could not leave Light alone.

Just as she reached the mirror, she heard the shattering of glass, and the silver liquid hardened. She desperately pushed the runes on either side of the mirror but nothing happened. Dread rose within her body.

"Light!" she shouted, her words echoing off stone walls, obscuring her ensuing whisper. "*I'm sorry.*"

She had no way of knowing if they were alive or dead, but even trapped in a krey ship, the fragments of Draeken were very dangerous. And Lira was a body mage with the power to manipulate every aspect of her physical form. They could survive anything, even a horde of goblins bearing anti-magic spears.

She hoped.

She clenched her eyes shut and slammed her fist against the mirror. What had she done? She'd been battling the goblins and the giant's hammer had come down, forcing her to dive away. But Lira had sought to pull the Gate out of the way, and Willow had tumbled right through, the force of the giant's hammer casting her out of the battle.

Anger spilled into her blood, but her instincts forced her to turn and evaluate her surroundings. She stood in a circular chamber illuminated by a central light orb. Gates lined the exterior, each with a symbol placed above. Four corridors exited the room, but the walls contained no windows. The room was otherwise empty, so she walked around the exterior, examining the symbols.

Some were obvious, like the one bearing a symbol of the Raven, the thieves guild in Keese, or the one depicting a black blade with a purple eye on the pommel, the symbol of the dark elf nation. Others were less obvious, like the Gate with the symbol of an ancient dwarven shield, and another with a curling flame.

The crossroads allowed the Order of Ancients to connect across Lumineia. She'd heard whispers of the Gate Crossroads from her time in the Order and would have had access to it after becoming a senior acolyte. But all that had been destroyed on her way out of Kordune.

A smile crossed her lips as she thought of Light, and what he'd done in the krey sphere. His unpredictability frequently resulted in more conflict, but it always brought a smile to her lips. She grimaced, and realized she already missed him. Had she made a mistake in ending their relationship?

Realizing she needed to focus, she shoved the thought aside. She could return to the Order in the Deep, but they probably already thought her a traitor. Or she could seek to connect with one of the other fragments, or even the Hauntress.

She prowled the room, examining all the Gates, gauging how well she would be received on the other end. Many she knew to be guarded, others she did not recognize. Entering could very well risk execution, or at the very least, capture.

Four corridors extended away from the Gate crossroads and she explored as far as she could down each. One led to storage rooms, while the other three were occupied by Order members. She spotted Bloodsworn assassins and Raven thieves, as well as a group of higher-ranking Order members.

She caught snippets of their conversations, most of which revolved around the recent destruction of Mistkeep. The current of anger in their voices was evident. The Order had thought the swamp fortress impregnable, yet Shadow and Light had left it in ruins.

What was news to her was the death of Relgor. Apparently, he'd been at Mistkeep, and Shadow had loosed a scaled reaver on him. Tardoq alone had survived the encounter. Hearing approaching footsteps, she ducked into a storeroom and let a pair of senior acolytes pass.

"Wylyn was furious when Serak told her," one said.

The second grimaced. "He was her son."

The first shook his head. "From what I hear, she was more angry at his failure than his death."

"What is Serak going to do?"

"Haven't you heard what Serak did to the Hauntress? Carn wielded his lightning magic like a blade and . . ."

Willow attempted to follow them but another came from the opposite direction, forcing her to remain in place. In the darkened opening of the storeroom, she frowned. Killing the Hauntress would be devastating to the fragments, especially Light.

Regret filled her chest and she leaned against the cold stone, wondering how she would get back to him. Or if she even could. It would take weeks to reach the northland again, and they would be long gone by then. She needed an alternative.

When the hall was empty she retraced her steps to Gate Crossroads. With so many moving through the chamber it was only a matter of time until she was discovered. She needed to pick a destination that gave her an advantage. But which one was the very question for which she lacked an answer.

The Hauntress might be dead, the other fragments were scattered, and the Order knew her to be a traitor. She could return to the dark elf capitol of Elsurund, and the Gate leading home was an inviting prospect. But doing so would take her further from the kidnapped queen, with no prospects or leads. The Order would probably seek her death and she would stand alone.

She scowled, feeling the press of time, and again circled the chamber, coming to a halt in front of those she knew, only to discard them for various reasons. Half of the destinations she didn't recognize. Of the remainder, some were heavily fortified, while others posed no benefit. Several times she returned to two Gates sitting next to each other. Herosian and Ilumidora.

Although distant from the north, they were the undeniable hub of the world. As capitol of the elven nation, Ilumidora was the center for nearly everything magic, while Herosian contained the mightiest military. The Griffin capitol of Terros had the largest trade and industry, but she guessed that Herosian and Ilumidora were her best options, sad as they were.

She released a harsh breath, feeling like she'd suddenly been cast adrift. She was a soldier without a war, with no way of getting back to Light or her primary task. So how could she get back into this fight?

Her choice was made when the Gate leading to the Deep flickered, and a group of dark elves appeared with a quartet of dwarves. Willow, halfway across the room, had no place to hide, so she feigned purpose.

"Oris," she said, nodding to the leader of the dark elves.

"Willow," he said, coming to a halt. "I didn't expect to see you here."

"I'm on assignment from Serak," Willow said coolly.

"Are you certain?" Oris said. "Because rumor has it you stood with the imposter."

Oris made a motion to those at her side. They spread out, subtly palming sword hilts. The four dwarves, all fire mages, drew heat from the air, preparing their magic. Willow stood her ground but shifted her hand to fall casually on her hip.

"Rumors rarely have truth," Willow scoffed.

"I also have orders from Princess Melora herself," Oris said. "And she wants your tattooed head on a spike."

"Many were tricked by the false Serak," Willow said.

Claiming to have been tricked by Light was risky but seeding her foes with doubt was her best chance at avoiding a conflict. She spoke with confidence, letting her words drip with anger, as if the imposter's trick had been a personal affront.

"The Kordune hall is little more than rubble," Oris said. "And you left with the false one."

"I thought he was Serak," she said, folding her arms. "He said we had threats inside the Order and we could not trust other acolytes."

"He made the *princess* wash the floor," one of the elves said. "You didn't figure it out then?"

Willow bristled at his tone. "Serak has done many things we did not understand, such as recruiting a guild of thieves from the surface."

Oris scowled and glanced to his own companions, all of which were members of the Ravens. Willow had chosen her words with care. When Serak had made clear his plan to bring the Ravens into the fold, many had disliked the order, causing miniature rifts in the ranks until Serak had ended the doubt with a lethal stroke.

Oris remained silent, a touch of doubt creasing his features. Willow managed to keep the smile from her face. If she really was on assignment by Serak—the real Serak—then striking at her would invite swift retribution. But if he believed her and was proven wrong, the consequence would probably not be lethal.

"She did just become a senior acolyte," one of the smaller dark elves said.

It was an excuse and Oris pounced. "Perhaps you are right. If the Queen's Hand clears Willow, who are we to argue?"

This shifting of blame did not go unnoticed by the four dwarves, who scowled and muttered to each other. They did not accept Willow's answers, but they didn't want to shoulder the risk either.

It was obvious Oris wanted to believe her, if only to save his hide, but he'd probably seen firsthand the destruction in Kordune, and he was loath to disobey the orders he'd received. Disobedience for a senior acolyte could be as dangerous as striking another acolyte. He needed a push.

"How can I know *you* are still loyal?" Willow asked.

Oris burst into a laugh. "Me? I've always been loyal to the Order."

"And what is your assignment?" Willow accused.

"I cannot disclose that."

She closed the gap. Dark elves drew their swords in a whisper of steel but she ignored the weapons pointed at her and poked Oris in the chest. "And you expect me to believe that? I wager those with you have accepted your orders on faith, never questioning if you are a spy for the queen."

A few cast suspicious looks at Oris, the tension in the room growing with every word. But the more doubt she deflected to Oris, the less would fall upon her. It was a dangerous play, but it might let her back into the Order, at least long enough for her to figure out where to go.

"Perhaps we should just let Serak decide," Oris said evenly.

"Indeed," she replied, retreating a step.

Oris glared at her, and then motioned the others to continue to their destination, the Gate bearing the dwarven shield. Willow folded her arms and waited, her features fixed with suspicion.

The group passed her by and Oris activated the Gate. But just as he went to step through, another Gate shimmered and Tardoq himself appeared, followed by two women—Wylyn and Princess Melora. The two were deep in conversation, and hardly looked up at the standoff except to acknowledge their presence. Then Melora's eyes settled on Willow.

"You!" she snarled. "I'll have you cut to shreds for what you have done!"

Willow's gambit was over. One look at Oris's triumphant expression made that clear. Her only choice now was to escape, quickly, before they trapped her. Unfortunately, Oris's forces were between her and the two Gates she'd thought were her best options. Realizing she would have to fight her way out, she drew a whip and a sword, the ink pooling into her hands and turning solid.

"Princess Melora," Willow said coolly. "Have your bruises healed?"

244

She had a moment to savor the princess's abject fury, red igniting the grey in her skin, her eyes burning with hatred. Then Melora jerked a hand to Oris, her words a cold proclamation of death.

"Kill her."

Chapter 33: Two Traps

Willow snapped her whip and flicked her blade, baring her teeth in a snarl. Oris had nine with him, four fire dwarves and five dark elves, and they quickly moved to surround her, closing the circle so Tardoq stood on one end. One leapt for her back and she snapped the whip in his face, forcing him back, blood trickling down his cheek.

"How many of you will die with me?"

Her taunt was meant to stall, but Oris raised his hand to issue an order. Instead, it was Wylyn that spoke.

"Hold your ground," Wylyn said, regarding Willow with interest.

They all froze, and Melora swiveled to face her. "Why would you spare her life?"

Wylyn ignored her. "You are the inked one, and tales of your abilities are wondrous indeed, but I wonder if you are as dangerous as the rumors imply."

She pointed her sword at the krey woman. "You'll see soon enough."

Wylyn chuckled and shook her head. "It is always surprising how those who have never been slaves can stand so defiant."

"I could kill you as easily as I could them," she said, using her chin to point at Oris.

"Try it," the dakorian said, hefting his hammer.

"This is Tardoq," Wylyn said. "My Bloodwall."

"I know who he is."

Willow spared the armored soldier a look. At ten feet in height, he would be taller—and larger—than even Queen Rynda. Bone plating grew out of his flesh, providing natural armor that covered his body. Some bore spikes, others were smooth. Two horns grew from his head. Willow would have expected eyes of brutality, but instead they conveyed a deep intelligence.

"Then you know what he is capable of," she said. "He is more than a match for you, but as much as I would enjoy the display, I like my son's idea of selling you to the Bone Crucible. To that end, I might give you one chance at life. Come willingly, and I will see that you are unharmed until the Crucible."

"*Unharmed?*" Melora's voice went up an octave. "She helped the fragment of Light impersonate Serak. She must be made an example of."

"Are you questioning me?" Wylyn asked, her voice turning dangerous.

"No," the princess said hastily, dipping her head. "I just think Willow deserves her chosen fate. And Serak—"

"Is not your master," Wylyn said, her voice gaining an edge, her eyes spinning with red.

Melora glared at Willow, and for an instant Willow thought the woman's anger would get her killed. Tardoq shifted his feet, his hammer rising a few inches, but ultimately Melora dropped her gaze, and Wylyn turned to face Willow.

"Now, what do you think of my offer?"

One of the dwarves was yanked into the ancient dwarven Gate, his cry of surprise extinguished as he passed through the mirror. All eyes turned to stare, but it was as if he'd just disappeared. Then another was yanked off his feet and hurled into the Gate.

"Stop," Tardoq snarled, pointing his hammer at Willow. "Or I will smash your bones to powder."

"I'm not doing anything," Willow said, raising her sword and whip.

"Liar!" Oris shouted and took two steps towards her before he too was yanked from sight.

One by one Oris's command were sent into the Gate. Bewildered, Willow cast about for any sign of the attacker, but there was none. Then she squinted and spotted a thread of what looked like smoke pulling the latest victim through the Gate.

Oris re-appeared, bellowing Willow's name. His voice died when a body collided with his. He released a grunt as an armored dwarf crashed into his face, and both tumbled through the Gate. Melora barked an order and the group spun, seeking threats, but a small crossbow bolt came from the darkness at the edge of the chamber and struck the light orb illuminating the room.

Glass shattered, and the room darkened. Lit only by the light from the Gates, the gloom heightened the tension. Shouts were hurled, and Willow heard hands clawing at the ground before the rest of Oris's force were sent into the Gate like trash.

Tardoq held aloft a small sphere which he tossed into the air. It burst with light that flooded the room—revealing a person standing next to Willow. Tardoq growled and spun his hammer, pointing the glowing weapon at the new threat.

"Shadow," he spat. "I was hoping for a second fight."

"The room was getting rather crowded," Shadow said casually. "You don't mind if I thin the herd?"

Someone attempted entering the chamber from the Gate, but they bounced off an invisible band, knocking them back the way they had come. Shadow smiled and turned to Willow, inclining his head in greeting.

"A pleasure," he said. "But I admit, I was not expecting to see you here."

"An unfortunate accident," Willow said, never taking her eyes of Tardoq, Wylyn, and Melora.

Then Willow noticed Wylyn's expression. She did not appear surprised, and her expression bordered on pleased, her eyes settling on

248

Shadow with a possessive glint. Almost as if she'd known Shadow would appear.

"Shadow," Wylyn said. "It's good to see you."

"Were you expecting me?" Shadow asked.

"Our meeting was no accident," Wylyn said. "In fact, I was informed that you were stalking this very hall, waiting for me to arrive."

Shadow groaned in annoyance. "You lie to save your pride."

"Would a liar know that you arrived through the Gate to the Deep?" She pointed to the Gate bearing the symbol of Elsurund.

Shadow's eyes narrowed. "A fortunate guess."

Princess Melora looked between Wylyn and Shadow in confusion. "What's going on?"

"Shadow was sent to the Deep after the events at Mistkeep." Wylyn's motioned to Shadow. "He was supposed to meet up with the fragment of Light but found that Light and Willow had destroyed the Order's hall in Kordune and fled. So he returned here, hoping to intercept me." Her smile was smug as she turned to Shadow. "Am I wrong?"

Shadow folded his arms. "Relgor was smug, too . . . before I killed him."

Her lips tightened. "I have many sons."

"Is that a challenge?" Shadow asked. "Because I don't mind killing them all. Unless Willow wants a few?" He raised an eyebrow to her.

"I don't even know what's going on," Willow said.

"Did you know Willow would be here as well?" Princess Melora asked, the sullenness in her tone making Wylyn bristle.

"I am not required to report my plans to a slave."

Shadow laughed at Melora's expression. "She's like a prized bull that just realized there's a dragon in the room."

Wylyn inclined her head as if it had been a compliment. "At least you know your—"

"This is awkward," Shadow said, wincing. "I was referring to Tardoq. Did he tell you *everything* about that night in the swamp?"

Willow listened to the exchange, confused by the words, but grateful she'd been fortunate enough to land in the midst of the conflict. She may not have known the intrigue, but she knew which way to point her sword.

"Speak your business so we can get to blades," Willow said.

"You're no fun," Shadow pouted.

Wylyn regarded the two of them with sharp distaste. "My patience wears thin. Your ally in the Deep was an informant for the Order and detailed your plans."

"Perhaps I trusted the wrong person," Shadow said, frowning. "Yet you only brought Tardoq? I'm offended."

"Don't be," Wylyn said. "If I were here to kill you, you'd already be dead. I wanted to deliver this."

She withdrew a small orb and tossed it to Shadow. He caught it, and glass revealed the image of a weaver laboring over a loom, her young son acting as assistant. He scowled, a current of rage appearing on his features before he controlled the emotion.

"They are not part of this."

"They are now," Wylyn said.

"Who are they?" Willow murmured.

"No one important," he muttered.

"You and your fragments have been a major obstacle to my plans," Wylyn said. "But I still believe you can be sold, as my son believed. Once I break you, I can bring the rest into my hands."

"You think I'm going to betray my brothers?" Shadow asked, incredulous.

"Serak already killed the Hauntress," Wylyn said. "And I won't hesitate to kill a few slaves."

A Gate opened and a group of humans entered. Wylyn snapped at them to leave and they hastily did, returning the way they had come. Wylyn never took her eyes from Shadow. Although Shadow's features were annoyed, Willow sensed a tension about him that was typically absent in the cavalier fragment.

Manipulation was a powerful tactic, especially if it succeeded against the fragments. If Shadow did follow Wylyn's command, he could very well destroy his entire family. Including Light. Once again she had the feeling she was fighting in a war that was far too big to understand.

When Shadow did not respond, Wylyn raised a hand to Tardoq. "Kill the mother and her child. Make certain it's painful."

"As you command," Tardoq said with a smirk.

"I can just hide them before Tardoq gets there," Shadow said.

Wylyn smiled as if she'd gotten what she wanted. "So you *do* care about them."

"Who are they?" Willow hissed.

"The family of a friend," he said.

"You don't have friends," she replied.

His jaw tightened. "I know."

"I'll give you a few days to think it over," Wylyn said. "But know that krey explosives are hidden in their house. If you attempt to help them escape, they will never see another sunrise, and your pet assassin will blame you."

Shadow regarded her until he folded his arms. "What do you want?"

"You can't be considering this," Willow said.

Princess Melora crowed with delight. "The infamous fragment of Shadow, finally brought to heel like a dog. This is a day I will cherish."

"Nothing is ever enough for you, Melora," Shadow said, all his customary amusement gone. "You were a princess fated for a crown, but you had to join the Order, hoping for even more power. Your insatiable hunger will be your undoing."

Melora's features darkened and she took a step forward, but Tardoq's hammer fell into her path, a reminder of who was in command. She trembled with fury but Wylyn seemed amused by Shadow's condemnation.

"You have the wit of an Empirical son," she said. "But sadly you lack the breeding. Come to the Herosian castle in six days' time. Midnight. You'll find me in the king's quarters."

"Where's the king?" Willow asked.

Melora smirked. "Another throne lies empty."

"And if I don't come?"

"Do you really need me to explain it to you?" Wylyn asked.

"What about Willow?" Melora growled.

"You want to kill her?" Wylyn asked. "Be my guest."

Wylyn folded her arms, making it clear Melora would face Willow alone. The woman regarded Willow, the anger blending with fear. Shadow laughed at her failure to fight, the sound a scathing taunt.

"You may depart," Wylyn said.

"I can't believe you're letting them go," Melora seethed.

Wylyn's chuckle was filled with menace. "It matters not where they stand, for Shadow knows he's on a leash."

Still feeling like she'd stepped into a conflict she didn't understand, Willow looked between Wylyn and Shadow, but Shadow did not speak. Catching Willow's arm, he dragged her towards the Herosian Gate, and without hesitation stepped through. Willow cast a glance at the entirely too smug krey, and then followed, wondering what had just occurred.

Shadow led them through the Herosian Gate. Leaving the crossroads behind, they stepped into a richly adorned room that bespoke wealth and pride. Fine silks covered the walls, the fabric rustling in the breeze. A quartet of guards were present, as were Black and Cutter, their masks in place, their weapons in hand.

"You may depart unscathed," Cutter said. "This time."

Disconcerted by the peace, Willow held her tongue as she and Shadow were escorted from the noble's home, across the grounds, and shoved into the street. The steel clanked shut, and Willow turned to Shadow.

"I really hope you can explain what happened back there."

"You landed in a trap I spent a week setting and have no idea what happened?" He grunted in disapproval. "I expected better."

He turned and strode away, and she jumped to catch up. "An hour ago I was on a krey ship in the north, and then I fell through a Gate and ended up here."

"A krey ship?" he asked. "I bet Light enjoyed that."

She grinned. "He did, especially when it crashed."

"I never get the good assignments," Shadow lamented.

"Wait," she said, catching his arm and bringing him to a halt. "You said it was *your* trap, not Wylyn's. I thought she had an informant that told her your plan."

"Do I ever tell anyone my plans?" he scoffed.

"No," she said slowly. "Which means you fed the information to the Order."

"To Wylyn," Shadow corrected. "Serak would have seen through the invitation, but Wylyn is too arrogant."

"And the mother and daughter?" she asked. "Are they real?"

253

"Of course," he said. "It wouldn't have been believable without them."

Willow grappled with the wealth of information. "So you have a friend—and you just handed their family to the Order?"

"Its brilliant, right?" he grinned and strode away.

Willow shook her head in disbelief. "That's unbelievable."

"I know," he said, misunderstanding her sarcasm. "Ready for what comes next?"

She released a long breath, wondering what she'd stepped into. She missed Light, but she'd asked for another chance to get back into the fight. She just never expected it would come from Shadow.

Chapter 34: The Fragment of Mischief

Willow liked Shadow—in small doses. The fragment of mischief was impossible to follow or trust, and he had an irritating habit of always having a plan, one he refused to share because he thought confusion amusing.

"I don't like this," she said for the tenth time.

"You've said that a lot," he replied. "Don't worry. It will be fun."

"It's only fun if you survive."

"I always survive."

She sighed, annoyed that he was right. He really did survive. He might not have had Light's luck, but his arrogance had its own route to victory. Mind may have been the brilliant one, but Shadow was very clever. She still hated his plan.

They stood in an alley across the street from the castle at Herosian. With high towers and thick walls, the fortress was enormous, the largest in Lumineia. Five thousand soldiers were stationed at the fortress, with three times that number positioned throughout the city. Yet somehow, somewhere, Serak had kidnapped the king. And not one of his soldiers knew.

The guards lounged by the gate and at the battlements, changing watch as if it were normal. Lower ranks complained in the absence of the officers, while the officers complained in the absence of the soldiers. All was normal except Wylyn wanted to meet them *inside* the fortress, in the king's very own chambers.

Since departing the noble's house controlled by the Order of Ancients, they had spent four days examining the castle at Herosian, studying the guard, working out their patterns. Shadow frequently departed without a word, returning without an explanation. Many nights she spotted him working on a cloak, and he was surprisingly protective of the task.

Shadow could get into the castle with ease, especially because the king had supposedly given orders for him to be ushered in. Even if they hadn't, Shadow could breach any fortress with his magic. But she was a greater challenge.

Although King Porlin had forged an alliance with the dark elves, many of his soldiers held a traditional fear of dark elves, making it impossible for her to walk inside wearing a guard's uniform. The fortifications were formidable, making it also impossible for her to breach the exterior, at least without help.

Like the city, the citadel was built in rings, each shaped like an octagon. The outer wall was a hundred feet tall, while the four inner walls were even higher. It boasted two entrances, one reserved for military, the rest for the populace. Inner gates connected between the courtyards, each guarded by a quartet of soldiers.

The innermost courtyard contained the castle. The giant structure had three great halls, as well as enormous towers and high, arched bridges connecting the turrets. The tallest turret contained the king's quarters, their destination.

"I could stay out here," she said.

"We both know I need reinforcements," Shadow said.

"You always preferred to work alone."

"Some things change," he replied with a dismissive wave.

She noticed more to his expression, and it aligned with the change she'd noticed in him. He was still cavalier and reckless, but he was also more thoughtful. He'd even brought back food for her after one of his absences. He'd denied it, but the change was undeniable. Still, Shadow didn't really need her, which made her think he wasn't telling the whole truth.

"Ready?"

"If I must," she said.

He grinned and exited the alley. Striding to the main gates of the fortress, he approached the guards. It was nearly midnight, and a half moon cast the street in silvery light. The soldiers allowed Shadow through, and Willow retreated into the alley. Circling south, she worked her way to the moat farther along the wall and reluctantly swam the swift current.

She reached the wall on the dark side of the fortress, where the moonlight failed to reach. Catching a crack in the stones, she held herself in the frigid waters until a thin chord of shadow descended to her. Catching it, she held on as Shadow pulled her up to the battlements.

Five feet from the top, the rope came to a halt. She dangled a hundred feet above the river, waiting as a pair of guards passed above, talking about a woman they had met in some tavern. Their voices hadn't even faded when the rope resumed its course and she clambered onto the top of the wall.

Shadow motioned her to the tower, and she ascended to the top of the turret that connected to another section of battlements. He cast his wings of darkness and soared to the next inner wall, leaving a line of shadow which she used to cross. Dangling above the courtyard, she pulled herself across the rope to reach the second wall.

They repeated the process each time, working their way to the innermost courtyard, where the giant castle resided. There Shadow left her on a balcony of the castle while he retreated and passed through the gates to avoid suspicion. When he returned to her side, they scaled the exterior of the tallest tower, which contained the king's private quarters.

Willow didn't care for heights, especially not when attempting to grip smooth stones. But Shadow's magic allowed her to grip the wall like it was a ladder, and she tried not to think about the drop. The wind blew and she glanced down, regretting the action immediately. Placing her cheek against the cold stone, she looked upward, gauging the distance, wishing the wind would stop tugging at her clothes.

The king's tower extended higher than the other turrets of the fortress. A second tower had been added after and attached to the outside of the main turret. Only forty feet high, the second turret did not reach the ground, and clung to the upper tower like an infant to his mother's side.

Willow reached for the angled beams supporting the addition and leaned backward over the drop. She wrapped her arms around the huge beam, her slim arms trembling. She hated this plan, and still suspected Shadow of an ulterior motive for bringing her along.

"Blasted fragment of Shadow," she muttered as she scaled the beam.

A gust of wind pulled at her cloak and she went rigid, gripping the support with all her might. The emptiness beneath her back seemed to reach for her, caressing her spine, willing her grip to loosen. She shuddered and reached for the outside of the appendage, where Shadow's gloves allowed her to grip the smooth stone. Shadow poked his head into view, nearly causing her to let go.

"What's taking so long?"

"Shadow," she said evenly. "Try not to startle someone clinging to the outside of a building."

"I still think you should have let me give you wings."

"I don't trust you that much."

"You used my ropes," he said.

"Better than your wings," she shot back.

Shadow grinned and leaned outward, casually, like the fall did not frighten him. She cursed his name, but that merely seemed to elicit more amusement. Then he pointed upward, toward the windows on the outside of the addition.

"This addition contains two floors," he whispered. "The bottom is the king's private library, while the top has the king's bedchamber and a private training room. While I'm talking to Wylyn, you can listen from here. Also, do me a favor and grab something from one of the bookshelves."

Her eyes narrowed. "Is that the real reason you wanted me to come?"

He shrugged like it didn't matter. "There's a large glowing shard on a bookshelf. Grab it and put it in your pack. We're going to need it."

"Now I'm stealing from the king of Talinor?" she hissed. "Do I have to remind you that I'm a sworn soldier to the dark elf crown? If I get caught, it could destabilize the entire treaty."

"Then don't get caught," he said.

Before she could respond, he let go and fell down the turret, his wings shaping off his back. He banked away and landed in the courtyard before the darkness folded around him. She released a long breath and reminded herself that Shadow was Light's brother. She couldn't kill him. Then she scaled the exterior of the wall to reach the correct window.

The wind tugged at her cloak as she peered into the darkened interior. As Shadow had said, the room was a small library, lit by a handful of light orbs, all dimmed for the night. The other source of light came from a large shard of pure yellow. Like a crystal of sunlight, it rested inside a darkened glass covering, obviously to prevent the light from flooding the chamber.

The place of prominence on the wall was reserved for the Gate. The mirror was unique, the silver liquid reflecting the room, the border bearing the symbols that chose the destination. The placement was obvious for its proximity to the royal bedchamber, allowing Wylyn a quick exit if necessary.

A doorway opposite Willow's window led to a corridor inside the king's tower. She also spotted a spiral staircase between the bookshelves that led upward, to the king's private bedchamber. She eased the window open and slipped inside. Her boots landed on the soft carpet and she dropped into the darkness beneath the window. Scanning the room, she crept towards the correct shelf before hearing a soft snore.

She froze and sought for the source of the sound. Then she spotted the guard sitting between two bookshelves. He sat in a chair, his chin on his chest. Shadow had said the soldiers in the tower were Wylyn's Order members masquerading as castle guards, but she wasn't about to kill him, just in case.

Voices came from above, and a moment later a door was opened. She heard Shadow's voice, followed by Wylyn's. An order was shouted and the guard in the library flinched. Rising, he feigned vigilance and strode to the stairs, ascending from view. A moment later the door shut, presumably because Wylyn had exited the bedchamber and now stood in the main tower.

Willow approached the strange shard and began to lift the glass, but a burst of light escaped the edge. She dropped it quickly and cursed Shadow's name. Then she removed her cloak and placed it over the glass. With great care, she removed the casing and collected the shard, keeping it wrapped in her cloak for safekeeping.

She retreated to the window, and then hesitated, glancing to the stairs. On impulse she ascended the stairs and entered the king's bedchamber. The room was lavish, with silk trappings on the bed and a beautiful painting on the wall depicting King Porlin with his son.

The door had been left ajar so she crept to the opening, the voices growing louder as she approached. Through the crack she spotted Wylyn standing across from Shadow, Tardoq at her side. Order members were present, as were Cutter and Black. She then spotted Mimic, also at Wylyn's side.

"No more games," Wylyn said, her tone annoyed. "We both know Elenyr survived Serak's attack. I want to know where she is."

"How should I know?" Shadow shrugged and swept a hand to the city. "I've been here, anxiously awaiting our meeting."

"You lie," Wylyn barked.

"I'm powerful, not omniscient," Shadow said. "I don't know where she is."

"Then find out," Wylyn said. "I want to know what she intends, and where."

"I'll need time," Shadow said.

"I'll give you ten days," she replied.

"That's hardly enough time to visit nearby cities and return."

"Then go quickly," Wylyn said. "The clock is ticking, and if you fail to return . . ."

Shadow groaned in annoyance. "I *know*. You'll kill Irenae and her son."

"I won't just kill them," Wylyn said, taking a step forward. "I'll make them die, painfully, stretch out their death until their agony seems eternal."

Shadow's smile was gone. "I'll be back in time."

"I know," Wylyn said.

Shadow's eyes flicked to the crack in the door by Willow, and then he turned and strode to the exit. He departed without another word, a surprise, given that Shadow always liked to have the last word. When he was gone, Wylyn chuckled to herself.

"And so a slave accepts its master."

"I do not trust him," Tardoq rumbled.

"You never trust a slave," Wylyn said. "They are to be used and discarded."

"And Elenyr?" Tardoq asked.

"She has no purpose," Wylyn said. "When Shadow finds out where she is, I will send you to do what Serak could not."

Chapter 35: Reluctant Allies

Willow backtracked her way through the fortress. Her fear remained sharp on the descent, but concerns of what she heard dominated her thoughts. She held her tongue until she and Shadow stood on the street in front of the fortress, where she rounded on him.

"No more games. You said Elenyr was hurt, but nothing more. And why did you need this shard? What's your plan?"

"That's a statement and two questions," Shadow said, his tone disapproving as he turned south. "Which do you want the answer to first?"

"I don't care," Willow said. "I just want answers."

He chuckled at the heat in her voice. "It's a shard of solid magic."

"What do you want it for?" she demanded.

"A gift for a friend," he said.

She came to a halt. "You wanted it for that thing you're crafting."

"Guilty," he said.

"You risked my life . . . for a gift?"

"It was made by Light as a gift for Porlin's father," Shadow said. "And since he isn't here, I needed access to his magic."

She reached for her bag but found it empty, and Shadow was already placing the shard in his own. She scowled at his ease in stealing, but he merely grinned and pointed forward.

"If you'd like the answer to your second question, it's right up there." He pointed to a noble's house further down the darkened street.

"And Elenyr?"

"Serak tried to kill her with a lightning mage. Nearly succeeded."

He said it dismissively, with his usual lack of concern. But she noticed a rigidity to his features, a stillness to his shoulders that bespoke a current of anger. Shadow never showed concern for anyone, but Elenyr was akin to his mother, and the attack had left him with a simmering fury.

"When?"

"Shortly after Mistkeep was destroyed. I didn't think the Order knew she'd survived, but Wylyn made it clear they did. Ready to learn my plan?"

The quick shift in topic reinforced her assumption about his anger, and she decided not to press it. He'd revealed more in the last five minutes than he had since she'd come through the Gate, and she didn't want him to stop talking.

"What do you intend?"

"I plan to kill Wylyn," Shadow said.

She scoffed at that. "She has her Bloodwall, hundreds of Order members, and thousands of Talinorian guards that protect the castle. How do you think to kill her?"

His smile was not kind. "She doesn't know it, but I maneuvered her into that castle so she would be where I could strike."

"You can't think to kill her alone."

"I don't," Shadow said. "That's why we are here."

He motioned to the noble's estate. Unlike the surrounding homes, their destination was crafted in the fashion of the elves, with trees and aquaglass shaping the outer walls. More trees grew on the grounds, becoming towers for the elves that patrolled the branches.

The home itself was built of fine wood and clouded aquaglass, the roof sweeping and pointed. Shaped like a long arc, the house faced a single blue tree at the center, the symbol for the House of Runya.

"Why would they help us?" she asked, but Shadow was already moving toward the wall.

"The House of Runya was founded by Thorilian and Venia," he said. "They were orphans with no house or home in Ilumidora, so they started with nothing. In a single century they built their home here and forged an alliance with King Porlin. Many of the elves in Ilumidora look at Runya with scorn because they make their home in the kingdom of man, but they also fear Runya's growing power."

Shadow reached for the wall and scaled with ease. Although the predawn glow had risen on the horizon, it was still dark enough to use his magic, and so he reached the top of the clouded aquaglass wall. She used the shadowhook he'd crafted for her and joined him on the battlements. From there they slipped into the estate.

"Why are we not using the gates?" she whispered, pointing to the guarded entrance.

"Thorilian doesn't care for me," he replied, bending the shadows to hide them from sight.

"Then why would he accept your plan?" she hissed.

"He likes Elenyr."

With Shadow twisting the shadows to ease their passage, they reached the home and scaled a large pillar, quickly reaching a room on the third floor. Shadow slipped over the railing of the balcony and crossed to the door, where he stooped to pick the lock. The light within indicated someone was awake, and Willow heard the shuffle of a chair, and a pair of voices speaking.

"Thorilian and Venia are intelligent and powerful," he said. "But when they learn the king has been kidnapped and Wylyn sits on the throne, they will agree to help Elenyr."

"Are you certain?"

He shrugged. "We need a small army to get in and strike, and they happen to have the best trained guards in the city."

She watched a pair of guards move from one treetop platform to another, their wary gaze scanning the dark grounds. Without shadow magic Willow would have been hard pressed to breach the estate.

"Every day, Thorilian and Venia stay late to review house business," he whispered as the lock gave a faint click. "Are you ready?"

"I guess," she said.

"Then good luck."

He swung the door open, caught her elbow, and pushed her into the room. The door shut behind her, leaving her alone with two startled elves. She caught a glimpse of finely crafted wood on the floor and walls, of paintings on the walls depicting three sons. At the center of the room, a broad desk had been built for two individuals to face each other. An office for two.

Both elves rose to their feet and drew weapons. Thorilian, by far the largest elf she'd ever seen, resembled a barbarian, and drew a massive sword from a scabbard leaning against his desk. Venia drew a smaller blade and pointed it to Willow.

"You are not the first assassin to come to our door," she said.

Thorilian's lip curled into a scowl. "The others are buried behind our home."

"I'm not an assassin," Willow said hastily, mentally cursing Shadow, who seemed to be chuckling from without the door. "I came seeking your aid."

The two elves had spread out to flank her, and she resisted the urge to draw an inkblade. "I am here on Elenyr's behalf."

"The Hauntress?" Venia asked, coming to a halt.

"A lie to lower our guard," Thorilian said, raising his giant, slightly curved sword. Willow recognized it as a katsana, a heavy blade meant for two hands, yet he wielded it with one.

265

"No," Willow said. "She was attacked by Serak and the order, who had a lightning mage in their midst. She was nearly killed."

Venia lowered her sword a little. "Is she well?"

"Recuperating," Willow said, raising an empty hand to Thorilian as if her tiny hand could stop him creeping forward. "I speak the truth."

Instead of looking to Willow, Thorilian glanced to his wife. "What do you see?"

Venia cocked her head to the side and seemed to stare beyond the walls of their home, her light blue eyes flickering with a white light. Then her expression turned shocked and she nodded her head.

"It is true. Elenyr is in Ilumidora. I've never seen her look so weak."

Thorilian scowled. "It could still be a trick."

"No trick," Willow said. "King Porlin has been kidnapped and Wylyn claimed the throne. I need allies to prepare an assault."

"There have been rumors of his absence," Venia said. "And many claim he is ill."

"You are too trusting," Thorilian said.

"But you trust me," Venia said, lowering her sword. "I cannot see King Porlin with my sight, but we both know strange mercenaries have become his personal guard."

"Who are you?" Thorilian demanded.

"Willow," she said. "I'm a friend of one of the fragments."

Thorilian's scowl deepened. "It had better not be Shadow."

The door burst open and Shadow swept inside. "You remember me? I'm flattered."

Thorilian growled but retreated. He slammed his sword into his scabbard so hard that the sound brought the guard to the door. Thorilian

266

barked an order and he withdrew. Venia too, looked on Shadow with distaste.

"Shadow," she said evenly. "We did tell you that you were no longer welcome in our house."

"Did you not listen to Willow?" he said. "She needs your help."

"*We* need your help," Willow said. "This was *your* plan."

Shadow ignored her. "Wylyn is the last of the outlanders. The other was killed in Mistkeep just weeks ago."

"By you," Willow said.

Shadow grinned but otherwise did not respond. "We need your help to prepare an assault on Wylyn, before she slips through her Gate and disappears again."

Thorilian folded his arms. "You are asking us to assault the king's castle. If we are caught, we would lose our entire house, our freedom. Two of our sons would be imprisoned as well. And that's if we aren't killed."

"Fear?" Shadow asked with a sniff. "I didn't think you to be the type."

Thorilian's features clouded with anger and he grabbed the hilt of his sword, but Venia placed a calming hand on his shoulder. Glancing her way, he settled back into his seat, his glare never leaving Shadow.

"The last time we helped you, our oldest son was exiled from Talinor," Venia said.

"He's now in the royal guard at Ilumidora," Shadow said dismissively. "And by all accounts he is headed for a high captainship."

"He can't come home because of you," Thorilian barked.

"This won't be like last time," Shadow said, and pointed to Willow. "Because we have the inkmage."

"Me?" Willow asked, already questioning the wisdom in enlisting the House of Runya.

267

"Why her?" Venia asked.

"Willow is a high captain and serves her queen," Shadow said.

"Another position to be risked," Thorilian muttered, but Shadow continued as if he hadn't heard.

"She is cautious and smart, and will help you craft the plan."

"So *you* don't get blamed for the failure," Thorilian muttered again, and again Shadow ignored him.

"She knows the Order and will help plan the assault."

Thorilian stabbed a finger at Shadow. "I will not—"

"Husband."

Venia's voice was soft, and Thorilian looked to her. "You can't be considering this," he growled.

"Our house is at risk," she said. "And what I see in Wylyn leaves a chilling terror. I believe they speak the truth, and so we must offer aid."

"But it's *Shadow*," he protested.

"I know," Venia replied. "And we aren't trusting him. We're trusting her."

She inclined her head to Willow, and a weight settled onto her shoulders. Shadow had brought her to the house, planned the meeting so they would follow her in the assault. But if they failed, Shadow would not bear the burden. Willow would be the one they trusted, and the one who had risked their lives and home.

"Willow," Venia said. "When I look upon you I see integrity and courage. We will ally with you."

Willow swallowed. "I will not let your trust be in vain."

"Excellent," Shadow said with a broad smile. "It's great to be friends again."

Thorilian groaned and looked to his wife. "I hate him. I *really* hate him."

"I as well," Venia said. "But let us begin. It appears we have an assault to plan . . ."

Chapter 36: Brothers

The wind blew past Light, pulling at his cloak and hair. His gaze fixed on the horizon, he did not hear Water approach until the fragment took a seat at his side. But Light did not look his way.

"Light," Water said. "You could have picked a better spot to be alone."

"The ship was too stifling," Light said.

"So you decided *outside* the hull was best?"

"It's better than inside," he muttered.

"Not to me," Water said wryly.

Water peered over the edge of the hull, his expression apprehensive. The ship wasn't too high off the ground, and according to Lira, it moved as slow as a broken wheel, but to Light they soared above mountain and valley, each more filled with snow than the last. They flew by a mountain, the snow cracking and tumbling down the slope at their passage.

The holes in the ship made the wind whistle, and patches of girders were visible beneath the skin of the hull. The short flight into the canyon had ripped it apart, leaving it broken and open. Light had used one of the holes to reach the top of the ship.

The sun was just beginning to dip into the mountains, the golden light tinting the snow. Trees were visible farther down, but the mountain range seemed to go for miles, the towering peaks a maze of crags and cliffs.

Light's brothers thought that noonday was his favorite time, but it was actually now, when the sun was just beginning to change color.

With his magic, he could see an abundance of colors, each with their own slight differences in power.

"Did you know I showed Willow all the colors of sunset?" he asked.

"Really? What did she think?"

"It was the first time we kissed."

"I take it she liked it."

Light sighed. "Am I hard to love?"

"Of course not—ah!"

The ship tilted slightly, and Water began to slide on the smooth surface. Light absently reached out and bent the sunlight, attaching Water's pants to the surface of the hull. Water clawed his way back to Light, dragging his body up the suddenly sticky surface, and then grinned.

"Thanks for keeping me from falling. You know how much I dislike heights."

Light lay back on the hull and stared into the sky just beginning to darken. Water sighed and reclined next to him, and for several moments they lay in silence. Then Water pointed to a cloud floating above.

"Do you remember when you wanted to touch the clouds?"

"Elenyr kept telling me no," Light recalled. "But I said the birds could, so I could."

"You should have seen her face when you cast wings and jumped into the air. I've never seen her so speechless."

A smile tugged at Light's lips. "I did touch the cloud, but it wasn't like cotton."

"You sounded so disappointed when you came back down," Water said with a laugh. "We had to remind you that you had just flown."

"I did enjoy that part." Light glanced at Water. He always looked so confident, so self-assured.

"Shadow cast wings that very night," he said. "And I was so jealous I didn't sleep the entire night."

"I didn't know that," Light said, sitting up to look at him.

"I was jealous of you a lot when we were young," Water admitted.

"Why? You were the one with honor, the one Elenyr liked best."

Water sat up as well, sparing the ground a glance before turning to Light. "She loves us all the same."

"That's not true," Light said. "Remember when I burned down her receiving room? She was furious."

"Of course she was," he replied. "But you also helped rebuild it, even if you did shoot nails into the wood with bursts of light."

"I missed the wood and hit Mind," Light said, grinning at the memory.

Light had forgotten all about that day. Mind had been so angry the entire home had begun to tremble, and Elenyr had made Light apologize and embrace Mind. Not ten minutes later, Shadow had stuck another nail in Mind's shoulder, and blamed Light.

"I still did the most destruction," Light said, his smile fading.

"You also learned the most," Water said. "And you brought happiness to the rest of us. We couldn't feel joy, not the way you could, but we felt it just being near you."

"Then why did Willow leave?"

"She fell through a Gate," he said with a laugh.

"That's not what I was asking," he said, annoyed.

"I know," he replied. "But it's weird being the one trying to laugh. When you are sad, it makes me *really* sad."

272

"I just don't understand," Light said, picking at the piece of hull beneath his legs.

The conflict had left much of the hull damaged, with large holes in the material. Lira had said the krey built their ships out of a nearly indestructible material, but time and weather had greatly weakened the ship.

"She wants a family," Water said. "And she doesn't think she can have that with you."

"How can I give her what she wants?"

"You might not be able to," Water said with a sigh.

"I would do anything to be with her." Light hit the surface of the ship to emphasize his point, causing echo inside the hull.

"Would you give up what you are, to be with her?"

"You mean my magic?" He jerked his head.

Water shook his head. "Would you do it, if you could?"

"You know we can't do that," Light said. "Mind told us our magics are threaded into the fiber of our being."

"Still," Water pressed. "Would you do it?"

Light looked to the deepening red on the horizon, wondering if he would do as Water suggested. His magic was everything to him. He breathed it in, used it in every aspect of living. To lose it would be like losing his legs—and being unable to craft legs of light to replace them.

But for Willow?

Just the thought of her made his stomach ache like his chest wanted to cave into his body. "I don't know," Light said. "Would you do that for Lira?"

Water shifted uncomfortably. "We weren't talking about me."

"Why not?" Light asked. "I've never seen you look at anyone like you do Lira. Do you love her?"

"I'm not sure," he said, looking away.

"She can live as long as you," he said. "So you don't have my problem."

"I have another," Water said.

"What is it?"

Water laughed wryly. "I've always liked your directness."

"And?"

He rubbed at his chin. "She's an Eternal, which means she protects our entire world from the Krey Empire. I live here, with you and my brothers, and Elenyr."

"You're going to leave?"

Alarm crept into Light's voice. He'd never thought of the possibility of losing one of the fragments, and the prospect left him terrified. He rose to his feet and began to pace over the top of the soaring ship.

"You can't go—what would that do to the rest of us, to Draeken, to Mind and Shadow. They need your fragment. Why would you even think about such an idea—have you told Elenyr? She would be devastated—"

"*Light!*"

Water was still sitting, but he was pulling on Light's leg. "Please don't go," Light pleaded.

"I'm not going anywhere," Water said. "She can't stay here, and I can't go there."

"Oh."

He slowly sank back to his spot, the magic giving a *slurrrp* sound as it bonded to his pants, holding him fast. They exchanged looks and laughed. Then Light pointed to the front of the ship, where Lira piloted the vessel.

"So you did to Lira what Willow did to me?"

"Not yet," Water said. "I've been avoiding that conversation."

"But you love her," he said.

Water didn't answer for a long time. Light would normally have jumped in, demanding an answer, but the expression on his face made Light sad. The oranges had turned to red, the sun kissing the mountains in the east before he answered.

"I think I do."

"Have you been in love before?"

"Not like this," Water said, a soft smile on his lips.

Light grew excited. "Really? It's about time."

"What's that supposed to mean?"

"You are the good fragment," Light said, patting him on the knee. "So it makes sense that you find a good companion."

Water laughed sardonically. "Sometimes I wonder if we're cursed, if we can never be whole on our own because we are just a part."

"I hope not," Light said. "Because I *really* want to get Willow back. Your suggestion about being dangerous did *not* work."

"I didn't suggest that," Water said with a groan.

"Don't worry," Light said. "I'll still listen to you, even if it causes a krey ship to crash and nearly kill us all."

Water wiped his hand over his face. "I hope you find a way to be with Willow," he said. "For both our sakes."

A scraping sound came from down the curve of the hull, and Lira poked her head through a hole. "What are you doing up there?" she called.

"Having a conversation," Light said brightly. "Want to join?"

"I don't think so," she said, eyeing the host of cracks and holes she would have to traverse.

"The ship hasn't died," Water called.

"Yet," Lira said. "But it's barely holding together. It's only a matter of time until it comes apart."

"Did you figure out where we're going?"

Lira smiled. "I think I did. The Forge of Light is a krey structure hidden far to the east, outside the known lands. At the rate we are going we can be there by morning."

"How did you figure all that out?" Light asked.

Lira swept a hand to the craft. "This ship was one of Ero's and Skorn's first explorer vessels, so it recorded all the potential sites for future constructions. I found one that matches the description of the Forge."

"You're brilliant," Water said.

Light elbowed him in the side and gave him a meaningful look. "Tell her she looks pretty," he whispered. "And that she has nice teeth."

"What?" Water asked.

"What did Light say?" Lira called.

"Nothing," Water said hastily. "We'll be down in a moment."

"Just be careful," she said. "We're a thousand feet up, and you can't cast wings like he can."

Water sighed as Light grinned. Then Lira retreated from view. When she was gone, Water turned to Light. "Did you really tell Willow she has nice teeth?"

"Of course," he beamed. "In the tavern where we first met. Her laugh was so beautiful."

"Only you could pull off such a comment," Water said.

276

This ship lurched, dropping several feet in a heartbeat. Water gripped a shard of hull like his life depended on it, while Light raised his hands and cried out, excited at the sudden drop. When it smoothed out Water looked to him.

"We'd better get down and help Lira," he said.

"Why?" he asked. "We should do that again."

"I would rather *not* attempt surviving another crash," he said.

"But the first one was fun," Light said.

"For you."

"Not you?"

"I was terrified." Water jerked his head as if the memory left a bad taste in his mouth.

The ship trembled again, and then swerved slightly to the side. Lira's voice came from below, a shout, her voice tinged with warning. Water began to drag himself towards an opening, and Light cast the sunset a reluctant look.

"Do we really have to work?" he asked.

"You already fixed the ship," he said. "I know you can do it again."

"I already solved it," Light complained.

"Maybe there will be a new puzzle," Water said.

"Don't tease me," Light said. On impulse he caught his brother's arm. "And I'm sorry about Lira."

"I'm sorry about Willow," he replied.

They shared a smile, the expression sad. Light pulled him into an embrace, clinging to his brother, grateful it was Water and not one of the other fragments. When they parted Water smiled and pointed into the ship.

"No matter what happens, you have me."

"That's because we're part of each other," Light said.

"I know," Water said with a grin. "So I guess you are stuck with me. Now let's go fix the ship."

Light sighed and followed Water into the ship. To his surprise Lira met them when they entered the hull, her expression confused. Water hurried to her, his features growing concerned as he pointed to the ship.

"Are we going to crash?"

"No," she said. "At least not yet. But I found something in Bartoth's notes that I think you should see."

"Why?" Light asked.

Her eyes settled on his. "Because it's about you."

Chapter 37: Missing

Light and Water followed Lira to the helm chamber, and Lira withdrew a large book. Obviously made for a rock troll, the text was also large, the notes in a scrawling script. Light grinned at the writing.

"His handwriting is terrible."

"Not as bad as yours," Water said, bending over the book.

"What does it say?" Light asked, craning his head to look.

"I keep telling you that you should learn all the languages," Water said absently. "It's what the rest of us did."

"Shadow doesn't," Light replied.

"He knows enough," Water said. Then his eyes widened. "This says that Serak is gathering his loyal acolytes and resources to a separate location."

"What does it say about us?" Light asked.

Water pointed to a place in the text. "Seems he's growing distrustful of Wylyn. Apparently Wylyn wants the fragments to herself. Both Wylyn and Serak have sought Bartoth's loyalty."

"Which one would he side with?"

"Serak," Lira said. "It seems he hates Wylyn."

"We all do," Water said fervently, and then pointed to a line of text. "It looks like Wylyn has some sort of plan to manipulate Shadow."

Lira was nodding to herself. "If Serak and Wylyn are fighting each other, they will be easier to conquer."

"But how do we take advantage of the conflict?" Water asked.

Light, quickly growing bored with the conversation, examined the desk of symbols. All were krey and he recognized a few. One in particular stood out, because it was blinking. Curious, he reached out to touch the symbol.

"—and where did you get that thing," a voice said.

"I stole it, of course—"

Lira lunged to the symbol and pressed it before rounding on Light. "Please stop touching things."

"But that was Shadow's voice," Light said. "Where did it come from?"

"It's not your brother," Lira said, and then sighed. "Who knows, maybe it is. How is it possible that you have so much luck?"

"Why would we hear his voice?" Water asked.

Lira pointed to the symbol. "That connects to a krey network. Anyone with a communicator would be able to speak to us."

"And Shadow has one?"

"If it was Shadow, then yes, he would have to have one," Lira said. "But it could be a trap."

"What if Willow is with him?" Light asked, growing excited at the prospect.

Lira looked between them and then shrugged. Light reached for the symbol but her hand closed on his wrist.

"Wait," she said. "Let me jam any other receivers. We don't want Wylyn picking up on this."

Her hands passed over the symbols and then she nodded to Light, who eagerly pressed the rune. Shadow's voice again entered the room, but he only spoke three words before it cut off again. Before Light could question why, his voice returned and then disappeared again.

"What's going on?" Water asked.

280

"He's activating it and de-activating it," Lira said. "And it sounds like he doesn't realize what it is."

"That sounds like Shadow," Water said with a grin. "And he did say he stole it."

Shadow's voice returned and Light shouted his name. For a moment there was silence as someone shifted in surprise. Then Shadow's voice came again, a trace confused.

"Light? Is that you?"

"It is and—"

"Hang on," Lira said.

She manipulated a group of runes. "I'm not sure if this is going to work, but if it does, we'll get to see them—"

The view of the ship gliding over the snowy mountains evaporated and was replaced with a room in an elven home. Shadow recoiled in surprise and dropped what he held—a small spherical object that clattered to the floor, briefly causing Light's body to flicker.

Delighted, he looked down at himself, and realized the communicator projected the image of himself, as well as Water and Lira. He reached to his stomach and felt it, but the projection could have passed through his body.

"Epic," he breathed.

"What is this?" Shadow asked.

Lira swept her hand to herself. "We are being projected using your krey communicator."

"My what?"

"That," Lira said, pointing to the orb on the floor.

"I told you not to steal it."

Light turned and spotted Willow standing across the room. Seized with excitement, he sprinted towards her—and collided with the side of the helm chamber. Knocked backwards, he rubbed his forehead.

"We're still on the krey ship," Lira said. "Our images are just being projected into their room."

"Oh."

His voice was so forlorn that Willow smiled. "It's still good to see you, Light."

He smiled broadly before remembering their last conversation. "You as well," he said tentatively.

"How did you get a krey communicator?" Lira asked.

"Stole it from Wylyn the last time we met," Shadow said.

"How many times are you meeting with Wylyn?" Water asked in surprise.

"Twice a week," Shadow said. "She thinks she has me leashed."

Water and Lira exchanged a look. "Bartoth seemed to think Wylyn would *actually* do that."

"I can't be manipulated." Shadow leaned back in his chair with a smirk. "I don't care about anything."

"True." Light grinned and realized his missed Shadow. He could be irritating, but he always made things fun.

"You're still on the krey ship?" Willow asked, walking around the room to stand beside Shadow.

"Light fixed it," Water said. "We're flying to the Forge of Light now." He briefly shared their escape from the canyon.

"I would have liked to see that," Shadow said.

Light flushed. "It was just a puzzle."

"Which you solved," Willow said with a smile.

"What happened to you after you fell through the Gate?" Light asked, eager to hear what had happened.

She briefly related her encounter with Shadow, and subsequent meeting with Wylyn. Then she described their plan to attack Wylyn, and their alliance with the House of Runya. Light noticed they stood in a room of polished wood paneling. A broad window revealed the setting sun, while elven paintings adorned the room. It seemed to be a receiving room for private quarters, with the customary couches and a crackling fire in the hearth. When she finished, Light pointed to the book.

"We learned that from Bartoth's book. Seems Wylyn and Serak are at odds with each other, and Wylyn plans to use Shadow against the rest of us. She is gathering allies in the Order of Ancients."

"You sound smart," Shadow said. "What happened?"

Light pointed to Water. "It was his idea."

"Jeric will want to hear of this," Willow said. "His message said he would arrive tomorrow."

"Jeric is there?" Light asked, perking up and looking to the door. "What's he been up to?"

"Taking care of Elenyr," Shadow said. "Serak tried to kill her."

Light looked up. "Is she well?"

"She survived," Shadow said. "Jeric is coming in her stead as we prepare our assault—"

"How bad was she hurt?" Light demanded.

"Light," Shadow said in irritation. "Your legs are inside a couch."

Light looked down and squeaked in surprise. His legs passed right through the couch. Distracted, he reached down but his hand also passed through the material. Then he realized Shadow had said it to distract him and glared at his brother.

"I hate it when you do that."

Shadow grinned. "But it's so much fun."

Light cast a rod of light and raised it, but Lira caught his arm and shook her head. "Swing that, and you'll break our ship, not him."

"What assault?" Water asked.

"Four days' time," Shadow said. "I'm to meet with Wylyn again but we're going into the castle with a small army. We intend to kill Wylyn."

"An assassination," Lira said.

"You sound disappointed," Water said.

"She's my responsibility," Lira said. "And I'm not there."

Light caught Willow's eyes and murmured, *I'm sorry*.

"Me too," Willow said softly.

"I miss you."

"I miss you, too."

His image flickered and for a split second he saw the interior of the krey ship. Then the room returned. Water and Lira began to speak in tense voices but Light stepped closer to Willow and lowered his voice.

"I was afraid you died on the other side of the Gate."

"I was afraid you died in the krey ship," she said.

Willow glanced over Light's shoulder, her features concerned. Water and Lira sought to talk to Shadow more but the image flickered again. Annoyed, Light reached out and touched the rune again, returning the image.

"I wish I could kiss you."

Willow looked away. "Light, you know what I said."

"Doesn't change what I feel."

"I do wish you were here," Willow said softly, reaching to touch the projection of his chest. "I don't trust Shadow as much as you."

"Hey!"

"Shadow," Water groaned. "We're running out of time. We need to know—"

"I'll find a way to reach you before your assault," Light promised. "All we have to do is get to the Forge of Light, rescue the queen, and use the Gate to reach Herosian. Then we can go after Wylyn together."

"Is that all that keeps us apart?" she asked wryly.

"For now," he said.

The image returned to the helm chamber and Light called to Lira in irritation. "Will you stop doing that?"

"I'm trying," she said. "But we're losing the connection."

The room returned with the beautiful Willow looking up at him. While Water and Lira hurried to talk to Shadow, Light reached out to touch Willow's hand, imagining her soft fingers on his. Willow looked up into his eyes and he smiled.

"Promise me you'll be safe."

"I promise," she murmured. "I'll see you before the assault."

"I look forward to it," Light said.

The projection died and the ship lurched. Light, his hand still where Willow's had been, closed his eyes, afraid that the rift between them would not be repaired. Seeing her had only reminded him of her decision, and the ache in his chest returned in force.

"What happened?" Water asked.

"I'm not sure," Lira said, reaching for the controls. "Something cut off the signal."

"Wylyn?"

"I don't think so," she said. "I'd guess it's something on our end. One of you should check the gravity sphere."

Light craned his neck to look into the belly of the ship and spotted several of the tubes on the walls breaking. Sparks and bursts of power appeared. Then another broke, spilling energy onto the floor.

"I think you should see this," Light said.

"Why?" Lira cast over her shoulder. "What's happening?"

"I think our ship is dying," Light said.

The ship lurched, but Light could not muster any excitement about the impending crash. He missed Willow and feared the rift between them would become permanent. Then he recalled her proximity, and the openness to her gaze. And a smile gradually returned to his features. Maybe he was wrong. Maybe she would change her mind . . .

"Light!"

He turned to find both Water and Lira staring at him. "What?"

Water groaned. "We need you to fix the ship, quickly."

"Right."

He hurried into the ship and jumped to the first broken tube, his thoughts on Willow. Just a few days. That's all it would take until he could be with her again. Then they would be able to assault Wylyn together. With renewed purpose he set to work, but with every repair, the ship continued to crumble, and he could not keep up.

Chapter 38: Crushed

"There's another one!" Water shouted.

Light leapt across the damaged ship to reach the sparking tube, using his magic to fix the breach. Even as he did, another broke, and then another. Light sprinted from break to break, fighting to keep his feet as the ship veered one way and then the other.

"Hang on!" Lira called back.

The ship entered a slim pass, plowing through the snow before striking a cliff on the right side. Sections of the material ripped off, leaving gaping holes in the superstructure and sending them careening into the region beyond.

Light clung to a section of steel as the ship rocked, and Water groaned nearby, his features twisted in dismay. Through the gaping holes in the ship's wall, Light spotted towering peaks and endless snow. Then Lira managed to slow their spin and bring them back into a stable flight.

"Can we *not* do that again!" Water called.

"I'm trying," Lira replied, "but the ship is coming apart."

"How close are we to the Forge?"

"Two days' walk. An hour's flight."

The ship lurched forward, the prow dropping several feet before Light repaired the next tube. But there were a dozen breaches forming, sparks bursting from every section of the interior hull, spilling onto the floor. The interior lines of power were now almost entirely crafted of Light's magic, but they too were wearing beneath the now-degrading power from the gravity sphere.

"I don't think we're going to last an hour," Light remarked.

"Just don't crash," Water said.

"We might not have a choice on that one," Lira called.

Water caught Light's eye. "We're weeks outside of the claimed lands. If we crash and can't find the Forge, we're going to be stuck out here for a while."

"Can we go sledding down the mountains?" he asked brightly.

Water sighed. "I think there would be plenty of time for that."

Light imagined crafting his favorite sled and careening down treacherous slopes, relishing the scrape of his sled on the snow, the rumble of an avalanche above. He paused in his work, wondering if he should let the avalanche catch him this time.

"Light!" Water shouted. "Now is not the time to get distracted."

Light grinned. "Right."

They continued to sink lower in the sky, drifting toward the earth while the mountains seemed to climb about them. Lira banked them southeast, curving around a rock formation to reach the lower ground beyond, the maneuver sending them over a group of trees.

The treetops grazed the bottom of the hull, catching on the holes beneath, and causing the ship to shudder anew. Like a dying beast, it was breathing its final breaths, and even Light knew they were going to hit the ground soon.

The right side of the ship lost power, and the entire thing fell, hanging by the left. Water cried out as he plummeted through a hole, and he caught the structure at the last moment. His body hung out of the ship, bouncing off trees.

"A little help?" he called.

"Of course," Light said.

He dropped to Water and reached through the hole. Not noticing Water's outstretched hand, he cast a giant wing out of sunlight, the appendage attaching to the right side of the ship and beginning to flap, raising them back to level, even if it went down and up with every stroke.

"That wasn't—"

The right side of the ship flapped upward, nearly tossing Water out of the hole. He hung on and worked his way inside.

"—what I—"

The right side dropped several feet, again almost tossing Water out of the window. He managed to grab another support and drag himself through the opening. He rolled onto the floor, his skin dark, his hands clinging to a section of flooring.

"—meant."

"Oh," Light said, confused. "What did you mean?"

"Whatever you did is helping," Lira called back. "But we're still going down."

Tubes of power were sparking and breaking on all sides. One piece exploded, sending shards of hull into the forest below. A large tree caught on the hull, peeling an entire section away. The ship resembled a skeleton with little skin, and more windows than walls.

"It's getting rather windy in here," Light said, dancing across the supports to reach a beam. "

"It's about to get worse!" Lira said. "You'd better get up here!"

"What about the repairs?" Light sealed a sparking section of tubing. He had to pass it over a wide hole.

"Too late for that!"

The urgency in her voice caused Light to cast wings and jump to Water. He was attempting to work his way across the supports and Light scooped him up, leaping to the helm chamber at the prow of the ship. Landing on the threshold of the opening, he deposited Water on the floor.

"Are we going to crash?"

"Don't sound so hopeful." Lira clung to the controls as one side of the ship flapped to stay aloft. "This isn't going to be as pleasant as the last one."

"The last one was *pleasant?*" Water demanded.

"Compared to this?" She pointed to what lay ahead.

She'd turned into a pass and curved around a mountain, but a shard of stone rose up in the center of the opening. A slim gap was on either side, but not large enough for the krey ship. Light stumbled as the wing he'd cast brushed the narrowing wall, sending snow falling into their wake. Annoyed, he dismissed the entire wing.

The starboard side of the vessel dropped, swinging so quickly that the bottom of the craft struck the mountain. Lira managed to retain her grip at the command sphere, but Light and Water tumbled into the side of the chamber.

"Great idea," Lira called to Light, and he beamed.

The starboard side of the ship hit the snow and scraped across snow and ice as the ship sped toward the narrow aperture. Lira cringed as they entered the gap, both the top and the bottom of the ship bouncing off the mountainside and the stone blocking the way.

Snow fell into the ship, tumbling through the holes and settling on the sparking tubes. Light heard a rumble of thunder and looked up through the window to the clear skies—and then saw the ice and snow coming free on the mountainside.

"I love a good avalanche," he said gleefully.

"Blast," Water said. "That can't be good."

A large boulder was visible in the rapidly expanding avalanche, and it fell directly towards their ship. Lira spotted it and risked pushing the sphere forward. They accelerated slightly, passing through the gap with a *screech* of metal, and suddenly they were free.

"We made it," Water breathed.

The falling boulder hit the rear of the ship, tumbling through a hole and striking the gravity sphere. The response was instant, and the entire ship dropped from the sky. It struck the slope and flopped onto its back. Upside down, it slid down the long slope like a giant pockmarked sled.

"We're in trouble," Lira said. "The sphere has been damaged and we have two minutes to get out before the entire ship implodes."

"And there's an avalanche behind us," Water said, pointing through the door at the back of the room.

Most of the hull was now gone, with just pieces stuck to the structure. The sphere at the back of the ship had a giant crack in it, and purple light seeped from the crack. Wherever the light touched, the structure began to bend inward.

"Is this a bad time to ask what implode means?" Light asked.

"We have to get out," Lira said. "Now."

"Where do we go?" Water asked. "We've got a cliff in front of us, an avalanche behind, and we're sitting in a ship about to implode."

"I still don't know what that means," Light called.

Water rounded on him. "It means the entire ship is going to crumple like an empty sack."

"Epic," Light breathed.

"Not epic," Lira said. "If we're inside, it means your whole body will be the size of an ant."

Light imagined such a crushing. "Won't that be painful?"

"Yes!" Water said.

Light sighed in regret. He would have liked to see the ship implode. Then he pointed to the command sphere. "Do you still need that?"

"No," Lira said. "But that's not going to help us escape this death trap."

The back of the ship was sinking towards the sphere, causing it to drag into the snow, slowing them further. A hundred feet behind, the wall of crashing snow reached for the shrinking ship. Light stepped to the sphere and cast a sword of light, which he used to cut the sphere out of its mooring. He smiled as he held it aloft.

"Are you getting a souvenir?" Water asked, incredulous.

"Yes," Light said. "But it's also useful."

Light pressed the rune on the outside of the sphere, causing it open like it had in Kordune. The outside plates began to expand. Light ducked and crawled through a gap. Water and Lira were forced to follow as the sphere grew inside the chamber. Far too large, it pressed against the walls and continued to swell, until the helm chamber cracked like an egg.

Standing on the platform at the center, Light smiled in awe as the sphere he loved came into shape around them, destroying the helm chamber and the prow of the ship. Water and Lira joined him, and she shook her head.

"Whatever you're going to do, do it now," Lira said, looking back at the gravity sphere.

The gravity sphere had devoured half the ship, the pieces folding onto the sphere and crunching together. Only seconds remained until it reached the helm chamber and the enlarged command sphere sitting on the front.

Light spun the small sphere in his hands, and the command chamber began to rotate, faster and faster. The gravity sphere devoured the next section of ship, now just a dozen feet from the exterior of the command sphere. Then the command chamber jumped free, bouncing them into the snow and sending them hurtling down the slope.

Light looked back and watched the ship get devoured by the gravity sphere—and then the gravity sphere get devoured by the avalanche. Water eyed the avalanche falling behind and shook his head.

"I'm beginning to think it's safer to be with Light than without him."

"I don't *always* put you in danger," Light said.

"Actually you do," Water said apologetically. "It's kind of your thing."

"I do not," Light said, indignant.

The sphere reached a cliff and flew into space, soaring in a grand arc before landing in an enormous pile of snow, sinking deep. Light looked up and saw the avalanche cascade over the top of the cliff and fall upon them, so he spun the helm, but the command sphere was too deep, and spun in place.

The avalanche hit hard, plunging them into absolute darkness. Light cringed as he heard cracking, but the command sphere held, and after several exciting seconds the rumbling came to a stop. With only the light emanating from the runes on the helm and the text around the interior of the room, Light just managed to make out Water's expression.

"I think I see what you mean," Light said.

Water laughed and swept a hand to the snow blocking the transparent material. "We're alive, even if we happen to be buried."

"We made it further than I thought," Lira said. "I think we're just a day out from the Forge."

"So how do we get out of here?" Water asked.

Light squinted into the dark exterior of the sphere, wondering how they could get out of the predicament. The cold was quick to sink in, but around the wheel it remained warm, reminding him of a cozy blanket at night. He yawned.

"Can I take a nap while you figure it out?"

The answer came from both of them.

"No."

When there was no response, both turned to find Light curled up on the floor, fast asleep.

Chapter 39: Serak's Lair

"How soon until we get there?" Light complained.

"We're in a *blizzard*," Water said, his voice tense as he struggled to control his water wheel.

After digging themselves out of the avalanche, Water had crafted his traveling wheel out of snow. Wide enough for all of them and sporting large spikes, the wheel allowed them to speed across the snow. Then the storm hit.

"Are you certain we're going in the right direction?" Light asked.

"Light," Lira said, "we trust you to get lucky and fix whatever havoc you cause. Please trust us to know the direction."

"And trust me to go as fast as I can," Water said, never taking his eyes from the ground ahead. "There are a hundred ravines and holes beneath us, but I can feel where the snow is safe to traverse."

Light tried to keep his doubts to himself, but he vacillated between excited to reach the Forge and find a Gate that would bring him back to Willow, and fear of what he would say when they met again. Lira and Water talked of Serak and Wylyn, but Light hardly spared them a thought. They didn't have much time to get back to Herosian, and Willow.

The wind howled as they sped across the snowy ground, passing around and through rocky formations, the grey stone cold and dark, barely visible in the gloom. Tired, irritated, and hungry, Light watched the snow billow about them as the storm gathered its fury, forcing Water to slow their path. The tempest obscured everything about them, but Water seemed to know where to go, curving their path ever upwards.

"We're on the mountain now," he said.

"How soon until we get there?"

"Asking a hundred times won't get you an answer," Water said.

"I haven't asked that many times," Light protested.

"Eighty-seven," Lira said.

Water and Light both looked to Lira and she shrugged. "I'm good with numbers," she said, apologetically.

"See?" Light said. "Not a hundred."

"Eighty-seven is not a victory," Water said.

The billowing tempest began to fade as they continued to climb, until they rose above a sea of clouds into sunlight. Water and Lira squinted and shielded their eyes, while Light crowed in delight and jumped from Water's snow craft, leaping into the air. Casting wings, he soared upward—and promptly crashed into the snow. Confused, he wiped the snow from his face as Water came to a halt at his side.

"What happened?" Water asked.

"My wings didn't work," Light said, rising and shivering as he shook the snow from his cloak. "And it's *freezing*."

"We're at a high altitude," Lira said. "The air isn't as heavy as what you're used to."

Light gathered the sunlight and wrapped it around his body like an enormous, glowing blanket. Only his head poked out from above, and the wings he'd forgotten to dismiss, which were now misshapen.

"So I can't fly?" he asked.

"Probably not," Lira said, her lips twitching as if she wanted to smile. "At least not with the wings you're used to casting. They'd have to be much larger."

The wind gusted, picking up snow and sending it in flurries around him. He shivered, and attempted climbing back into the wheel, even more miserable than he'd been before. Water protested as his overstuffed frame attempted to enter the small space.

"Light," he said, "you'll have to at least get rid of the wings."

"Oh, right."

He dismissed the wings and then settled into his seat. Water again accelerated them up the mountain, which he now saw was a three-sided peak. Other mountains were also visible in the distance, rising from the storm clouds like enormous teeth.

"When do we get there?"

"Eight-eight," Lira said.

Light grunted, irritated that Lira was counting how many times he'd asked, but couldn't resist Water's laugh. The two-wheeled craft banked to the right, the spiked wheels spinning quickly, sending snow kicking up into their wake. The frigid air washed over Light.

"We've found the mountain," Water said. "Now how do we find the Forge?"

"It's been lost for thousands of years," Lira said. "Only Ero would know its location."

"Could we contact him?" Light asked hopefully.

Lira shook her head. "I have a device that allows me to connect with him, but he wasn't responding."

"Is that normal?"

She gripped her seat as they burst through a snowdrift. "All the Eternals live in precarious circumstances, so we do not activate our communication devices unless necessary."

"So we're on our own," Water said.

Light shrugged. "I'll search the north side, you take the south."

Light leaned out and began casting hawks, their wings larger than normal. One after another he sent them soaring away. Ten became twenty, and then a hundred. Water brought their vehicle to a halt and cast snow foxes on the opposite side, the sleek animals darting away into the snow.

"Don't let your birds get spotted," Water warned.

The small army of animals raced away, combing the surfaces of the great mountain. Some perished on the treacherous slopes, while the rest searched through the snow. Water accelerated, bringing the wheel up the slope.

"Maybe we should split up," Lira said. "It's a big mountain."

"I don't think that's a good idea," Water said. "I'd rather not risk Serak's Order spotting us and attacking."

"Besides, it's freezing," Light said, his teeth chattering.

They searched across the slopes and crags of the mountain, which Light took to calling Light's Bane. Even with Light's and Water's entities their efforts proved in vain, and by nightfall they were forced to dig in and attempt to weather the frigid temperatures of the night.

"What if we don't find it?" Light asked.

"We will," Water said. "We have to."

Light rolled himself in his giant blanket of light, in the house of ice his brother had fashioned to shield them from the wind. He fell asleep wondering how the search would have been different with Willow at his side, and hoped she was well.

For the next two days they searched Light's Bane, working their way higher and higher. The storm below finally dissipated, allowing them to continue their search lower down. On the third day, they found what they sought.

"I expected something bigger," Light exclaimed.

"There's more underneath," Water said, his voice tinged with awe.

"It's just a door," Light exclaimed.

"A door that leads inside," Lira said.

They sat huddled behind a snow topped boulder, looking across a shallow ravine to what was unmistakably a balcony. It pressed out of an enormous bank of snow, revealing a single door. Light had expected a great fortress or structure, but instead it was just a tiny balcony. He turned to Water but his brother stood in awe, staring at the door like it was the city of Ilumidora.

"What do you see?" Lira asked.

"Beyond the door it's . . ." he shook his head, unable to voice it.

"How can you know what lies beyond the door?" Light asked.

"It's *made* of ice and snow," Water breathed.

Light grinned, suddenly eager to see the legendary Forge of Light. He began to step forward but Water caught his shoulder, dragging him back. He shook his head and pointed to the doorway.

"Let's *try* to enter unseen, shall we?"

"Great idea," Light said, and reached to the sunlight.

A quick charm cast a cloak above them that bent the light, shaping an illusion of a snowdrift around them. They weren't exactly invisible, but with the wind kicking up flurries of snow, a slow-moving drift would be difficult to spot. Sufficiently hidden, the trio worked their way down the ravine and back up, an agonizingly slow approach that left Light annoyed and impatient. Water smoothed the snow in their trail.

They reached the balcony but no guards were present, so Water climbed over the railing and stepped to the door. He cast his favorite staffblade, this time, of snow.

"Take it slow," he said, glancing meaningfully to Light. "It would be much better if we know where the queen is before we attempt a rescue."

"And we need to find a Gate back to Herosian," Lira said.

"But hurry," Light said. "We don't have much time before Willow, Jeric, and Shadow begin their assault on Wylyn."

Water nodded in agreement. "Find the queen. Get her out. Escape through the Gate. Return to Willow."

"And don't get angry," Lira said.

"Why do I feel like you are repeating our plan for my benefit?" Light asked, folding his arms.

"Because we are," Water said. "The last two times we had a plan, you destroyed it because you didn't listen."

Light opened his mouth to argue, and then considered their recent escapades. Taking his silence as understanding, Water reached for the handle. The barrier should have been frozen shut, but it only took a small tug to swing the door open, allowing them inside. As Water had said, the walls were pure, hardpacked snow, white and beautiful.

Sunlight managed to pass through the snow, illuminating the short corridor, and causing Light's eyes to widen. The trio slowed as they reached the end, and Light lifted his gaze to the grand hall.

Snow, bound by magic, formed the walls and columns, the sweeping pillars and arches. Ice shaped the windows, allowing the brilliant rays of sun to cascade onto the pristine interior of the great hall.

Statues lined the exterior, each more intricate than the last. Some were dakorians, their bodies covered in their bone armor, their huge hammers hanging from their hands, their teeth bared in a snarl. Other statues were of krey figures arrayed in robes of pure white snow, their features arrogant.

The beauty of the room was captivating, mesmerizing in its simplicity. An entire hall built of white. It was the hall of a king, an emperor, and Light yearned to watch the light dance against the flawless creation.

"This wasn't built by the krey," Lira said, her voice tense.

"So?" Light breathed. "It's beautiful."

"It looks new," Water said. "The snow, the ice, all of it made recently."

"So is this the Forge or not?" Light asked.

"I'd say not," Lira said, and then pointed to the statues. "But it looks like Serak's lair."

Unable to stay still in such a location, Light stepped around his friends, who were both peering down the hall. Deep in a hissed conversation, neither noticed his absence until he appeared in the center of the hall.

"*Light!*" Water hissed. "Get back here."

Light didn't hear him, and reached to a pillar, touching the surprising texture of hardened snow. As a child he'd built many houses out of snow, but this was like a structure of his dreams, and it made him giddy with excitement. Then a hand settled on his shoulder and Lira and Water sought to drag him out of sight.

"Do you even know how to sneak?" Water hissed.

"Don't hide on my account," a voice said.

The trio spun to face the figure now sitting on the white throne. Clad in white armor, the man had a sword of shining aquaglass, the blade pulsing with power. He smiled and rose to his feet, gesturing in invitation.

"It is a pleasure to have you in my home."

"Serak," Water said evenly. "You seem to be waiting for us—"

"Did you build this hall?" Light asked excitedly. "It's stunning."

"Thank you, Light," Serak said, not taking his eyes from Water. "And yes, I built it, in the last two days, in fact. I couldn't very well receive my most prestigious guest into a krey stronghold. I wanted to receive you in style."

"And your servants?" Lira asked. "Surely they are about to attack?"

Serak's smile was disturbing. "Not this time. After all we have danced, it's time you recognize your future ally."

"You?" Water scoffed. "We will never be allies."

"I wasn't speaking to you." Serak smiled and descended from his throne. "I was speaking to Draeken."

Chapter 40: The Shadow Catapult

Willow watched the castle at Herosian from the balcony of the House of Runya. As the only elven noble's house in Herosian, the estate was unique in many respects, and boasted more trees than the other noble's houses, the branches preventing the few stars from lighting the ground.

A flicker of motion in the sky drew her gaze to the keep, where dark wings flew away from the castle. She shook her head, not surprised that Shadow had once again defied Wylyn's command to stay in the fortress. He flew north, undoubtedly to Lorica's family home, the weaver hall of Irenae.

Shadow hadn't told Willow the truth, but she had seen the orb when Wylyn had given it to him. Shadow always abhorred connections, so it hadn't taken her long to figure out the weaver woman and her son were linked to Lorica, Shadow's new friend. The assassin.

She retreated from the balcony to the large room at the top of the House of Runya. Spacious and vaulted, the room had been cleared to allow space for a large table at the center, on which sat a map of the fortress at Herosian.

Venia, mother of the House of Runya and formidable warrior, stood over the map. Dressed for combat, she wore dark green armor and carried her favorite bow on her back. She looked up from the map to glance at Willow.

"Is Shadow on his way?"

"It appears he's going to be late," Willow said.

Venia chuckled to herself as if she'd expected the action. "I have a son like him, unreliable and reckless. But he always comes through in the end."

"Tell me," Willow said. "Why did you agree to this plan?"

Venia turned to the map hanging on the wall behind her. Unlike the one on the table, the one on the wall depicted the whole of the claimed lands in Lumineia. Capital cities were displayed in vivid colors, each a living representation of the city. Terros showed the new district being built, with tiny workers laboring over the walls. It was powerful magic that few knew Venia possessed.

"I have never seen a great deal with my physical eyes," she said. "But I behold much. On the throne of Talinor an ancient sits, plotting enslavement for all. I cannot stand idle while such a threat resides in my home city."

"And me?" Willow asked. "Many of your people abhor my race."

"Especially one with your tattoos," she said with a knowing smile.

The comment cut to the heart of Willow's concern, so she inclined her head. "Indeed."

"Do you know what I see when I look at you?" Venia blinked her blue eyes, the strange tint to the color making them appear abnormally bright. "I see a woman of integrity willing to sacrifice everything for the home she desires."

Willow looked away, uncomfortable with how much that mirrored her doubt regarding Light. Their relationship had always been easy, but she'd destroyed it out of fear. Again, she questioned if she was wrong.

The door opened and Jeric entered with Thorilian, head of the House of Runya. Thorilian had the build of a barbarian, his broad shoulders making him intimidating to any of his own people. Jeric was tall, but still shorter than Thorilian.

"Any news from Elenyr?" Willow asked.

"She is on her way," Jeric said, his tone one of disapproval. "She is still weak, but well enough to travel."

"I wager she wishes she could be present for the battle," Venia said. "She is the protector of us all."

"I suspect she will not arrive until after the assault," Jeric said. "Nor would she be ready to fight if she did." Then he noticed Shadow's absence. "Has Shadow not arrived?"

"He is also on his way," Willow said, secretly hoping he would delay for some time. She still held hope that Light would return in time for the conflict, even if it seemed increasingly unlikely.

"We shall begin without him," Thorilian said. "We all know the risks of this endeavor."

"If we fail, we lose our home and our freedom," Venia said.

"A great risk, a great reward," Thorilian said, and stabbed a finger at the map. "Let us begin."

Willow listened to him review the plans with half an ear, her thoughts on Light. It had been days since she'd spoken to him. She doubted he had been killed, but why had he not come? Had they found the forge?

". . . everything hinges on Shadow removing their defenses on the east wall," Thorilian was saying. "When the guards are subdued, we use the shadow ropes to ascend past the outer wall. Then we use the catapult to reach the castle. Remember, no one dies. These are common soldiers, and if anyone falls to our blades, we could set Talinor on a course for war."

Kill the guards and they failed. Get captured and they failed. Reach Wylyn but let her escape? They still failed. The only chance for victory was to prove the king had been kidnapped and force the city to recognize the threat of the Order of Ancients.

"Shadow and Willow have confirmed that Wylyn has three hundred Bloodsworn assassins and Order members guarding the inner tower," Jeric said. "Ostensibly they are mercenaries to increase the king's protection, but they really act as a buffer between the king and his real guards."

"Are you certain Serak does not know of Wylyn's deal with Shadow?" Jeric asked.

Willow nodded. "We cannot be certain, but I do not think Serak knows."

The door opened and Shadow stepped into the room.

"You're late," Jeric said.

"They had to threaten me," Shadow said, a smile lighting his features as he recalled their ignorance. "They think I'm still loyal to them."

"Are you?" Jeric asked.

Shadow feigned a wounded expression. "Of course not."

Willow watched him. She guessed he'd gone to Irenae's home, but none but her knew that secret. Shadow himself probably didn't know that she knew. Willow had never seen Shadow act protective about anyone, even his own brothers. She wasn't sure if she found it disconcerting or hopeful to see one of the fragments change.

Shadow's frequent absences had not gone unnoticed by their allies, and Thorilian folded his arms, a trace of suspicion in his eyes. He didn't like Shadow, but he was enough of a tactician to recognize him as an asset.

"You like to play both sides," Thorilian said.

"He is always on our side," Willow said.

Jeric nodded his agreement and motioned to Shadow. "Is it set? Is Wylyn in the castle?"

"She is there," Shadow said.

"Light's information was accurate, then," Willow said. "And Wylyn has not told Serak of her deal with Shadow. If he had . . ."

"Serak would likely have stopped her from coming to Herosian," Shadow said. "He is too clever for his own good."

"Then Wylyn's distrust is our advantage," Jeric said.

"We strike now," Thorilian said. "Before she can slip away again."

"Light has yet to arrive," Willow said. "And he should have been here yesterday."

Her tone was worried, but Shadow swept his hand to the room. "We have enough. Wylyn will not survive the night."

"Are you certain you wish to do this?" Jeric asked, looking to Thorilian. "If it is discovered you aided our attack, the consequences could be devastating."

His wife leaned in, her eyes forceful. "We did not claim our home out of fear. Is this so different? We will not stand idle when such a threat has risen."

"Indeed," Thorilian said. "Our guard is ready."

Willow folded her arms. "We should wait for Light."

"Your concern is admirable," Shadow said. "But he is a fragment of Draeken. He is more than capable of watching his own back. Literally. You should see him cast magic to watch his own back." He tapped his chin in consideration. "Actually, you might not want to witness such a thing. It's rather disturbing."

Jeric grinned and turned to Willow. "I know you are concerned, but if we wait, we risk losing our best chance. Wylyn moves often, and with her network of Gates provided by the Order, we have no way of knowing where she will go."

Willow looked away, her eyes dark. "Light would not miss this."

"You think him in danger?" Thorilian asked.

"That is my fear," the dark elf said.

Jeric and Thorilian exchanged a look, and then Jeric shook his head. "If he is in trouble, killing Wylyn will only help. Doing nothing merely serves our foe."

Willow regarded her surface cousins, and then finally dipped her head. "There is truth to your words."

"Then gather yourselves," Jeric said, turning to Thorilian. "We have everyone we need so the assault may begin—"

"One more," Shadow said, and stepped to the window.

"We cannot wait," Thorilian said. "No doubt Wylyn has a Gate up there. If she even hears us coming she'll—"

"Husband," Venia said, placing a hand on his arm. "Patience, my love."

He scowled, and Jeric turned to Shadow. "Who are we waiting for? Fire and Mind are occupied, as are Lira and Water. We cannot wait, especially after what happened to Elenyr . . ."

Jeric's jaw tightened and he looked away. Shadow scowled as well. Willow noticed the exchange, the hatred, the anger. In that moment she realized Serak had made a mistake. The Father of guardians hadn't made a mistake in *trying* to kill Elenyr. He'd made his mistake in failing. If she was dead Jeric and the fragments would be out for blood. But alive, she could lead them, and they were just as angry. Serak had been an enemy before, but now? A small smile found its way onto her face as she imagined what Light would do to Serak.

"One more," Shadow repeated.

"The assassin?" Jeric asked. "What makes you think she will come?"

"Because I extended an invitation," he replied.

"And that is enough?" Willow asked.

She was surprised. There had been no word of the Angel of Death since the destruction of Mistkeep, but her ruined wings had been found. Many assumed her dead. Despite the rumors, she and Shadow were friends. But did she know that Shadow had used her family as bait?

Shadow stepped to the window and looked to the sky. "She's already here."

He opened the window and cast a giant hand of darkness that pointed to the balcony. Jeric snorted as the hand lead Lorica to the top

306

floor of the House of Runya. She alighted, her wings folding into the cloak on her back, her eyes sweeping the room.

Willow watched the woman. The assassin appeared much the same as she had in Mistkeep, but there was a lightness to her expression, a forcefulness to her gaze. It was the features of one who knew their purpose.

"Shadow," she drawled. "Did you have to point the way?"

"I wouldn't want you to miss this," Shadow said, motioning her into the room.

"What if I decided not to be an assassin anymore?" she asked.

He pointed to the wings and winked. "If you were no longer an assassin, you wouldn't be wearing those."

Willow noticed the wings, unsurprised to see the project Shadow had been working on. They had his shadow magic, as well Light's magic from the shard Willow had stolen. Shadow would never admit it, but he cared about the assassin, and that growth implied that Light could grow as well. She looked to the window, hoping in vain that he would appear.

Jeric looked her up and down, nodding his approval. "Then let—"

"Wait," Shadow said. "Can I say it?"

Willow hid a smile. Since she'd tumbled through the Gate, Shadow had been irritating, aggravating, and insufferable. But he also gave glimpses of Light, and for that, she was grateful. She hoped that wherever he was, he was well.

Jeric sighed. "As you will."

Shadow pulled a cowl of darkness to cover his features, his smile evident in his tone. "Then let it begin."

Chapter 41: Cornered

Willow and her command of Runya elves crept to the moat surrounding the fortress. The captain, a woman named Lin, cast a charm that hardened the water into aquaglass, allowing them to dart across. All six huddled in the shadows of a turret as Willow raised the bracer Shadow had given her.

Imbued with shadow magic, the shadowhook sent a thread of darkness up the stone and attached to the darkness near the top. It yanked Willow off the aquaglass ledge and she sprinted up the stone, a hundred feet straight to the top.

She slowed as she reached the circle of battlements, listening for the passage of guards. The fortress had roving and stationary guards, and she'd chosen this spot to breach because the roving guards tended to stop and talk to those positioned in the turret.

Hearing voices inside, she ascended to the top, where a lone guard stood watch in the circle of fortifications. His companions had descended the steps at the wall battlements, leaving him to watch alone. His sense of duty was rewarded with a blow to the head, and he collapsed into her arms. Grunting from the weight, she gently lowered him to the stone, and then used a dart to prick his skin, ensuring he would sleep for the next hour. Then she advanced to the steps and peered into the inside of the turret.

A single torch illuminated the group of five guards, who were well into a game of dice. She smiled to herself and returned to the wall, lowering the rope she'd brought with her. One by one the elves ascended to join her, and she made hand motions to indicate the five guards were below. One of the elves pulled a thin tube from her side and inserted a small dart. The others did the same, and the entire group took up position at the trapdoor or windows. At Lin's hand signal, five darts pierced skin, but only four collapsed. Bewildered, the last guard stared in confusion, the dart hanging from a fold in his tunic. Willow dropped down the stairs and leapt to him, her hand closing over his mouth just as he went to shout. He struggled, but she jammed the dart into his back, and his eyes rolled back into his head. He fell on his face, his helmet rolling away.

"Put them above and signal the others," Lin whispered.

The elves pulled the unconscious men up onto the turret, the last dropping to the stone as the rest of their group climbed over the railing. Fifty elves, led by Thorilian and Venia, as well as Jeric and Willow. Against a force of thousands.

Two humans arrived last. Both were loyal servants to the House of Runya and had volunteered to take the place of the unconscious guards. They stripped a pair of uniforms and donned them as Venia stepped to the ledge and touched a light orb. For an instant, a light glowed to life. Then Shadow swooped over and landed in their midst, his shadow wings folding behind him. Lorica landed at his side, both bearing matching grins.

"This isn't supposed to be fun," Thorilian growled.

"It always is," Shadow said with a smirk.

He stooped and began pulling on the darkness, fashioning great beams and supports, as well as a powerful cord. As the catapult came into shape, Lorica released a low whistle of appreciation, and reached out to touch the war machine.

"It looks dwarven made."

"Mine is better," Shadow said.

"Don't get arrogant," Venia said.

"He can't help it," Jeric said.

"Willow?" Shadow pointed to the war machine. "You're first."

Willow gathered her courage and climbed the catapult into the obscenely large bowl, and then swallowed as her heart accelerated in her chest. Shadow's head poked into view, his delighted features barely visible in the gloom.

"It's just how we practiced."

"No it's not."

"And don't scream."

"I never scream," she said flatly.

Despite the confidence to her words, her nerves rattled against her bones, and she waited for the mechanism to release. Each passing second it seemed like her heart wound tighter and tighter until—

Snap

The mechanism released and she was launched into the air. A scream bubbled up against her lips but her jaw was clenched tight, so she tumbled through the air in silence, terror and wind robbing her of breath.

She caught glimpses of the inner walls of the fortress before she began to spin, her arms flailing as she sought to regain her balance. For a single terrifying instant she questioned whether this was how she would die, smashing into the king's fortress, her crumpled remains falling hundreds of feet to a second, final impact on the courtyard stones.

She reached the apex of the curve and began to fall, her heart leaping into her throat. She managed to partially right herself and spotted the wide balcony that was her destination, the darkness preventing her from seeing where she would land. She clenched her entire body and cradled her legs—and the giant hand of darkness caught her like a ball, slowing her momentum and depositing her inside the guest quarters.

She rolled on the carpet and then spread her arms wide, her face on a rug. For several seconds, she fought to breathe. The carpet was soft on her face, a welcome that did not negate the fear she'd just experienced. Then she crawled to the edge of the room and sat in silence, breathing her gratitude at feeling solid objects around her body.

Jeric came next, but he came out of his roll on his feet, his face flushed with excitement. She felt a touch of envy at his ease. Then he walked across to her and settled into position behind the same couch.

"That was more fun than practice."

"Your sense of adventure is going to get you killed."

She jerked her head at the memory of practicing in the fields outside Herosian. The distance had been the same, but Shadow had been watching over every attempt, and caught those who looked like they might not land in the shadow hand.

The rest of the Runya soldiers landed, each breathless, their faces rigid and white. Shadow and Lorica came next, both flying around the shadow hand and entering like they owned the castle. Shadow came to a halt next to Willow.

"Any sign of the cleaning servants?"

"None," she said.

The guest quarters were spacious and decorated with memory orbs of the kingdom. The cleaners usually performed their task during the day, and they hoped the rooms would remain vacant, allowing them to enter unseen.

The guest quarters were also located just a short distance from the king's tower. More importantly, they were close to the king's library, and the Gate. Once they captured the Gate, they would be able to go for Wylyn, who would no longer have an escape.

Venia landed in the hand of shadow and came out on her knee. She scanned the room before rising and slipping behind a couch. She nodded to the others, her features flush with either fear or excitement, Willow could not tell.

"Just Thorilian now."

A key sounded in the lock and the group froze, dropping from sight in whispers of cloth. Then a servant entered and ignited a light orb, making his way towards the cabinet set against the wall. He didn't see the giant hand of shadow on the balcony beyond, or notice it disintegrating from the light in his hand.

Venia's mouth widened in horror as she watched the shadow hand crumble, but Lorica darted past her and rolled onto the balcony. For a split second her frame was visible before she leapt skyward, her wings darkening the moment she passed out of the pool of illumination. There was a grunt, like one body catching another, and the servant looked up.

He scanned the room. Then he licked his lips and retreated with the bottle in hand. When the door shut, Lorica lowered Thorilian to the balcony and then staggered to her knees, winded from the impact.

"You weigh more than a dwarf," she said.

"Last time I trust a shadow to catch me," Thorilian said.

"You can't blame that on me," Shadow protested.

"We don't have time for this," Jeric said, stepping to the door. "Remember, Willow and Lin will seal the Gate. The rest of us will strike at Wylyn. She's bound to have Tardoq with her, and probably a few of her remaining dakorians. We might not get another chance, so let's make it count."

He finished picking the lock and then eased it open. The corridor beyond was adorned with Talinorian banners interspersed with swords and shields. He motioned to Willow and she took the lead, slipping into the open and hurrying down the corridor. Shadow turned in the opposite direction, where he would seal off the portcullis, slowing soldiers from coming when the sounds of battle filled the fortress. The rest followed Lorica upward, veering up the stairs and out of sight.

Willow continued to the end of the hall and entered the stairs of a turret, following it upward to the level above. Then she turned down a side corridor, slowing as she spotted the two guards flanking the room ahead, the entrance to the king's library, where Willow had stolen the shard of light. She motioned to Lin, and the woman spun her aquaglass blade. She looked to the others, and they all nodded their preparedness. Willow reached to her dagger and palmed one of the darts. Laced with an elven poison, it would take down a rock troll, although she doubted it had the strength to incapacitate a dakorian.

She surged into a run, sprinting the length of the corridor on soft feet. One of the guards turned, his eyes going wide. But Willow was too close, and she passed the man, the dart striking once at the cheek. His shout died on his lips and he collapsed. The second man was already

312

drawing his sword, and Willow parried the blade before spinning inside his guard and pricking his hand. He too collapsed, and Lin's elves were quick to drag them out of sight.

Willow exchanged a look with Lin on the other side of the door. This was as far as Shadow had managed to breach in the last few days, so they had no idea what lay beyond the door, except that it contained the Gate. It could be empty, or it could have its own guard.

Her jaw tightened as she thought of Shadow. His request to steal the shard of light magic had put them at risk. No doubt the theft had been noticed, and now they might be facing anyone. Lin caught the handle, and Willow slipped through, her crossbow and dagger in her hands. Her gaze swept the room, registering the Gate against the wall, the bookshelves laden with tomes, and the spiral stairs in the corner. She also noticed the trio of occupants, all standing in the middle of the room, all bearing white masks.

The Queen's hand.

Mimic stood with Cutter and Black, their posture relaxed, their weapons in their sheaths. Willow and Lin had talked a great deal about what they could expect, and one thing had been constant. Stop the Gate. Stop the reinforcements.

Ignoring the trio just beginning to turn, she leapt across the room, sprinting past them. Mimic shouted in dismay but Willow was already past, and reached the Gate before they could react. Mounted on a small stand, it was obvious the Gate was meant to be transportable in the event Wylyn wanted to leave quickly. That very caution proved Willow's ally, and she snapped her whip, coiling it around the base. With a yank she sent the Gate tumbling onto its side, and on its face. Lin, on the opposite side, leapt to a bookshelf set against the wall, and dropped it onto the back of the Gate, the crash reverberating into the fortress as the other elves entered the room.

"Willow," Mimic spat the name like a curse. "You have lived far too long."

"I could say the same for you," Willow said, retreating and drawing her sword from her flesh.

"Cutter," Mimic said coldly. "This woman is beneath my talents. Kill her." There was no response, and Mimic looked to him, her voice gaining an edge. "Did you not hear me?"

Cutter looked to Black. "Is it time?"

Black reached up and removed his mask. "I'd say it is."

Mimic whirled to face them, but the blade was already reaching for her, cutting deep into her side. Mimic cried out in shock and pain and fell to her knees. Stunned by the betrayal, Willow stared at Cutter and Black as they took up position on either side of Mimic, their blades raised in execution.

Chapter 42: The Forsaken

Willow's eyes flicked between Mimic and the other two members of the Queen's Hand, uncertain how to respond. Was it a ploy to get them to drop their guard? Or were Cutter and Black on her side? She glanced to Lin but the woman merely shook her head in confusion.

"You would betray the Order?" Mimic demanded.

"We were never part of it," Cutter said, tossing his mask aside. "You betrayed our people, the kingdom, the queen."

"And you killed the rest of the Queen's Hand," Black said, his features twisted in anger. "You really thought we would follow you?"

"They lacked my vision," Mimic said.

"We were a family," Cutter growled. "And then we found two of our brothers with knives in their backs."

He stepped in and punched Mimic, cracking her mask and sending her to the floor. He knelt at her side and ripped the mask away, revealing the scarred and mottled flesh, and the hate filled eyes.

Willow shifted her feet, feeling like she'd stepped into a fight that was not her own. She'd never seen the Queen's Hand without their masks, and now she understood the reason Cutter and Black fought so well together. They were obviously brothers, both bearing the same strong features, although Black had a scar across his jawline.

"You should have killed me with the first blow," Mimic said, holding her side.

Cutter didn't take his eyes from Mimic but spoke to Willow. "I assume you came to kill Wylyn."

"We did."

"Then go," he said. "Permit us to kill the one that killed our own."

"What if it's a ploy?" Lin asked.

Willow regarded the two soldiers, but she did not sense deceit. They had followed Mimic because they had no choice, feigned support for the Order, all to find the time they could claim vengeance. And they had chosen this moment, chosen to trust Willow.

A distant clang of steel caused them all to look upward, and Willow realized the her allies had attacked Wylyn. She could either stay here and fight all three or assist in the battle against the krey. But could she trust them? She recalled the moment in her trial, when Cutter and Black could have killed her, and chosen to spare her life.

"Go," she said to Lin. "Join with Lorica."

"Are you certain?" the elf said.

"They will be facing dakorians and Tardoq," she said. "And it appears we have allies here."

Lin hesitated, and then ordered the rest of her elves out the door. The group departed as quickly as they had arrived, and Willow straightened. Inclining her head to Cutter and Black, she stepped to the door.

"Willow," Mimic called, and Willow came to a stop on the threshold. "Before you depart, you should know one thing."

"What's that?" Willow asked cautiously.

Mimic raised her hand from her wound and tossed a small vial to the floor. Empty, it clattered to a stop, a drop of pink liquid falling out of the opening. Willow's eyes snapped to Mimic as she raised a hand, revealing blood, but her wound had healed.

Cutter thrust his sword toward Mimic's chest, but she caught his arm and twisted, forcing him into a bookshelf. Then she twisted her arm, revealing the tattoo of a dagger. Drawing it from her flesh, she used the blade to deflect Black's strike. Willow leapt into the room, closing the opposite flank as Cutter and Black drove Mimic towards the window.

Mimic smiled and pointed upward. "Do you hear the conflict raging above? All that magic, including Venia's sight, and Shadow's power."

She drew a dagger from her waist and sent it hurtling at the light orb hanging from the ceiling. It shattered, plunging the room into darkness. Before Willow could move, a large clawed hand closed about her body and sent her into a bookshelf. Her body crashed through and she landed in a pile of heavy tomes.

She hit hard, her vision flickering. Cutter and Black both retreated, drawing light orbs to combat the dark entity. But a spike of shadow pierced Cutter's arm and lifted him up.

"You thought you could stop me?" Mimic's voice was harsh and grating. "You are like toy soldiers compared to my power."

The spike of shadow pierced the wall, leaving him dangling several feet above the ground. He ducked a strike meant for his head, and sought to dislodge the shard of darkness, his features a mask of pain.

The light from the open doorway was not enough to stop the magic of shadow, but it was enough that Willow could make out her foe, a great scorpion with huge hands instead of pincers. The tail snapped once, catching Black, the blade grazing his side, but his anti-magic blade flashed, severing the tail.

Willow shook her head, desperately trying to clear her vision. She caught a glimpse of a snapping tail and rolled across the shelves, the tail stabbing into books and wood. Pages and bits of wood filled the air, providing her a chance to retreat against the wall. She'd lost a grip on her weapons and they had sunk into her flesh, so she drew her hand crossbow and a dagger, rising to fire at Mimic's form.

Bolts thudded into the shadow body, failing to pierce Mimic's skin. Mimic growled but could not turn to Willow, as she was forced to deal with Black, who used his anti-magic blade to carve his way through her entity. Bits of shadow flesh fell to the floor and disintegrated, allowing him the chance to dive in with a shout.

His anti-magic blade plunged through the entity's body, right where Mimic should have been. The shadows crumbled away, leaving empty air and a bewildered Black. Willow shouted a warning as Mimic dropped from the ceiling above and struck him in the back, her shadow-enhanced fist sending him through the window.

Glass shattered as Black disappeared, and Cutter dropped to the floor, charging Mimic. She cast more shadow limbs but he cut them apart, driving Mimic toward the wall. Willow leapt to the window and leaned out, and spotted Black clinging to the railing. She dropped her weapons and drew her whip, lowering it to him.

"Hurry!" she shouted.

He grasped the whip and climbed. As he pulled himself through the window, his eyes widened, and he dove forward, knocking them both out of the way. She tumbled to the floor as a giant hammer smashed through the wall where she'd stood. Stones and broken glass fell from the gaping hole, allowing the chill wind to enter the room.

"You really thought this was your moment to betray me?" Mimic snarled.

She'd managed to cast a knight to duel Cutter, and the two battled between the bookshelves, the books taking the brunt of the damage. Then she turned to Black and Willow, both rising near the stairs. Mimic summoned a great panther, sending it towards them.

Willow spotted a light orb against the wall. It had been darkened, and she snatched for the sphere of glass. Activating it with a touch, she tossed it at the panther, and in the same motion drew her large crossbow from her shoulder.

The ball passed through the panther's jaws as it pounced, the creature falling apart, the magic unable to withstand the bright light. The sphere arced towards Mimic, who raised her hand to catch the orb, her expression one of disdain. But from darkness to sudden light, she was momentarily blind.

Willow fired, the large crossbow bolt shattering the orb just as Mimic caught the ball. The bolt passed through her hand and sank into Mimic's shoulder, bits of broken glass pelting her face and neck. She cried out in anger and pain, dropping the broken glass onto the floor.

"I think we picked the right moment," Cutter said, his face a mask of pain from his wounds.

"Shadow is not the only magic being used above," Mimic snapped.

She darted for the stairs that led to the king's bedchamber. Willow leapt to follow, but Mimic snatched up a sword that had hung on the wall and slashed the wood in her wake. The weapon glowed bright blue, mimicking the sharpening augmentation on Cutter's sword. As Willow reached the stairs, they collapsed. Unwilling to let the woman escape, she leapt to a bracket for a light orb, using it to swing herself upward. Kicking off a broken stair, she surged up the remaining steps and alighted near the bed.

The room had once been regal and richly draped, but Wylyn had taken much of it down, replacing the royal trappings with fine cloth. The cabinet of rich ales had been replaced with a statue of herself.

The door to the receiving room lay ajar, the wood on fire, the hinges broken. Through the opening Willow spotted Shadow on Tardoq's back, unsuccessfully hacking at the bone armor on his shoulder. Lorica attacked from the top of the vaulted room, her blade sweeping through two Order guards before swinging for Wylyn.

Tardoq's hammer clipped Lorica on the side, sending her crashing into a couch. Then he reached up and caught Shadow about the waist, launching him at the wall. Most of the Order members were dead, but Tardoq fought with unparalleled ferocity, moving as if with body magic, swinging with more force than a rock troll. Alone, he stood against the guards of Runya, and even Thorilian and Venia could not get close.

Willow had thought Mimic would join Wylyn. Instead she stood at the desk in the corner of the king's bedchamber. She scribbled a note on a scrap of parchment, the words spotted with the blood from the cuts on her hand. Then she spun and pointed to Willow, her hand now wreathed in flames.

She cast a small entity of fire, the tiny golem collecting the note and streaking to the stairs, disappearing. Cutter cried out in dismay, and Willow heard a shift in glass, as if the golem had lifted the Gate.

"Calling for help?" Willow taunted.

"Did you know the people fear you?" Mimic's sickly features twisted with anger, the image all the more fearsome due to the cuts from the shattered light orb.

"They fear what they do not understand," Willow said. She drew her chakram and her sword, setting the chakram into a spin.

"The renowned inkmage," Mimic said mockingly. "So fearsome, so deadly, yet so foolish."

Willow hurled the chakram, the spinning blade cutting through the fine cloths as Mimic ducked. She retaliated with a burst of fire, burning the cloth behind Willow as she dived to the side. A blue blade pierced the floor, Cutter's sword carving through the stone like it was hot flesh.

"You don't know me," Willow snapped.

"I know everything about you," Mimic said. "Your mother the soldier, your father the cook. You crave a home like theirs, but you refuse to see the truth. People like you don't get a happy home."

Stung, Willow hurled the chakram at her foe. As Mimic sent fire to deflect the spinning blade, Willow dropped her weapons and drew her hand crossbow, firing a small bolt at Mimic. She saw it coming and twisted, the bolt scraping her side and leaving a bloody furrow. Cutter's blade finished its turn and a chunk of stone fell, leaving a large hole in the floor.

"You choose your fate," Willow said. "I choose mine."

Black leapt through the hole and rolled to his feet, flanking Mimic. The woman bared her teeth in a snarl. Before they could attack a body came tumbling through the broken door. Venia rolled across the floor, crying out as her body came to a stop at Mimic's feet. Thorilian bellowed her name but Mimic cast a sword out of fire and aimed it at the stunned Venia.

"My fate is to kill," Mimic said.

She leaned into the killing blow, but Willow's whip coiled around Venia's ankle. Mimic's sword grazed Venia's throat, drawing blood but failing to pierce her heart. Venia slid across the floor and Willow leapt to protect her.

320

"You will not touch her," Willow said.

Mimic burst into a laugh. "A dark elf protecting a surface elf. Your compassion is disgusting."

"But not unappreciated," Venia said, climbing to her feet. "Willow, you'll find what you need on the table in the corner."

She pointed to a gauntlet set on a shelf by the king's bed. All black, it seemed to absorb the light in the room. Willow's eyes widened when she recognized it as a Darkfist, a glove that spread anti-magic onto any weapon.

Black never took his eyes from Mimic. "How did you know we'd need it?"

"I see much," Venia said. "But not with my eyes." She smiled and picked up her sword before retreating the way she'd come, joining her husband as Tardoq charged through the furniture.

"Get the Darkfist," Black said.

"You'll never touch it," Mimic said.

She sent a burst of flames at the table supporting the gauntlet, surrounding it in a ring of fire. The flames did not approach the gauntlet, which seemed to absorb the heat, but the fire became a wall that blocked the way.

Black surged forward, his anti-magic blade spinning and striking at Mimic. He called to his brother and an answer came from below. Then Black used his chin to point to the hole in the floor.

"Stand there," he called.

Willow rolled past a blast of fire and stood next to the hole. Out of the corner of her eye she spotted Cutter slice a hole in the floor. Mimic shouted in dismay as the Darkfist fell through the hole. In the room below, Cutter caught the glove and tossed it through the original opening, into Willow's waiting hands.

She caught the gauntlet and shoved her hand into the glove. At the same moment, she heard a dwarven voice bellow from the room beyond. Mimic reached to the floor and it rose between her and Black, while a needle of stone appeared behind him. Willow shouted a warning but the needle pierced his back, and lifted him off the floor.

Willow darted in and drew her blade from her hip. The inksword normally appeared almost liquid, but now the gauntlet extended its magic onto the blade, making it appear obsidian. She slashed through the needle and it fell, knocking Black through the hole. Mimic dived away, and dropped down the stairs, with Willow on her heels.

Willow was faster, and she leapt to the library below. Mimic sought to escape through the door into the corridor, but Willow drew her whip and snapped it in the opening, forcing her to turn. Unable to flee, Mimic cast a sword of fire and fought.

Willow brought all her skill to bear, decimating every bit of magic Mimic sought to cast, tearing through entities and weapons, driving Mimic towards a bookshelf. Without her magic, Mimic's skill was for naught, and she could not withstand Willow's attack. With a feint high, she pulled a knife from her skin and drove it into Mimic's chest.

The woman cried out and fell, the knife falling back into Willow's flesh as she placed both hands on her sword. She stood over Mimic, who gasped for breath. The woman scooted away until her back hit the wall. Mimic reached for the Gate with a trembling hand, and Willow noticed that it was not on its back, the silver liquid reflecting the room. Black lay on his side, while his brother held his wound, keeping him alive.

"Kill her," Cutter said, his voice raspy. "She's too dangerous to let live."

"I know," Willow said.

She held her sword to the woman's throat, but hesitated. She was a soldier, not an executioner, and only the queen could order one's death. Black then called her name, the urgency in his tone causing her to turn—and see a man step out of the Gate, the one man she feared.

Chapter 43: The Snow Dragon

"What do you want with Draeken?" Light asked.

Serak descended the steps of his throne, his eyes settling on Lira. "She has the answer."

"Me?" Lira jerked her head. "You don't know anything about me."

"You are an Eternal," he said. "Sworn to protect our world from the Krey Empire. I know everything about you, the reason you fight, and how you have failed . . ."

Lira bristled. "We have kept Lumineia safe."

"You have delayed the inevitable," he said. "And that is hardly a victory. One day, the krey will arrive in our skies, and your paltry group of Eternals will be as a candle in a hurricane."

"So you brought the krey early?" Water demanded. "You opened the door for them."

"Every war can be won," Serak said. "And I am the only one willing to use the right gambit."

Light abruptly noticed that he was alone. Both Lira and Water had drifted apart, moving to flank Serak, who did not seem concerned that he would soon be surrounded. Light hissed to his brother.

"Where do you want me to stand?"

"It doesn't matter where you stand," Serak said. "Draeken might be powerful, but the two of you?" he shook his head with a chuckle. "I admit, however, that I do look forward to the coming duel. It has been ages since I have faced a true challenger."

"Why are you taking monarchs?" Water asked.

"Because what is coming will require their support," Serak said.

Lira shifted another foot, advancing around Serak's left side. "You think kidnapping kings and queens will earn their loyalty?"

"Loyalty isn't given," Serak said. "It is taken, by those with the power for true leadership."

Light craned his head to look down the door at the back of the hall. "Are we really at the Forge of Light?"

"Sadly, no," Serak said. "That would be a different mountain. I've removed access to the krey structure—for you and my Order, and placed the Gate here. Some things are better left forgotten."

Light couldn't keep the disappointment from his face. "Why?"

"Because a certain dark elf tumbled through a Gate," Serak said. "She saw enough to find her way back, and that was not something I could permit."

"Willow?" Light asked, excited. "Have you heard from her? When can I—"

"Light," Serak drawled. "Stay focused now. Your brother is about to strike and I'm not done talking to Draeken."

"We aren't Draeken," Light said.

"But you are his fragments," he said, "and when you merge again, your memories will become his."

"Your offer in Keese," Water said slowly. "That was to Draeken, wasn't it."

"It took you this long to figure it out?" Serak smiled. "Mind and Shadow truly did get the bulk of the intelligence."

"What offer?" Light asked.

"Serak asked me to join him," Water said. "At the time, I wondered why he would ask me instead of the others."

324

Light laughed at the prospect. "He asked *you* to join *him*? You're the fragment of honor."

"But I'm still a fragment of Draeken," Water said.

Light's amusement faded, his smile turning into a frown. Serak wasn't trying to enlist the fragments, he wanted Draeken. He'd always wanted Draeken. But surely he knew what happened when they joined together.

"Draeken cannot survive when joined," Light said. "We just shatter again."

"Light," Water hissed. "Stop giving him information."

Serak ignored him. "Do you know why Draeken cannot remain whole?"

That brought them all to a halt. Lira and Water were now on either side of Serak, while Light remained in front. The tension in the room was at a breaking point, but Serak's question stilled the waters.

"You think you know us better than we know ourselves?" Water asked.

"I know what you do not, what the Hauntress has kept from you." His eyes flicked between Light and Water. "And I am willing to tell you the secret she fears."

"She always has secrets," Water said. "We trust her."

"Even when the secret is about you?"

"You've spent a lifetime manipulating others," Lira said. "They're not going to believe you."

"I am gifted with deceit," Serak mused. "Doesn't mean I'm lying now."

"I will never believe you," Water said, his voice uncharacteristically harsh.

"I know," Serak said, his smile disturbing. "But again, I'm not talking to you."

325

"I think it's time we stop talking," Water said.

Water pulled from the snow in the floor and pillars, bending the magic to his will. One of the pillars began to change, the hardened snow turning semi fluid, morphing into a towering golem. Instead of hands, long spikes extended from the arms, the sharpened blades glittering in the sunlight.

Lira drew her sword, her body shimmering with brown light. When she spun her sword, it moved with inhuman speed, the weapon blurring. Light, unwilling to be left behind, gathered sunlight into his hands, shaping a pair of great cats at his flanks. Then he conjured a wolfsteed and mounted.

But Serak was no normal foe, so Light conjured a giant hammer, a crossbow, a sword, a pair of daggers, a few knives, a mace, because he'd always wanted one, and then a rock troll greatsword, which promptly fell to the ground, plunging into the snowy floor. He shifted the weapons in his hands and reached for the handle but noticed Water's expression.

"What?"

Water shook his head and turned to Serak. "Whatever plan you have, it ends here."

"And will you kill me?" Serak asked, holding up his wrists like he was ready to surrender. "Or attempt to imprison me in anti-magic bonds?"

"I like the first option," Lira said.

Serak smiled, and then spread his arms wide. The great hall began to tremble. The walls opened in jagged lines, like teeth from a great beast. The roof flattened and straightened, the snow billowing into the chamber. Then the sides began to open, like the jaws of a mighty beast. The floor tipped upward, sending Water, Light, and Lira tumbling back towards the entrance. The teeth widening so the trio fell through the opening and into the snow.

With weapons cascading off Light, he pulled himself free of the snowdrift and looked up as the jaws of the gigantic dragon rising from the snow, the walls of the great hall shifting and moving into teeth, the roof turning into the snout and eyes. It tossed its head, the snow falling away in huge piles to either side, revealing the breadth of his enormous frame.

His body rose from the mountain, huge hind legs of snow grasping sunken boulders, the tail flicking, nearly causing an avalanche. Enormous wings unfurled and spread wide as the beast released a thundering roar.

"He's better with water than you are," Light said to Water.

"That's impossible," Water breathed. "No one has that much power."

"It appears someone does," Lira said, her voice tense.

The dragon stilled and Serak appeared in the beast's maw. "Do not feel bad," he called to Water. "I am a full guardian, and you are merely a fragment."

"What do we do now?" Water asked.

"We ride the biggest dragon ever," Light breathed.

They stared at him, and he raised an eyebrow. "Is that not what you were thinking?"

"*No*," Water said. "We weren't looking at a snow dragon the size of a hill and thinking we should *get on its back*."

"Oh," Light said, disappointed.

"Whenever you are ready," Serak called, leaning against a tooth that was taller than he was. "I'll even give you back your entity."

The dragon opened its jaws and spit the pillar-turned-golem. It landed in the snow and managed to right itself, rising to its now unimpressive height of twenty-five feet. Then the dragon shifted to the side, sparking an avalanche down the slope that covered the golem. The dragon dug its claws into the snow, catching the embedded boulders before circling again. The trio huddled behind a boulder as if it could spare them from the beast's might.

"He has far more power than we thought," Water said uncertainly.

"I think that's an understatement," Lira said.

"We need Draeken," Light said.

"That's exactly what he wants," Water said, his forehead creasing as he eyed the enormous creature. "We need to show him that just the fragments are strong on their own—"

"Look!" Light called.

The dragon had come to a halt, and now a second person had appeared next to Serak. The Father of Guardians appeared displeased but accepted what was unmistakably a bloody scrap of paper. He sighed and then raised his gaze to Water.

"My apologies," he said. "But it appears Wylyn has made the mistake of inventing her own plan. I must depart, but I'm sure you will enjoy playing with my creature. You might think to simply depart but know that one of my Gates is in its belly. I know you will try and fail to reach it, so do enjoy the long journey back to the claimed lands."

He turned and left with the visitor, and the dragon remained in place, obviously so Serak could leave. Any second it would begin to fight, and as Water argued with Lira on a course of action, Light spotted one of his weapons.

"Hey, my sword."

"We don't have time to find your weapons," Water cast over his shoulder.

"But look!"

"No, Light," Water said. "We need to get inside that thing to reach the Gate."

"Okay."

From the wealth of sunlight, Light cast a beam of light. The conduit burst from his hands and passed straight through the open jaws of the beast. It coiled around the rock troll greatsword, still embedded where it had fallen.

Reaching out, he sent a coil of light around his companions and then cast wings on his back. The rope yanked them off their feet, the wings keeping them from dragging. Water and Lira sucked in their breath as they hurtled through the jaws of the beast. Light released his magic and they fell onto the bottom of the great hall. The floor looked much the same except it was now curved, and he pulled the greatsword free and slung it onto his shoulders.

"Ready?"

Water began to laugh and clapped him on the back. "Always, brother."

Lira took the lead. "I will never doubt your impulsiveness again."

"We need to hurry," Water said. "It's only a matter of time until Serak steps through the Gate and—"

The dragon rose onto its hind legs and charged down the mountain, throwing its head. Light, Water, and Lira were tossed about, bouncing off the walls, floor and ceiling, rolling towards the snapping jaws. Light slammed the greatsword back into the floor as the entire hall swerved and fell.

"If we fall out, we'll never make it inside again!" Lira called from where she'd snagged a hold on a window.

Water landed on his feet and snow froze him to the floor, his magic holding him bound as the dragon sought to dislodge them from its mouth. He pointed to the beast's throat, a corridor leading downward into the fortress.

"The Gate must be down that way."

He cast a cord out of snow and sent it into the opening at the dragon's throat, where it hooked on a light orb. Using the rope, he worked his way towards the rear of the chamber, collecting Light and Lira on the way. Light grinned when Watter also bonded his boots to the floor, allowing him to walk as the beast twisted and jumped, tossing its head back and forth. It wasn't as much fun as it would have been to ride the mighty dragon on the outside, but a close second.

They reached the corridor and continued down the throat to the belly. Apparently deciding it could not dislodge them, the dragon reached to its own body, tearing great holes in an attempt to remove them.

An entire section of wall ripped away, nearly taking Light with it. Wind and snow gusted inside but Light jumped past the breach. The room beyond was gigantic, even bigger than the jaws. Windows and walls flexed like muscles, breaking as the beast clawed at its own stomach. On a pedestal at the center of the dragon's belly the Gate stood, the silvery surface reflecting the icy room.

They sprinted towards it but a clawed hand tore into the stomach and grabbed the Gate. Light hurled his greatsword. It dug into the beast's hand, trailing the rope of light. Light and his companions caught the rope as the beast dragged the Gate out the hole, yanking the three of them from their feet.

Wind gusted against them as they burst into the open, and the dragon brought its claw downward, obviously intent on crushing them. But Light shrank the rope and landed on the dragon's claw. He kicked off the large sword, diving through the Gate. Water and Lira followed, disappearing as the great beast smashed the Gate on a boulder.

Chapter 44: Falling

Willow's eyes snapped to the Gate when Serak stepped into the room. His eyes swept the group, passing over the two brothers, and then settling on Willow, still standing over the wounded Mimic. Mimic looked at Serak with hope in her gaze and raised a trembling hand to him.

"Master," she called.

Serak's lip curled in distaste. "Three traitors and a failure, all in one room."

"Master, please," Mimic said.

"You are no longer mine," Serak said. He withdrew a pair of anti-magic shackles and tossed it to Willow, who caught them in surprise. Then his gaze settled on Mimic. "A failure such as yours does not deserve death."

Mimic crumpled to the floor, and Willow dropped the shackles onto her wrists, where they robbed her of her magic. The woman did not resist and merely stared at Serak, her gaze filled with pleading. Serak's lip curled in disgust and then he looked upward.

He reached to the stone at his feet and the floor rose upward at an angle, bypassing the bedchamber and entering the king's receiving room. Through the gap, Willow caught a glimpse of a raging battle, of Shadow and Lorica battling side by side. Serak's sudden appearance caused all to retreat.

"Go!" Cutter called. "Before Wylyn escapes."

The spiral stairs to the king's bedchamber were destroyed, so she sprinted into the hall and hurtled down the corridor. From there she raced up the stairs to the main entrance to the king's quarters. From below, she heard the shouting and clanging as someone sought to breach a portcullis, the sound followed by the crunching of brick. Jumping up the stairs, she raced to the double doors, skidding to a halt at the burning portal.

The room beyond was filled with broken furniture and the bodies of the slain. Order members were easily distinguished by the Talinorian guard uniforms, while Runya soldiers were among them. Fire licked at the furniture, the walls, and the fine tapestries. A painting of King Porlin lay on its side, the frame broken, the paint dripping into the flames. Half the light orbs were damaged, casting the spacious room into flickering light.

Lin and a pair of elves were caring for the wounded, and she noticed Willow in the doorway. She pointed to the king's training room. Willow dodged through the dead and wounded, jumping a fallen dakorian to reach the chamber, where the battle had come to a halt.

The training room sat next to the bedchamber, also above the Gate room. The wide space was open, the floor containing a training circle. Racks of weapons adorned the walls, and cabinets of more expensive blades sat in the corners. Shadow and Lorica stood with the remaining members of the house of Runya, including Venia and Thorilian, who were both wounded, and Jeric. The entire group faced Serak and Wylyn, who stood on the balcony. Tardoq flanked Wylyn, his bone armor bloodied in a dozen places.

"You made a deal with one of the fragments without my knowledge?" Serak asked, his tone dangerous.

"I am not beholden to a *slave*," Wylyn said. "And *someone* had to deal with the threat."

"You consider me a threat?" Shadow asked, feigning embarrassment. "How touching."

Wylyn stabbed a finger at Shadow as if his comment proved her point. Serak clenched a fist, causing Tardoq to raise his hammer in warning, but Serak didn't even look to the towering Bloodwall.

"I *brought* you here, *told* you of your son's impending betrayal, yet you *dare* to speak of me as a slave?"

"You *are* a slave," she spat. "You thought you had all this power, but while you've been away I have taken everything. The Order of Ancients that worships me now *belongs* to me."

The words could have been a lie, but the way she said it, like she'd been waiting for the moment to speak, was too triumphant, too arrogant to be untrue. Willow glanced to Jeric, but even he seemed surprised. Willow expected Serak to strike, and the others in the room tensed for the ensuing conflict. Instead, Serak laughed, the sound so laced with scorn that Wylyn flushed.

"You think to fight Draeken on your own? You think that taking my Order will make you powerful? You know nothing about this world, and I will enjoy watching your fall."

"You are nothing without your Order," Wylyn said haughtily.

Serak regarded her with a strange expression that made Willow shudder. It was as if Serak was not surprised at all by the change, as if he'd known the moment was coming, or even planned it. His eyes flicked to Shadow, the only fragment in the room. Then he glanced about the room as if just noticing where they stood.

"Every piece is worth losing," he said. "As long as it brings victory."

"What's that supposed to mean?" Wylyn asked.

"That you're just a pawn," he replied.

"And you're just a slave."

Serak glared at her, and then raised a hand to the doorway where Willow stood. Stone cracked, the sound echoing in the stillness. On the threshold, Willow looked down and watched the stone break beneath her feet. Her eyes widened as the crack spread, parting stones like a blade through parchment.

Like the Gate room below and the bedchamber at the side, the training room was attached through supports embedded in the tower wall. As Serak clenched his fist, those supports snapped.

Wylyn's eyes filled with red, and a trace of yellow when the section of tower began to lean away from the King's Tower. They were four hundred feet off the courtyard, and Serak was about to let them fall.

"Call me a slave one more time," Serak said.

His hand extended towards the cracking wall, where stones were tumbling away, revealing just three supports remaining attached. If they broke, the entire addition would plummet to the ground.

"Wylyn, perhaps you'd like to take this inside?" Jeric called. "Before things . . . descend any further?"

The words were an invitation for Wylyn to withdraw from Serak, to join with Jeric. Wylyn spared the elf a look. Those come to kill her were arrayed closest to the door, while Serak was positioned on the outside of the room, closest to the balcony. Jeric was offering aid against Serak, but she would have to make a choice. The hatred in her eyes burned bright, and then she turned back to Serak.

"When my army comes to harvest this world, you will be the first to be sold, for you are—and have always been—a *slave*."

The word hung in the air like an anvil about to fall. Willow held her breath. They all stood on precarious footing, and Wylyn had just struck the last support. Then Serak began to laugh, the sound tinged with dark amusement.

"Everyone with power believes themselves impervious to those they call inferior. Enjoy the fall, Wylyn, and remember, those that kill you, are those you called slave."

He clenched his fist one last time, and the three supports snapped. For a single, terrifying instant, the adjoined tower seemed to hang in space, and then the earth reached into the sky and claimed what it now owned.

The tower dropped down the side of the great turret—and jolted to a stop, the beams snagging on the protruding stone. Willow spotted Cutter and Black inside the King's Tower, both staring in horror from their position in the hall. Mimic lay bound between them, equally as shocked.

"No one move," Thorilian hissed. "The slightest motion could tip us over the edge."

Serak, still standing in the same spot like his boots were bound to the floor, cast a disdainful glare at his enemies and strode to the balcony, where a finger of stone carried him away. The shift in weight caused a grinding of stone, and the turret began to lean outward.

"Tardoq." Wylyn snapped. "Get me out of here."

Tardoq caught Wylyn about the waist and dived towards Willow, his heavy footfalls shaking the entire turret. Unable to avoid the dakorian, Willow was knocked into a rack of heavy weapons mounted on the wall. The stones holding them had come free and the impact of her body knocked them loose.

Tardoq slid out the doorway and dropped into the crack between the two turrets. His hand caught the threshold, swinging himself into the library through what had once been the door. Three heavy footfalls sounded, and then nothing, indicating he'd escaped through the Gate.

"Blasted dakorian," Jeric growled, holding to a bracketeted staff. "Don't move unless . . .

A grinding of stone caused them all to draw in a breath. The floor tipped to the side, drifting further and further. All recognized what was coming and Thorilian stabbed a finger towards the King's Tower.

"MOVE!" he bellowed.

Unable to balance on the protruding supports, the turret slipped free. Willow's feet came off the floor and she floated upward, her hair rising about her, and everyone in the room fought for a grip. The weapons where she'd fallen bounced about. She cried out as her legs tangled with them, all falling in a heap as the adjoining turret began to lean away from the fortress, the gap between the door and falling turret growing wider. Then the stone turned into a blur as they plummeted.

Willow fought to pull herself free as Shadow and Lorica reached for Thorilian and Venia. They dived out of the balcony that was quickly pointing towards the courtyard floor, while Jeric reached for Willow.

He caught the weapons but it was too late for him to save her, so she struck him in the jaw. Unprepared for the blow, he tumbled out the doorway. He rotated so his feet landed on the castle wall. She'd known his boots could bond with stone and had seen him run vertically before. He sprinted straight down the stone, calling her name. Willow closed her eyes, and waited for the impact, wishing her last thoughts were not tinged with regret.

The falling turret twisted, the sudden shift in momentum causing the weapons to slide, freeing her. She opened her eyes to see the doorway filled by a being of pure, yellow light. Her heart soared as he darted to her side with shocking speed, scooping her up and wrapping them both in a sphere of power.

The turret struck the courtyard floor with a *boom*, shattering into stones, broken beams, and pieces of glass. The impact sent bricks hundreds of feet high, breaking windows in the castle and clattering off the innermost wall.

Talinorian guards huddled out of sight before rising to see the pile of rubble, and the bulge at the center. Shadow and Lorica dropped to the pile and shoved stones aside, uncovering a ball of light half sunk into the ground. Inside, two people were locked in an embrace, oblivious to all as they kissed.

Inside the sphere, Willow finally pulled away. "Light," she breathed, all the yearning, regret, and hope infusing the word.

"I missed you," Light murmured.

"And I you," she said.

His eyes were soft, filled with hope, yet also a powerful peace, like they should never have been apart, and were now whole. All her doubts about a family were gone, not discarded, but settled. She didn't know how, she didn't know when, but she knew Light was her family, her home.

Someone was calling her name from above the sphere but she could not tear her eyes from Light. Her tactical mind knew they should be moving, fleeing before the Talinorian guards flooded the courtyard, but her body refused to respond.

"Sorry I'm late," Light said. "But I think you'll enjoy the tale I have to share."

"I'm sure I will," Willow said.

"Light!" a voice called.

He rolled his eyes and released an annoyed grunt. "Can you not see that I'm busy?"

She giggled, and then marveled. When was the last time she'd giggled? She was a grown woman of three hundred years, but in that moment she did not feel her age, and merely wanted to reach up and pull Light back into another kiss.

She recognized Water outside the sphere and motioned upward. "Your brother wants to talk to you. It seems urgent."

"*This* is urgent." He kissed her again.

She sighed and shook her head. "Later, I promise."

"An oath accepted," Light said, and they finally parted.

The sphere that had protected them separated into a thousand sparks, each floating away as tiny glitters of moonlight. She watched in awe, knowing he'd done the display just for her. Water and Lira stepped through the curtain of sparks and Water pointed to the sounds of thudding boots.

She reluctantly turned and watched as thousands of Talinorian soldiers appeared through the floating lights. They spread out to surround the pile of rubble. Shadow and Lorica had landed with them, as had Thorilian and Venia. Jeric stood in their midst, his expression one of irritation.

The high captain, a man named Kelg, barked an order and the army leveled spears and swords at the intruders. Willow had met him before and knew him to be an honest man, but he now stood, his features twisted in confusion.

"Lower your weapons! And place these anti-magic shackles on your wrists!"

Black shackles were tossed to them, clattering onto the pile of rubble. Shadow snorted in disbelief and lowered his voice. "I think we can win."

"We are not killing innocent soldiers," Water snapped.

"Where did you even come from?" Shadow asked.

"Through the Gate," Lira said, turning to examine the surrounding men. "We made it through as it was falling and managed to catch the wall. That's when Light saw Willow."

"Last warning!" Kelg said. "Submit or be slain!"

Willow gripped Light's hand tightly. She knew he would not abandon her, but the look in his eyes suggested he would lay waste to the army to protect her, and she didn't want that on her conscience, for however long she would survive in the battle.

"We should escape," she murmured. "Three of you can fly."

"Nowhere to run to," Thorilian said, reaching to his wife. "Our house is fallen."

Jeric groaned and strode forward. "I was really hoping I wouldn't have to do this."

He picked his way down the rubble, approaching Captain Kelg. Weapons were leveled at him and warnings were shouted, but he ignored them all. Coming to a halt a short distance from the captain, he withdrew a small object and tossed it to the soldier.

The man caught it and stared in shock. Then he held the circle of steel aloft, revealing an amulet bearing the insignia of Talinor, the king's seal, proving the bearer as the Steward to Talinor, second only to the king himself.

"Captain," Jeric said, "please remove my army from my courtyard."

Kelg, his features twisted in disbelief, obeyed the order, and shouted for the soldiers to withdraw. As they filed out, Willow and the others turned to stare at Jeric, who sighed in regret and turned to face them.

338

"I think there are some things I should explain."

Chapter 45: Reunion

Light, delighted at the turn of events, listened to Jeric's explanation, which proved to be rather exciting. Turned out he'd saved Porlin's grandfather from an assassination attempt by a rival, earning him the seal. He glossed over the details, as Jeric always did, but Light knew the battle was over. He was back with Willow, and that was all that mattered.

"You didn't think to mention that you were the Steward of the kingdom?" Thorilian demanded.

"Wouldn't have helped us get to Wylyn," Jeric said. "She would have escaped through the Gate long before we reached her quarters."

"Well played," Shadow said, inclining his head in respect.

"I enjoyed the conflict," Lorica said, eyeing the surrounding soldiers. "But it's time for this assassin to depart."

Light glanced their way but Shadow was already retreating into the darkness, and a moment later two pairs of wings soared into the night. Light raised his hand in farewell as Venia stabbed a hand toward Jeric.

"You still should have told us the truth."

"I have many truths," he said. "None of which are fit to be shared."

Venia cocked her head to the side. "My eyes have always shown me much, and I see a wealth of deceit in your soul."

"Thank you," Jeric said with a smile and a bow.

"That wasn't a compliment," Thorilian said.

"At least you get to keep your house," Jeric said. "And I won't even raise taxes on your home for the intrusion into mine."

Thorilian issued a bark of laughter at the absurd comment. Jeric grinned and turned to Kelg, who also wanted answers. As Jeric left with his new captain, Light swept a hand to the pile of rubble.

"I don't understand what is happening, but it's clear you've had fun in my absence."

"Not the word I would use," Thorilian muttered.

"What *did* happen here?" Water asked.

"Our assault on Wylyn failed," Venia said.

"You reclaimed the throne," Lira said, eying Jeric as he spoke to Kelg. "I'd call that a victory."

"We're alive," Venia said. "And that is victory enough."

Thorilian grunted and turned away. "We have wounded to care for."

Casting them a grateful look, Venia followed him back into the castle. Light took that opportunity to wrap his arms around Willow and gaze into her beautiful eyes. He launched into the tale of their journey after Willow had departed, and didn't hear Water.

"Light? Perhaps this can wait until morning? Light?" He shook his head and looked to Lira. "I think he ignores me on purpose."

"Let him be with Willow," Lira said. "Let's get our own answers."

Water nodded and departed with Lira, leaving Light alone with Willow on the pile of rubble. He wanted to be with her, to tell her everything, and it wasn't until he was describing the battle with the snow dragon that he noticed the black gauntlet on her arm.

"And then the dragon—what is that?"

She smiled and held it up. "A Darkfist. It makes my weapons anti-magic."

"Epic," he breathed.

He reached out to touch it but the material burned his fingers. Sucking on the burn, he marveled at its craftsmanship, impressed by the quality of the weapon. It was an object made to be wielded by one without magic, to kill one with. One like him. But he didn't notice that.

"Where are Black and Cutter?" she asked, as if suddenly noticing their absence.

"Who?"

"They are the fourth and fifth members of the Queen's Hand," she said.

He stared at her in confusion and she smiled. "The ones I fought in my trial."

"Right," he said, anger hardening his features. "I hate them."

"Not anymore." She pointed to where the tower had fallen. "Turned out they were on my side the entire time. Mimic killed the second and third members of the Queen's Hand, so they joined to survive. When I arrived they decided to reveal their allegiances. They saved my life and helped me get this," she held aloft the Darkfist.

"They hurt you," he said. "I still hate them."

"Our apologies," Cutter said, limping into view with Black and Mimic in tow. "We could not reveal ourselves at that time."

Light folded his arms and fixed them with a glare. Jeric noticed their captive and called out to his guards. Obviously unhappy with following the orders of an elf, they reached for Mimic to take her into a cell.

"We'll take her," Black said.

Mimic, whose head was bowed, trudged with Black after the guards. Cutter raised his hand to Willow, an act of gratitude that made Light bristle. Cutter shifted the bandage on his shoulder and then offered a smile.

"You have our gratitude."

"What will you do with her?"

"Take her home," Cutter said. "And make sure she receives a proper execution."

"Why do you suppose Serak abandoned her?" Willow asked.

Mimic scowled while Black shrugged. "Who can understand such a twisted mind? And we needed some good fortune."

"Don't let her escape," Willow said.

"We won't." Cutter inclined his head to Light and then followed his brother.

"You're pleased they are alive," Light hissed.

"They saved my life. How could I not be?" She reached up and wrapped her arms around his shoulders. "I'd rather talk about your sudden appearance. Your timing could not have been better."

"I just followed Serak," he said with a bashful shrug. "And it seems he was the reason the room was falling in the first place."

"Indeed."

Light suddenly noticed she was smiling, her expression open, her eyes soft. In that moment he realized she hadn't pulled away, and they talked as if they had never parted. Afraid to hope but unable to stop the words, he voiced his doubt.

"Wait, why are you kissing me?"

She tilted her chin up. "Because I want to."

"But what about what you said before?"

"I was wrong," she said. "I want *you* to be my family."

Guards cursed as he began to glow, the light becoming blinding as he grinned. Someone called out a warning, while others shouted and shielded their eyes. Willow, also with a hand over her eyes, laughed quietly.

343

"Light?"

"Yes?"

"Do you mind dimming the sun charm?"

"Right." He did as requested and the night sky returned.

"And Light?"

"Yes?"

"I love you."

"Water was right," Light said, beaming. "Being dangerous did work."

Her laughter echoed off the castle. "Come, we should offer aid."

Still struggling to keep his glow in check, Light picked his way down the pile of rubble to Jeric, where Willow asked what they could do. Minutes later they were in the king's tower, caring for the wounded.

The next few days were a blur for Light, and he hardly noticed the rubble being cleaned up, or Jeric—an elf—sitting on the throne of Talinor. The House of Runya remained in good standing, and a proclamation was released to the people revealing their king had been taken, but a steward now served in his place. All efforts were being made to return King Porlin to the crown.

Light heard snippets from Water and Shadow, both of whom were helping to ease tensions in the city. Lorica disappeared, while Lira stayed to help Water. If Light had not been so enamored with Willow, he might have noticed the current of worry and tension seeping in. But he did not, because his attention remained fixed on Willow.

Until Elenyr arrived.

Chapter 46: Elenyr's Return

Shadow and Light gathered at Water's request, the three of them standing on an empty battlement near the summit of the Herosian castle. Light had reluctantly left Willow in their quarters and arrived to watch the storm clouds drift towards the city.

"Is this going to take long?" Light asked.

"I was going to ask the same thing," Shadow said. "I have things to do, you know."

"You don't," Water said. "We need to talk about what has transpired, and where we go from here."

"Jeric is now Steward over the largest kingdom in Lumineia," Shadow said with a shrug. "The kings and queens are now all kidnapped, all except the elven queen at Ilumidora."

"Don't forget that the Order of Ancients is now controlled exclusively by Wylyn," Water said. "And Serak is still missing."

Light shook his head. "Why does that matter? They are both our foes."

"Indeed," Water said. "But one of Willow's old contacts in the Order made it clear that Serak hasn't been seen since the conflict here. It's like he just vanished."

"I wish Mind were here," Light said. "Or Elenyr."

"She already is," Water said.

"What?" Shadow asked, rising to his feet. "When?"

"Why do you think I called you here?" Water asked, his smile wide. "She just arrived and asked to meet us here." He gestured to the empty turret.

"Where is she?" Light asked, eager to see Elenyr. There was so much he wanted to tell her.

A faint footfall echoed on the stairs and the trio turned to see the Hauntress carefully ascend to the top of the turret. Her appearance brought a smile to Light's lips and he bounded across the room to embrace her.

"Elenyr!" he cried. "Where have you been, you were missed so much! And you wouldn't *believe* what I saw in the north—"

He noticed her wince and abruptly withdrew. He stared at her, looking her up and down, noticing the bandages, the rigidness to her expression, as if she were still in pain. Anger pooled in his belly and magic sparked across his arms.

"Who did this?" he demanded. "I will cut them to pieces—scorch them to ash and then kill them. I will find them in their haunts and lairs, rend them asunder until—"

"Light," Elenyr said with a smile. "I am well."

"Oh," he said. "Then would you like to sit down?"

She shook her head. "I have sat enough for a lifetime, and there is much to discuss."

"Should I get Lira?" Water asked.

"No," she said. "This conversation is for the fragments of Draeken."

"That sounds ominous," Shadow said.

Elenyr stepped to the battlements and leaned against them, the motion controlled. Light had never seen her so weak, and the anger came again, powerful and sharp. As if sensing his anger, Elenyr gave him a reassuring look.

"You have struck a blow to the Order," she said. "And under Wylyn's command, the Order has now seen conflict."

"It's easy to worship what is absent," Water said. "Now that their god stands in their midst, they discover her cruelty."

"Indeed," Elenyr said. "But Jeric has learned that the Order does not possess the monarchs."

That was news to Light. "So Serak has disappeared, yet somehow still holds every king and queen of Lumineia?"

"Except the queen of the elves," Shadow corrected.

"Exactly," Elenyr said. "And it falls to us to bring them home. Already tensions rise in the kingdoms, and if nothing changes, we will see the people go to war."

Light nodded. "Willow said her people now know the truth, and many have begun rioting. Princess Aranian is attempting to regain order in the Deep, but the absence of the queen will make the task more difficult."

"We must act quickly," Elenyr said. "But I am not well enough to fight, at least not yet."

"Where would you have us go?" Water asked.

"One question we must first answer," Elenyr said. "Why did Serak not kill you in the north, or Wylyn when he arrived here?"

Light frowned in confusion. "What do you mean?"

"Jeric detailed to me the events of your attack," Elenyr said. "And it seems clear that Serak could have killed Wylyn—and all of you in the turret. Instead he departed. Why?"

"You think he still needs Wylyn," Shadow said, his tone of understanding.

"But for what?" Water asked. "When we were in the north, Serak implied that he wants to fight the krey. Why would he prepare to fight the krey, and then ally with one here?"

"It has something to do with the Shard of Midnight," Light said.

All three looked to him, and he shrugged. "We know that's what Wylyn seeks."

"True," Elenyr said. "And Fire and Mind are currently seeking the tower. When we learn its location, we can take measures to stop Wylyn."

"And Serak?"

"For now he has withdrawn," Elenyr said. "He has left Wylyn with more power than she has ever had, and forced us to deal with the threat."

"I hate being manipulated," Light said.

"Even when I do it?" Shadow asked with a smirk.

"When did you manipulate me?" Light asked.

"No one likes being manipulated," Water said. "And when we were in the north, Serak tried to talk to Draeken. The way he spoke it was . . .," he shook his head as if trying to figure out how to finish, ". . . disturbing. Like he knew something about Draeken that we did not." He looked to Elenyr. "Something you had kept from us."

Shadow sat up from his seat on the battlement. "Elenyr has her secrets, but not about Draeken."

"That's not true," Elenyr said softly.

The three fragments stared at her, and Light blurted. "What?"

"Don't be so disappointed." Elenyr shifted her leg and grimaced. "You have always known I keep secrets."

"But not from us," Shadow said angrily. "Not *about* us."

"Shadow," Water said, "we have to trust her."

"*You* have to trust her," Shadow said. "Because you're always the one with that insufferable honor. *I'm* the one that doubts."

348

The heat to his tone made Light wince. Shadow rarely displayed such anger, especially to Elenyr. But did Light feel different? He knew Serak had been manipulating him, but was Elenyr doing the same?

"What's the secret?" he asked.

Elenyr's features were pained. "I cannot tell you."

"You won't tell us?" Water asked, surprised. "Why keep it from us now?"

"Because she loves her secrets more than us," Shadow said.

"I'm sorry, Shadow," Elenyr said. "But attempting to goad me into sharing will not work this time."

Caught, he scowled and looked away. Water and Light exchanged a look. Both knew Elenyr kept the truth from them, but she'd never done it so blatantly, and never with something about Draeken.

"Serak knows this secret?" Water asked slowly.

"I've begun to think he does," Elenyr said. "And that is what makes him so dangerous."

"And you won't tell us?" Light asked.

Elenyr sighed and looked away, her eyes on the approaching storm. "When I became your caretaker, there was much I didn't know about you. The guardian charm that created you was untested, and not even its creators understood what it would do. I spent the first few years just watching you, measuring your responses, hoping you would survive."

"You thought we would die?" Water asked.

"The guardians before you could not endure the power," she said. "And I worried about you constantly. Then you shattered, and it gave me a unique chance to help each of you control your own power, so that when you became Draeken, you would not be consumed by the magic."

Water leaned against the door frame. "What does that have to do with the truth?"

"Draeken is unique, as are the fragments," Elenyr said. "I have spent a lifetime at your side, and there are still aspects to your being I don't understand. In time I hope you—and I—understand them all. But we must proceed with caution. Knowledge can be dangerous, especially about one as powerful as you."

"You said knowledge always enlightens," Water said.

"Indeed," Elenyr said. "But you cannot learn what you are not ready to understand."

"Sounds like an excuse," Shadow said, his forehead knit.

"This is one truth you will learn on your own," Elenyr said. "And for now, you must trust in that answer."

Shadow stabbed a finger at Elenyr, but Water spoke first. "We will."

Light, confused by the exchange, shrugged. Shadow reluctantly fell silent. Elenyr nodded her gratitude and then asked for each of their respective tales. Light, already eager to share, launched into the events of Kordune and his side of the story in Mistkeep. Elenyr laughed at the story of Bartoth, and Water shook his head in amusement. Then Light spoke of the krey ship.

"I can't believe you got to fly a krey vessel," Shadow said, leaning back against the stone with a scowl.

"He did fix the thing," Water said.

Light flushed at their praise, and then at their prompting, continued the tale. With a cold wind curving across the battlements, and gloomy clouds in the sky, the foursome talked and laughed about the various exploits, and soon the worry over Draeken's truth was forgotten.

Shadow lurched to his feet. "Water suggested you do *what?*"

"Be dangerous to win Willow back." Light shook his head in disapproval. "I must say, it was a terrible idea."

"That was not my idea," Water sputtered.

"It certainly was," Light insisted.

"Reason seven why we should never listen to Water," Shadow said, and raised a hand as if counting them off. "He is insufferable. He is never as much fun as me. He always does the right thing even when . . ."

Elenyr was laughing, as was Light. Water groaned and hung his head, but he too had a smile on his face. Light relished the moment, especially when Elenyr began to share her own tale. All three fragments sat with wide eyes, reminding Light of moments in their youth. They were warriors, guardians from another age, but they were first and foremost a family. Light would, of course, kill Carn for what he'd done, but for now he stayed, unwilling to depart.

Like always, his concerns faded quickly, even if his brothers remained somewhat tense. One glance at the king's tower revealed that they were winning, and the conversation eventually turned to their foes. Wylyn had suffered a blow, several dakorians had been killed, and Serak had disappeared. Serak's vaunted Order was now under Wylyn's leadership, but Jeric had learned the Order members did not care for her command. Many times in the conversation his thoughts returned to Willow, and he smiled to himself, grateful for their reunion.

"Light," Elenyr drawled. "Please don't damage the king's castle."

Light looked down to find a sword in his hand. Set against the stone, he was obviously getting ready to carve a section of the battlements in half. Chagrined, he dismissed the sword and sat again, irritated at his discomfort.

Too excited at his future with Willow, he failed to notice the dark stirring in his chest, or the increased irritability that seemed to find its way into his behavior. As they spoke of finding the monarchs and the Shard of Midnight, he shifted uncomfortably, blaming the stone parapet because he did not recognize the whispers within.

Draeken had heard Serak's invitation.

And he wanted to answer.

The Chronicles of Lumineia

By Ben Hale

—The Shattered Soul—

—The Master Thief—

—The Second Draeken War—

—The Warsworn—

—The Age of Oracles—

—The White Mage Saga—

Author Bio

Originally from Utah, Ben has grown up with a passion for learning almost everything. Driven particularly to reading caused him to be caught reading by flashlight under the covers at an early age. While still young, he practiced various sports, became an Eagle Scout, and taught himself to play the piano. This thirst for knowledge gained him excellent grades and helped him graduate college with honors, as well as become fluent in three languages after doing volunteer work in Brazil. After school, he started and ran several successful businesses that gave him time to work on his numerous writing projects. His greatest support and inspiration comes from his wonderful wife and six beautiful children. Currently he resides in Missouri while working on his Masters in Professional Writing.

To contact the author, discover more about Lumineia, or find out about the upcoming sequels, check out his website at Lumineia.com. You can also follow the author on twitter @ BenHale8 or Facebook.

www.ingramcontent.com/pod-product-compliance
Lightning Source LLC
Chambersburg PA
CBHW020825180626
46814CB00001B/111